Obsidian Reign

Book One in the Crimson Shadows Trilogy

Madalyn Leigh

Madalyn Leigh Books

To my family. Thank you for believing in me, even before the first word was written.

Contents

Prologue

My mouth waters in anticipation as I raise the plump berry to my lips, eagerly awaiting the sweet juiciness I know will burst from beneath the bright skin. The moment shatters when Dad's whispered alarm fills my ears, a harsh tone I barely ever hear him use. Firm fingers quickly wrap around my wrist and shake it until the fruit falls from my grasp.

My wide eyes flash up to Dad, searching his now relieved smile, until settling on the discarded berry. As my heart thumps unevenly in my throat, it takes a second for me to realize how close I was to death.

I learned to be grateful for what I have a long time ago because you never know when it will end. My mother would whisper that to me at night as she tucked me into bed, humming a soft lullaby that never failed to pull me toward sleep. It always stuck with me, years after she stopped walking me to my bedroom in the corner of our small cabin, the words she uttered before my heavy eyelids would drop.

When it will end, she would say, not *if.*

"See the color of these berries, bumblebee? That means

they're poisonous, so watch out." Dad's voice drags me from my inner thoughts, and I eye the bright red spheres that hang innocently from a bush.

"They look just like cryberries," I state, leaning forward to inspect the impostors more closely. "How can you tell the difference?"

Dad laughs, the deep rumble making my lips stretch involuntarily into a smile. "Similar, but not quite the same. Look closer, Cassie. These are bigger and brighter. They want you to choose them, to fool you into believing they will be even more delicious than a cryberry. Just because something appears better doesn't mean that it is. Now, let's go home before your mother starts to worry. The sun will set soon."

He slowly gets up, stretching out his knees as he goes. I follow suit and snatch the leather pouch full of our non-life-threatening berries from his hand. I love how he lets me come with him when he forages, teaching me all that he knows about plant life, and in return, I try to be as little of a burden as possible.

We walk the short trek back to our house in comfortable silence, one of Dad's arms slung across my shoulders. I lean my head against him and focus my eyes on the ground as we weave past shadows the trees cast, always staying within the light. I can feel the warmth seep into my back as the sun creeps below the trees, the shadows on the forest floor lengthening in a gentle reminder to hurry.

Then I'm talking again, quietly chatting about the latest thing I learned in my studies with Mom and a plot twist from one of my favorite mystery books that I'm rereading for the tenth time. Dad just nods his head, chuckling when I throw in a joke to keep him entertained.

Only when we pass through the wooden threshold and

I'm swept into my mother's arms do I realize there was a slight tightness in my stomach while we were walking home.

"Welcome back," Mom gushes, bending far enough away to brush a strand of brown hair from my face. I stare up at her hazel eyes, only a few shades darker than mine, and take a deep breath, leaning into her comforting touch. She ushers the two of us into the house and softly shuts the door. "Dinner is almost ready."

I watch my parents hug with a small smile, struggling to smother my unease. I've never liked the silence. Being outside for fifteen years without problems hasn't quite subdued the fear, not fully, even though my parents have tried to prepare me for everything.

At a young age, they explained to me what happened to our world, how monsters swallowed humanity thirteen years before I was born. I've yet to see an Obsidian in real life, but sometimes, when it's silent, I think I can hear them moving in the distance, snapping a tree branch. That a shadow slightly more formed than the others is our death inching closer to us.

My eyes flash to the front door, muscles tensing like a demon is already on the other side, waiting for the perfect moment to strike. Waiting for the end.

Almost as if pulled there by a force, my eyes switch from the door to one of the many torches that line the inside of our home. The torch in the living room is dimming, signaling it's time to switch in new pieces of wood. My increased heartbeat evens out as my gaze settles on the flickering flame. The comfort that swathes me rivals my fear when looking into the inky darkness of night. The flames protect us from the monsters that revel in the shadows.

As long as we have fire, we will survive.

Chapter 1

Daggers and Emmerick

My consciousness comes back quickly, as if it was holding its breath for as long as it could and then had to gasp for air. Eyes snapping open, I stare at the black mat that's sprinkled with small red drops.

My blood, I think slowly. The flashback of being with my parents years ago floods my vision, but I force the images away, trying to focus on the multitude of voices shouting above my head.

"She's fainted!"

"It hasn't even been thirty seconds!"

"Someone get the Serous. What a waste of resources."

Without fully understanding the situation, I jump to my feet with my hands curling into fists. From the few snippets I could concentrate on, there are only a couple of options for where I am. The same places I've been for the last three years since joining the academy.

All of them suck.

I blink rapidly to clear the black spots in my vision until I see the large, muscled man looming across from me. Brown hair shaved close to his head, a twisted smirk distorting his features. Emmerick, such a lovely human being and classmate, looks ready to smash my face in for a second time tonight, but he holds his ground.

"I think you've lost, Cassie." The oaf doesn't even look out of breath.

"I'm standing, aren't I?" I bite out through clenched teeth, wiping at the blood trickling from my nose.

My eyes dart around the poorly lit room, toward the other students who exude annoyance at my pathetic display of strength, until they land on the one instructor in the old gymnasium. I'm not sure 'instructor' is the best word for him since he's about as caring as an Obsidian.

Lywell Raddo, a middle-aged man with glasses and a lanky frame, leans against the door with an air of indifference. When a challenge is in session, he always plants himself in front of the only exit. I wonder if it's a conscious decision to make sure no one can leave.

Eyes so dark they almost look black lock with mine, and he tilts his head to the side, curly flaxen hair falling across his forehead. "The rules state that the match ends if an opponent forfeits or goes unconscious. You, my dear, were clearly out of it, even if just for a second. That means Emmerick wins, continuing his undefeated streak." Raddo pushes the wire-framed glasses farther up his nose and gives me a wicked grin. "Better luck next time."

I glance around the room, doing my best to hold my tongue. Six other classmates of mine watch with bated breath, not hiding their hope that I'll restart the match anyway.

I step back, putting on my most charming smile. As my mouth widens, I feel the sting of a split lip. "Well, I'll be going to bed then, if that's it. Pity, I was ready for round two."

Turning around, I march toward the exit until I'm directly in front of Raddo. He peers down at me for a second before stepping to the side. Opening the door, my head stretches to look behind me. "It's been fun. Thanks for the splendid memories, as always. See you next week?"

I slam the door before anyone can respond, sagging against the wood once it's closed. *What a mess.* I barely remember what happened in the fight prior to my quick snooze, though I'm sure it went exactly how all of my other challenges had gone. With Emmerick feeling the need to release some steam on the nearest individual, and that was me.

I really need to learn to stand farther away from him.

I remember what my mind had conjured up while I wasn't awake, though. My chest squeezes as my dream comes back to me. My parents. The nightmare of their deaths almost three years ago resurfaces every night, but seeing them in a daydream is new.

My fingers twist within the gray sweatshirt above my heart. The pain that seizes me when I think of them never goes away, but it always fades. I wait as long as I dare—I refuse to let anyone in that challenge room see me like this—until the throbbing settles into a dull ache. *Three seconds will have to do.*

Blowing out a breath, I force the tension from my body and push off the door, slowly making my way back to my dorm room. Normally, I'd do a training session before going to bed, but more than anything, I'm ready to shut my brain off for a few hours.

My feet guide me to my room as I walk the empty stone hallways, the soft tapping of my steps echoing around me. It's late enough that I doubt anyone will try to stop me. The guards who protect the school are more focused on not letting anything get in when the sun's gone rather than stopping our illicit fights. That's why the challenges only happen at night.

It doesn't take long to reach the dorm wing. The school is only big enough to fit about two hundred humans in total. Between the five grades of students, instructors, and guards, there are about a hundred and thirty of us.

I quietly slide the door to my room open, careful not to wake up my roommate and best friend, Sara Rosen. It doesn't matter. Sara sprawls on her bed, lightly snoring. I've always envied her ability to sleep so soundly, especially since I rarely get five hours of rest a night.

Heading into our adjoining bathroom, I walk toward the small flower box containing our light source, Azura. It's a mushroom that emits a blue glow, almost as luminous as torchlight. I pour water from the sink into my hand and let the droplets splash onto the wide blue caps.

We'd get into big trouble if we let our light source die. It's a common plant that grows easily, but with how much we use, there's not a lot left over to replant a room.

After ensuring the Azura mushroom's health, I strip my dirty clothes off and step into the shower, carefully washing the minor scrapes that line my arms and face.

Exhaustion aches in my bones when my head finally hits the pillow. I try not to think about how easy it was for Emmerick to defeat me in the fight. After three years as a student at Hallow Academy, experiencing countless painful challenges, my skills are still lacking, no matter the effort I put in.

With only a few months of school before we graduate and join the losing side of the war, I know I'm not ready to make a difference.

If I'm going to become a hunter who won't die on their first day outside the walls, I need to become stronger.

"I'm curious. What were you dreaming about that put you in such a deep sleep?" Sara turns her head to study me as we walk the long hallways of the school.

I'm usually out of bed and halfway through a training session when Sara gets up, but today, she had to throw me out of bed to wake me. And I mean, she physically tossed me onto the floor, which was an exciting way to greet the day.

I was dreaming about the same thing I was during the challenge: my life before the academy. I've never talked with Sara about my parents or how they died, so I skim as close to the truth as possible without going into details. "The day before I joined the academy. It brought back some unhappy memories."

We follow the white granite path through a large stone archway that leads to an outside trail with an overhead balcony. The entire academy looks reconfigured from a giant stone castle, complete with torches and display cases of distinct Obsidian-slaying weapons. I'm unsure if they are proper weapons or just for show, but a few times, the temptation almost had me picking the lock.

"Ah, I see," she breathes, and I bet she does see.

Only those who either can't get an apprenticeship in a specialized school—like researcher, blacksmith, historian—or have nowhere else to go join a military academy, training to become a soldier in the war against the demons that plague Arrynd, our country.

The instructors say we lost contact with Ortibam, the only country connected to ours, days after the spread began.

And because Arrynd is surrounded by the Night Sea—a deadly ocean that is impossible to cross except through a thinly raised stretch of land called the Bone Strip, also overrun by Obsidian—we have no way to ask for military help or resources.

Any attempt we've had at trying to cross the sea with hastily made boats or sending scouts to sneak their way through the Bone Strip to Ortibam has gotten us nothing but more casualties. We haven't stopped trying, but Arrynd has been on its own for the last thirty-one years, and we're losing the fight. Soldiers are the only thing that stands between our complete extinction and a minuscule chance at surviving.

I wonder if Sara's entrance to the school resembles my own. Hunters, whose primary goal is to travel the country protecting families and farms from Obsidian attacks, were too late to save anyone but her.

When I become a hunter, I wonder how many times I'll be too late to save someone.

I sigh and stuff my hands into my gray hoodie's pockets, suddenly wishing I hadn't brought up such a depressing topic. "You know what? I just think I didn't sleep well last night, and now my brain is malfunctioning. Don't worry about it."

Sara purses her lips, her chocolate brown eyes not easily deceived. "Uh-huh, sure. I've never known you to sleep well, Cassie. You and sleep are like," she pauses and wiggles her fingers at me, "hot and cold, day and night, daggers and Emmerick."

I laugh and bump into Sara with my shoulder. It's true; Emmerick would never choose a weapon length less than two feet. It just doesn't fit with his superior-in-all-things-mighty personality.

Thinking of Emmerick brings up last night's challenge,

and the humor drains out of me. Sara knows I get challenged, though she doesn't know about this latest one.

She's seen me come back from some nasty fights in the past and has threatened to tell the headmaster about them, but I've always talked her out of it. The backlash from the other students would be extreme, and I'm not convinced Headmaster Hallow doesn't already know it's going on. While he may not intervene, it would be odd for the challenges to be happening for so long without him hearing about them. Professor Raddo knows, so why couldn't Hallow?

Besides, the challenges help me practice my skills in high-stakes scenarios. The system mainly showcases the strength of bullies, but that doesn't mean I can't get something out of it. Thinking of the silver lining keeps me from cracking under the humiliation.

We continue down the stone awning that lines the inner perimeter of the academy. The pillars on our left obstruct my view of the expansive green grass, but I can hear some of the younger kids discussing different tactical drills they must have just learned in class. Thunder cracks overhead, warning the students that rain might encroach on their discussion.

I lean out towards the grounds to stretch my head past the covered walkway to the sky, eyeing the dark storm clouds in the distance with a frown. I pick up my pace. At eighteen and in the fifth-year class, I rarely use the courtyard since it's the prime hangout spot for anyone under the age of fifteen. Team drills occupy most of the green space when class is in and out of session.

Sara and I move swiftly toward our classes' gym, the door just after the entrance to the mess hall. Past the two rooms, the colonnade splits into three separate pathways. The left trail continues to ring around the courtyard in a square that also leads to the faculty and guard wing. Going straight is a small dirt trail that heads toward the garden. The right follows the walkway until it travels back into the main building.

I long to follow the dirt trail, sit by the flowers, and listen to the soft babbling of the pond. It's been a while since I've been there. It is the most serene place in the academy, yet most people forget it even exists. There isn't much time for relaxing when you're at war.

Stuck in my head, I collide with a lithe body exiting the cafeteria. I stumble back a few steps but catch my footing before I end up embarrassingly on my butt. My mouth flies open, a snappy response on the tip of my tongue. It dies as I lift my head to stare at the two figures in front of me.

"My goodness, Cassidy, I'm very sorry about that. I should have been paying attention to where I was walking. Are you alright?" A hand comes down on my shoulder, and Officer Zypha Felvor's pale green eyes survey me with worry.

As head of security, she's clad in her usual black uniform, her red hair pulled into a tight bun that highlights the silver strands lining the sides.

"I'm fine, Officer Zypha. It was my fault." I smile and deftly slide out of her hold, glancing behind Zypha to find her second-in-command. The black-haired man is only a few years older than us, but he's risen through the ranks quickly.

Adrian Camson stands rigidly off to Zypha's left in the same standard officer uniform, his hands clasped behind his back. His sharp blue eyes roam over Sara before locking onto mine, but he remains silent.

In fact, I don't think I've heard him say three words to me since the day I joined the academy. The thought tugs my mouth into a frown, and his gaze dips to it before pulling back up to my eyes.

My cheeks flood with heat without permission, the mortification of the flush almost doubling the warmth on my face. I focus on the head officer, who continues to apologize. *Stop overreacting, Cassie! He did nothing to warrant a stupid blush.*

"Well, it's good to see you both either way. How are your classes going?"

Before I can respond, Sara loops her skinny arm through mine, shoots Zypha a dazzling smile, and drags me down the hallway. I sputter, attempting to break free, but she holds on tight. *How can someone so tiny be so strong?*

"It was nice seeing you, Zypha." Sara twirls around and waves at the stunned woman, still pulling me along. "Unfortunately, we have sparring class to get to. You know what Professor Tala will do to us if we're late!"

Zypha blinks in bemusement before waving back with a grin. She shouts something about the importance of good attendance as we disappear into the gym.

I tug on my best friend's arm to get her to slow down, partly grateful she pulled me away from what felt like the beginnings of an epic embarrassment. "Sara, we still have ten minutes left before class. What's the rush?"

She lowers her speed to a casual stroll, weaving through black leather sparring mats to reach the back of the room and running a hand through her short brown hair. Even half-irritated, my best friend is beautiful.

"Zypha is kind and all, but she tries too hard to be involved in our lives. Besides," Sara shivers and wraps her arms around herself, "Adrian stresses me out. He's way too intense to be around."

I tilt my head and purse my lips, drumming my fingers on the sides of my gray training pants. I always found Adrian's fierce gaze comforting. He appears to be someone you can count on, albeit not for a good laugh.

I've never seen him in action, but I've heard whispers of

his power and agility, that he's killed an Obsidian in less than ten seconds, and no human has ever matched him in combat. They even said that Hallow Academy begged him to join a year earlier than the required age, too desperate to wait. If those stories are true, I wonder why someone with such great strength would spend his days as an uneventful security officer.

Chapter 2

A Fierce Tongue

I spin around and face Sara while walking backward. My mouth pulls up at the corners as I give a teasing laugh. "Adrian can't creep you out when we've been preparing for years to kill a lot *scarier* things."

"That's different," Sara huffs out with a grimace. "The Obsidian are supposed to be scary. It's like their job. It wouldn't hurt Adrian to smile once in a while."

I chuckle, my gaze bouncing through the vast gymnasium. Mats evenly space the stone floor, and equipment fills the perimeter, ranging from shelves of various swords to worn wooden targets. As we near the back wall, it's impossible to ignore the paint splattered against the stone. Every graduate from Hallow Academy has painted their name on the stone blocks, a last rite before they're considered a fully fledged soldier in the war. Twenty-five years' worth of academy history is strewn across the wall, each name written in either black, red, or white dye.

Adrian's name is displayed first in his class from four years ago, which isn't surprising given the rumors about him. Our current professor, Tala, is there too, nine years before him and also placed first in her year.

Chelsea and Amber are already wrestling, forgoing their weapons on the side of the ring. There are multiple training facilities throughout the academy, enough that every class can train in one simultaneously. The seniors always receive the largest gym, which I assume is so we can see the graduation list as daily motivation.

Because it isn't just a proud archive of the academy's graduates.

It's also a memorial.

More than half of the names have the academy's symbol stained red beside them: an 'H' and 'A' overlaying each other. Those are the warriors who have fallen in battle, and most of them are students who were lower than tenth place in the rankings. All twenty-five students ranked last have a symbol by their name.

I clench my teeth and move toward the side of the room, focusing on my usual stretching routine. I eye Amber as she circles Chelsea, whose chest is heaving with wheezes. Amber is a flash of red as she steps close to Chelsea, throwing her off balance and then sweeping her legs out from under her. Chelsea lands on her back with a thump, her long black hair splayed out behind her, and I wince. Why they would want to waste all their energy before class begins is beyond me.

The nearest corner puffs with dust as my discarded hoodie lands in a heap. I lower myself to the floor, grab my toes, and rest my head on my knees. Releasing a deep breath, I close my eyes and sink into the stretch.

My goal today is to not need the infirmary. Honestly, that's my goal every day. For my first year at the academy, I spent more nights there than in my dorm room.

My senior year has gone a little more smoothly, but the

nurse likes to point out that we still have a few months left of the school year. *It's nice to know she believes in me*, I think with a sarcastic chuckle.

The room fills with chatter as the rest of the class files in and starts their warm-ups. I glance at Sara, whose sparring steps look more like a dance than an attack routine. She's incredibly elegant but still strikes like a panther.

I smile as I remember the first time I faced her in the sparring ring. I finally thought I'd found an opponent that I could beat, but boy, was I wrong.

Tala, the senior professor, strides into the room with purpose and conversations quickly die out. She spares me a withering glance before planting herself in the center of the chamber.

Most of our class is terrified of being reprimanded by Tala's fierce tongue. For me, I've verbally sparred against our instructor so many times that I can predict what she'll say to me before she says it. She's hated me all these years—beginning on the day I said yes to joining the academy—and I still don't know why.

I haven't had to deal with her dislike of me until my senior year, when she officially became my professor. Before that, she normally ignored me as much as possible while her gray eyes shot daggers from afar.

Hands perched on her hips, she tells us all to take five laps around the courtyard. Complaints erupt throughout the room, but one look from Tala shuts them up. "Do you think I care that it's raining out? Do you think the demons will wait for perfect weather to slaughter innocent people? Get your sorry butts out there right now!"

The class scrambles through the door, establishing a brisk pace under the stone canopy. A sigh pulls from my lips as a wild crack of thunder rumbles the ground under our feet.

Sara and I were out here just minutes ago, but it feels like night has captured the afternoon. Black storm clouds whirl above us, and the courtyard is vacant of the young students practicing their skills earlier. The sound of the rain pelting down on earth and stone overpowers my senses. I take in a lungful of air, the scent of a storm prickling my nose. The pillars do very little to keep the cold raindrops from pelting us sideways as the wind picks up in fervor.

I glance up at the wall's ledge and scan the guards that stand rigidly in the rain, watching over the perimeter. A thunderstorm is never good for the academy: darkness and lack of sight with the rain are a dangerous combination.

Sara cups the side of her face to keep the water out of her eyes. "Professor Tala is in a worse mood than normal. What's her deal?"

I smirk as I watch the students in front of us hug the side of the school to escape the brunt of the storm. I push wet brown strands of hair that escaped my ponytail from my eyes in one fluid, forceful movement. Even though it's pouring, I still relish the sensation of my feet hitting the stone, my muscles straining with exertion, pushing my body forward. Warm-up is my favorite part of the class.

"Her deal," I shout over another boom of thunder, "is that the rain probably ruined her perfectly styled hair. 'How am I supposed to fight back a horde of Twos without chipping a nail?'" I whine in my finest high-pitched Tala impersonation.

Sara laughs, telling me to keep quiet before someone overhears.

"That's not funny, Cassidy." Joshua rotates his head to look back at me with a disapproving scowl, his curly black hair bouncing with every step. Like most of the men in our class, he's bulky from years of training. I remember his face as a classmate who witnessed my epic fail of a challenge last night.

"Oh, you've done it now," Sara leans in to whisper in my ear.

Oh, yes, I did. Ugh, I'm gonna get a lot of crap for this. Of course the teacher's pet is the one to witness my great impression.

"Sounds to me like you've lost your sense of humor. Do you want my help to find it?" I give Joshua my sweetest smile and bat my waterlogged eyelashes at him. He huffs and runs faster, like he can't stand to be near me.

That's just great. When Tala hears about this, I can kiss my daily goal goodbye.

No one knows for sure where the first Obsidian came from, or if it's inflicted anywhere else but Arrynd. There are rumors about how they came here, though. That the sin of our country drew the worst race of monsters from hell, or the black souls of the dead molded together to create a nightmare come to life.

Either way, the Obsidian arrived. I've only seen them once in my life, the day my parents died. Since then, I've dedicated the last three years to learning everything about them in order to destroy them.

The first recorded incident was near Pellema, a small town fifty miles from Hallow Academy. Before anyone knew what was happening, the monsters took over Maltava, the largest trading city in Arrynd, where there was no stopping the spread. It was only a matter of time before the entire country collapsed in on itself, leaving us on the edge of extinction.

They don't seem to be sentient, just attracted to humans. One bite from an Obsidian transforms a human into one of their own. The person becomes encrusted in the black rock of the Obsidian's skin, and they pounce on the nearest victim within minutes.

A single creature turned ten people, who then turned a hundred people, until the monsters became a colossal problem. Regular weapons can barely crack their stone skin, but through extensive trial and error, we found that fire is the easiest way to kill them. It melts their skin, breaking through their armor, and allows us to take them down from the inside.

Fire also naturally repels the Obsidian and daytime makes them weaker. Attacks often happen at night, as they meld with the shadows, stalking their prey. Having a source of light at all times increases the chance of survival tenfold.

Even knowing their weakness, we find ourselves on the losing side of the war. Things look bleak, but humanity isn't known for giving up.

My face scrunches as I pluck at the black tank top that's suctioned to my stomach. We've been out of the rain and back in the training room for an hour now, yet I still look like a drowned rat. Tala vetoed allowing everyone to change clothes after our warm-up laps, saying this is a great 'deal-with-an-unfortunate-situation' exercise.

We started with practicing our sparring techniques, but have now switched to one-on-one sparring matches. In this drill, everyone gathers around the middle ring, and we watch our classmates get beaten up as we take notes on what *not* to do. People always seem to take more notes when it's my turn.

The aim is to last three minutes in the ring without stepping out or becoming unconscious; if both people are still standing, it's a draw.

Each year focuses on a different aspect of our military training. Students in Year One learn everything about the enemy, from their average height to the difference in their speed when the sun is up. They also learn useful practical skills, assisting in the academy's greenhouse and workshop. Year Two works with weapons, since wielding Obsidian swords and arrows is dangerous and takes a lot of dexterity. The weapons are on fire, after all.

Year Three memorizes different tactical skills, learning to fight with order and structure so no one in your group dies. Year Four students put those drills into action. At the end of the fourth year, students should be proficient enough to go out with any team and kill quickly and efficiently.

Year Five is all about placement as an academy graduate. You show off your fighting skills, endurance, and anything you can to get a high enough ranking to choose the job you want.

To make sure no one slacks off, the rankings are secret until the end of each month, where the scores reconfigure based on how well you did the month prior. Normally, the rankings don't change too much. Top students stay on top and those on the bottom…

Let's just say those on the bottom are trying *really hard* not to be there.

Tala walks around the ring, her gray eyes swinging between Sara and Joshua as they take turns dodging and jabbing. Her face is gentle compared to when she looks at me, but a small frown etches her mouth. Obviously, the lack of intensity is not making her happy.

The rain has made the students sluggish, as if their punches are moving through water. It's been about two minutes so far, and with a quick survey of the room, I can tell that most fights will probably end in draws. A lot of kids are sitting, some twisting water from their shirts, the clothes making puddles around them.

The only two people on their feet are me and Emmerick, though I suspect Emmerick has never sat down in his life. His oversized frame oozes intimidation, with a neck the size of a tree trunk. He looks like a bear that has the uncanny ability to walk on two feet.

Just observing Emmerick makes my mind travel to the elixir Serous and all the times I've had to take it after sparring with him.

I've never heard of the medicine before coming here, but thirteen years after the Obsidian arrived, more powerful, mutated monsters emerged. Some gained back senses, like their sight or hearing, or their skin became fireproof, making it almost impossible to kill them until you chip enough of their natural armor to use the fire internally.

Hunters captured some of the more unique demons and found that one of them could regenerate from any cuts that weren't lethal. They extracted its blood and transformed it into a regeneration elixir, one significantly less potent than its origins. It's saved more lives than we can count. The best part is that, because of its intense level of filtration, there's no chance of transforming, no matter how much someone takes.

What I hate most about Serous is how the medicine has brought out aggressively violent tendencies in almost everyone. Except for being maimed, Serous cures all injuries, so why not break bones in the worst way possible? Why not go for a savage attack to let out all your anger and frustration over the misery that looms during such a calamity?

The instructors promote the drug as an opportunity to not hold back, to train like your opponent is genuinely an

Obsidian. All it does is let the tyrants of the class torment the weaker opponents with zero consequences.

I understand wanting to prepare us for the pain we're guaranteed to endure outside these walls, but do we truly have to suffer in here as well?

I won't need Serous today, I chant, the determination pulsing in time with my heartbeat. While I size up my classmates' fatigue for my future fights, I notice a tall figure in black standing near the entrance, surveying the match.

Adrian is leaning against the doorway, his arms folded over themselves. He's been coming to our classes regularly once sparring starts, and I assume he's here to scout for Officer Zypha's security team.

Not that I would know. The guards rarely interact with students, more focused on keeping the Obsidian out than on what the students are doing. They leave that up to the instructors. Besides Adrian and Zypha, whom I only know because of my first night here, I have never talked to another guard.

I frown, absently picking at my wet shirt. Adrian also never interacts with the group and silently watches until he sees fit to leave. His presence always throws me off, like he's judging us.

Tala calls time, and both Joshua and Sara immediately sag, breathing hard. Sara shuffles off the mat and lies on the ground, closing her eyes. A thought pops into my mind that makes my lips curl upwards. *With everyone so tired, I might win a match for once.*

My eyes are still on Tala, so I notice as soon as she spots Adrian in the room. Our instructor smooths out her shirt and puts on a beaming smile. I roll my eyes, tipping my face away so she doesn't see my response.

Does she not realize how obvious she is? The man is ten years younger than her. Talk about creepy.

"Alright, guys, that match was overly uneventful for my taste. Let's mix things up, shall we? Emmerick, you're up."

"Finally," Emmerick rumbles, stretching his thick arms. He sneers at his closest companions, distorting his too-small face on his too-big head.

As I watch Tala's lips curl maliciously, a pit in my stomach tells me exactly who he's going up against.

Chapter 3

Brutal Dance

"IT'S ONLY FITTING THAT THE HIGHEST-RANKING STUDENT goes up against the lowest-ranking one. Isn't that right, Cassidy?"

The class perks up like wolves who just got thrown an enormous chunk of fresh meat. Sara pales, scrambling to her feet. She opens her mouth, but I raise a hand with a small shake of my head.

"Of course, Tala. I've been wanting to test my new skills out on a dummy, and he's the best one we've got," I explain in my most charming voice, shoving down my disappointment. *With him as my opponent, my chance of winning has decreased dramatically. But it hasn't reached zero.*

A few nervous laughs litter the air as Tala scowls, and Emmerick's eyes narrow like he's trying to figure out who got hit with the punchline.

I don't make eye contact with anyone as I walk onto the mat, fully focusing on my opponent. I grimace when I enter the ring, my wet shoes squeaking against the floor.

Going up against Emmerick isn't new. Between his *many*

challenge requests over the years, including last night, and Tala's affinity for broken bones, specifically my broken bones, I'd say we've grown rather close. Oh yeah, the hungry, savage look in his eyes as he cracks his thick knuckles *definitely* means I'm his best friend.

Tala steps into the ring and gives us both a pointed gaze. "Okay, you know the deal. You have three minutes to get your opponent to tap out. Emmerick, good luck. Cassidy... try not to die."

I give her a mocking, two-fingered salute before she slips off the mat and blows a whistle.

Emmerick charges quickly, sparing no chance for me to take the offensive. I dive out of the way and roll up to my feet, crouching with my hands raised into fists. While Emmerick has brute strength, he's not the fastest adversary I've had to face. If I can keep myself from being grabbed, I can last three minutes.

Emmerick turns and barrels toward me again. I step to the side and punch him in the left shoulder. My knuckles sting from the contact, my upper body rearing back when he pins me with a wicked glare.

"Nice try." My opponent smirks. He doesn't even flinch at my attack, only wetting his lips as if he can already taste my blood.

I'm so dead.

The brute swipes at my head with his meaty paw as I duck and kick out at his leg, grinning when my foot finds purchase. Emmerick stumbles back but immediately straightens, not the least bit fazed.

My grin slides away. I had hoped my attack would have done some sort of damage. He contorts his whole body as he puts as much force behind him as possible for a punch to the stomach. I zero in on his fist, knowing it could end the fight if it hits me straight on.

I dodge the assault, but something slams into my head, the impact knocking me to the ground. I look up at him in dazed confusion. It takes a moment to understand what just happened, and I want to slap my forehead when I realize my mistake.

I was so focused on his hand coming at my stomach that I didn't notice his other fist was swinging toward my temple. *Tricky bastard.*

I attempt to climb to my feet, but Emmerick kicks me in my side and sends me flying across the mat. My elbows dig into the leather until I stop sliding, my body centimeters from leaving the ring. Cheers from my classmates fill the air, and the approval elicits a deep chuckle from Emmerick as he slowly saunters toward me.

I flick my gaze to the class and scan their features. Most aren't watching the fight, either bored or too tired to care, but some have the same hungry expression Emmerick wears. Sara is watching my opponent, her eyes wide with fear and hands wrapped together in silent prayer.

I unsteadily jump to my feet. Staying on the ground will not only lead to my defeat but also a very painful pummeling. My stomach spasms from the movement and a metallic-tasting liquid slowly fills my mouth. I swallow it quickly, refusing to let Emmerick know he made me bleed. Before I can place a hand on my stomach to brace against the pain, he comes at me again.

It becomes a brutal dance. I dodge, dodge, dodge, then stumble, leaving myself open for an attack, which Emmerick happily exploits. Each ruthless strike radiates through my limbs, the bruises blooming across my skin.

To make matters worse, tears of frustration prick the back

of my eyes. I know it's been longer than three minutes, yet Tala hasn't stopped the fight.

She wants to see me lose.

My legs shake as I stand again after another vicious knee to the thigh. Sweat pours down my face and back, though the shirt is already soaked from the rain. I shove the anger and exhaustion down, not wanting to give Tala the satisfaction of seeing me cry.

I lash out with my fist, but I'm slower than before. Emmerick wraps his hand around my wrist and yanks me closer to him. The action catches me off guard, and I stagger forward far enough for him to wrap a beefy hand around my throat.

He lifts me off my feet like I weigh nothing. I thrash in his grip, struggling for air. Panic swelling within my chest, my legs swing wildly while my fingers dig into his forearm, but his hold is unbreakable.

Black spots cloud my vision as a female voice screeches out. "It's been five minutes, Tala. The match is over!"

A few agonizing seconds go by until I hear a blaring whistle echo through the room. Emmerick begrudgingly lets go, and I crumble to the ground, gasping against the burn of oxygen forcing its way into my lungs. Sara wraps her arms around me. She's shaking, but I can't tell if it's from fear or anger. I bring a hand to my throat, massaging the aching muscles.

With Sara's help, I limp off the mat.

Tala gazes at me with disinterest. "Do you need to go to the infirmary?"

"I've never felt better," I declare. My ragged voice is just above a whisper, throat spasming with each syllable.

Tala sighs and calls out the next match. While there's Serous in each gym, anyone who needs it must go to the nurse's office for a check-up in case the medicine doesn't fully do its job.

I ignore the two students sparring as my gaze travels to the entrance of the gym. Adrian is still there, but he's not watching the match; his calculating blue eyes are on me.

I give what I hope is a smile, although his expression doesn't change. His face is stone, unyielding. I wish I could tell what he's thinking, but I bet it's along the lines of just how weak I am.

The thought twists my insides more than Emmerick's kick, and I swivel back to the pair of attackers just in time to see Amber get hit in the temple by a lithe Naire with enough force to fall unconscious.

Tala yells at someone to give the girl Serous and then take her to the infirmary. We watch in silence as she gets carried away.

As Tala continues to pair students up, I let a small smile creep onto my face. That's the first time I've gone up against Emmerick during class without ending up in the hospital.

I may have gotten my butt handed to me, but at least I hit my goal.

The five-minute trek through the school grounds takes longer than normal as I hobble along beside Sara. She doesn't ask before sliding past a creaky and unused door, holding it open for me behind her.

I prefer to stay hidden after a rough fight in front of the class, and I'm grateful Sara doesn't question this habit. Any show of weakness always excites the other students, as though an injured person is just begging for a challenge.

We walk silently through the dusty, thin hallway. I lean forward to gauge Sara's expression, but she's too far ahead of me to see. She hasn't spoken to me since class ended, but I can feel some sort of animosity emanating from her.

I quietly huff and rub my twinging side. After the match, I could tell I wasn't as badly injured as I had predicted. That's normally how it is for me, though. I have an annoyingly low pain tolerance that makes me believe the wound is worse than it is, but when I check, sometimes it hasn't even broken skin.

By the time we get to our room, I'm jumping on the balls of my feet, antsy for Sara to say something. It isn't like I *volunteered* to go up against Emmerick. What was I supposed to do? Say no? That word doesn't exist in Tala's world.

I go over to my side of the room—which is in considerably more disarray—and grab the tiny vial half full of clear liquid on my wooden dresser. The top spins off with a flick of my hand, revealing an attached dropper, and I put a drop of Serous on my tongue. I can't help the quick distortion of my features as I carefully place the bottle back on the dresser and dramatically fling myself onto my bed.

Rolling over, I squint at Sara. She's hugging a pillow tight to her chest and sitting cross-legged on her sheets, regarding me cautiously.

The silence makes me nervous, so I shuffle through topics to talk about. "Nurse Dorna gave me a secret stash of Serous for emergencies, though I basically use it every day. It may taste like Obsidian toenails, but at least it does the trick," I offer to make her laugh.

When I get no response, I ease onto my back and throw an arm over my eyes with a soft sigh. "Just give me a few minutes for the medicine to work, then I'll be ready to head to dinner. I can meet you down there if you're hungry now."

"Are you not the least bit upset that Emmerick had no intention of stopping earlier? He could have killed you, and

Tala looked ready to let him!" Sara suddenly yells, throwing her pillow at me.

It hits the wall beside my head with a light thud and partially lands on my knee. The bright white pillowcase is in stark contrast with my black ones, and even after being thrown across the room, it still has fewer wrinkles than my bed covers.

She springs from her mattress and starts pacing. I watch as her hands close into fists and tears well in her eyes. *Wow, she's really upset by this.*

I rise and join her in the middle of the room, planting my hands on her tense shoulders. "I'm fine," I say sternly, getting her to stop and meet my eyes. "Emmerick is an idiot, but he's not a killer. He's just trying to scare me, and Tala knows it. I appreciate your concern, but I promise I'm okay. The Serous is already working. I'm all healed up."

I spin around with my arms out for show. It's true, though. The pain in my stomach is completely gone, along with all the bruises that peppered my limbs.

Sara frowns, but I can tell I've distracted her from her prior distress. "Serous shouldn't work that fast, especially in such a tiny amount."

I shrug. "I told you my injuries weren't significant. Now, come on, I'm starving."

I grab my gray hoodie and sling it on. The coloring options for clothes and accessories include white, gray, and black. The academy loves its neutral colors.

Sara gives me one more skeptical look, biting her lip. I don't give her the chance to continue the conversation as I walk out the door. My roommate sighs behind me but follows without commenting.

We amble through the large, main hallway and pass by one of the multiple display cases. I slow down to gaze through the glass at the wide range of weapons. There are mostly different sizes of swords and daggers, and a few arrowheads. I've used all of these weapons before, but most feel clunky when I wield them.

Frustration swarms behind my eyes at the sight of the steel, the sharp edges glinting lethally in the torchlight. As Tala so gently puts it, I'm more likely to hurt myself than an Obsidian with a weapon in my hand. While my performance as a fighter has slowly increased over the years, I'm nowhere near where I need to be to become a powerful hunter.

But I made a promise to myself and my parents. Giving up isn't an option.

I wade closer to the glass, biting the inside of my cheek in concentration. *What can I do to give myself some sort of advantage? Think, Cassie, think. Anything is better than nothing.*

I do my best not to imagine how my face likely resembles a thoroughly constipated Belar chicken and focus on finding an answer to all of my problems. At the internal sound of crickets, a defeated sigh escapes my lips and I push away from the wall, reluctantly following Sara down the hall.

As we near the dining hall, I hear the echoing of over a hundred voices spilling out of the open doors. Students sit themself based on age and class, and as seniors, we are at the last long table in the expansive room.

The corners of the cafeteria hold wooden tables with large pots that store our usual food. There's an instructor beside each one, with students picking a corner at random to serve themselves whatever is inside the dishes. The instructors regard us silently, confirming we only take a rationed portion.

Agriculture is scarce now, with the shadow monsters following livestock wherever they are. While Obsidian attack humans first, they won't hesitate to kill animals as well.

Fields with farmers are another prominent target, which

means most have guards stationed by them. Our academy is as self-sustaining as possible and has a large greenhouse at the back of the school that the first-year students assist with. There's also a simple workshop, where kids learn to sharpen and care for their weapons. When I told the Headmaster about my experience with plants, he assigned me two weeks in the workshop with the second-year students until I joined my official classmates in the third-year group.

Sara and I stand in the shortest line of the four and fill our plates with scrambled Belar eggs and lumpy porridge. Sometimes there is meat or fresh fruit, but it's never consistent.

We head over to our table, the quietest of the bunch. Our classmates pick at their food, staring off in different directions with disinterested expressions. It's the complete opposite of the first years who laugh and chatter amiably.

We set our plates down at the end of the table, close to the wall. I end up next to Naire, tall with short, spikey black hair and a nose ring. She slides closer to the person on her other side when I sit down, and I roll my eyes at Sara, who takes a seat across from me. At least she's lucky enough to sit by Jared, one of the few who doesn't seem to hate us.

"Hello, Sara, Cassie," he says with a polite nod.

I tilt my head and smile back, pleased he used my preferred nickname. Sara shovels a large bite of porridge into her mouth and gives him a half-wave.

The rest of the class ignores us, returning to their quiet argument of who would win in a fight: a rabid dog or a Zero. I answer their debate in my mind with a soft snort. That's an easy one.

While some Obsidian developed one or more senses, Zeros have no mutations or enhanced abilities. The rabid dog would win, since Zeros are weak if they don't have numbers on their side.

Satisfied with my answer, I take a bite of the eggs, which are cold and bland. Rare commodities like herbs are difficult to come by nowadays, so flavorless food is a staple. I take a second, then a third bite, too hungry to care.

A sharp kick lands on my shin, and I yelp, glaring at Sara. She discreetly points to Jared. I look at him. He's grinning and I realize he must have been talking to me.

"I'm sorry. Did you say something?" I wipe my mouth with my napkin as I lower my fork. By the speed at which I was mindlessly shoveling tasteless eggs into my mouth, I must've appeared crazy.

"I was just saying that I like a girl with an appetite," he laughs, gazing down at my nearly finished plate.

Eyes wide, I turn to Sara, who's silently choking on food. From her reaction, that's not what he said the first time.

Once the initial shock goes away, I eye Jared as he winks. When he pivots to talk to Bryce, a long, lanky kid with acne, I study his form. Jared's short, an inch or two above my five-and-a-half-foot frame, but he seems taller with the way he carries himself. He's also muscular with light blonde hair barely scraping above dark green eyes.

Overall, he's pretty attractive, but I don't know why he'd be flirting with me. I can sum up the number of times he's acknowledged me on one hand, including tonight.

Unsure of what to do next, I lock eyes with Sara, who's now sporting a stupid grin. She wiggles her eyebrows and makes kissing faces. I force down a laugh and I shove another bite of food into my mouth.

Jared must be in a good mood, and he's sharing the love.

Chapter 4

Transferring Conviction

LYING IN BED THAT NIGHT, MY EYES STARE UNSEEINGLY UP AT the ceiling as I chew on my lower lip. Sometimes I can't fall asleep, not with what awaits me when my eyes close.

After having the daydream of my parents yesterday, I have no desire to see their mutilated bodies tonight.

I roll over and tightly hug a pillow, squeezing my eyes shut. To keep my mind from imagining their deaths, I focus on another memory, only hours after their demise.

My first day at Hallow Academy.

I stare at my hands, limply folded with my palms up and still smeared in ash from earlier. My head hangs low, pulling my body down to slump in the chair, chin straining in its efforts to rest against my chest.

The ash has colored my hands a dull black from the hours I'd spent on a horse. The coal paints a picture on my hands, and one shaking finger traces the design on my left palm as I sit listlessly.

I'm not entirely certain where I am—the transfer from the horse to this room was just a blur—but the confusion dissipates under the weight of my indifference. Nothing matters, not without my parents.

"Miss Hale," a voice says in front of me.

I look up, my neck seizing painfully at the effort. Within seconds, the surprise dwindles into a comfortable numbness. For the first time since sitting in this plush leather chair, I focus on my surroundings.

The room is medium-sized, with floor-to-ceiling book-cases crafted from rich mahogany lining the walls. I slouch in one of the two tan chairs facing an enormous desk where a man sits in a crisp black suit. His short, dark hair is slightly graying on the sides, his mouth slanted in a frown. His hands rest on the desk while his fingers lightly tap an odd rhythm.

My eyes drop to the surface of the glossy table. There's an emblem etched into the surface: an embellished 'A' above an 'H' with a simple line cutting horizontally through the center.

Concern—*is that annoyance as well?*—shines in his light blue eyes, and, from the inflection in his tone, this wasn't the only time he's spoken my name.

At least I'm assuming it was him, because the man and woman flanking his sides don't seem so worried.

"I'm sorry about your parents, Cassidy." The man in the suit speaks again. "My name is Devero Hallow. I'm the head-master of this academy."

There's an extended pause as Devero stares at me expec-tantly. He's probably waiting for me to say something, maybe ask what academy he's talking about, but I stay silent. My lungs ache as they fill with air, a slow pain that expands with my breath until I'm afraid my lungs will burst, and then I slowly breathe out through pursed lips.

I center all of my energy on keeping myself breathing. In, out. Everything else—talking, walking, *emotions*—is of little importance.

After an awkward minute, he leans back and smooths out his tie with a light cough. "Yes, well, our students normally start their training earlier than your age of—" he glances at some notes scattered across the table, "fifteen, but I'd like to make an exception in your case if you are interested in joining our school. You'd be an excellent fit here, I think."

Once more, he stops. With three sets of eyes on me, I shift uncomfortably in my seat. How could he know I'm a good fit when I've been doing nothing but sitting in this chair?

I force my mouth open to say something—an action that hurts more than it should—though what words will escape is unknown to me. Before I find out, the woman to his right gives a harsh laugh.

"Oh, please, Dev, you're trying too hard. Even if this girl wasn't a mute, she wouldn't last a day here. Look at her. Pathetic."

"Tala." The sharp warning from the headmaster rings through the room. He continues talking, but I don't hear him as another sensation washes over me. This time it's like acid pouring over my skin.

I turn my head to meet the gaze of the older woman. Her eyes are gray and thin, pink lips pull into a sneer. Her hip rests on the side of the desk, arms crossed over a snug black leather outfit that clings to her lean frame. The other hip has a holster and a long sword attached to it.

Tala, I assume, raises her eyebrows, as if daring me to fight back.

"What did you call me?" My voice comes out rougher than I expected, more gravelly from disuse.

I wait for the incredulous anger to disperse under the numbness, but it doesn't. It floods my veins, pushing adrenaline through my body.

The woman laughs again. "She's deaf, too. That's just great." Her voice is high and light, like it's made to sing lullabies rather than spout insults. She flicks her blonde hair behind her, and I'm struck by how someone so stunning could be so cruel.

Tremors overtake my hands from her taunts. I clench them into tight fists and grit my teeth, doing my best to hold my tongue. The last thing I need is to make a record of the fastest person accepted and expelled from some random academy I've never heard of.

Truthfully, I should thank her, right? While her words are a slap in my face, at least I feel alive again, my body waking up from its anesthetized state.

Yet she's looking at me with such hatred, a searing fire with the sole goal of burning me from the inside like dead, dry vines. It's insane and confusing and, as I fight back my frustration, very undeserving. I've known this woman for less than a day, but it's as though I kicked her puppy, then spat in her face.

Devero shuffles some papers before he clears his throat. "That will be enough, Tala. You're excused."

Tala rears her head back in astonishment, like she can't believe the headmaster isn't taking her side, and I let a tiny smile curl my lips at her scolding. It helps to ease some of the resentment building inside of me.

Tala and Devero stare at each other, and some silent form of communication I don't understand passes between them.

She glances at the man who hasn't spoken yet on Devero's other side, but his eyes never leave me.

His expression is stoic, except for a small part that looks to be trying to figure me out. He still says nothing.

Tala's nostrils flare and she pulls herself to her full height, fixing me with a glare. "You don't belong here. You better say no to our dear Headmaster, or your life will be hell." She strides across the room towards the heavy double doors and slams them behind her.

I can't help but note the wide berth she gives me when heading for the doors. *Is she afraid I'll hurt her? Or that I'll wipe my grimy hands all over her?* Tossing the thought aside, I smother another grim smile. *I just went through hell a few hours ago.* There's nothing she could do to top my family being ripped from me right in front of my eyes.

My gaze locks with the man beside Devero, and my inward grin disappears. He stands tall with his arms behind his back. The man doesn't seem much older than me, maybe by two or three years. He's wearing a similar suit and sword set to Tala's, just less form-fitting. His black hair is short, the tips almost falling into his eyes. His bright blue eyes are impassive, showing no emotion, as if they've seen too much, regardless of his young age.

I wonder what my eyes must look like to him. Blank? Vacant? I tear my gaze away.

With Tala out of the room, the anger fueling my vitality seeps from me like a wilted flower deprived of the sun. Devero also watches me, though his eyes are more curious than intense.

He rests his shoulders against the chair and folds his hands in his lap. I wonder if he'll bring up Tala's attitude, but he doesn't seem perturbed by his employee threatening a student. His relaxed posture almost irritates me.

Devero turns his head toward the man, a slow grin pulling at his lips. "So Zypha's letting you off her leash for once? You've only been shadowing her for a short time, yet she's already given you an assignment. Jeez, Adrian, you must feel so proud."

I peek at Adrian, whose attention narrows on the headmaster, giving him an impassive glance. I can't tell if the headmaster is joking with Adrian or purely taunting him. Devero sighs at Adrian's lack of response and turns back to me.

"I'm sure you're wondering who we are and what we do," Devero splays his hands in front of him. "We are Hallow Academy, founded by my father after the calamity started. We're a military academy, meaning we train kids into adulthood to protect what's left of humanity and fight back against the rising number of Obsidian that's plagued our country for thirty-one years. First years start at thirteen. You'll be two years behind your classmates, but if you work hard, you might graduate when you're eighteen. You can refuse, of course. I will be more than happy to arrange for you to leave for the fields."

I openly gape at the headmaster as he finishes his spiel, trying to wrap my head around what he just said.

Training to kill Obsidian.

The monsters that just *murdered* my parents.

My body quivers at the memory, still fresh in my mind. I push down the thought of the creatures before fear takes hold of me. I want to tell the headmaster 'no,' that I'm not strong enough to do what he thinks I can do.

The fields are another unknown in this new life, but they have to be better than hunting Obsidian. What am I supposed to hope for? The chance to avenge my family? I'll just be another casualty in a war we can't win. Their sheer numbers alone overpower us easily.

A shiver slides across my freezing skin, only adding to the tremors wracking my thin frame. The only desire I have now is to curl up into a ball and ignore the world forever.

"There's a reason you survived, Cassidy."

My head snaps up at the voice that clearly didn't come from the headmaster. This voice is deeper, smoother. Adrian puts one hand on the desk and bends forward, trapping me in his gaze, turning me to ice. A piece of his black hair falls across his forehead, and my breath catches at his fierce expression.

"Those demons killed your family, but you're not the only one who's gone through this. It happens all the time. This is an opportunity for you to do something about it. You can stop it from happening to another child, mother, or brother. You can fight for humanity, or you can tend to the fields and forget about the thousands of lives that are being taken every day. Taken, then turned against us. What will you do?"

Adrian's eyes burn with passion and anger, as though he's willing and able to transfer some of his courage to me. His face is fierce, jaw clenched with conviction. It makes my fear fall away when the staggering image of myself as a warrior like him pops into my mind.

A warrior. It's an odd feeling, going from hopeless to motivated in one breath. But Adrian is right. I may never avenge my family, but I can at least stop it from happening to someone else's. Maybe if I can save just one life, that will bring meaning to my existence. That, even if for a second, I can make a difference.

What would make my parents proud? Being alive but living in constant fear, or sacrificing myself to save another?

I straighten in my chair and turn to the headmaster. He looks bored, like he's waiting for the conversation to be over.

"I'm in." When I flick my gaze to Adrian, he nods in satisfaction, crossing his arms again. I incline my head back and stand. Sucking in a deep breath, my lungs fill with new purpose.

Headmaster Hallow rises to his feet, but he doesn't move as he studies me. "The world has fallen into chaos, Cassidy. Your classes may seem arduous now, but our methods work. We don't train kids, we train *soldiers*. Those who can pass the trials at the end of their senior year receive the best fighting chance to survive the hellish world outside these walls. Do you understand?"

I watch the headmaster with wide eyes. Is this why he didn't discipline Tala? Because being brutal is a good thing?

And what about these trials? He doesn't go into detail about them, but I assume they're important, maybe even dangerous.

The idea makes me hesitate, makes me consider if this is really what I want to do. Hallow said I can easily go to the fields. I'm sure I wouldn't have to fight there. But I remember what Adrian said about being able to make a difference in someone's life.

I don't want what happened to my family to happen ever again. Not if I can do something about it.

I mull over Hallow's words, flipping through my options.

"I understand, Headmaster."

"Then you're ready to join this academy."

Chapter 5

Aggressive Certainty

A DEEP ACHE RESONATES IN MY CHEST BEFORE I EVEN OPEN MY eyes. It pulsates through my heart and up to my head, my temples throbbing with each heartbeat. I hoist myself off the bed only after the headache subsides, glancing over at Sara's sleeping form to make sure I didn't wake her.

That's it. There's no way I'm sleeping tonight.

I shuffle into our adjoining bathroom and grip the sides of the stone sink, glancing at myself in the mirror. Tired hazel eyes stare back at me. Pale, clammy skin gives the impression of a ghost, not helped by the dull blue glow of the Azura plant.

I quickly turn and rush out of the bedroom, smothering memories that threaten to grip my mind. I don't like to see my reflection; it reminds me too much of my mom.

My footsteps echo loudly in the empty halls as I jog down the steps leading away from the dorm. Thoughts about dinner last night invade my brain, how Jared continued to rotate between Sara and me and his friends.

Sara spent the rest of the night gushing about how cute he is, and I spent the rest of the night absentmindedly nodding along. He seemed to flirt with us both equally, though, which means he's probably not interested, just a tease. Hopefully Sara doesn't take his antics too seriously.

It was the strangest evening I've had in a long while.

Turning right, I let my feet guide me into a narrow hallway that leads to a smaller version of the main gym. It's just big enough to fit a sparring mat in the center of the room, with multiple wooden target boards mounted to the back wall. Practice dummies line the left wall, and the other has a long shelf stocked full of weapons, each stamped with the same school emblem as Hallow's desk.

I call this place my personal training center because it never gets used during my usual training hours. And my hours include after the sun goes down and before the sun comes up.

As I skim the weapons shelf, I mull over the memory that drove me from my bed. The day I learned about the academy. One thing in particular doesn't sit well with me, no matter how much I review the memory: how *empty* I felt in Headmaster Hallow's office.

Now, I wouldn't call myself a ball of energy, but there was something off with me, even if it was the day my parents died. After I left the office, the emptiness faded, and I've never felt the sensation again.

I know I'm missing a puzzle piece, but I don't know how it should fit or what shape it should be.

With a frustrated sigh, I push the memory to the back of my mind and begin my morning practice. I stretch quickly, then grab a few throwing knives from the weapons shelf. The blades are dark gray and sleek, the sharp edges glinting off the torchlight.

Knives are one of my favorite weapons. Nothing is better than tossing daggers coated in fire at a target. We're banned from using flames without an instructor present, though, so I can't hone that skill on my own.

I place myself in the middle of the mat and face the target boards. Releasing a controlled breath, I launch five knives in quick succession, each one flying through my fingertips to land solidly on the board. I shake out my hand and scrunch up my nose as I go to gather my blades, judging the far distance between them and the center dot. *Have I ever hit the bullseye?*

"Why are you awake at this hour?"

A voice jolts me from my thoughts, startling me. I ignore the fifth knife still stuck in the wood and spin around, bending my knees as I lift one of my four knives.

Adrian's examining me intently, one hand resting on the doorframe and his head tilted like he's trying to solve an unsolvable riddle. It's not the first time he's given me that look. Others have too, but with him, it seems less...demeaning.

I straighten up with a relieved sigh and return to my last lodged knife. "What time is it?" I ask over my shoulder.

"Four in the morning," he responds, emphasizing the first word. His voice is thicker than normal, which I attribute to the hour. The deep timbre reverberates against the walls and surrounds me with his husky voice.

The power he exudes, even in the middle of the night, is overwhelming. I clear my throat, unable to meet his gaze as I return to my position in front of the targets.

"That sounds about right. This is my normal training time. The real question here is, why are *you* up?" I don't wait for his answer as I throw my next round.

They are wilder than the first set, one knife even

bouncing off the board to clatter against the ground in a mocking laugh. I silently curse the universe for my wretched aim while sulking over to gather the blades.

"Security's doing rounds, and I saw the light from the main corridor." I hear him come farther into the room and barely hold in a groan, wishing he would leave me alone to train in peace. I always feel so disoriented when he's around. "Your throws are fast but too rushed. You might take out a Zero, but nothing more than that. Sleep would help you focus better on the target."

Knives in hand, I spin toward him once more and press my back into the mounted target, crossing my ankles. The rough wood against my shoulder blades, deep rivets from years of use, helps to keep me grounded. Adrian wanders past the mat, one hand massaging the other as he regards the weapons shelf casually.

"Gee, thanks for the advice." It's impossible to keep the sarcasm out of my voice. He glances at me with a raised eyebrow before returning his attention to the weapons again. I ease up on my bitter tone, but only slightly. "If you knew me, you'd know that I'm lucky to get four hours of sleep a night. I decided a long time ago to use that extra time to train rather than lie in bed. It seemed more productive. Besides, I'm just having an off day."

I twirl one of the daggers in my hand while Adrian picks up a sword and runs his thumb along the flat edge of the blade.

"One off day," he declares, holding the sword up to the torchlight, "could cost you your life out in the field. Or someone else's."

Flushing with anger, I viciously stab four of the knives back into the board, keeping one in hand. *I don't need him to tell me I'm still not able to protect anyone.* By the time I turn around, Adrian is back on the opposite side of the mat, close to the door. His fast movements are giving me whiplash.

"Why are you here, Adrian?" It's the only thing I'm able to express without insults flying from my mouth. I take a deep breath to cool down. Throwing a tantrum is the absolute worst thing I could do at this moment.

"I saw your match today with," he searches for the right word, "Emmerick, right? Your moves are sloppy, and you're not strong enough to go up against someone like him. Which means you're not strong enough to go up against an Obsidian."

"Wow," I respond with a low whistle. "Don't hold back now."

He gives me an 'I'm being serious' look. "Your senior trials are coming up, and you're not ready. If you try to take them, you'll fail. If you somehow pass the trials, you'll die within your first week outside the academy."

I can feel the anger crawling up my skin like a rash at his words, my pathetic attempt at calming down getting unceremoniously chucked out the window. His words, his lack of faith, sting. Even as my ire rises, my mind flashes to the graduation lists in the main gym, to all twenty-five students who have died as the last-ranked person, including the one from last year. I'm sure Adrian is thinking the same thing as I am. *Well then, I'll just have to beat the odds.*

I bare my teeth at him in an aggressive smile. "Well, not with that attitude."

"Cassidy, you could have died today."

I throw my hands up in the air in exasperation. *First Sara, now Adrian.*

"It was a practice fight! I wasn't in any real danger!" I

can't count how many challenges I've faced with Emmerick that have gone exactly like that, including the night before. While this may be news to them, it's an everyday occurrence for me. "If I *were* in danger, then I—"

"You would have what?" He cuts me off, crossing his arms. His face hardens. "Escaped that chokehold on your own? Hoped that Sara would save you?"

I point my dagger at him, trying to keep the tip from trembling. "Of course not. I would have figured something out. I've been training for years and can handle my own."

Adrian studies me silently, his eyes narrowed. With his thick, black eyelashes, they almost look closed. He marches toward me with intent. I keep the knife up, a shield against his measured steps. Adrian stops right before the tip of the blade touches his chest, his tall, muscular frame looming over me.

Talk about intimidation. I don't think he's ever been this close before, and the scent of pine trees permeates my senses and threatens to distract me.

"For the amount of training you've had, you're incredible. But your classmates have been training for twice as long. They have years of experience on you, and you can't close that gap. I'm sure the headmaster will allow you to take a few years to hone your craft before you graduate. Otherwise, your current skills will get you killed when you go up against a demon that's ten times stronger than Emmerick."

I gape up at him, my dagger lowering in shock. He wants me to hold back a few *years*? After all the work I've put in to catch up? The harsh training sessions, the long hours, the extra beatings from my classmates…all for *nothing*?

When I joined the academy, I vowed to myself and my parents that I would graduate with my class and become a hunter as soon as I could. Waiting until I'm ready may seem like a reasonable option to him, but not to me. Not when I know how many families are being torn apart by monsters that I could've eliminated if I hadn't postponed graduation. On top of that, I've never seen another student repeat a year, and I'd rather be remembered as the first student to survive their cursed ranking than a coward.

Unable to speak through the disbelief, I pivot around and collect all of my knives. I brush past Adrian and deposit the blades into the exact position I found them, picking up a wooden longsword designed for practice dummies.

It takes a few minutes for the storm inside of me to quiet enough to face Adrian again. When I do, I find him still standing by the targets. I match his icy glare with one of my own.

"I think you should leave now, Adrian. I have more training to do." My fingers squeeze the hilt tightly while my free hand gestures to the door.

Adrian exhales sharply, his jaw clenched together. He holds my gaze for a second more before he strides out of the room, leaving as wordlessly as he arrived.

With the harsh echo of a slamming door ringing in my ears, I stumble backward until my shoulders hit the wall and I slide to the floor. Thumping my head against the stone, I squeeze my eyes shut. That conversation was the last thing I expected to hear.

Why does he care if I graduate, die, or stay in my fifth year forever? I shake my head, not understanding Adrian at all.

I fortify myself before using the wooden sword to pull up from my crouched position. Rolling onto my heels, I take in the surrounding area. I have spent so many hours here that it's a part of me. Adrian called me incredible, which means he noticed the progress I've made.

I go over to the first practice figure in the line and furiously swing my sword at its neck. The dummy knocks to the side before righting itself. I relentlessly bash the leather, taking out as much anger as possible.

My wrath continues for hours and through multiple weapons. I fly through the room, attacking and throwing and hitting everything I can reach. By the time Sara arrives to remind me of our approaching morning meal, I head out with new conviction.

I'm not giving up. I'm not even close to hitting my potential. It doesn't matter how many extra hours I'll need to spend practicing or if I have to subject myself to more sparring matches.

I will graduate on time and become the greatest hunter of my generation.

The next week passes in a blur of training, classes, and avoiding Jared as much as possible. Though that's become rather difficult since he walks with us to class and sits by us in the dining hall, keeping me and Sara entertained with his jokes and random thoughts. I don't laugh nearly as much as when the three of us are together.

While I now value him as a friend, our little circle's dynamic has become slightly awkward.

I've been noticing Sara smile a little too widely at him and immediately turn her gaze away when he talks to me. She's never brought up her feelings on the matter, but I can tell it's bothering her when his attention is on me. The problem is, even though Jared is flirty, I can tell it's harmless fun. Yet, any time I try to say that to Sara, she always changes the subject before I can finish.

So I've decided that after dinner tonight, I'm going to tell

Jared to stop flirting with me. However our talk goes, I hope he still wants to stay in our group. I've enjoyed his company, even if I bear no romantic feelings for him.

But I'm nothing without my spectacular ability to avoid uncomfortable situations.

With unimaginable stealth, I run into the mess hall, grab a simple wheat roll, and dash into an unknown hallway before Sara and Jared arrive. A perk of training so early in the morning is that I'm alone in the cafeteria.

A small part of me huffs in annoyance at my theatrics, but a bigger part cheers at my brilliant idea. I'll stay clear of Jared until dinnertime, so breakfast and lunch are on my own.

Chewing on the hard crust, I meander aimlessly, my eyes trailing the dusty stone walls. It's the end of the week, which means our classes are usually more extreme than normal.

Once, Tala snuffed out all the torches, and we had to spar the other students using the entire gym in complete darkness. That's not an experience I want to repeat, especially not right now. My muscles ache from the extra hours I've put in at the gym, and I'm more exhausted than normal. As much as I need the practice, I'm not sure how much more my body can keep up.

Don't think about that. You need to get stronger.

A whisper goes through me, wondering if Adrian is right and if I should stay back at least another year, but I shut the thought down immediately. There's no room for doubt if you're putting everything, even your own life, at stake.

My teeth ache as I clench them tight, my hand squishing the bread roll into chalky crumbs. It's been a week since I silently declared my intentions to graduate, to become stronger, but all I have to show for my efforts is continuous muscle pain.

At this rate, the best I'll do is clean the hunter's barracks, and that's if I'm lucky.

Blinded by my disappointed aggravation, I don't notice the other person in the hallway until it's too late. Papers and wheat flecks go flying as we collide with enough force to send us both sprawling.

Chapter 6

Ancient Ease

I SCRAMBLE TO MY FEET, MY EYES LOCKING ONTO THE MIDDLE-aged woman gathering books and sheets from the floor. Only when her striking violet eyes meet mine, her lips lifted in a sheepish apology, do I place her as my old classroom teacher, Heather Bosts.

She's the fourth-year instructor, the only other professor I've had for a full year besides Tala. I joined halfway through the third year, and, still grieving my parents, spent a lot of it curled in on myself. Not that my first teacher, Raddo, helped in any way; he was just as annoyed as my classmates to accept the late addition.

My current sunny disposition took a while to manifest.

"I'm so sorry, Cassidy. I didn't see you there." Her gentle, melodic voice is the same as ever. She gingerly hands me the last of my breakfast, but I'm too stunned to notice.

"You remember me?" Out of all her students, I was undoubtedly the worst one. Not having as much time to learn the drills taught in the third year showed when we graduated to the next class. No one wanted to be on my team, and for good reason.

Eventually, I realize how rude I'm being, dumbfoundedly gawking at Bosts as she struggles to juggle her books. I jerk forward to help her, but she waves me off with fingertips just barely visible under the volumes.

"Of course," Bosts chirps while regaining her balance, brown ringlets of hair defying gravity with their excessive bouncing. She peers at me over her large stack of leather-bound books. "You were one of my best students."

I gape with my mouth flopping uselessly. *No point in trying to close it if she's going to continue shocking me,* I think faintly. Surely she has mistaken me for someone else. She was always kind to me, but she was kind to everyone.

She laughs at my expression. "Don't give me that; you were a star in the classroom. An extremely quick study, and your determination was a sight to behold."

"Um, thank you." I fight to keep my nose from wrinkling, which would easily give away my displeasure at the compliment, understanding that her words are meant to be encouraging. "But that hasn't helped me succeed. I mean, I'm ranked last in my class, and I can barely hold my own against an opponent in the ring."

"It sounds like you're basing success on brute strength, but that's only a small part of the equation. The strongest Obsidian in the world can't win against a better strategist. If you have to choose between brawn or brain," my past mentor leans in like she's sharing a deadly secret, "be grateful you have brain."

Her words rush through me, though I don't believe she's fully correct. In this world, power matters more. But just like strength, knowledge can be acquired through hard work.

I'm confident that most of my class, including myself,

care very little about anything unrelated to Obsidian. What better way to learn than through practice, right?

"Professor." The word is slow, drawn out, as my mind whirls with the beginning of a plan. "Do you have any books that aren't being used in your classroom?"

"I can do you one better if you're interested. The library is just down this hallway and to the left." Her arm swings out in a sweeping gesture behind her, and I follow the movement.

It doesn't take a genius to know she must have gotten her books from there. *Speaking of which, why did nobody tell me we had a library?* I smile and thank her before dashing off. If I want to check out this mysterious library before class starts, I have to speed up.

The large, wooden double doors are simple enough to spot, and with only a quick hesitation, I shove them open.

There's no mistaking what this room is. Soft, dim light stretches into shadows, creating an ominous feeling that doesn't fit the vibe. Its circular shape holds floor-to-ceiling shelves, all stuffed with different colors and sizes of books.

There's a brief stone floor until it drops to the next step, which is identical to the top tier except the bookshelves only reach to about my neck in height, still allowing full view of the room. The last stair leads to the center, where four tables neatly align in two rows, each sporting paper, writing utensils, and an oil lamp.

I stare at the lamps in surprise. Those are devices of the Old World, the one before the rise of Obsidian. Technology took a giant step back once the war began, as most of the blacksmithing community focused on weapons and keeping Obsidian out of the cities rather than on luxuries.

What is Old World equipment doing in a place like this?

I cautiously enter the room, the silence becoming a

warning bell drumming against my skull, and head to the second tier. I wander through the shelving, my eyes trailing the covers. Most of them are blank, which is confusing to me. *How will I ever find what I'm looking for if I don't know what the books are?*

Incensed, I grab a thin, light green book at random, finally able to read the title, handwritten in gold script.

"The Top Ten Coldest Winters in Ortibam. A riveting read, I must say."

An old voice, like worn leather, wraps itself around the intimate, curved room. I jump, the book nearly slipping from my fingers.

Along with a hammering pulse being trapped in my throat, I'm almost knocked sideways with irritation. *How is it so easy for people to sneak up on me?* Maybe I can find a book on increasing my passive perception because this is getting ridiculous.

I tip my head to the side, following the direction of the voice, my face wiped clean of emotion. The speaker didn't *sound* threatening—no need for them to know they had successfully snuck up on me. *Thank the universe I didn't drop the book. That would have been a dead giveaway.*

"And you are?" I keep my voice casual, vaguely bored, as if the stranger across the room is of no importance to me.

The bass-pitched voice chuckles softly before a figure steps into the lowest section of the room, his body alight enough from the lanterns to give me a discernible view of his features. The oldest man I've ever met, with his ancient characteristics, immediately puts me at ease. *Definitely not a threat.*

His skin, a deep golden brown, folds endlessly over his hands, face, and head. The smile lines are extensive around his mouth and eyes. Long, brown robes scrape against the floor in soft swooshes as he moves, and a thin golden chain wraps twice around his neck.

"I am Zacharias Cane, but you may call me Zachary," he states in a deep voice.

"Cassie Hale," I respond out of courtesy, but my eyes narrow a fraction. Never trust someone who sounds trustworthy, not at first.

Zachary doesn't seem perturbed by my apprehension. He leans forward, his eyes a shade lighter than his robes and bright with intrigue. "Ah, the only student I have not met. Curious, what brings you here?"

"You've met every student?" His words distract me from whatever I was originally going to say, which would have probably been a very lame attempt at intimidation.

"Indeed. The founding headmaster made it a rule that in the first year of training, each class is summoned to the library as a way of reminding them of this useful tool, but alas, I seldom have visitors. The current Headmaster Hallow doesn't care for books, and neither do the students, unfortunately. You must have fallen through the cracks because of your late arrival."

So, everyone knows about the library but ignores it anyway. Makes sense since I've never heard about it until today. I guess the teachers were so busy trying to catch me up with the classes I missed that they didn't remember to take me here. And if the headmaster doesn't think the library matters, why should they?

Zachary is eyeing me with a strange expression: half smile, half focus. It takes a second for me to remember I never answered his original question.

Why am I here?

A reasonable enough inquiry that deserves a reasonable

enough answer, but I hesitate, gripping the novel in my hand tightly.

Do I even know what brought me here? I wanted to learn...what? What could I learn here that I haven't already or could easily gain in the classroom?

Nothing that I come up with sounds even remotely reasonable—or comprehensible—so I decide to ask another question instead of answering. It seems odd to have any volumes in here not related to the Obsidian, and I can't get the query out of my mind.

"Why is there a book about Ortibam's unfortunate climate changes?"

Ortibam is the country on the other side of the Bone Strip. Arrynd was their biggest import of cloth and wool, since Ortibam is infamously known for its deadly winters, ten times worse than our own.

"You can learn a lot from things that appear to be useless," Zachary states lightly.

I wait for him to elaborate, but he only strides a few feet to one of the wooden tables and sits down, gesturing to the seat across from him.

The sensation of having no control over the conversation is a little unsettling. It's like we're in a battle over who can have the most evasive answers, and I'm rapidly falling behind.

Huffing, I slide the book into its spot on the shelf and join him. The old man smiles warmly as though we just sat down for tea.

"When the war started, we lost much information. As a scholar, it's my sworn duty to protect what we have left, no matter what it is. Most books, paintings, and architecture stay within the cities and scholar academies, where security is extensive. But what would happen if we stockpiled all of our history in one place?"

He pauses, and I bite my lip, watching his face morph from friendly to solemn. "Too much creative exposure?"

"It means we could lose everything in a single blow. The scholarly community dispersed as much of our history as possible, so when this nightmare is over, we won't have to start from nothing."

"And the aristocrats let you do that?" I ask doubtfully. I'd have thought some greedy noble would object to the decision

Local government controls its walls and the surrounding land for all ten cities in Arrynd. Headmaster Hallow reports to the lord of Netiva City, the largest city in the country and only two days by horse from here.

Outside any walls, there is no authority, but there are hardly ever problems because of it. Most people living out there focus only on survival.

"No one at the time cared about our past when our future was in shambles. We took matters into our own hands after the creation of scholar academies." Zachary's lips pull down at the corners, his eyes glazed in recollection of terrible memories.

"And having Old World technology here? Is that part of preserving our past?" I gesture to the lantern.

Zachary smiles, pleased with my question. "Yes and no, though I must admit you are very sharp. These lanterns were a trial of combining what we used to know and what we know now. Tell me, what do you know of the Eloyla plant?"

I try not to scoff at the simple question. "It's our lifeblood. Inside the thick leaves is a paste that we coat on our weapons and torches. The fire clings to the paste, making it a lot less likely to jump onto our clothes or the floor, and the paste can keep the fire burning for hours longer than any other material."

Zachary nods. "This Eloyla lantern doesn't use oil but a mixture of rope and paste to create a wick. There are few in production, so I count myself lucky to use them."

I open my mouth to ask more questions, specifically why he has them, but I jolt from the chair as a shock goes through me. It can sometimes be hard to tell what time it is, but after so many years, I get a cold shiver down my spine that warns me Tala's fury is going to be upon me soon if I don't hurry.

Zachary leans back in his chair, his face returning to a friendly smile. "It was nice talking to you, Cassie. Please come visit again soon."

"Thank you, I will."

I sprint through the heavy double doors and into the hallway. *What a strange encounter.* I never found what I was looking for, but meeting Zachary was worth it.

I find my two friends leaning against a pillar lining the courtyard, waiting for me before class starts. I groan, suddenly reminded of the day. *Oh, goodie, what torture will Tala have in store for us today?*

All I want is to keep talking to Zachary, but I hastily push the scholar from my mind. It's going to be a rough class if I can't pull myself together.

My pace slows as I watch Sara and Jared's conversation. From their body language alone, they seem so comfortable around each other, with Jared poking Sara's cheek while she swats at his hand and laughs. His smile, so genuine and easy, is the complete opposite of his confident grin when he looks at me.

The exchange makes me want to throttle Jared. It's obvious he likes her. That's simple enough to see from the interactions they have when the two of them are alone. So why does he still flirt with me?

I sullenly slide past them with a brief hello. Sara snorts at whatever joke he says that I don't hear. I'm too distracted by my thoughts and our upcoming class to pay attention to their conversation. Sara and Jared follow close behind, chatting away.

As we near the propped door that leads to the gym, Jared slings his arm around my shoulders and draws me to his side.

"What's wrong, Cassie? I could have cheered you up with my perfectly timed quips, but we haven't seen you all morning!" He chuckles to himself as he leads me through the archway and into the gym.

"I was busy, but you and Sara seemed to be having a great time together while I was gone. It's good to see you flirting with someone else for a change."

Whaaat am I saying? The words, while said innocently, could easily be mistaken for jealousy. Which is the exact opposite of what I should say to him!

I quickly glance at Jared, ready to take my words back, but before I can, his arm springs from my shoulders. "I'm not flirting with anyone. You guys are my best friends."

His confusion, lips turned down as if the thought never occurred to him, baffles me into silence.

Is he seriously that thick-headed? He may think he's just been joking around with me in good fun, but his actions have been hurting Sara, and that pisses me off. *Who's not waiting for dinner to put this idiot in his place? Oh, right, me.*

I grab his arm and open my mouth, but get cut off by a smothered giggle. My head snaps to the side to watch my class leering at Jared and me. A quick scan around shows Sara on the opposite side of the room, not looking at us.

"Is someone having a lovers' spat? Do that on your own time, kids," Tala shouts with a smirk.

Our instructor stands at the front of the class with Adrian, his gaze pinned on the rack of swords in front of them. Adjacent to the weapons is a bin filled with black hefty jackets on Tala's right.

Dropping Jared's forearm, I follow Sara to the edge of the room. I try to catch her eye to communicate that this was the absolute *opposite* of a 'lover's spat,' but she gives me a brief, strained smile and plants her eyes firmly on Tala.

I whip my head around to glare at Jared, but he doesn't notice, still lost in thought. *Positively wonderful, Jared. Way to make my life more complicated than it has to be. Good job, buddy.*

Chapter 7

Not Without a Fight

I peek up at Adrian, who is still blankly studying the weapons. It's the first time I've seen him since his confrontation a week ago, and I feel painfully unprepared in his presence. Maybe even a little aggravated.

There's no way I've come close to where I want to be this week, and here Adrian is, probably ready to watch me suffer and make his point.

Too bad I have a nasty habit of being stubborn. I cross my arms and hide a smirk, focusing on the bare wall to my right as Tala takes a step forward.

"You officially have two months before your trials, and after that, you'll be able to choose your job based on your ranking in the class. The higher you're ranked, the more likely you'll get the career you desire. The top four spots may choose a job in the city, and the next six are open for academy work. Those of you in last," Tala sneers, invisible to everyone except for me since her eyes are also shooting hateful but smug daggers in my direction, "will become hunters."

Murmurs trickle through the class. Hunters have the most dangerous job; they roam the country actively tracking Obsidian hordes to eliminate them before they can become a threat to cities, fields, or nomadic settlements. Some hunters even protect scattered farms or homes that are frequently attacked.

Those sitting in the middle ranks can join an academy as a security officer or even become a professor if they possess the knowledge to teach.

There are also jobs in the military, who guard the large stone walls that surround the cities or keep the peace between the citizens inside. Only the highest-ranking academy graduates can work in the city, though you don't have to choose it if you don't want to. At a high enough ranking, you get the top pick of any job you want.

Adrian was at the top of his class, but he still returned to the academy as a security officer.

You would think that the top students would become the hunters, with the strongest out there actually making a difference against the Obsidian. I have a hunch it has more to do with the city's agenda. How can an academy run without supplies? Where do those supplies come from?

I'm positive that the cities are poaching our best students for the resources needed to keep this school going. And I'm sure the academies want semi-decent graduates teaching and protecting the students. So that leaves those in last place in charge of mitigating the hordes of death, which, left unchecked, could easily overrun a city.

It's funny how the world works.

But that's not how my world is going to work. No matter what, I will become a hunter.

"So it's time we start seriously training you all for specific

Obsidian attacks. Today we will engage in a mock battle called 'Kill the Commander,'" Tala explains, putting her hands on her hips. "Officer Zypha couldn't make it today, so Officer Camson has graciously offered to fill in for her. We will split into two teams, each led by either me or Adrian. One team will be the Obsidian that attempts to 'bite' and protect the Commander, while the goal of the other team is to take out their leader."

She gestures to Adrian, who steps to the side to reveal a practice dummy painted all black with a red dot on its upper neck. All eyes snap to him. The knowledge we have on Commanders is sparse since they rarely appear in front of humans.

"Commanders," Adrian says in an authoritative voice that draws everyone to attention, "are our most recent mutation. They are a type Four Obsidian, the most powerful one we know of. While they're not strong in the sense of their killing abilities, as they can barely move or see, their brain stem is still intact, giving them the ability to communicate with lesser Obsidian to plan strategic attacks. All monsters are susceptible to a Four's directive, turning the Obsidian into an easily controlled army."

He walks over to the dummy and points to the red dot. "Destroying their brainstem will sever their connection with their minions, making the horde momentarily confused and easier to kill. If you find that the Obsidian are attacking with a sort of purpose, then you know a Commander is not far behind. The closer you get to their leader, the more ferocious their fighting is. That's when you know you're going in the right direction."

I stare at Adrian in astonishment, along with my classmates, as we take in what he said. I knew that the Obsidian had mutated due to the virus reattaching parts of their brains to create heightened senses, but constructing a brain stem capable of cognitive function? *How is that possible?*

Tala waits for questions as we process Adrian's words before she claps her hands together. "Alright, let's pick teams. Adrian, since you were so gracious enough to help us out today, why don't you pick first?"

Adrian scans the crowd, his eyes resting on me for a brief second before moving on. "Jared."

Disappointment flows through me as Jared joins Adrian. I don't know why I thought he would pick me. A tiny part of me wants to show him why I deserve to be here, that I'll do anything to graduate.

"Emmerick," Tala shouts.

They continue to progress through the class, picking one after another, with Adrian sometimes calling out people by their features. He chooses Sara halfway through, and she gives me an apologetic glance before moving to her new team.

Each selection causes more frustration to bubble up inside me. I was prepared for Tala not picking me, but this is humiliating.

In less than a minute, the only two left are me and Astrid, a short, timid girl who's one spot above me in the ranking. Black bangs hide her eyes, and she never interacts with the class unless she has to.

"Astrid," Adrian says without hesitation, and my chest squeezes tight.

"I guess I'm stuck with the one nobody wants," Tala snickers. I keep my head held high as I slide in beside Chelsea and Naire, refusing to meet anyone's gaze.

It's not like I'm new to being shamed, and from the things

I've been through, this doesn't even make it into my top ten most embarrassing moments. The thought actually makes me feel better.

"Since I chose first, you can pick what side you want to be on," Adrian announces to Tala, his expression never wavering.

"Let's see." She taps her finger to her chin. "We'll slay the commander. You guys can be the demons."

Adrian nods and picks up the painted mannequin, ordering his team to follow him out of the room. They all grab wooden swords on their way out.

Once they're gone, Tala tosses out the jackets. I throw mine on, and it feels heavy, like it's made from lead. "While we aren't using fire in this fight, these jackets are similar to the fireproof ones you use in practice. The weight of the jacket helps to take a bite from an Obsidian without the venom getting injected into your system. We left the masks that attach to your collars off for today, but you must always wear them when you're in battle to protect your neck, mouth, and nose against fire and bites."

When she's done handing out the jackets, she gestures for us to grab a wooden sword. I pick one up that's a little smaller than the others in a feeble attempt to help out my sore muscles.

Even with the lighter blade, my arms ache against the weight, and it takes effort for the strain not to show on my face.

I also snatch up a dagger and tuck it into the waistband of my pants at the small of my back. It's always smart to carry an extra weapon, even if the battle isn't real.

"For this game, you get 'bit' if the other team hits you in a place that is not covered by the jacket, including your face, neck, and hands. You 'kill' the other team if you hit them at a vital point, like their neck or head. In this scenario, we are going up against a horde of Twos, so they technically are supposed to have two senses that have been hyper-developed to track down and kill humans."

"What happens if we get bitten?" Emmerick gruffly asks as he swipes his large wooden sword cleanly through the air.

"Well, then you sit out for five minutes, wait for the transformation to kick in, and you join Adrian's team. Normally, if you get bitten by a Two or Three, you still change into a Zero. We're not sure why, but we assume it takes time for the virus to mutate, even with the injection of an already mutated virus. However, for the sake of this game, you'll start as a Two."

We gather around Tala after she grabs two steel short swords. Out of the ten on my team, I end up as a straggler, flitting around the outside of the half circle. Even though I hate my group, with it including people like Emmerick and Joshua, I'm itching to test my skills out in a proper fight.

"Final rules," Tala says with a flourish of her swords. "Adrian will hide the Commander somewhere in the east wing. You're prohibited from going anywhere else in the school; we've received special permission from the headmaster to battle outside of the gym in this section only. Adrian will stay with the Commander and send his team out to hunt us down. We are going to send one of our own to hide in a random gym while everyone else lures each Obsidian in there individually to be killed in a surprise attack."

Tala pauses with a slow smile. "Cassidy will be the brave soldier to wait for the attack in the gym. I want you to stay in gym E5. Hide somewhere well and be ready for the opposing team to rush in."

I wait to see if she's serious because, in my humble opinion, this plan sucks. But my comrades remain silent and look at each other with meaningful grins.

Good grief, they're not even trying to hide it.

After a period of awkward silence, Tala continues slowly, condescendingly. My fingers twitch against the hilt of my sword. "Now you go on ahead while the rest of us figure out the minor details. These don't concern you."

"Whatever you say, boss." With the willpower of an absolute *god*, I smile, give a fake bow, and trot out the door without another glance. Once I'm through the door, I decide to take the back hallways so I don't run into anyone accidentally.

After the not-so-subtle performance of my comrades, I know that I'll end up stuck in the gym with no actual task to do while my allies completely forget about me.

Striding forward silently, I contemplate screwing this 'plan' and going back to help them, but I also think my team would strike me down and call it an accident. No way I can take on both sides simultaneously, and I've had enough embarrassment for one day.

It's best if I stay out of their way and take the ridicule of running from the battle later.

I clench my free hand as I march through the hallways, attempting to keep my thoughts from morphing into anger. *How am I supposed to prove myself if no one gives me a chance?*

Flinging the door to the gym open with frustration, I stalk into the room. I only get a few feet in before skidding to a stop, my blood turning into a frozen sludge that weighs heavily in my veins.

The Commander rests in the center of the room, a black beacon under the bright torchlight.

The rest of the room is empty of Obsidian, except for

Adrian, who stands before the Commander with his sword pointed at me.

My eyes bulge from their sockets, jaw dropping. *Why is he here? What in the world is going on?*

Adrian lowers his sword and sheathes it like he's unperturbed by the enemy being twenty feet away from him. *Or maybe he's just not worried about me,* I think sourly.

Questions form in my mind, tickling the tip of my tongue, but he speaks before I have the chance to voice them.

"Tala knows me too well. She sent you into the belly of the beast to be slaughtered," Adrian mumbles as he leans against the Commander.

I pause, the gears in my head working overtime to process his words. Tala knew he'd be in here? What was her goal then, to make me suffer a crushing defeat? The thought makes my lips pinch together. I lift my sword with two hands and bend my knees.

"Maybe so, but I'm not going down without a fight," I snarl, gnashing my teeth. He straightens and draws closer, still not taking out his sword.

"I'd be disappointed if you did," he exclaims, raising his hands in defense.

I dash forward, my weapon swinging in a wide arc. Adrian bends backward at the waist, and my sword flies right over his chest. I press the offensive, attacking through the pain in my screaming muscles. *Curse those extra hours in the gym!*

"I thought you'd be faster than this. You *have* been training, right?" He ducks another attack with ease, his movements flowing like water.

I let out a growl, pushing myself harder. I'd have a better chance of harming the air as he blurs with each step. *Or maybe my vision is going out.*

He maintains his speed while I feel myself wearing down

with each minute that passes. We dance around the room, but eventually, I stop in the middle to catch my breath. Lurching a step forward with a gasp, my legs quake from the extensive effort. My grip on the hilt loosens, and I'm afraid it will slip from my hand without me noticing.

I force my sweat-drenched face to look at Adrian in the corner of the room. He's eyeing me darkly, the planes of his face highlighted sharply from the torchlight, his arms crossed.

"I expected more from you, Cassidy," Adrian says with a sigh. He shakes his head, finally drawing his sword.

My heart rate quickens as I realize he's about to finish the skirmish. I haven't even landed a blow on him. *It can't end like this! I won't let it end like this.*

My mind spins as I think of a strategy, anything that could help me win. But the goal of this exercise isn't to defeat Adrian. I shouldn't be focusing so much on him. Even on my best day, I couldn't take him down on my own.

I stop breathing as my eyes rest on the Commander, who's placed a few feet too far from where Adrian is. The fight had moved him away from his leader. I'm definitely in no shape for a sprinting contest, but a slight pressure against my lower back gives me an idea. *If you have to choose between brawn or brain, be grateful you have brain.*

I can tell the moment Adrian recognizes what I'm about to do. He lunges towards the Commander at the same time I launch my sword through the air towards the single red dot on its neck.

With his eyes finally off me, I bolt after him. Well, it's more of a fast wobble, and I send a silent prayer that it's enough.

Adrian catches my sword out of the air by its hilt and

whips around, but I'm already right in front of him, my dagger placed firmly against his throat.

"I expected more from you, Adrian," I wheeze. My attempt to throw his words back into his face isn't as satisfying as I hoped it would be, the deafening silence broken with each loud gasp of my ragged breath. "You lose."

Chapter 8

Echoed Memories

Neither of us move, our eyes locked in a battle of wills. This is where my stubbornness comes in handy. Either he's going to break it, and hopefully soon, or I *will* fall unconscious at his feet.

Adrian's eyes narrow, his chest heaving. Finally, he steps back, handing me my sword and sheathing his. My blade is crafted from smooth wood, and his is metal. They must not trust the students to avoid maiming each other.

I let my weapon clatter to the ground as I sink to my knees with a weak laugh. Black spots dot my vision, but even that isn't a cause for concern. Only one thought continues to run over and over in my mind.

I beat Adrian.

I crawl over to the wall not littered with training supplies and slump against it, my body unable to support me anymore. *I doubt I'll be able to get out of bed for a week after this.*

Adrian ambles closer to me, gracefully sliding to the floor, his hands clasped together and elbows on his bent knees. If I had an ounce more energy, I would've used it to ponder how

I look like death warmed over while he isn't even sweating. But I'm too tired to care right now.

"Aren't you going to kill the Commander?" Adrian asks from my right, his voice annoyingly unwinded. "That's the whole point of this drill."

"No, I'm sure the others will come soon to end it. They probably wouldn't believe me if I said I beat you anyway."

Adrian glances at me curiously, and I rub my upper arms.

"Besides," I add, uncomfortable under his scrutiny, flashing a teasing smile as I switch the subject, "the only thing that matters to me is that *you* know I beat you."

He chuckles, resting his head against the wall and closing his eyes. "You did, and I'll never forget it." After a second, he starts again. "How did you evade my team? I had them posted in multiple corridors to block off entry to this room."

Pulling my lower lip into my mouth, I consider his words. Honestly, I hadn't thought of that as I cruised through the hallways earlier. I assumed I was heading in the opposite direction, and that's why it was so empty.

I end up with a shrug. "I normally take the lesser-known hallways when traveling through the academy. And I also left less than ten minutes after you and your team, so you probably weren't fully set up yet."

Silence swallows the space after my answer, and with it drifts faint shouting from the distance. The sound twists my stomach. My team must have made contact with Adrian's group, which means my glorious minute of victory and satisfaction will be gone.

Not willing to let this moment of happiness go, I review our fight in my head. It was amazing to spar with someone of such incredible talent, someone who pushed me harder than ever.

I learned more in that three-minute match with Adrian

than I did in all my years of solo training combined. The idea is astounding and leaves me slightly breathless.

Adrian's eyes open and land on me. "You did well today."

The elation inside me dies as his previous words rush into my mind. "But not good enough to make you believe I'll graduate, right?" I say flatly, curling my hands into fists as his lips press together.

I prepare myself for another disagreement on the subject. *There's no way I'm backing down from this.*

He sighs deeply, rubbing one of his hands against his forehead. "I know you could. But there's not enough time to teach yourself everything you need to know in two months, Cassidy."

"I prefer Cassie," I mutter, sidetracked from my next argument point.

A clever thought pops into my mind. One stemmed from our sparring match, and my breath falters at the possibility. My knees pop as I jump up and begin pacing the diameter of the mat. Adrian stands when I do and leans against the wall with his arms crossed, though I can sense his eyes on me.

Oh man, this just might work. I whirl around, a smile creeping onto my face. The officer observes my complete mood change warily.

"Train me," I urge, my hands spreading out and palms facing the ceiling.

"What?" Adrian stammers, clearly taken aback by my sudden proclamation. I've never seen him look so flabbergasted before.

A fire works its way up from my toes as the idea slowly expands in my mind. I can't imagine how much stronger I could get with the aid of the best warrior in the academy.

"You said it yourself. I don't have enough time to learn it *alone*, but I know I can with the right teacher. Please," I look at him with wide eyes, hoping I can convey just how important his help is to me. "Help me do this."

He studies me uncertainly, his dark brows drawn together. "I'm not an instructor. Tala—"

"Would rather see me prance through the forest at night than pass any test," I intervene. "She would never help me. Being a hunter strong enough to save others is all I ever wanted, and you could help me achieve that. Please, Adrian."

The more I watch his face morph back into its original stony, blank quality, the more discouraged I become. *He's going to say no.* I should have known Adrian wouldn't want to train some random eighteen-year-old on how to pass the trials. *I* wouldn't want to do that.

I try to keep the disappointment off my face and hold some semblance of dignity together. But I must be doing a shabby job because Adrian's eyes soften into something resembling...

Oh no, is that pity? Universe, just strike me down now and save me some suffering.

I contemplate sprinting from the room and spending the rest of my time at the academy hiding from Adrian out of sheer mortification, but the door to the gym bursts open, and half of my team rushes in with battle cries.

Tala follows closely behind them, her eyes scanning the room. She raises her two swords when she sees Adrian and my classmates create a semi-circle around him. He throws up his hands before she can advance.

Adrian nods to me, but I refuse to meet his gaze, to see the *pity* dwelling there. "She already killed me. The Commander is still in play."

Tala glances at me in shock before it transforms into a glare. Everyone in the room pauses until Emmerick surges forward and stabs the Commander in the throat, cheering wildly.

The losing group shuffles into the room with glum expressions, grumbling apologies to Adrian as they survey the winning team jumping around, pumping their fists in the air.

No one on my side acknowledges me, and I'm just fine with that. In fact, I would feel a lot better if there were more walls between me and everyone else. When I asked Adrian for help, I never thought he would feel *sorry* for me, and that's a gigantic blow to my ego.

Tala shouts at us all to return to our usual classroom, and I sullenly follow behind Sara. I can't stop myself from stealing one more glimpse at Adrian, who's still looking at me. There's something else in his eyes now, less sadness and more... conflict? *Is that a good thing?*

I watch as Tala places a hand on his back and whispers something in his ear. Feeling nauseous, I don't see his response as I jog from the room, readying my aching muscles for more sparring matches. *This day is undoubtedly going into my top ten most embarrassing moments.*

Everything is black. I can't feel, see, or hear. For a split second, my heart stops, thinking I've turned into a Zero. Slowly, my vision comes back to me.

I'm back in my home, my home before the academy. The confusion changes into fear, like someone dumped cold water over my head. I try to scream, but I'm unable to move my limbs. I'm trapped behind the eyes of my younger self as I take in my surroundings.

Scattered remains of burned bodies litter the entire living

room. Most of the house has burned black from a fire still licking up the back windows.

Turning my head, I spot the remains of what used to be my parents in the corner, their scorched skin halfway covered in black rock from the semi-transformation.

Even then, the horror that I know I should feel suffocates under a blanket of numbness. Invisible chains bite against my skin as the events unfold, tying me down inside the shell of my body, reminding me that even though my younger self can't feel anything, I still can.

The painful emotions well up inside me like a dam about to burst, and I ache to relieve the pressure. I want to scream, to cry, to run away, yet I can do nothing but sit silently and suffer.

Adrian and Tala barge through the burned remains of a door with their flaming swords raised, their bodies and faces up to their noses covered in black leather. They stop short and absorb the scene before them. Tala moves first, swiping a cloth over her sword to douse the fire and striding over to me with a concerned scrunch of her forehead.

I witness Tala reach me and place a hand on my shoulder. She instantly jerks away as if I stung her, eyes wide. Tala gawks at me before she stands, murmurs something to Adrian I can't hear, and stomps out the fire raging on the other side of the room.

Adrian pulls down his mask and studies me with a slack jaw: an unharmed girl in the corner of a massacre. From inside, I try to shout his name, to cry out, but all I do is blankly stare at him with paralyzed limbs. It's the haze that continues through my meeting with Hallow when I'm first introduced to the academy.

Adrian carefully steps over piles of cinders as he methodically makes his way to me, black boots crunching over ash and char. He kneels in front of me, his bright blue eyes roaming over my body, searching for injuries.

I shrink away from him, my gaze sliding past him to my parents. I don't remember how the fire started or why I'm the only one alive.

"Are you hurt?" His soft voice is soothing, but my mind cannot comprehend his words. I look at him, powerless to speak. He exhales and moves in, wrapping his brawny arms around my small frame and hoisting me into the air.

I don't struggle as he carries me from the house and gently places my listless body in the saddle of a sturdy black horse. I've never seen a horse before, and I'm mesmerized by its glowing blue mane. The horse flicks its head, and the luminous strands lift into the air in a brilliant haze that highlights my stained skin. Swathes of leather cover the saddle, and I keep my hands tucked into my stomach.

How foolish it seems now to care if the leather is ruined by charcoal.

I watch Adrian and Tala exchange more words before they swing onto their respective horses, with Adrian carefully sliding in behind me. My head bobs limply as the trees blur past the racing horses.

I imagine the Obsidian on the other side of the trees, waiting for us to stop so they can feast on our flesh.

I suppress a moan as I roll off the bed and onto my sore feet. The room is pitch black, though I can hear Sara's faint snoring across the room as I silently get dressed. The image of my parents' bodies still echoes in my mind like an unpleasant aftertaste, and I shift uncomfortably in my training sweats.

It's not the first time I've dreamt of that night. That one haunts my dreams more than any other nightmare.

You would think being exposed to it so much would desensitize me to the pain, but every time I wake up from it, I'm left winded with a small throbbing in my head.

I blindly root around the top of the dresser until my fingers encircle the Serous. One drop of the awful medicine falls onto my tongue, and I swallow it quickly before bolting from the room, not waiting for the potion to fix my blurred vision.

I was so fatigued after the mock battle that I skipped dinner and fell asleep. Unconsciousness is also a great way to stop thinking, especially if you make a fool of yourself in front of your role model.

Sara didn't fight me on it, although I saw her trying to mask her worried expression with a smile. She's told me before that I'm too thin, and with all the work I've been doing, I know that skipping meals isn't good for my health. I make a mental note to eat all of my breakfast later.

I let my mind wander to anything but Adrian as I meander my way through the vacant halls, trusting my feet to know the way. I toss my hands up with an exasperated huff after remembering my time at the library and why I was avoiding the mess hall yesterday.

I completely forgot to talk to Jared!

I drag a hand down my face as I think of a time to corner him today, frustration filling me. *I can't neglect this any longer. Today, for sure,* I declare, my fingers balling into fists.

I mentally rehearse my 'focus-on-the-one-you-really-want' speech, opening the door to my favorite training center. My brain sluggishly processes that the torches are already lit.

As my eyes adjust to the brightness, I squint to find

Adrian leaning against the wall and polishing his sword with a white rag.

"What are you doing here?" I ask, unable to keep the surprise from my voice.

Seeing him now after all the crap that happened yesterday is like a punch to the gut. Just being in his presence is a reminder of everything I'm not: strong and powerful.

"I knew that you'd come in here to practice eventually. Don't worry," he says, flipping his rag through the air, "I haven't been waiting long."

"Uh-huh," I hum, pursing my lips. I keep my voice light. "I guess I should have phrased my last question better. *Why* are you here?"

Adrian casts his rag onto a side table, depositing his sword back into its covering. He settles a hand against the weapons shelf. "I need you to be honest with me. Have you at all considered waiting to graduate?"

Well, that's an easy one. My head slants to the side as I fire back in response, "Of course I thought about it. But then I thought about how much I *don't* want to do that, and I discarded it from my mind forever."

I match his grave expression with my determination, refusing to back down. He may not want to train me, but he can't stop me from training myself.

He shakes his head. "Go to bed, Cassie." I scowl and begin to raise my objection, but he continues. "Zypha permitted me to work with you twice a day. We'll start our training later today at six in the morning, but I want you sleeping reasonable hours. You'll get nowhere if you are sleep-deprived."

"You can't—" I start, until I realize what he said. I stare at him in surprise until my lips stretch upwards to the point I'm afraid they'll tear. "Are you serious?"

"I'm always serious," he says in a monotone voice.

I laugh, giddy with relief. *I never thought he'd say yes.*

Adrian's lips tug up on one side, giving me a crooked smile that makes my heart skip a beat. It's the first smile he's ever worn in my presence. The urge to run up and hug him, to thank him profusely, fills me, but I have an inkling that wouldn't go over well.

"I'm not staying up on purpose, though," I sigh. My fingers rub over the pad of my thumb. I feel uneasy sharing a piece of myself that only Sara knows, but I want him to understand. "I have nightmares almost every night. Normally about the day my parents died." I wrap my arms around myself as if that will shield me from the ache of their memory. "I can never fall asleep after them."

He nods, fishing through his front pocket. "I thought that might be the case," he exclaims, pulling out a bottle.

He holds it out for me, and I take it uncertainly. The jar contains white pills that are striped with black. I've never seen them before, not even in the infirmary.

At my confused expression, he states, "Zypha had them specially made for me a few years back. I used to have nightmares, too."

Adrian blinks, jaw working like he's stunned by his admission to any weakness.

If he's surprised, that's nothing compared to my brain combustion. My head rears back at his honest confession. I yearn to push the subject, to learn more about this small connection we share, but his hard expression and crossed arms let me know he doesn't want to talk about it.

"They are sleeping pills. Take one in the evening and it will help you sleep through the night."

I hug the bottle to my chest, touched by his thoughtfulness. "Thank you," I whisper.

He looks away with a small nod and an almost uncomfortable twist to his features. "You should try to sleep now. It's only midnight, and the pills usually last at least five hours. I'll see you in the morning."

I leave without saying goodbye, the bottle tight in my grip.

I'm going to train with Adrian tomorrow. I repeat the phrase over and over in my head like a mantra.

By the time I reach my dorm, I'm a ball of energy, wishing we could start right now. My hands shake as I withdraw a tablet and pop it into my mouth. Adrian's uneven smile is the last thing I remember before I succumb to the darkness.

Chapter 9

Haunted Pain

HE'S TRYING TO KILL ME. I FLING MY ARMS UP JUST IN TIME TO block his kick to my head, the force of the blow sending me crashing to the ground. I scramble out of the way, hearing the crack of his fist against the mat from where I was seconds ago. *He's seriously trying to kill me.*

"Faster," Adrian shouts as I launch to my feet, barely missing his elbow.

Feeling the wind of his attacks inches from my body reminds me how close I'm getting to breaking a multitude of bones. While I'm grateful he's not holding back, I've never undergone training like this, and my performance conveys it.

My legs give out, and I fall to my knees hard with a startled gasp. I hold up a trembling hand. Panting tears up my dry throat while my nose scrapes the black mat.

"We've been at this for an hour," I wheeze, watching my sweat drip steadily onto the floor until I can tug my head up to meet his blazing eyes. "I need a break."

Adrian crosses his arms, which pulls my gaze to his black shirt that strains against his muscled chest and arms. I force my eyes back up to his unimpressed face, hoping my cheeks are flushed enough from exertion that he won't notice the heat flooding them. The light sheen of moisture on his forehead is the only indication he's been sparring.

"Less than two months, Cassie. That's all we get."

"I *know*," I growl a little too forcefully. I wipe the sweat from my eyes with my drenched shirt, but it just smears the perspiration around my face. "Shouldn't we be using weapons? I know I spar my classmates for endurance, but I won't engage an Obsidian without a weapon."

Adrian studies me with his usual steely demeanor before squatting at my eye level. He rests his forearms on his knees and waits until I meet his gaze to continue. "Imagine you're assigned to protect a family that's been reported too close to a wayward Three. They send you alone because you can eliminate Threes, and hunters are stretched thin. When you arrive, you find no Three, but a mob of Zeros surrounding the house. They're mindlessly beating at the windows, and you can hear kids screaming from inside. You decide to fight without calling for reinforcements. They're weak, of course, but deadly in large numbers.

"Once you make your presence known, all the Obsidian turn to attack you: a fresh, easy target. You slash and slash, but they're relentless. It's all you can do to dodge their shadowy fingers as they tear at your clothes, and just when you think you're about to be overwhelmed, you drop your weapon. Now it's you against twenty, and all that's standing between your death and that of the innocent family is any combat techniques you've got..."

His voice trails off, faint and strained. Adrian's distant stare sharpens on me. "So what do you do?"

Silence fills the room as I process his words. His expression when he talked, his hesitation at the end, makes me waver.

"Did that happen to you?" I ask, dumbfounded.

The same look of surprise flashes across his face, like he can't believe he shared a piece of his past, and his lips pinch. He clenches his jaw, and I fall back onto my butt.

Adrian was a hunter?

"Knowing how to protect yourself in any circumstance is vital. You seemed proficient with your swords, so I thought we'd start with hand-to-hand combat. You've never practiced that outside of class before, right?" Adrian notes, changing the subject.

"What happened?" I blurt out, unable to stop myself. He gives me a quizzical look, and I rush to explain. "After you dropped your sword. What happened to the family?"

Adrian gradually rises, pushing off his thighs. He walks over to the target boards and remains turned away from me when he responds in a tone full of steel. "There were too many. By the time I reached them, they had already transformed."

My heart sinks at the answer. If the family turned into Obsidian, he would have had to kill them, too. I step up beside him and gently place my hand on his shoulder.

"I'm sorry," I whisper, not knowing what else to say.

He glances at me in astonishment. I watch his composure break, and a strange battle of conflict invades his eyes as he surveys me. His mouth opens, features softening. I hold my breath and wait for him to open up to me more.

But Adrian's lips snap closed and he slides away from me. My hand falls limply to my side, a small inkling of disappointment wiggling into my heart. He clears his throat, throwing me a stern look.

"You should get ready for breakfast. We'll continue our

training before and after your classes. Tonight we'll work on knife throwing." He brushes past me and strides out the door.

My eyes linger on the exit long after he's gone, powerless to move. By the time I shuffle forward, my mind is whirling with more questions. If Adrian graduated at the top of his class, why become a hunter? Why did he stop being a hunter? Because of the family that died? Why did he return to the academy instead of joining the city? With his skills, I'm positive they would have let him in.

When I arrive at my room, I drag my feet into the shower, pouring water over our Azura plant as I go. The steam relaxes my muscles and eases my mind. Stepping out of the water, I quickly dry off and get dressed, letting my wet brown hair dampen my gray shirt.

Sara's sitting on her bed when I emerge, and we exchange greetings before leaving for breakfast. On our way to the cafeteria, I realize I barely know anything about Adrian or his life.

"Why the long face, Cassie?" Jared's question startles me out of my reprieve.

With all my unanswered questions about Adrian, I could barely think about anything else at breakfast. Which made me about as much fun as a rock, but a girl can only process so much at once.

Halfway through breakfast, I snuck into the garden, the one place that never fails to ease my troubles.

Yet here we are, with one of those troubles staring me right in the face.

"I came here to be alone, Jared. I'm very sorry, but could we talk later?"

I sigh when he walks further into the garden, sitting beside me on the stone bench. At least he gives me space.

"I understand, and we can if you want, but I've been trying to get a second alone with you for a while. It seems at every chance you get, you run off somewhere."

My gaze roams over Jared. He's chewing on the inside of his cheek, his face scrunched like he's nervous.

Guilt hits me. I've been so focused on Adrian, between asking him to train me and discovering more about his past, that I have completely pushed setting things straight with Jared to the side. My friends don't deserve that.

I clear my head of Adrian and turn to Jared. "Of course we can talk. And I've been wanting to talk with you, too."

"Oh?" Somehow, Jared looks even more anxious. "Well, I'll go first, then."

There's a long pause, and as much as I want to fill the silence, I wait for him to ask his question. Finally, he says, "Does it truly look like I'm flirting with you and Sara?"

Of all things, I laugh. I know I pegged him as not being serious about his intentions, but I never could have guessed he was unaware of how his actions appeared.

Jared's face flushes as he turns to me. I give him a teasing smile, and the tightness around his shoulders relaxes. His lips curve slightly at the edges. "Okay, I guess I was. But I promise I didn't mean anything by it with you, and I'll watch my words more carefully. If I ever say anything stupid, I give you full permission to call me out on it."

Tension releases from me as well. I didn't even have to give him my speech. My comment before the 'Kill the Commander' exercise must have bothered him more than I thought. It's almost endearing that he's coming to me to clear it up.

I think more about his words and can't help but probe further. "You don't mean anything by it *with me*? Did you mean it with someone else?"

I hold my breath as I wait for his response. *Please say Sara.*

"I love being around both of you." Jared draws the sentence out like he's thinking through each word. He glances at me. "It hasn't been long, but I feel closer to you guys than anyone else at the academy. You've become family. But with Sara, it's different."

I exhale slowly as he continues, his gaze traveling to the small pond in front of us. "I thought I loved you both the same, but it's not the same. Cassie, you're like my sister. I don't want Sara to be a sister. I want more."

Something shifts in my heart at his confession. My world of people I love has doubled without me even noticing. Jared's right; he's the brother I never had.

"You're family to me, too. And I can see why you like Sara. She's amazing." My smile stretches wide at the dreamy look on his face. "I think you should tell her how you feel, Jared."

His expression creases with stress as he blinks a few times. He stands and starts walking out of the garden with short, jerky steps. I follow, calling out from behind him. "What's wrong?"

As he walks, his voice floats back to me. "I just admitted you guys are my family, and you want me to risk losing that? I came to you to apologize, not to mess everything up."

I speed up as we reach the courtyard, which is empty except for a few guards stationed on top of the wall. I can hear the faint chatter of the students still at breakfast from the half-open mess hall doors.

"Jared, you have to take a chance if you want to be with her. Give her the option to choose what she wants, too."

Jared's stride doesn't break, so I grab his wrist and pull him to a stop. My eyes do a quick scan of the guards on the wall unconsciously, and from this distance, I'm able to discern the people standing watch. None of them I recognize, except for one.

He's too far away to hear what we're saying, but I know he notices me by the way his outline stiffens. Does my new trainer usually keep watch on the wall during the day? I can't remember seeing Adrian there, but I guess I've never been that aware of him until now.

In my hesitation, Jared closes the gap between us, determination and a hint of fear radiating off him. "You don't understand, Cassie. I am *not* losing my family again."

Each clipped and harsh word slices through the air, brooking no argument.

Adrian disappears from my thoughts at Jared's declaration. No one talks about their past here. Either it's too painful, or forgetting is much easier than dealing with it. But Jared's admission pulls the image of my parents to the forefront of my mind, and I gasp at the onslaught of grief.

"Believe me," I wheeze, my hands shaking with emotion. "I understand."

Jared shakes his head, his eyes filled with remorse. "Of course you do. I didn't mean to—"

"Look," I interrupt in a stronger voice, pulling myself together. "Don't waste a chance for you both to be happy. We don't exactly live in a world where we can take it easy. You might never see Sara again after we graduate. Are you fine with never telling her how you feel?"

He stills, the weight of what I'm saying seeming to dawn on him. As thrilled as I am to have Jared as a brother, the fear of losing another person I care about is just as potent.

I would give up everything to tell my parents one more time how much I love them. From the look on his face, he would too.

"You're right," Jared whispers, a sheen of haunted pain filling his eyes.

"Then go get her," I state, letting his hand drop. If I can stop someone from living in fear, and not have any regrets, then I'll consider my job as a hunter started. I give a bitter-sweet smile. "And as her best friend, I give you my full support."

Out of nowhere, he grabs my shoulder and pulls me in for a hug. I stand frozen before I wrap my arms around his lean frame.

"Thank you," he says, gratefulness dripping from his voice. "I'm glad I got to know you. The rest of the class has no clue what they're missing."

"You're—" My eyes open and fall on Sara, staring at us in horror from beside the mess hall doors.

I pull from Jared's hold, and he looks down at me in confusion. It doesn't take long for him to follow my gaze to Sara, who, in the seconds it takes for him to turn around, has masked the shock behind a slate of emptiness.

"You both were gone a while, so I wanted to check on you. But it looks like I'm interrupting something important. My apologies." Sara wheels around and stalks down the courtyard toward the dorm rooms.

Jared immediately sets in motion, sprinting toward her. I follow close behind, a sick feeling curling in my intestines.

Jared catches up with her quickly. "Sara, wait! It's not what you think! We were just talking and—"

Sara whirls around, anger beginning to seep through the

cracks in her blank expression. "It didn't look like 'just talking' to me. Who you want to be with is fine, Jared, but don't string me along." Her clenched teeth muffle the words. I don't think I've ever seen her this angry before.

"Sara, Jared's telling the truth." I get one sentence out before Jared jumps in again.

"All Cassie did was help me realize the one I want to be with is you, Sara. I like her, but it's not how I like you," Jared pleads with his arms out.

Faster than either of us can react, Sara springs forward and slams her knuckles into Jared's cheek, striking him completely off his feet. He lands on the ground with a thud, cupping his face as he gapes at Sara.

I glance at the guards, prepared for them to break up the fight, but they aren't looking in our direction. Adrian is gone.

I gawk at my best friend in astonishment. "Sara..." I start, but she's not paying attention. Her narrowed eyes pin Jared to the grass.

"If you don't have any feelings for Cassie, then you've been messing with her this whole time. To me, that's *worse*, Jared." Her statement is soft, scarcely hinting at her anger. I'm unable to move as she turns away without looking at me and marches away.

Sara pauses and half-turns back to Jared's taut profile. "Like I would believe your words," she adds, the tone full of remorse. Then she's gone.

I focus on Jared, who hasn't looked at me once since Sara knocked him off his feet. I wait for him to get up, to brush the whole incident off, but his rigid form doesn't budge. His fixed gaze remains on the spot Sara was last standing. Shock emanates from his face, so raw it hurts to look at.

"Jared," I whisper, inching toward him. My feet lock up, eyes widening, as I watch tears roll down his face.

"Leave me alone, Cassie, please." His broken words are almost too painful to listen to.

"I'll talk to her, Jared, I promise," I announce, because I can't take looking at his tears. I told him to live without regrets, but pushing him to confess might have cost him everything.

I am not *losing my family again.*

So much pain for such a simple misunderstanding. Sara has to understand what happened. I refuse to let this moment be the end of them. I wait for Jared to respond, but he ignores me.

Holding back my tears, I walk on stiff legs toward the dormitory, leaving Jared crumpled on the ground.

Chapter 10

Pressing Clarity

I FIND SARA CURLED UP IN THE CORNER OF HER BED, AND MY heart hurts just looking at her. I gently lower myself onto the edge of her mattress, nervously nibbling on my lower lip.

"I'm sorry, Sara, but I swear nothing is going on between us. Jared came looking for me to apologize for his actions and to say you're the one he wants. He hugged me as a thank you." My words are gentle, a plea that she hears me.

"That may be the case, but I don't care. He may not have meant it, but he still messed up." Sara's voice is tiny, and I can't stop myself from crawling closer and hugging her. Her arms loop through mine, and she squeezes tight.

All the sadness she tried to hide when Jared was around me flashes through my mind. I'm confident that Jared would have stopped immediately if he knew his actions were hurting Sara. We sit quietly for a while as I try to find something to say to comfort her.

"You should have seen his face when he was talking about you," I mumble. "He loves you."

Sara yanks herself into a sitting position, tears welling in her eyes. "And what about you?"

I blink. "What about me?"

My roommate grabs one of her pillows and clenches it against her chest. "How do you feel about Jared? He was flirting with both of us. I won't let him be the reason we lose our friendship."

I'm almost tempted to ram my head into the stone wall. Of course Sara would stop herself from truly falling for Jared if she ever thought I was interested in him.

All the times I've tried to broach the subject of Jared and her changing the subject make sense now. She wasn't too shy to talk about him; she just didn't want to hear that I liked him too. More guilt wraps around my lungs, squeezing until my breath becomes shallow. Why didn't I communicate my feelings better? This wouldn't have happened if I had talked with them.

"Sara, Jared is like a brother to me, and he feels the same way. I'm so sorry, I should have told you that from the beginning. You have my word that I do not and will not hold any romantic feelings for him."

Sara sighs, letting her body slump against the wall. "I believe you, and I'm not upset with you, but Jared still hurt me. If you could give me space, I'd like some time to think about what I want."

My throat convulses. Both of my friends are pushing me away. *What if they don't want me in their lives anymore?* The thought makes me nauseous.

I swallow hard before choking out, "Sure."

Walking to the door, I turn the handle with shaking hands and step through the threshold. Before I close the door, I stick my head back in. While she may not need me right now, I won't leave without sharing my feelings.

95

"I'm here for you, Sara. No matter what you decide, I love and support you."

Sara, blankly staring at the wall, refocuses on me and gives me a small smile. "Thanks."

I shuffle toward the gym and rub my hands together anxiously. I need to pull myself together before my training with Adrian. He won't care what happened to my friends. He expects me to put training as my top priority.

By the time I reach the gym, I'm able to shove most of my feelings deep down. Resting my fingers on the door, I exhale before pushing it open.

Adrian is already there with a collection of knives on a small wooden table. He doesn't look up when I enter, so I take my time surveying him. As soon as my eyes fall on him, some of the stress raging inside me calms.

I feel closer to Adrian after this morning when he opened up about his past, and I give him a meek smile when his eyes shoot up to mine.

"Good, you're here. Let's start," he announces brusquely, his voice sharper than normal. I eye him uneasily, my smile dissipating, but his face gives nothing away. He tells me to pick three knives and choose a target.

I scan the table. The daggers range from seven to twelve inches, some jeweled and others less conspicuous. I pick up three sleek, smaller knives and spin toward the target.

Out of the corner of my eye, I catch sight of Adrian. His stoic face is unnerving and sets me on edge.

With apprehension coursing through me, I hurl my blades. Each one bounces off the board and scatters onto the floor. I freeze, biting my lip. *That's not going to look promising.*

Adrian scoffs, and I whip my head around. He's scrutinizing me with narrowed eyes and lips pulled into a scowl. The fierce expression is almost scary enough to force me back a step. "If you're not taking this seriously, then I'm wasting my time."

"I am taking this seriously!" I shout, furiously picking up my fallen daggers.

"It's obvious you're distracted," he growls, gesturing at my less-than-stellar performance.

I flinch at his tone. His attitude differs completely from this morning's practice. I rack my brain to figure out why, but I can't think of anything.

Already stressed from earlier, my temper quickly flares. "What the hell is your problem?" I snap back, my daggers clinking together as I squeeze them.

For a tiny moment, I consider throwing a knife at him. I'm positive he would dodge it, and maybe it'd pull him from whatever funk he's in.

"I expect you to put aside whatever problems you're having in your life when we're training. We will get nowhere if you can't."

His words have a final tone to them, a heavy weight that settles uncomfortably on my chest. It hasn't even been a day, and he's already having second thoughts.

"You're right. I'm sorry," I reply stiffly, turning to face the targets. Every part of me wants to fight back, but I'm too afraid to push Adrian any farther. *I don't want him to leave me like my friends.*

I hold up my knives and release all my tension. *I have to make these throws count, or else Adrian could give up on me.* In a bout of defiance, my fingers refuse to quit their trembling.

A large hand presses down on my own before I can let the daggers go, and I jerk my head up to Adrian.

"I promised to train you until graduation, and I won't go back on that promise. Why are you so sidetracked?" Adrian's glacial eyes bore into mine, but his expression is gentle.

With his assurance, I let out a breath, the fear of him stopping our training sessions leaking out of me.

I rehash the last hour, skimming through the event so I don't end up crying. I have a less-than-zero desire to cry in front of Adrian.

My instructor listens patiently without interrupting, his face never wavering as I go through my story, except for a slight tick in his jaw.

"So he was pursuing both of you, then decided to focus on Sara, and then hugged you in front of her?" Adrian says, his voice hard.

"No," I snap, annoyed that he's lessening the work Jared's done to figure out his feelings. "Jared always chose Sara. He was just afraid of our dynamic being ruined by unrequited feelings."

"But Sara's upset that he was stringing you both along, right? It sounds like he's in the wrong here," Adrian responds, seeming to get equally frustrated.

"Jared didn't realize how his actions looked to us, but once I told him, he stopped. In my eyes, he did the best he could." My voice rises by the end of my words, my fingers balling into fists.

A warning flows through me, begging me to run from this conversation now, before I go too far. I can feel my emotions, the ones I had hastily shoved away, struggling to break free. But Adrian steps forward, his face contorting in anger.

"It sounds to me like Jared doesn't understand how lucky he is to have you both."

"You don't know what you're talking about," I grind out. All I can hear is Jared's statement over and over again. "You don't know what he's lost."

"We've *all* lost someone, Cassie. You don't get to *live* in this world without losing everyone you love," Adrian growls, his past, his sorrow echoing through his words.

I don't hear it because the control on my emotions snaps.

"But this time, it's *my fault!*" I scream, unable to hold back all my fears and the pain of potentially losing my friends. Of still having the image of my parents' smiling faces mocking me ever since Jared brought up his own family.

All my actions over the past few days hit me with perfect clarity. "*I* was the one too scared to speak with Jared because I didn't want to lose his friendship. Sara was hurting, but every time I could have talked to Jared, I focused on something else. It was only after Jared told me he liked Sara that I pressed him to share his feelings, even though I couldn't do that myself."

My voice cuts off as my breath hitches, my body unable to stop shaking. I try to look at Adrian, but find my vision is blurry with tears. "I think I destroyed my family."

Suddenly, I'm encompassed in warmth. Adrian's arms tighten around me as I sob. I haven't cried since my parents died, and the thought only makes the tears fall harder. I reach my hands up to grip the back of his shirt and smash my face against his chest. He says nothing, one hand sliding across my back in slow circles.

We stay like this until my eyes dry and my breathing evens out. Finally, Adrian pulls away, and I'm left feeling empty.

"It's not your fault," he says gently. "And it's not Jared's either. If the bond you three have is as strong as you say, then not even this can break it. Have faith, Cassie."

I sniffle and wipe my wet cheeks with my sleeve. While I'm still scared, some of the agony inside has disappeared. I'm grateful for Adrian's comfort, but now that I'm not blinded by my anger, his own remark comes back to me.

"Who did you lose?" I ask in a whisper.

It takes a moment for Adrian to understand what I mean. *You don't get to live in this world without losing everyone you love.* He smiles, but it's strained. "It's been an emotional day. I'll tell you some other time."

I nod. While I'm disappointed he doesn't want to talk about it, I understand not wanting to relive the past.

"So, would you like to end our session for the night? I know it's been a hard day." Adrian moves to put the knives away. His gentle tone almost makes me smile.

"No, we don't have many training sessions left. And Sara said she'd like some time to herself."

"Okay." Adrian tilts his head in acknowledgement and takes a deep breath, picking up a knife. "Hold the knife like this." He demonstrates by pinching the flat hilt of the blade with his thumb and forefinger. "It will give you better accuracy."

He goes through the proper technique of how to keep the knife from hitting the target hilt first. After letting my hand mimic the throwing actions without a weapon, I pick up my first knife, relax my stance, and fling it. The steel lodges into the wood right outside of the middle circle. I turn to him with a victorious smile, and he dips his head in approval.

We practice with multiple sets, going through the entire table of daggers. By the end, I'm sweating, but my aim has improved considerably. The strenuous exercise also helps to keep my mind from everything that happened today. Energy thrums through my body. *If I progress this much in one day, where will I be in a few weeks?*

Adrian and I take our time placing the daggers back on the weapons shelf as I shake out my nearly numb arm.

"Knives are incredibly useful for Obsidian that have senses, like a One or higher. Ones are easier to kill because they only have a single sense, which also gives you an advantage because of their limited perception. They rely on that sense so much that if you can impair their ears, nose, or eyes with a well-placed knife, they will be momentarily blind. That is your opening to strike them down," Adrian explains after we finish cleaning up the gym.

I've never seen an Obsidian besides a Zero, and I'm curious about how different the higher levels appear. Can you tell the difference between a Two and a Three?

My head turns to ask Adrian my question, but it dies in my throat when I catch him regarding me with a strange expression. "I'm sorry about what I said earlier. I'm sure Jared knows how fortunate he is to have you."

"I feel the same way about him." My response is slow as I trace the small, red scratches that crisscross my fingers from the knives. My gaze lifts to lock with Adrian's. "I feel lucky to have you in my life, too."

Adrian smiles, so small, yet it still makes my heart stumble. He bids me goodnight and leaves me to finish my cooldown stretches in silence.

When I wake up the next morning, refreshed from the use of the sleeping pills, I notice the skin on my fingers is smooth and unblemished, with no signs of knife cuts. I try to remember if I took Serous last night, but I can't recall.

I dismiss the thought, knowing I have much more important things to focus on. *I take it so often that it's just muscle memory now.*

Two weeks have gone by since my first day of training with Adrian and the fallout between me, Sara, and Jared. Two incredibly long, painful, frustrating weeks.

Sara spent the first week distancing herself from Jared

and me, by extension, since I wouldn't stop trying to plead Jared's case. Her attention in class was nonexistent, and she barely gave anything during sparring matches.

There's no way her rank didn't suffer from that, and I told her as much. She got angry, saying I didn't know what I was talking about. But after that, her focus was solely on classes. She became almost as ruthless as Emmerick.

If that's her excuse to not talk to Jared, then at least it's a productive one.

On the other end, Jared and I have gotten closer. Our friendship has strengthened significantly throughout this whole ordeal. Though he's not as talkative and is less likely to jump in with a joke. I know he's miserable because Sara's ignoring him, but he also has a look of determination that makes me hopeful.

I've been rotating between feeling sick and being exasperated in rapid-fire succession. It took the full two weeks to process my guilt over everything that happened, and now that I have, I'm just annoyed. There's no reason for her to be disregarding Jared for so long. She should at least give him the decency of one conversation.

The only good thing to come out of these weeks is that I'm winning most of my sparring matches now, which means my rank has risen considerably. I'm in the middle of the pack, much to my elation and Tala's displeasure.

After the latest ranking announcement, her attitude has decreased significantly, and she's tougher on me than ever. I don't think she knows about my training with Adrian, but she knows that something has changed for me to have gotten so much better in such a short amount of time.

Through it all, Adrian doesn't let my concentration waver. He reminds me every day why I want to get stronger. The best parts of the day are the mornings and nights when we work together. He's encouraging and patient, especially in my hand-to-hand combat skills, which are still severely lacking. Most of our sessions contain sparring, with Adrian insisting on the importance of defending myself without a weapon.

"Trust me" is always the response he gives when I question his methods. And I do trust him.

This evening involves another night of sparring. I've gotten faster and last longer in the ring. I can even land a solid punch on him once in a while.

I twist free from Adrian's grip on my wrist, directing a knee to his thigh. He doesn't move fast enough, and it nicks him, causing his leg to buckle. I use the opportunity to propel an elbow toward his throat. He ducks, rolling down the length of his spine before using his hands to launch himself onto his feet in an impressive flip.

"Show off," I shout as I block his strike to my neck.

His grin is fuzzy as he dashes forward, continuing his onslaught of sharp jabs. The force of his attacks pushes me back, but I keep pace, concentrating hard on my defense.

I unconsciously retreat another step. My right knee gives out, and I tip forward, the opposite of where I thought I would fall. The unexpected action throws me off-balance, and my hands instinctively fly out to stabilize myself.

I register my mistake too late, watching Adrian's look of alarm as he also realizes he won't be able to halt the attack that's a centimeter from my skin.

Chapter 11

Exposing Within

I DON'T EVEN HAVE TIME TO BRACE MYSELF BEFORE HIS FIST slams into my upper cheek a second later, and the pain immediately radiates through my face. I soar backward, a loud crack piercing the air as my head collides with the stone wall.

Bright lights flash in my eyes, encompassing my vision, and I crumble into a mess of limbs. Throbbing pulses in my head with each pump of my heart.

I'm going to vomit all over myself, I think as bile surges up my throat. Then Adrian appears in front of me, and I swallow the disgusting liquid as fast as possible.

Vomiting on myself is one thing, but I will *not* throw up on Adrian.

"Oh, Cassie, I'm so sorry." I feel his warm hands palm my cheeks, and I recoil from the pain. He jerks his hands away as if I burned him.

My vision gradually returns and finds his face, but I can't make my eyes focus on his panicked expression.

"You probably have a concussion." The rushed words make it difficult for me to follow him. His hands hover over my body like he's afraid to touch me. "I need to get you to the infirmary."

I barely hear his harsh curse at not bringing Serous to our training sessions as I focus on keeping the room from spinning.

"Just give me a minute. I'll be fine," I assure him. At least I think I will, though the words sound garbled to my ears. I blink rapidly, trying to clear my vision. I smile at him, but his anxious frown deepens.

That's not a good sign. Am I bleeding out of my eyes? My fingers dab the skin under my left eye socket and find it dry. I let out a relieved sigh, which somehow causes Adrian more distress.

"Let me see your head." He scampers behind me without unfurling from his crouch. His fingers gently probe the back of my skull, and I lean away instinctively, biting my lip to keep in a whimper. But Adrian doesn't notice my flinch, nor does he touch my skull again. I roll my head around to figure out what's wrong.

"There's no wound," he mutters, a hint of doubt in his words, spoken soft enough that I strain to hear it. "Not even a scratch. The damage has to be internal, then."

Nodding to himself, he wraps one arm around my shoulders, the other sliding under my legs, and tugs me closer to him in an attempt to lift me. I lightly bat his shoulder, mumbling more reassurances.

"What the hell is going on here?" A voice shrieks behind us from the direction of the door, and I wince at the sound. With how my blood curdles, it must be Tala.

Adrian pauses his effort to hoist me up but keeps his arms around me.

"She hit her head. I'm taking her to the infirmary," Adrian remarks in an impatient voice. I narrow my eyes until my vision fully zeros in on Tala's stricken expression.

"Oh, poor baby," she mockingly croons, one hand on her heart. "That's what you get for going up against the big boys, Cassidy."

"Really? You want to be like that?" I demand, my voice still slightly warped.

I try to push away from Adrian, but he just holds tighter. Tala's upper lip curls at the movement.

"Look at her, Adrian. She's faking it to get your attention. It's pitiful," Tala scoffs, placing her hands on her hips with a disgusted shake of her head.

I struggle against Adrian's grip until he reluctantly lets me go. I shoot to my feet, but stumble as my head spins and a tingling sensation washes through my extremities.

Adrian places a hand under my elbow to steady me. He's glaring darkly at Tala, his mouth set in a grim line.

"Don't—"

"If you weren't such a nightmare," I snarl, not wanting Adrian to intervene on my behalf, "then maybe Adrian would like you better."

Tala glowers at me, her eyes burning with enough hatred to set me ablaze. "You think you're tough now, don't you?" Tala says in a smooth, quiet voice, walking to the center of the mat and taking off her jacket. A twisted version of a smile leisurely spreads across her face. "How about you show me what you got right now? Let's just see how much your precious trainer has taught you," she spits out and levels me with a hateful gaze, her eyes a swirling storm.

Then her anger twists into something deeper, deadlier. "You think you have everyone fooled, but I know the truth. While Adrian may trust this little charade you're putting on, I'm not buying it. You're a monster, something worse than an Obsidian, and I'm going to expose you for what you truly are. There's no escaping the truth now, Cassidy. I challenge you."

There's a brief moment where no one moves, and the only sound is the blood rushing past my ears. Deafening and maddening, the sound churns against my skull in a death march, nearly drowning out Adrian's harsh inhale.

I close my eyes to regain my stability, preparing myself for the inevitable.

Monster? That's a new insult. Her fuddled words are incomprehensible, though I'm not sure if it's because the room is swimming in and out of focus or if she's spouting nonsense.

"You can't challenge a student! Are you mad?" Adrian's heated words resonate distantly, his tight grasp on my arm sending fire racing through me.

Surprise bubbles through my broken thoughts at his comment. *So they both know about the challenges.*

"There are no rules that prohibit it, and the headmaster forbade the guards from interfering in any challenge, so you'd better sit back," she snaps, waiting for my decision. "Come on, Cassidy. Are you going to run away like the piteous little thing you are?"

I jerk forward, but Adrian's fingers squeeze my elbow, holding me back. "You're injured," he murmurs against my hair. His hot breath tickles my ear, and I suppress a shiver. "Don't let her goad you into this. No one would know you declined it."

For some unfathomable reason, she's got a crazy grudge against me, one she believes this fight will solve. If a challenge is what it takes for her to stop targeting me, then I'm willing to take the risk.

I don't break eye contact with Tala as I roughly whisper to Adrian. "I don't care that I'm injured. Refusing this challenge would just show us both that she's right. I accept," I add, loud enough for Tala to hear.

Adrian's fingers spring from my arm, and I lurch forward

with the support gone, feeling cold without his touch. I right myself as Tala cackles, which only fuels the rage inside me.

Adrian steps back, his face blank, but I can see the turmoil in his eyes. He can't help me now, even if he wanted to. I've accepted, and by the rules, any interference from one side will mark their immediate loss.

There are only two ways this could go: one of us will either concede or fall unconscious, and I have a hunch there will be no forfeits.

I step into the ring and Tala hurls herself at me with a growl. I stagger to the side to avoid her clawed fingers, but she doesn't give me the chance to recover. She kicks out, the wide arc of her foot ramming into my shoulder.

Crashing to the floor, I use the momentum to roll onto my knees, swiping my leg under hers and throwing her to the ground.

My legs tremble as I rise from the floor, my breath wheezing in swift gasps. My headache drums harder each time my fist or Tala's connects with flesh, and my vision blurs once more. Tala seems to grow more agitated as the fight goes on, especially whenever our skin makes contact.

I lash out, knowing I won't last much longer, clipping Tala in the jaw with my knuckles. Blood dribbles from the corner of her lip, and she wipes at it with the back of her hand.

Pain streaks across her features, pain and wild anger.

While her face is even, I can see a lethal glow in her eyes. I gulp and raise my fists higher. My stomach twists as we stare at each other, and a small section of me shuts down to prepare for her next, most likely final, attack.

Adrian shouts something I can't hear past the ringing in my ears. Tala leaps at me, tackling me to the ground. She straddles my waist and strikes a blow to my nose.

I feel, rather than hear, the snap as blood instantly gushes from the wound. I struggle under her weight, but I'm too weak to throw her off me. A sickening gurgle spills from my lips as I choke on the blood pooling in the back of my throat.

Tala pummels me, raining down one ferocious punch after another. I raise my hands to block her blows, but she easily swats them away.

"Change." She whispers the word with each hit, an echo against the forceful strikes. "Change, change. Come on, change, damn it!"

Numbness envelopes my face as I close my eyes, waiting. For what, I'm not sure, though it doesn't matter too much now. Even at the end, all I can think about is Sara and Jared and how they deserve to be happy together.

The weight of Tala on my midsection is suddenly gone, and the attacks have blessedly stopped. I roll onto my stomach and cough, splattering the black mat with bright crimson blood and sucking in a breath tinged with the taste of metal. I look up, finding I can only open one eye.

Adrian pins Tala to the ground, his forearm resting firmly on her neck. Both of their faces are red as they bellow back and forth at each other.

I fall onto my back and stare at the ceiling, tracing the cracks in the stone wall that create a map with their webbing. The room is chilly enough that the blood on my shirt prickles uncomfortably against my skin. I blink, struggling to figure out what I should do next.

I'm still in a challenge. Ah, yes, that's what I'm doing. I've been in this position before. Hurting a lot, but lucid enough to understand why forfeiting isn't an option for me. I have to get up and keep fighting.

It takes a few tries to get my knees under me. My heavy head draws down, and I find my hands pressed into a puddle of red liquid. *My blood,* I think dazedly.

I wrestle with my limbs, aggravated at their inability to follow directions. Finally, I'm able to drag myself to my feet.

Adrian's head snaps up when I stand, alarm washing over his features. His mouth moves and I squint my good eye, trying to discern what he's saying. My face feels puffy, and I can't open my jaw to ask him to repeat himself.

Tala is still struggling below Adrian's grip, reminding me of my purpose. I step forward, but that little movement is the last straw for my body, and my legs give out. Adrian lunges towards me with his arms outstretched as I collapse, my eyes rolling back into my head.

Resting on the couch, I open my eyes to my mother's lips pressing a gentle kiss to my forehead. She leans over me, her long, graying brown hair framing my face, and I smile up at her.

"If you sleep now, you'll never be able to fall asleep tonight, sweetie," she chuckles, her hazel eyes shimmering with mirth.

I look out the window to see that the sun is just beginning to set, painting the sky golden yellow and bathing our small cabin in its warmth. The blue haze of Azura mushrooms peaks out above the windows from Dad's meticulously maintained flower boxes.

I stretch with a yawn and stand, my bare feet slapping against wood as I meander into the kitchen to put away the freshly washed clay plates. Mom twirls through the room, humming the melody of a song from her childhood.

The front door cracks against the wall as Dad surges in. His clothes and face are dirty, his brown eyes frantic. I notice in an afterthought that the sack he uses to gather berries is missing.

"They're coming, Nema," he gasps, slamming the door closed and locking it before rushing into the next room. My mom's face pales and she sprints after him, asking him what happened.

I stand frozen in the kitchen, my fingers tightening around the plate. With the harrowing tune of my parents' urgent and frightened voices echoing in the other room, I set the plate down and examine our small home.

From the kitchen is a clear view of the dining and living room. Our cabin is modest, with little decoration, but even then, it's cozy and warm. I love how safe I felt in this house. And my parents, Rogen and Nema Hale. I will cherish every memory I've made here with my wonderful parents.

I'm choking on air as my throat spasms painfully, realizing my thoughts are leading toward a farewell.

The sun has lowered enough to cast long shadows through the trees surrounding the house, and I approach the tall glass sliding door to watch for movement. A loud thump ricochets off the front door, and I twist around, waiting for it to fly open.

Seconds tick by, the silence overwhelming, suffocating me, and when nothing happens, I let out a breath. Relieved, I turn back to the glass door.

A scream erupts from my throat.

I trip backward and onto my butt, digging my nails into the worn wood under me as I scramble away. More Obsidian than I can count swarm the other side of the door. My yelp must have set them off because they slam into the glass with fervor. I can't tear my eyes from their hideous beings.

Jagged shards of rock-like flesh cluster entirely around their elongated bodies. Their eyes are gone, and they stare at me with gaping holes, the sunken cavities inducing a panic as if I've jumped into an ice-cold bathtub. With mouths hanging open, they expose needle-like black teeth eager to rip into flesh. Their noses and ears are missing, giving their heads a more symmetrical sphere.

Except for the ones that are missing half their head, curved in as though erosion etches itself into their skulls.

A hefty weight comes down solidly on my shoulder, and I jerk away with a smothered squeal. Dad kneels beside me, putting one finger against his lips.

Dull steel presses against my leg, and my eyes widen with fear as he places a long sword into my palms. I shake my head, but he grunts and wraps my fingers around the leather hilt.

I hold it away from my body like it's a venomous snake, eyeing it with dread. I've never used a weapon before. Any time I've ever asked, my dad would just pat my head and say, "When you're older, Bumblebee."

Regret reflects in his eyes now, and a lone tear trails down his anguished face, highlighted by the fire in his hands. "I love you," he mouths before tugging me behind him in a crushing grip. Mom grasps another torch, and she kisses my head on her way to stand by Dad. Shoulders aligned, they both hoist the torches into the air, the fingers of their empty hands weaving together.

The glass shatters with a deafening boom.

The smell hits me first. I gag at the stench of death that overpowers my nose and stings my eyes, as though people are rotting inside their stone carcasses.

The Obsidian stagger in, overcoming my parents almost immediately, seizing their struggling bodies and sinking their sharp teeth into their limbs.

The demons' moans drown out my screams as I howl my

parents' names, their faces mirroring each other's agony. My father attempts to light himself on fire, but an Obsidian bites into the fleshy part of his wrist before he can.

The torch tumbles to the floor and fizzles out, with Mom's light not far behind.

The sword drops from my lax hand, and I crawl backward until my back hits a wall, eyes never wavering from my parents. Their bodies sprawl on the ground, skin already turning to an ashy gray and hardening. The Obsidian lurch away from them, repelled by the corpses now that the monsters have successfully turned them.

My trembling changes into convulsions as I stare death in the face, its gaping sockets sucking the life out of me. The Obsidian in front of the pack clinks its teeth together, lifting an arm.

A deep, chest-racking sob rips from my throat as its claws graze my neck. Something inside me begins to burn, my nerves searing with fire, and I let out another piercing scream.

Everything is black. I can't feel, see, or hear. For a split second, my heart stops, thinking I've turned into a Zero. Slowly, my vision comes back to me.

The charred bodies of Obsidian litter the entire living room, the flower-patterned furniture in a blaze. My parents lay in the corner, their features halfway through the transformation.

A haze settles over me as Tala and Adrian fly through the doorway, my mind numbing the pain that festers just below the surface.

Chapter 12

A Little Mystery

MY BODY SHAKES AND I STARTLE AWAKE, HEART STUCK IN MY throat. Sara towers over me, bending close with one hand on my shoulder.

"Are you okay?" Sara queries, her brows pinched together. "You were crying out in your sleep."

I examine my surroundings with panicked eyes, only settling down when I take in the white walls, lined hospital beds, and the powerful scent of Serous. Thick, scratchy fabric tickles my arms, and I lean back onto an unforgiving pillow. *I know this place all too well.*

"What happened?" My voice cracks, and Sara offers me a glass of cold water. I sip it with a satisfied hum, the cool drink soothing my dry throat.

"Well," she perches herself on the edge of the cot. "I was called here by the nurse, who said you got into a skirmish with an instructor."

The memories slam into me at her words, and I groan, running my hands down my heated face. *Oh, right, I remember. I got my butt epically handed to me by the devil.*

I quickly summarize the details, though the fight is still fuzzy. Tala thought that something miraculous would come from the fight. I wonder if she got what she was hoping for.

"Tala challenged you? How does she know about them?" Sara's mouth drops, and I shrug.

"I don't know, but I'm not surprised she did. I bet she's been aching to do that ever since she met me," I huff and fall back onto not-so-soft pillows.

My head hits the metal bar above the bed. I grimace, rubbing the spot. *Looks like anything can take me down*, I think in annoyance.

"But she lost, right? I mean, she almost killed you, and that's against the rules."

I shake my head while running my fingers over the rough blanket. The itchy texture is almost comforting. "She *didn't* kill me, though. Since I was still conscious and never forfeited, I'm pretty sure she's safe. And besides," I add softly, "Adrian intervened before it was over. That alone makes her the winner."

"We have to tell Headmaster Hallow! There's no way he'll let this slide." Sara scrunches up her face in distaste.

"Tell him what? That the students have been doing underground fighting matches for years, and Tala somehow knew about them and used them against me? We'd be condemning all the students, and who's saying he'd do anything about it?"

I don't tell Sara that Tala has already admitted to the headmaster knowing about the challenges, and has forbidden anyone from interfering. The fact would just upset her more.

Sara opens her mouth to argue, but I cut her off with a look, not in the mood to keep rehashing it. I'm curious to see if Tala brings it up to anyone, but something in my gut tells me she won't. In her mind, the fear would be much greater as our personal secret.

I also shove aside all her insults. I don't care that she thought I was faking an injury or that I'm a monster. Her words mean nothing to me now.

Nurse Dorna bounces into the room, her shoes tapping lightly on the ground and her light brown skirt swishing around her ankles. I sigh in relief at her perfect timing, and she beams at me.

"Oh, joy! You're up a lot faster than I thought you'd be. Only out for a few hours. I say, dear, that Serous works wonders on you. I gave you half a bottle; that's how badly you were hurt. You need to be more careful in your classes. Other students won't go easy on you, that's for sure. It's not all bad, though. A strong young man who seemed very concerned about you carried you here. He was *quite* the looker if I say so myself."

Nurse Dorna elbows Sara and gives me a wink. I flush while Sara's eyes are about two seconds away from popping out of their sockets. Listening to the nurse talk about Adrian's attractiveness isn't something I want to do, *ever*.

"When can I leave, Nurse Dorna?" I ask in an endeavor to save my ears from bleeding.

"Well, you look great. How do you feel?" I give her a thumbs-up and a winning smile. She laughs, smoothing out her gray bun. "You can leave whenever you want. Though I'd be a fool not to ask: could I take some blood samples? When I graduated from the research academy, they gave me some of their simpler equipment, but I don't have enough test subjects to use it on. I'd love to see what makes you heal so fast. Maybe we can even do some experiments!"

She gives me a grin that borders on maniacal.

"No, thank you, but I appreciate the suggestion." I spring from the bed, ready to rush out of there.

"Oh, also," Nurse Dorna claps her hands together in a revelation. I half turn and witness her excited, plump cheeks turn pink. "I almost forgot, silly me. That officer said he had business to attend to and left shortly after dropping you off. He's the one who told me to call your friend in here to sit with you. He asked me when you would be awake, and I assured him you'd sleep through the night. Now I'm a liar. You only slept through half of the night! If he stops by in the morning, would you like me to pass anything along?"

I hesitate, biting my lip. "No, I'm sure I'll run into him eventually."

"Well, alrighty, dear. I'll see you again soon. Not because I want you to get hurt, but because I enjoy your company. And because I love to observe your healing in action. It's just a marvel! I could just sit and watch you for hours as…"

Sara and I sprint from the room, Nurse Dorna's monologue echoing behind us until the door to the infirmary slams shut.

Outside the hospital door, Sara and I exchange a glance before we burst into giggles.

"That was…entertaining," Sara exclaims once our laughter dies down.

I hum in agreement. *It's always an adventure when I get stuck at the clinic.*

We take our time traveling back to our room, the silence expanding between us. Once we file into our bedroom, Sara heads straight for my bed and sits down. She pats the spot beside her and stares at me expectantly.

"You're ready to talk?" I ask hesitantly, though inside I'm filled with elation.

Being in the infirmary was the most time we spent together in weeks. I missed my best friend, but never wanted to force her into talking before she was ready.

"I didn't mean to shut you out. I got scared that my rank was dropping and somehow convinced myself that if I wanted to reach my goal, I had to push you both away."

"Your goal?" I ask, trying to hide my curiosity.

Sara casually said before that she wants to live in the city, but she's never once mentioned a reason for it. I guess I just assumed she wanted the security of living behind walls like everyone else.

"It's...not important. I'm sorry for being so withdrawn, but I'm here now. Nothing like hearing that your sister is flirting with death to really put things in perspective."

Sara knows I want to be a hunter, and that's about the extent of it. I fully understand her not wanting to share her reasoning.

I give her a smirk. "What can I say? I'm a tease." I walk closer to her and finally sit on the bed. "All I want is for you to be happy, Sara. I know I've said it a thousand times, but I think Jared will make you happy."

"I agree," she responds with a sigh.

I nod, ready to accept her wish not to talk about the subject. I get halfway through the action before her words finally hit me. "Wait, you what?"

"As angry as I was, I still wanted to be with him. I just couldn't get past the fear that maybe you both could one day become interested in one another. While I backed away and threw myself into training, I thought that could give you both time to be sure about your desires."

I blink, unsure if I want to hug her or smack some sense

into her. "Are you serious?" Sara shrugs, studying anything but me. "Sara, look at me. I'm honored you would give me the space to do that, but my feelings for him haven't changed at all. If anything, I would say it made us more sure that we're just friends. He only thought of you this whole time."

"Really?" Sara asks, as if reluctant to believe me, even though she wants to.

"I think you should talk to him and hear it for yourself. Maybe then you can trust what we both are saying is the truth."

"Yeah, okay, maybe. I-I still need some time." She bites her lip and fidgets.

What's stopping her? I promised myself I wouldn't meddle again, but this time, I have an inkling it's going to go better.

I jump up with a smile. "Are you afraid to ask him for a conversation?"

My best friend stands as well, her eyes wide. "Wh-what? No, of course not."

Busted. Trying hard to smother my grin, a plan blooms in my mind. "For real, Sara. Do you want to talk to him?"

She seems to debate it in her mind before her shoulders sag. "Yes, I would like that very much."

"Then leave it to me," I announce before swinging around and kneeling to pick up my shoes.

"You're not doing it *now*, are you?" Sara demands, bewildered.

"Of course not," I reply, wiggling my feet into my sneakers. "The plan starts in the morning, so that gives you plenty of time to think about what you want to say. Until then, I'm heading to the gym."

"The gym?" Sara seems more confused by that than if I were to sneak Jared into the girls' dorm.

"I just woke up, and my body can't train itself." I jump up and throw on my hoodie.

Sara pauses, disapproval shining from her narrowed eyes, but she just nods in reluctant agreement.

"Besides," I add, hand on the doorknob, "you heard the nurse. I had half a bottle of Serous, and now I can hear colors. This is the perfect opportunity for me to burn off this extra energy before my training with Adrian. You do *not* want to know what gray sounds like."

I point to her pajamas with a wrinkled nose. She snorts, shooing me out.

Halfway to the gym, I stumble upon a familiar hallway. Peeking down both empty aisles, my mind makes the snap decision to change destinations.

I would have bet my next fruit slices that the old wooden entrance would have creaked in protest at each fraction of movement, but the doors to the library swing open with surprising ease. It's been weeks since my first and last visit to the library. I pass by the corridor leading here almost every day, yet I honestly forgot it existed. I recall my promise to come back and visit Zachary, and guilt tugs at my abdomen.

The faint crackling of oil lamps greets me as I enter the room, but it's otherwise vacant. Zachary must be asleep like the rest of the academy. I recall Nurse Dorna saying I only slept through half the night.

It was a stupid idea to come here. Did I think Zachary would be like me and never sleep? Maybe a tiny, tiny bit, yes.

With a huff, I spin around and march out of the room. It's only when I'm nearing my training area that a small realization hits me, the tickle of a feather against my mind. The last time I was there, the library looked empty then, too. When I went to pick up a book, Zachary seemed to appear out of nowhere.

I wonder if there's an attached chamber, like a secret door. A little mystery to be solved. My lips spread into a smirk.

My dad had a miniature collection of books stored at our cabin, most of them mystery novels. Since I loved to read when I was younger, I had to keep rotating those five books, giving me an affinity for riddles and unsolvable puzzles.

I'm still smiling when I reach the gym, which is as empty as the library. The grin slips; I had hoped Adrian would be here. The hazy image of him ripping Tala off me flashes through my mind.

So many emotions swirl through me, raging and tumbling like a river through a hurricane. Anger, embarrassment, shock. But the worst of them all is that even though I'm angry at Adrian, I still want to see him and his lopsided smile.

Another weakness, how much I rely on him. *I can't depend on him forever if I want to be strong.*

I stretch before choosing a dummy to practice some more difficult spins that Adrian recently taught me, their intensity impeding my mind from thinking. My limbs shake as my eyes dance through the room, unable to stay in one place. The challenge replays over and over in my mind.

I used to be challenged all the time when I first got here. I was the new girl trying to join an advanced class, a thing that rarely happened. That's when I got to know Nurse Dorna well.

Those challenges weren't pretty, but they never sent me packing. Soon, the excitement of trying to throw the new girl from the academy to the fields vanished, leaving me to be beaten solely in sparring class—except for Emmerick's continued challenge requests.

Through all of that, I've never been so utterly pummeled,

even by Emmerick. With Adrian there to witness it, no less. He had to help me. I couldn't do it on my own.

I imagine Tala's face and hit the dummy harder. Her obsession with attaining my demise annoys the crap out of me. *What have I done to her to deserve this kind of treatment? Besides calling her ugly once...or twice.*

I rub my temple, kicking the mannequin in the head with my shoe. *Maybe I should start being nice to her, and she'll follow my example.* I imagine myself complimenting Tala on her stellar teaching skills and almost retch. *Nope. That's impossible. I'm going to table this so I don't get sick all over my training partner.*

My mind inevitably wanders to my parents, as it always does when I'm alone with my thoughts for too long. Thinking about that night spurs the memory of the dream I had only a few hours ago.

I blacked out. The Obsidian were close to killing me, I blacked out, and then woke up to Tala and Adrian's arrival. Did someone come and burn the place before reinforcements arrived?

My knuckles slam into the dummy's chest, and it topples to the ground. I pause, then sit on its overturned base. *Maybe I'll ask Adrian what he remembers about that night.* I pull the dummy back up and start the sets again.

The hours pass quickly. Once it's a reasonable enough time to enact my plan, I rush back to the dorm to grab Sara. I explain my idea and, once I finally convince her to go through with it, we part ways.

Please let this work.

Chapter 13

Where It Counts

I'M LYING ON THE GROUND, TRYING NOT TO THINK TOO MUCH, when the sound of footsteps reaches my ears. I stretch, pulling myself into a sitting position.

"You're early," I remark.

"When you call, I'll always answer. What's up?"

I crane my neck around and find Jared leaning against the doorframe, watching me with a sad-tinged smile. I scramble to my feet, itching to wipe that expression off his face.

"Sara's waiting for you in the garden."

Jared slips off the doorway, faltering before catching himself. He stares at me with a slack jaw. "You're joking."

"Would I joke about this, Jared?" I give him a look, but can't stop the small smile at his immediate hopefulness. "I just wanted to be the one to tell you. While I don't know what she's going to say, she promised to hear you out."

"That's all I need." He steps into the room. "You made this happen?"

I shake my head. "She was ready herself. I just gave her a little push."

Jared chuckles, tilting his head. "Thank you, Cassie. For everything."

"You too," I respond.

"Well, wish me luck!" Jared says breathlessly, excitement replacing his usual sorrow.

He gives one last wave, turns around, and runs right into Adrian.

Jared stumbles back, off balance, while my trainer stands steady as a rock. Adrian is at least six inches taller than Jared, looming over him with a menacing presence.

Maybe I'd be scared if that glare was pointed at me, but since I'm in the clear, his intimidation makes me stifle a snort.

"Can I help you?" Adrian growls, his sharp eyes mirroring a storm.

"N-no, sir. I was just leaving," Jared stammers, giving Adrian a wide berth as he slides past him.

"Good luck!" I shout after Jared. He pumps a fist in the air before disappearing. "I think things are going to work out between Jared and Sara," I explain with a smile at Adrian's questioning gaze.

"That's great." His gentle voice sounds far away, and I suddenly remember what happened the last time we were in this room.

Awkward silence settles over us as I think of something to say besides: "Thanks for carrying me to the infirmary while I was dying. Sorry if I bled on you."

Something about the tense room tells me that the joke might be too soon.

"I stopped by the infirmary, but the nurse said you left hours ago. Have you been here this whole time?" Adrian gives me a once-over, like he doesn't trust I should be up and walking.

"Mostly." Adrian won't care about my quick detour to the library. "It was too late to take a sleeping pill, and I was wired from all the Serous I had."

We meet in the center of the mat and start warming up. Adrian's palms face me, and I lightly jab at them randomly, bouncing on the balls of my feet.

"Serous shouldn't be able to heal you in such a short period, no matter how much you take." He swallows hard, glancing away from me. "The damage was pretty extensive."

"The nurse says that my blood is super compatible with it or something like that. I've always healed fast, which has come in handy." I punch in quick succession before peeking up at him. "Where's Tala?"

Adrian's face darkens and he crosses his arms, forcing me to either stop or continue my practice on his chest. "Getting ready for her morning classes, I'd guess. I took her to the headmaster to be disciplined, but he didn't care since you had no lasting injuries."

His lips thin in irritation. *I wonder if that's the business Nurse Dorna referred to.*

"You told the headmaster about the challenge?" I ask in shock.

Adrian shakes his head, displeasure lining his mouth. "He went to this school when his father was the headmaster, and the challenges were around back then, too. Devero liked the challenges, and when he became Headmaster, he prohibited anyone from stopping them. The man appreciated the idea of an instructor challenging a student. Another form of discipline," he spits the words out, fists clenching.

I step away from him and grab my elbow to stretch my

shoulder, mulling over my next sentence. I knew the head-master wasn't stopping the challenges, but I never thought he'd be promoting them. He probably saw nothing wrong with what happened. I agreed to the challenge myself, and then Adrian broke the rules by stopping the match.

Adrian's intervention materializes in the front of my mind, and I get frustrated all over again.

Should I apologize? Say I'll try harder next time? Adrian stays silent, watching me. With each quiet minute that passes, I grow more agitated.

My mouth opens before I can stop it. "You shouldn't have intervened, Adrian. I was fine."

Whatever he expected me to say, it's not that. Honestly, I wasn't expecting it either. But once the words are out, I realize how much I wish he'd let me fight my battle alone.

He barks out a surprised laugh before staring at me in astonishment. "You were *fine*?"

"Yes, I was! I accepted the challenge, and you broke the rules. You didn't think I could take care of myself!" Anger burns through me as I say the words that have been on my mind since I departed from the hospital. If I'm going to lose, then I want it to be on my terms.

I spring to my feet, ready for a confrontation.

Adrian strides up to me, his chest heaving. "I know you can take care of yourself, but I'm not going to watch you get beaten to death."

"That's not your call, though, is it? As much as Tala detests me, she wouldn't kill me. You made me look weak in her eyes and in both of ours!"

My shout echoes through the small room. I ball my hands into fists as a wave of helpless rage washes over me.

I can't believe he doesn't understand what I'm trying to

say. With a challenge, no part of me will ever give up. It's the one thing that always kept me going through all the pain and misery I've had to endure. It's like I've taken ten steps back from all the successes I've accomplished.

I spin around in wild anger, not wanting to talk about this anymore. There are only so many ways I can state how his help made me feel frail and vulnerable.

As I stalk towards the door, Adrian seizes my upper arm in a steel grip that jerks me to a stop. Straining against his hold is futile. I can't move an inch. He towers over me, and I crane my neck up to look him in his frigid eyes.

A chill runs through me at his expression.

"Accepting help isn't a weakness, Cassie," he says. My breath stops at his words, and the tightness in his voice halts my efforts to pull away. "There are people in this academy who don't want to see you put your life at risk. Why do you feel you have to do everything alone?"

His accusation makes me hesitate. I think about Sara, Jared, and even Adrian himself. My closest allies.

"I'm not alone," I breathe, unsure of what he's getting at.

He squeezes my arm before letting go and backing away from me, his face cut from stone. "You are where it counts. Don't forget that your actions affect others, too."

A crease forms between my eyebrows, and my jaw clenches until my teeth creak. I storm out the door without responding, my unspoken words burning up the path behind me.

I fly through the hallways, letting my feet guide me as my mind whirls. What does he want me to do? Ride on the coat-tails of someone else until graduation and then find a cushy job in the city? *That's not why I joined this school.*

I came in here wanting to be a hunter, to protect the

people who need it. You put yourself at risk every day as a hunter, and Adrian will have to get used to that. If I allow someone to protect me now, then I'll never be able to protect myself when I'm alone outside the walls.

I inhale deeply, slowing my pace. More students are walking through the hallways now, yawning and chattering as they make their way to the main hall for breakfast. I follow the walkway outside to the courtyard, the cool air calming my nerves.

My anger fades along with the morning fog. The sun peeking up over the stone wall helps give me clarity again.

Adrian is only looking out for me. I shouldn't be upset with that. He just doesn't understand my urge to be strong, to stand confidently on my own two feet, to defend everyone I love with my own hands. At least, not to the extent I'm feeling.

The sound of kids giggling reaches my ears, and I stop when I see four young teens running through the grass, small wooden swords swinging around them. In the center of them is Tala, who is smiling, affectionately pulling a kid into a hug when they get too close to her.

Tala. *Smiling.*

The scene makes me do a double-take. My mind files through memories of her, trying to match a similar scene. The realization that I've never seen Tala genuinely smile before hits me hard.

She looks so happy, something I didn't think was possible. Why does she refuse to smile like this in class?

Tala looks up and catches me gawking at her, and her delight morphs into distaste. She pats one boy on the head and walks away towards the faculty wing of the academy. The kids appear briefly confused before they resume their game without another thought.

I scowl and keep moving, following the hungry crowd into the main hall. Most of the lines are already long, so I put little effort into choosing one.

As I slowly creep toward the food, my fingers tap rapidly on my arm. It's so frustrating to see Tala be nice to others when I get nothing but resentment. The more I think about it, the more aware I am of the fact that she only ever throws me disgusted faces. I take the brunt of her bad moods, and I get the short end of the stick on her good ones.

Porridge splatters onto my plate as I aggressively fling food from the serving spoons. *If this is her way of motivating me to be better, which I highly doubt, then she should pick another strategy.*

I'm distracted all day, unable to fully focus in sparring class. Tala ignores me, leaving me to practice kicks on a dummy. The only good thing about that is it gives me time to think.

I contemplate my blowup with Adrian. *You're alone where it counts*, he told me. Am I? I know Sara and Jared have my back, so what does he mean?

And why do his words bother me so much? Sure, I respect him as a soldier, but his opinion holds more weight than even what Sara says. I want Adrian to see how strong I've become, for him to feel like he can depend on *me*. I want to watch his back and protect him.

I have to care about him more than just as an instructor to have these feelings. But something's off when I call him a friend, like that title doesn't fit. *Ugh, I'm not making any sense.*

My whirling thoughts nag at me the entire day.

With an hour to go before my evening training session, my shoulders are tight with stress. I haven't seen Adrian since our argument this morning, so I'm not sure how it's going to go. I wipe my sweaty palms on the tops of my thighs as I pace my room and take a shaky breath to calm myself.

This is ridiculous. There's no reason for me to be so nervous. At this rate, I'm going to burn a hole through the floor. If Sara were here, she could distract me with how she and Jared left things, but I haven't seen her since class ended.

I'll just have to find something else to distract me, then.

I pause my tirade with a slow grin.

"Like a mystery," I declare to absolutely no one before rushing out of the room.

The hallways are empty as I travel quickly through them. The vacancy isn't uncommon; most students don't roam around after dinner.

Thankfully, I reach my destination without problems. The inside of the library is as uninhabited as ever, which is perfect for my stealth mission. I gingerly close the doors behind me, wincing slightly when they thunk together.

My hand lightly traces the bookshelves as I make my way around the circle. I'm not entirely sure what I'm searching for. A weirdly sized book, a loose shelf?

I stop when I reach the area where Zachary was standing when we first met. *Unless he was crouching behind the half shelf, the door should be around here.* I quietly get to work, pulling out books and outlining shelves for weak points.

Nothing magical happens. *Maybe it's a trapdoor,* I think as I drop into a crouch and scan the floor.

Three shelves down, I spot thin scuff marks that arc away from a bookshelf. I waddle closer in my squat, my fingers running over the marks. *Found it.*

I excitedly tilt all the books and inspect the shelves, but still, nothing moves. Frowning, I grab the inner shelf and tug it toward me. Slowly, with my heart skipping a beat, I'm able to pry the shelf open like a door. I can't fight the smile that blooms across my face. *I found a real-life secret door!*

Half of me assumes this small room will be Zachary's bedroom, allowing him to stay in the library at all times for any visitors.

I'm very wrong.

Chapter 14

Concealed Scribe

WHERE THE LIBRARY HAS NEAT ROWS OF BOOKS AND symmetrical tables, this room is uniformity's greatest enemy.

Shelves of different lengths hang from the walls, with papers, scrolls, and small metal trinkets scattered in various forms of disarray. Some papers look a breath away from flying from their perches. A compact wooden desk takes up most of the space in the middle of the cramped room, the edges chipped and worn.

I also get a strong whiff of musty old paper. I'm amazed there aren't moths fluttering next to the pot of Azura mushrooms precariously hung on an iron pole in the corner.

The dim glow illuminates a man in brown robes hunched over a piece of parchment paper spread flat on the table. I wait for him to lash out or gasp in surprise, but it seems he didn't hear the door open.

Did he not notice me opening the door? I didn't think I was quite that incognito. Befuddled by the librarian's concentration, I stand silently and observe his movements. They are slow and methodical as he uses one hand to move across the paper, and the other to draw circles in red ink.

I walk further into the room, making my steps softer than the scratch of his quill, and can finally see that Zachary is marking different sections of a map. Some are red, others black, and they make misshapen rings around a focal point.

"It is good to see you again, Cassie." Zachary's eyes peer up at me, hands still poised over the map. His usual smile is in place, but there's something odd about it.

I examine him more closely as he goes back to his work. The lines around his mouth seem deeper, his brown eyes swimming in apprehension. Something awful must be happening for him not to be perturbed by a student breaking into his office.

"What's wrong?" I ask, unable to help my curiosity, but also feeling shame for my poorly thought-through actions. *Well, I can't take it back now. Maybe I can help.*

Zachary collapses into a chair I hadn't seen coming in and sets his pen down, the large black feather ominously splayed on top of the circles.

"There has been more Obsidian activity around the academy." My eyes widen at his comment, but he waves away the panic with a flick of his fingers. "Not enough to be concerned about, but enough to produce a conversation on whether actions should be taken."

"How do you know?" At my question, the older man beckons to me and picks up his pen, pointing to one of his newly drawn red circles.

"This color means there was spotting of at least two or more Obsidian in that area in the last month, up to ten miles from the academy. The circles are retraced in black ink after a month with no more activity."

I can instantly tell there are more red circles than black,

almost twice as many. While the look of it frightens me, I suspect his reasoning for only 'starting a conversation' rather than asking hunters to clear the area is because the red is a lot farther away from the academy than the black.

"Does this mean they are closing in?" I whisper to hide the slight tremor in my voice.

I've had one experience with Obsidian in my life, and that encounter cost me my family. With our academy having one entry point, the main gate, its breach would be even more catastrophic.

"Not exactly," Zachary postulates, scratching the stubble on his chin. "Within the last ten years, we've had Obsidian sighted much closer than this, and nothing came of it. The sightings could even be the same ones that have moved. The best course of action is to report the findings to Devero and let him make the final decision."

I'm torn between pushing the subject and respecting Zachary's conclusion. Since I probably shouldn't be hearing this as a student, and I barged into his study without warning, I decide to go with the latter.

"So, this is what you do? Track demon movement around the school?" I can hear the doubt in my voice, but honestly, this seems more like a task for Zypha and her security team than a librarian.

"What did you think my job was?" Zachary questions, leaning forward and raising his dark gray, bushy eyebrows.

"Um, book duster?" I want to kick myself once the words are out of my mouth. *Could I have picked a more offensive description?*

Thankfully, Zachary doesn't seem to mind. "Yes, I do that as well," he nods with a chuckle, "but really, I'm just the scribe of the school."

"Scribe?"

"The security team patrols the perimeter and gathers the whereabouts of nearby Obsidian. They bring that information to me, where I put it on a map and hand it to the headmaster. After that, we send it to Netiva City."

"The city? Why?" I'd have thought the city would have its own security team doing that. Why would they rely on us for reconnaissance?

"Lord Netiva likes to stay informed, not just on the land surrounding the city, but on any area in his jurisdiction. The more statistics we give him, the more he rewards us."

"That's where you got the oil lanterns from." I hum as Zachary's previous words dawn on me.

Zachary said there aren't a lot being produced. The city must give them as a reward for the school's details. *What an interesting exchange system.*

"Very perceptive." Zachary smiles before going back to his map.

I take in the room again, suddenly realizing how many rolled-up papers are here. "Are these all maps from your recordings?"

I have an unexpected urge to withdraw the maps and line them up to see how Obsidian activity has changed over the years. Would I find a large influx of monsters during the time my parents died? Or were we even close enough to the academy to become a statistic, tucked away and molding on one of these poorly maintained shelves?

I swallow my bitterness and focus on Zachary, who has been nothing but kind to me. He doesn't deserve my ire, especially since I don't know my house's location from here besides a loose guess of *south-ish.*

"No, they're not only maps," Zachary answers. If he notices my brief downward mental spiral, he doesn't comment, and for that I'm grateful. "There are also reports of different Obsidian types, their weaknesses, and the best strategies to defeat them."

"Best strategies? Against a horde or individually?"

"Both. Scholars on our side of the country send information back and forth to help further the effort of eliminating the Obsidian. I keep a detailed record of everything I receive, in case we ever need it one day. The scribes who work in the hunters' barracks also track the deaths of hunters. It's how we keep a tally of the death count, and they send the names of the deceased to their old military academy." Zachary points to a shelf untouched by the chaotic mess, with a stack of scrolls neatly aligned. Each paper is short and thin, held together with twine.

"You're saying these are the names of all the students who died after graduation?" My eyes widen as I take in the paper, not needing much imagination to know what happened to the soldiers. By my count, there are about fifty small scrolls.

He nods solemnly. "Every six months, we receive the count, and there's never been a time when a scroll was blank. Though there is no guarantee that all the graduates have died. Any soldier who does not come back from a mission is recorded as dead."

My lips purse. The last part I knew, since every year the professors repeat the same warning about trying to escape our duty. Soldiers rarely work alone, regardless of their placement, because the only way to know if someone has absconded is to have a witness. Not that fleeing is a better option. It's treason—the worst thing a soldier can do to Arrynd—and we've been told there are special units in each city tasked with hunting down escaped soldiers within their region.

I refuse to run, to allow others to die in a cowardly

attempt to save myself, so I'll never know whether the special unit is true or a clever tool used to keep us in line. I lean back until my shoulder blades grace the nearest shelf, my eyes traveling back to Zachary. "So you know a lot."

The librarian laughs, slowly standing as the chair groans under the release of his weight. He rolls the map into a tight cylinder and grabs a small container beside the ink, scooping out some sort of sticky putty that keeps the scroll together.

Zachary gives me a grin that makes my lips tip up. His playful side mitigates the age in his face. "I know a few things, depending on the category. For example, I know the headmaster wants to talk to you."

"Really? I haven't heard about that." I shouldn't be skeptical of Zachary anymore, though. He must have psychic powers that are beyond me.

"I'm sure of it. While you're there, give this to him and save my knees from the hike." Zachary hands me the scroll, and I take it gingerly. The rough paper scratches my palms.

I glance at him curiously. "Are you sure you want me to? What if something happens to it?"

The older man sits back down. "I trust you," he states simply.

My heart warms at his confidence, and I hug the map close to my chest. "Thank you. Next time I'm here, I'll remember to knock."

Zachary's laughter follows me out the door.

While I prefer to delay my destination, I force myself into a brisk stride. I haven't been in Headmaster Hallow's office since my first day here nearly three years ago. My thoughts swim with the possibilities of why he wants to talk to me now, and worst-case scenarios tug at my fast pace. But my training with Adrian is rapidly approaching, and I don't have time to dawdle.

I arrive at the headmaster's office after getting stopped by two separate guards, who both asked me what I was doing. Only when I showed them the scroll, stuck together by putty I guess only Zachary uses, did they let me pass.

This is why I take the deserted routes, I think sourly as I rap lightly on the large doors. A distant greeting calls for me to enter. I push the wood open, praying this won't take too long and I'll make it to my practice on time.

The office looks exactly like it did three years ago, right down to Hallow sitting in his large leather chair. He appears surprised by my entry.

"Cassidy. Can I help you?"

I walk up to Hallow's desk and hand him the map before sitting in one of the plush chairs. "Zachary Cane wanted me to give this to you. He also said that you wanted to talk to me."

Hallow throws the scroll into a drawer without looking at it and sinks into his chair. "Ah, yes, I want to talk with you about your challenge with Tala."

In seconds, my stomach twists into knots. That's a topic I had hoped he wouldn't bring up. I keep my mouth shut, and eventually the headmaster resumes.

"Adrian told me the whole story. I spoke with Tala as well, but I thought I'd also get your side of things." He stares at me hard enough that I feel uncomfortable under his scrutiny. It's as though he wants a specific answer, but I don't know what he wants.

"Tala challenged me and I accepted." I begin slowly, inspecting the headmaster's reaction.

"Have you told anyone about this?" Hallow asks, his voice still even.

I think about Sara and wonder if she'd get in trouble for knowing. "No."

Hallow stays silent for a second before nodding. "It would look bad if word got out that instructors were challenging students. I think it's best we keep this to ourselves, don't you agree?"

Head tilted, my fingers tap against the large armrest as I contemplate my answer. Is he going to ask how I felt about everything, or if I feel safe in the academy?

By the look on his face, I don't think so. It sucks that someone who doesn't care about the students is the Headmaster just because their father was.

Feeling deflated, I answer his question for the sole purpose of being able to leave sooner. "Of course, Headmaster."

"Then you're excused. Try not to anger my staff next time, will you?"

I rise to my feet, stiff with irritation. Shooting him a tight smile, I turn around and walk out of the room.

Once the heavy doors shut behind me, I bend my knees and wrap my arms around them. My eyes squeeze shut, but a few traitorous tears leak out.

As much as I told Adrian that I didn't want help, a small part of me still assumed Hallow would feel something when he heard what Tala had done. It hurts, the callous indifference of someone who should protect the students.

I shouldn't have expected anything else. At this school, you can't wait around to be saved.

I take a couple of deep breaths, shoving the pain down deep inside. I don't have time to feel sorry for myself. If I can just get stronger, then I won't need to rely on anyone.

Ugh, I'm going to be late! I break into a sprint as soon as I'm able to stand again, racing through the hallways. When I reach the entrance of the gym, I remember my fight with Adrian this morning, and more unease floods through me.

Torchlight pours out from under the door, which means he's already in there.

Catching my breath, I wipe the sweat from my forehead with quivering fingers. *I hope my tardiness doesn't make this situation worse,* is all I can think as I tug the door open. My heart jumps when I see Adrian, and I blame it on the mad dash to get over here.

He's casually leaning against the opposite wall with his arms folded as I cross the threshold. I try to gauge his mood, but he doesn't have any expression. I can't tell if I should be happy or anxious about that. He doesn't *seem* to be upset, at least.

"I'm sorry," he says as I get closer to him. My mouth opens to stop him, but he continues. "I shouldn't have gotten upset with you. I know you can handle yourself."

"Well, I'm sorry, too," I respond, my body relaxing. "For blowing up on you. You're just looking out for me, and I appreciate it."

Adrian nods, the ghost of a smile on his lips that I mirror. For a second, we just stare at each other, his azure eyes against my hazel ones. My smile fades as I think about the scene with Tala and the kids earlier, how she played with a serenity that disappeared the moment she saw me.

Adrian picks up on it immediately. "Something else on your mind?"

"Why does Tala hate me?" I shake my head. "I mean, I understand my personality isn't always charming, but she *loathes* me."

Adrian sucks in a slow breath and runs a hand roughly

through his midnight hair, making the strands stick out in every direction. He pauses, so I wait and watch him debate what I assume is whether to tell me his theory.

While I'm not always known for my patience, it's worth it to hear what he has to say. Whatever he's thinking will be ten times more accurate than anything I can come up with.

Finally, he sighs again. "I think she's threatened by you."

"Threatened? By *me*?" Disbelief echoes through my startled laugh. *That's definitely not accurate.* "I think you're just a little off with your facts. Do you not remember yesterday?"

"Not of who you currently are, but of what you can become."

I feel like I can find an insult in there somewhere if I look hard enough. My face scrunches in confusion. "I don't understand."

Adrian studies me, like he's not sure if he should explain. Eventually, he turns and gestures towards him. "Walk with me," he says, stepping through the exit.

I waver, wondering why he doesn't want to talk here. After swift deliberation, I jog to catch up.

We amble through the vacant halls—aside from the guards who nod to Adrian—with the moonlight bathing the concrete ahead of us. Adrian waits until we are alone before sharing his story.

Chapter 15

Breathless Connection

"Tala and I weren't supposed to be there the night we found you. We aren't hunters, after all. But the people assigned to protect your family got ambushed by a group of Twos and were too injured to continue. They called Devero for reinforcements, since we were the closest facility that dealt with Obsidian in the area. He sent us out as soon as he could."

Adrian's faraway voice has me too terrified to speak. I wait for him to resume, not wanting to ruin the moment with my questions. "We thought we arrived too late to save anyone. We saw the damage to the house, the fire inside. I scoured the perimeter for lingering Obsidian while Tala went inside to kill any remaining demons and scout for survivors, though we weren't hopeful. But you were still alive, unhurt, surrounded by flames that killed all the Obsidian. We found your parents soon after that."

Pain constricts my heart at the mention of my parents. Adrian gives me a sideways glance. "Tala and I put together that you and your family had set that fire. And before the fire killed the Obsidian, you survived their attacks. A scrawny young girl evades Obsidian who kill even the most seasoned fighters. Tala was insistent that we drop you off at the nearest fields, but Devero immediately advocated for you to join the academy. He believed there was something special about you. He used to say that about Tala, who was a prodigy at your age."

"Tala wanted to do what?" I ignore the rest of what he said and file it away for future examination. What I can't ignore is that Tala tried to ship me off to be a farmer before I even entered the academy.

"When hunters find older orphans, protocol is to take them to the farms as workers. It's normally only the young kids who transfer to whatever military academy is the closest. The schools used to accept them, but almost all the older trainees died in their first year after graduation. We now require all five years of training. You're the first student Devero has accepted since the change."

I pinch my lips at his explanation. It makes sense when I think about it. Besides myself, I've never seen a late addition to the school.

"Tala fought hard to persuade Devero to follow protocol, but he would hear none of it. That's one of the few times I've ever seen her so angry."

I hold in a snort. I've seen Tala angry plenty of times. *But why would she not want me at the academy so badly? Was she truly just threatened?* At least I understand why she's been so hateful since our first encounter, but it still feels like I'm missing something. *There's no way this all stems from jealousy.*

We reach the courtyard, and Adrian stops, resting against a pillar with his arms secure across his chest. He continues talking through my inner monologue. "Based on what we saw, I think you have the potential to be stronger than any of us.

Stronger than me, stronger than Tala. For people like her, it's difficult to allow someone else to take the spotlight that they've been standing in their whole life. And I'm not positive she knows what she's doing half of the time."

I blink rapidly, unsure of what to say. I'm reeling from everything he told me and having a hard time processing it. *If those hunters hadn't been attacked, then maybe they would have reached our house in time.*

Maybe my parents wouldn't have died.

I wrap my arms around my stomach, squeezing against a surge of nausea.

"Special, huh?" I chuckle weakly. "That's a lot of pressure. I can barely survive sparring class." I aim for a smile, but it falls short.

If Devero assumed there was something special about me, then he must have lost faith a long while ago. Maybe that's why he doesn't care about Tala challenging me.

Our silent walk around the courtyard eats away at me. I think of something to say, but my scattered thoughts jumble the words in my mouth.

As we loop back around, Adrian exhales a long breath. "You should get some sleep. We'll start again in the morning."

Relief and irritation mix inside me at the idea of finishing early for a second time. Adrian turns to leave, but I lightly press my fingertips to his forearm. "Thank you for asking the nurse to bring in Sara while I was sleeping."

Nurse Dorna had said a lot of words then, but those specifically stuck out to me.

"Of course. I didn't want you to be alone when you woke up. Are you sure you'll be well enough to train in the morning?" He surveys me intently, waiting for my answer.

"We're almost at the one-month mark. I can't miss a

training session. Honestly, I feel great now." I shake my limbs out, rolling my shoulders.

"Okay, then. Tomorrow we'll work on how to escape when someone has you pinned." He gives me a brief nod and heads off toward the security wing.

I stand still until the loud hoot of an owl from the garden startles me out of my trance, forcing my feet to shuffle toward my bedroom.

At a slow, dazed pace, I peel my clothes off and lumber into the shower. Ten minutes later, I slide into bed and pull the blanket over my head, refusing to dwell on the conversation I had with Adrian. I barely register that Sara hasn't come in for the night as sleep takes over me.

I have a lot to think about, but not right now. Now, I am going to fill my face with chicken. That better be chicken I smell, or I'm going to lose it.

I briskly enter the crowded dining hall, the excited chittering floating about the room confirming the meat as much as the smell does. My mouth waters, and I silently praise my nose for not losing its touch as the scent washes over me.

I've been jittery since I woke up, and training with Adrian this morning was just as uncomfortable as I predicted it would be. I groan, pushing the heels of my palms against my eyes at the thought of this morning.

We finished early for the third time in a row because I couldn't pull myself together. While Adrian was his usual self, I couldn't look him in the eye, let alone try to escape from underneath his body as he pinned me down. Not even the exercise could hide my blush as I felt his hard muscles press against me. *I just couldn't focus!*

When he questioned why I was so off, I muttered some

lame excuse about how Serous must be affecting me and rushed out the door, leaving a confused Adrian behind.

I stifle another groan at my eccentric behavior. At this rate, I can either calm down or kiss my chance of passing the trials goodbye. I need to get it through my thick skull that we are just friends—*friends, I say*—if I can even call us that.

Honestly, I'm not too sure. Sometimes Adrian is as serious and harsh as a dictator, other times we are joking like best friends.

I sigh and wait in line while eyeing the room for Sara, but she's nowhere to be seen. She still doesn't arrive when I sit down at our usual spot. Conspicuously, Jared isn't here as well. *That could either be really good or really bad. Maybe Sara is hiding Jared's body.*

I munch on a thin, bland strip of chicken with great satisfaction. It might not have the best flavor, but it's still delicious. It's been at least three months since we last had any sort of protein besides eggs.

When I inhale my last piece, nothing can keep my mind from wandering to what Adrian said about the night we met.

He thinks my parents and I started that fire, but I remember them getting bitten before there were any flames. Didn't their torches die out? And I for sure didn't set one before I blacked out. I groan, rubbing my fingers over my temple. *There are so many pieces missing here.*

Another thing Adrian said pops up in my mind. He told me that Tala went into the house first while he surveyed the area, but I remember them arriving together. *Did she come in and then leave again? Why wouldn't she have helped me?*

I bite my lip, my brain cramping from the overwhelming thoughts.

The bench screeches as I shoot to my feet. I need a distraction, or else my brain is going to explode. Tossing my disposable tray in the compost pile, I head for the garden.

Maybe I can try to make mini boats out of leaves and push them around the pond.

Yeah, that sounds relaxing.

Or maybe you've officially lost it.

I'm still debating my questionable sanity when I break through the thin layer of trees that separates the courtyard and the garden. It takes a painfully long time to realize that there are already two people sitting on the bench, their bodies *very* close together.

"Uh…" The single syllable fills the air as my mind sluggishly processes that I've just interrupted my two friends locked in what looked like a steamy embrace. *Talk about awkward.* "Sorry, wrong garden."

Spinning around to hide my instant flush, I only get one step before Sara calls out to me, her words bordering on a laugh. "It's alright, Cassie. We're the ones who stole your favorite spot."

I take my time turning back around, hopefully long enough for them to sneak a last-minute kiss in. Embarrassment doesn't even begin to cover how I'm feeling. I'm also frustrated that I ruined one of their moments, which are probably few and far between.

When I'm finally facing them again, they are both the picture of innocence, though Jared's face looks almost as red as mine feels. "So I take it the talk went well?"

There's a second of silence before the three of us burst into laughter. Relief washes over my mortification. The fear that my little circle of family would never recover finally seeps out of me.

Without thinking, I go over to both of them and pull them into a group hug. "I am so happy you guys worked it out."

"Yeah, me too," Jared wheezes with a laugh. "Now stop crushing my windpipe."

I hastily pull away, but I can't stop smiling. "Well, I think I'll head to class early. No, no, don't get up. You guys just go back to enjoying each other's company."

They chuckle as I retrace my steps.

When I'm alone again, all the problems and fears plaguing me creep back into my mind. Only this time, I'm not so afraid.

My eyes widen into saucers as I gawk at the towering oak trees surrounding me. I inhale the scent of earth and fresh air and exhale with a wondrous, breathless laugh.

I'm outside! I'm home. Memories of hiking with my parents around our house flood back to me, and I blink back tears.

"Whether you become a hunter or not, you need to know how to survive on the land in case of emergencies. Even city guards have to travel between cities sometimes, exposing them to the dangers of the outside world. We will spend the next week during class out here, where each day we'll focus on a survival skill that may very well save your life. So pay attention." Tala stands rigid in front of the class, her feet spread in a wide stance.

She hasn't looked at me yet, which is strange. *I normally get an evil glare this far into class.* "Today, our focal point is finding food. We are going to identify berries and mushrooms that are edible and which ones are poisonous."

Tala waits for the class to murmur in agreement before shooting me a venomous scowl.

I hide a smile with my hand. *There it is.*

She tells us to go find different berries within the area and bring them back so she can help us identify characteristics of poisonous fruit.

"Stay within range of the guards," she shouts as we scatter, "unless you want to become an Obsidian's next meal."

I glance at the security team, which creates a wide perimeter around us, their black clothes half hidden in the trees. I briefly ponder if Adrian is here before my mind travels back to our assignment.

I bounce off in excitement, advancing further into the woods. I've been foraging with my father since I was six; the forest is like my second home. My father taught me the skills to stay quiet, recognize when danger is highest, and determine how best to stay in the sun to avoid attracting their attention.

I used to think we would always be safe, but sometimes even the best scout can't predict a random attack.

Pulling my mind to the present, I bend down to look at a small cluster of mushrooms, but immediately shake my head. Dad drilled mushrooms into my skull more than any other plant, since it can sometimes be tough to differentiate between delicious and fatal.

My eyes scrutinize the asymmetric yellow spots that sporadically dot the mushrooms. *These are undoubtedly poisonous.*

I crouch around to wave my friends over and show them my discovery, but find that the entire class has barely moved from the center circle. They all stand awkwardly, some shuffling close to a berry bush.

Confused at their actions, I'm about to head back to them when I remember that we only get one week out here, two hours a day. I brush off their hesitation and keep moving outward, naming as many plants and fungi as I can.

My nimble fingers pluck wild yonberries from a small

bush tucked under the base of a tree. Unable to resist, I pop one into my mouth, humming as its tart juiciness erupts across my tongue. I happily decide they are my favorite of all my discoveries today.

"You're pushing past our perimeter," a deep voice states, coming from right behind me.

Berries spill from my hand as I flinch, so engrossed in my harvesting that I didn't notice anyone walk up to me. I pick up the berries that fell from my cupped hand, lightly blowing off any dirt still clinging to the purple fruit.

Spinning around, my eyes slide past Adrian to my classmates, who have moved as a group to another bush just inches away from their first one.

"Why aren't they exploring? They look so nervous." I toss another berry in my mouth, perplexed.

"They don't have a connection to the outside world like you do. Most of them only have memories of being protected by walls. To them, being out here like this is threatening. Without happy memories to change their perception, they will always think of the outdoors as Obsidian territory."

"Huh, I've never thought about it like that before," I murmur distantly, devouring another yonberry. At the rate I'm inhaling these little fruits, I'll have to pick more soon.

Is that why I don't fear being out here? Because of all the memories I have? I imagine myself not having any impression of being outside, and the only thing I can attribute to the woods is when the Obsidian crawled out to kill my family. I shiver. *Yeah, I can understand where they are coming from.*

"How will they tolerate their jobs if fear guides their judgment?" I propose with genuine curiosity.

Adrian tilts his head in contemplation, his knuckles grazing across his chin. Sunlight washes over his face, highlighting his jawline and full lips, his dark hair dripping in golden rays of light. I force out a slow breath and tear my gaze away.

We're only friends, I remind myself fiercely.

"The anxiety never truly disappears, but as you become more confident in your skills, you discover the Obsidian should fear you, too." His eyes sweep behind me before locking with mine.

"If I were an Obsidian, I would undeniably fear you," I respond.

Adrian's lips stretch into a crooked smile at my serious tone. I return it, pushing down the butterflies that threaten to overtake my stomach. The sharp edges of his face soften when he smiles, and it leaves me stunned every time.

Desperate to stop my body's reaction to Adrian, I switch subjects. "Are you sure it's safe to be out here, with more Obsidian surrounding the school than normal?"

Adrian narrows his eyes. "How do you know about that?"

Oops. Will Zachary get in trouble if I say who told me? I shrug. "I know people."

While I try to look as impassive as possible, Adrian seems torn between scolding and laughing at me.

"Uh, huh. We took care of any threats to the class's excursion," he states calmly, gaining control of his emotions a lot faster than I could have, while also not giving me any extra information to work with.

A mountain is easier to crack than this guy.

"And by 'took care of,' do you mean killed?" I'm not sure why I asked the question. In what other ways do you get rid of Obsidian?

At least, that's what I thought until Adrian answers with, "Not exactly. We transferred them somewhere else."

Transfer Obsidian? How does that work?

Exploding with more questions, I'm unable to voice any

of them, as Tala chooses this inopportune moment to yell at me to rejoin the group. I pull one corner of my lips up at Adrian and hold out my hand, offering him a yonberry. He pinches it tenderly, and I glide past him, holding the fruit close to my chest.

I glance up at the cover of trees, the rays of bright light streaming down through holes in the leaves. I smile. *There's nothing like the beauty of the outside world to wash away my problems.*

Chapter 16

To The Best of Us

"I DID *NOT* ENJOY OUR CLASS TODAY, AND WE'LL HAVE TO BE outside for an entire week! I feel so exposed out there," Sara complains, biting into a piece of bread.

I don't respond as I lie on the long stone bench with one arm covering my eyes, basking in the sun beating down on me. With the weather slowly growing colder, I need to soak up as many rays of light as possible. Being in the garden is the closest I can get to experiencing the peace of being surrounded by nature.

The garden is empty almost every time I come here. Most people would rather be in a training room than relaxing. A small pond nestles in the corner, along with another bench and a thin gazebo. Flowers of all kinds and colors bloom sporadically around the pond, and a line of trees blocks the view of the courtyard.

I listen to the tranquil sound of water trickling from a tiny waterfall above the pond while Sara and Jared argue over the possibility of us getting ambushed while trying to dig up mushrooms. Sara giggles at whatever Jared says.

Hearing the happiness in her voice soothes me, and I smile. I don't contribute to the conversation, content to just listen to them talk.

"So, Cassie," Sara drawls. Noting the smirk in her voice, I lift my arm to study her. She's sitting at the bottom of a pine tree by the pond. Jared's head is in her lap, and she's stroking his blonde locks absentmindedly. "I saw you talking with Adrian in class today. You guys seem…close."

I eye her, not liking her tone. "Of course we're close. He's training me."

"It seemed like something more to me." Sara smiles, the fingers not in Jared's hair lightly tapping against her cheek.

Is she implying what I think she's implying? I glare at her, ignoring the fluttering in my chest at the idea of *something more,* and look to Jared for support. The boy's eyes are closed and he's happily humming to himself, not the least bit paying attention to our conversation.

"He's my *trainer,*" I heavily emphasize to her the same words I tell myself, "but if you want to stretch it, then I guess we're friends."

I return my hand to its original position, hoping she takes the hint. The sun is suddenly hotter than it was ten seconds ago.

I never talked with Adrian about whether we're friends or not; it feels like a weird topic to bring up. I don't even know if Adrian is dating someone else. The thought that he is makes me feel sick. I think of Tala, how she feels about him, and can't help but wonder how he feels about her.

I roll onto my side, careful not to fall off the bench. Propping up my head with a palm, I lean toward them. "I think Tala has a thing for Adrian."

Sara's eyes widen as she jerks, knocking Jared's head completely off her legs.

"Hey!" Jared shouts, rubbing the back of his head.

Sara ignores him as she gasps, "No way."

"Oh yeah. I think that's why she challenged me. She saw us training together."

Sara laughs and slaps her knee. "That explains the look she was giving you while you and Adrian were talking!"

"What look?" I demand, baffled.

"Like she was figuring out the best pedestal to mount your head on," Sara giggles, wiping her eyes.

I let Sara have her moment, tapping my fingers against the warm stone. When she sobers, she regards me with sympathy. "That must be so strange for you. Knowing your trainer and your nemesis could be all intimate."

My fingers clench and my lips twist. "Yes," I say sourly, "it's very strange."

Later that night, as my friends and I walk toward our dorms after dinner, we stop dead in our tracks when a scream resounds through the corridor. My legs move on their own, sprinting down the hallway and flying through the door to a random gym, Jared and Sara's footsteps directly behind me.

If I had taken a second to analyze where I was, I would have noticed which room we were running to. My breath whooshes from my lungs as I take in the ring of students around the small gym.

No one pays attention to my entrance as their cheers and laughter finally reach my ears. Another yell erupts from inside the ring, but the roar of the crowd smothers it.

"A challenge," Sara whispers behind me.

Jared stands beside Sara with his arm around her waist as

she clamps her mouth shut. My lips pinch, and I stalk toward the younger kids.

Sara's hand whips out and wraps around my wrist, her wide eyes locking with mine. "You're not stopping it, are you?"

I shake my head and pull from her grasp. My last challenge is still fresh in my mind, and so is the humiliation of having someone intervene on my behalf.

There are a lot more people here than for my challenges with Emmerick. All from different ages, too. New challengers always generate a good crowd.

I spot Raddo in the corner, watching the fight from behind his glasses, and my stomach burns just looking at him. The third-year instructor is present for every challenge. He doesn't stand by the door like he usually does, and I wonder if that's a conscious choice.

The echoes of a fight are unmistakable by the time I reach the front row and find the two challengers. They don't detect a newcomer among the crowd as the large male laughs and shoves a petite girl off her feet. She stumbles before righting herself unsteadily.

The boy's black hair hangs limply around his greasy face, and his long, lanky arms wave for the crowd to cheer him on. I assume they're in their first year, which means he's trying to prove his strength in front of his peers by beating up weaker opponents. He wouldn't be the first one to do so.

The cornstalk-yellow hair of his opponent is messy and dirty, and covers most of her features. When she peeks up at the boy, I can see her strained features with light blue eyes set slightly farther apart.

The crowd shouts its approval at the actions of the boy, who, I gather, is called Ian from their bloodthirsty cries. His black eyes gleam with each cheer.

"Give up, Risa," he goads while stalking toward her.

Risa tries to retreat, but the crowd is unyielding. They thrust her forward with enough force that she pitches toward Ian, who grabs her shoulder and pulls her close to him. He leans in and whispers something in her ear. I can't see Ian's expression, but Risa's face morphs into sheer terror. He lets go, and she drops to the mat without his support, her hands covering her mouth.

I bite my lip hard as the boy kicks her in the abdomen. She rolls away from the force of the blow, but doesn't stand up. Only her heaving chest shows she's still conscious. Wrapping my arms tight around myself, my eyes bore into her curled back.

Forfeit, I beg in my mind. My gaze flashes to Ian. *He's not going to stop*.

Risa stays silent until Ian steps on her fingers, the action fracturing at least three fingers by the cracks that follow. A hand flies to my throat at the guttural scream ripping through the girl. "Stop," she begs in a breathy voice, "please, I forfeit."

"Why?" Ian's lips pull into an overstretched smile. "I'll just keep coming back. Every day, I'll snap a new bone in your body. The nurse will heal you just for me to break you all over again."

My exhalation falters at his laugh. I try to stay out of my head, out of memories that feel far too similar to this unfortunate girl's experience.

Tears stream down Risa's cheeks as a sob racks her frame. "No," she cries. "I-I can't take it anymore. I quit."

Judging by Ian's triumphant smile, he had wanted more than just winning the challenge from the beginning. His head slants to the side as he nods to Raddo that the challenge is over. The instructor pushes his glasses up his nose and saunters over to Risa, grabbing her by the shoulder.

Risa doesn't seem to notice, too consumed with her weeping.

"As you can see, Professor Raddo, she's forfeited. You'd better take her to the headmaster because she's also done with this school." Ian shakes his head in mock sorrow. "Poor thing just couldn't handle the stress of it all."

"Happens to the best of us, I'm afraid," Raddo states with a regretful smile that I know is fake. His eyes scan the crowd and stop when they meet mine. Raddo's grin stretches, and I can almost hear him in my mind, goading me to quit too.

I whirl around and shove my way through the crowd and out the door, not waiting to watch Raddo haul the girl to the headmaster's office. My head shakes when I pass Sara and Jared, who look at me with the same expression of knowing sadness.

"Are you okay, Cassie?" Sara asks.

I sink to the floor of an abandoned hallway. My shoulders slump, and I rub my eyes wearily, letting my head knock against the wall. Sara and Jared sit beside me, their faces lined with worry. I want to wipe away the pity, but I understand their concern. After all, my challenges were never pleasant for anyone, except Emmerick.

"I'm fine," I sigh.

My friends have never participated in a challenge before. Challenges are actually quite rare. Normally, they're only used when bullies feel the need to drive someone out of the school. The criteria for whom they choose? I doubt they have one, just easy targets. Like Risa. *Like me.*

Sara has been there for me since my first fight. Even now, her eyes still hold the same love and care they did that first day when she helped me bandage my injuries.

I loop my arm through Sara's. "I think Tala's challenge

dug up some old wounds, but I promise I'm okay. Thank you for caring, Sara. I love you." She squeezes my hand and lays her head against mine. My heart warms at her touch. "And I guess I love you too, Jared."

He snorts. "You guess? Glad to know our friendship is so solid." He sounds offended, but I can hear the smile in his voice. I give a weak, playful smirk, grateful for the two of them.

Pulling my legs in for a stretch, I chew on my lower lip while Adrian deposits the swords we used in training tonight on the shelf. I was late to practice, but Adrian didn't scold me like he usually would. Something on my face must have warned him not to push me.

He walks over without speaking and sits down, mirroring my stance. We stretch in comfortable silence for a few minutes while I shuffle through my chaotic thoughts.

"A girl left the academy today," I blurt out, not looking at him.

"I know. I was with Zypha in Devero's office when Lywell Raddo brought her in."

"Is she going to the fields?"

Adrian nods. "They all do."

I rest my back on the floor and lift my leg into the air, tugging it to my chest until my muscles protest. Those who quit the academy end up tilling the farms scattered across Arrynd.

The professors explain it with statements about how we serve society either way: by feeding the people or protecting them. Though I don't think any of the students believe that. Quitting the academy signifies you weren't strong enough to handle the pressure, or at least that's what I hear from others.

My own opinion on the matter isn't as rigid.

I raise my head to peer at Adrian from around my leg. The sudden need to defend Risa bubbles up inside me. "Her classmates drove her out of this school; she didn't leave because she wanted to."

"She wanted to escape them. That was her choice," Adrian says, sitting cross-legged with his back straight and elbows on his knees.

I frown. "So her two choices were to quit or endure suffering every day?"

Adrian tilts his head as he regards me, his sharp gaze calculating. "She could have fought, and they would have backed off eventually. Only the strongest can survive this school, this profession."

"I used to be her, you know." The words slide from my tongue before I can stop them. My head thumps against the mat and I lower my leg, exhaustion leaking into my voice. "My classmates weren't too happy that a newbie with no prior training was joining their class. They said I didn't belong, which in a way was right. I got challenged almost every day that first year. And when they weren't throwing out challenges, they took their frustration out in the sparring ring. I was in the hospital two or three times a day."

I chuckle bitterly at the memory. My gaze locks with Adrian, who's watching me silently with dark eyes. "Only bullies use the challenge system, and those bullies break people who don't deserve to be broken. Someone has to stop it."

My teeth press into my bottom lip to cut off my rant. I'm sure Adrian doesn't want to hear my resentment over the challenges that no one cares about. I utter an apology and stand, shaking out my limbs.

"Well, I should head to bed. I need to be prepared for our next outdoor activity tomorrow. Have a good night, Adrian." I give him a tight smile and twist around.

Adrian grabs my wrist before I can make it to the door, his touch sending tingles through my arm. I turn my head to look at him over my shoulder. His gentle words brush my cheek as he leans closer. "I'll talk with Zypha, see if she can reason with the headmaster and put an end to them."

A small, genuine smile tugs at my lips as I nod, ignoring the squeezing of my heart at his proximity. His black hair is slick with sweat, his eyes shining with their usual fire.

I hold my breath, waiting for his next move, but he drops his hand and steps away, bidding me goodnight.

Blinking back the dismay, it takes a moment for me to find my feet again and leave the training room. Flashes of Adrian's face, his touch, play through my mind.

I scrub my forehead with my hands and let out a groan.

My *'just friends'* mantra is falling apart at the seams.

Each day, we learn a new survival skill: from hunting small game to setting up camp to deciding how many people should take watch at night. I love every second of it, absorbing as much information as possible and combining it with what my dad taught me.

This is our last day out here, possibly until we graduate. A twinge of sadness fills me as I observe Tala kneeling on the ground, describing the best way to check to see if an Obsidian horde has recently passed by.

"Obsidian don't pay attention to where they step, so

discovering broken branches in a large path could mean a horde just stampeded through," Tala explains, using one hand to break a branch in half. I smirk as she prattles on.

Scanning the perimeter, my eyes rest on Adrian. He's to the right of the group, but he's not looking at us. His attention lies farther out into the forest, face pinched in concentration. I've never seen him so intensely focused before.

Something's wrong. The sight of it curls my toes as cold blankets my skin in a chilling caress.

"Are you listening to me, Cassidy?" Tala snaps her fingers at me, her voice doused in annoyance.

I ignore her and keep my eyes fixed on Adrian. *What does he see?*

Tala marches over to me, her nose nearly touching mine. "If you think—"

She doesn't finish her threat. Multiple cracks reverberate through the forest like drums to a death march. And out of the shadows, as if materializing straight from our nightmares, appear the Obsidian.

Chapter 17

Shaken Truths

"Everyone inside, now!" Adrian roars, pulling his leather mask above his nose.

It's been a while since we worked with our specialized weapons. I stare in awe as Adrian grips the hilt of his sword and rapidly draws it from the sheath, causing flames to ignite across the blade. The scabbard, lined with flint, catches the weapon on fire once the metal reaches a certain speed. The Eloyla paste coating the sword keeps the fire clinging to the blade.

Adrian shouts orders as he disappears into the trees, only the haze of his flames visible.

My knees lock as the woods explode into fire and chaos. All the guards follow Adrian's directive and brandish their blazing weapons. On the wall, more guards race around with torches to light the arrows. Though if we are in close range with the Obsidian, the guards risk shooting one of us instead.

Screams split the air, combining with the sickening crunch of steel against rock. How they got so close without us noticing their presence only adds to the confusion.

"But it's daytime!"

"How many?"

"What level are they?"

"What senses?"

"Help me!"

"It's a Two, no, a Three!"

The cries swirl together in the mayhem. I spin in a circle, trying to locate Sara and Jared through the havoc. Naire pushes me to the ground in her haste to reach the large metal gate, and I land heavily on my knees, my frozen limbs not budging. My classmates sprint toward the school, where the two guards at the entrance urge them on with frantic waves of their torches.

Officer Zypha rushes through the opening with two short swords, each one dripping fire. She immediately engages in combat with the nearest Obsidian, her weapons slicing through nothing as the monster rears back to avoid the attack.

I watch Sara, who reaches the safety of the walls, grab Jared's hand and turn around. Her eyes scan the scene until they fall on me, her face draining of color.

"Cassie!" Sara screams. Jared snaps his head up at her voice and steps forward with resolve.

"Stop," I shout back, not wanting them to risk their lives for me. Jared advances an inch before the unyielding grip of a guard clamps on his shoulder.

I'm distracted from my friends as another guard moves to stand in front of me. He raises his sword, the crimson blaze flickering in his brown eyes, and the mole above his upper lip twists with the determined set of his mouth.

"Don't worry, miss. We'll protect you." The barest hint of an accent rolls over me, his words forcing me into motion.

Finally regaining my senses, I spring to my feet, my

gloved hands gripping the hilt of my weapon. "I can help," I announce, thankful they supplied us with actual swords in case of an emergency.

My sword pulls from its sheath with a ring, and I soak up the heat radiating off the blade. The fire is comforting, a shield between me and the monsters eager to taste my blood. I have to blink hard to tear my gaze away from the mesmerizing red tendrils.

The young guard gives me an appraising look before dashing off into the fight. I follow along, yanking my mask up above my nose, heart beating wildly in my throat. *This is what my training has led up to. This is where I can show how much I've grown.*

When I near the battle, I slow, my feet turning to blocks of cement.

There are only four Obsidian, but they don't resemble the ones I remember at all. There are at least three guards on each one, and the Obsidian are going up against them easily.

The biggest thing that makes me hesitate is the fact that they're fast. *The demons aren't supposed to be fast, especially during the day.* They dodge swords and swipe with such accuracy that I almost believe they can see, their towering forms stretching at least seven feet in height.

Their skin is smooth stone, less like chunks of small rocks stuck together and more like one sculpted piece. Instead of empty eye sockets, they have giant black eyes, which are somehow even more disturbing to look at. The skin over their noses and ears is open and folds outwards in a cup around the holes.

These must be the Threes. They have three senses: sight, smell, and hearing.

My gaze switches to Adrian as he fights off a Three on his own, his sword impeding the Obsidian from reaching the school. When comparing the other guards' skills, no one comes close to his speed and agility, not even Zypha. His ferocity is palpable, energizing me and the officers.

He's unbelievable, I think in amazement.

"What are you doing here?" Tala pulls down her mask to scowl at me. "You'll get someone killed."

She roughly shoves me toward the academy. I trip over myself and land on the forest floor with a grunt, barely able to keep my weapon from lighting the grass on fire.

Stop falling, Cassie! Letting out a curse, I scramble to my feet.

I'm about to tell her that now's not the time for one of her moods when a black creature slams into her side. *Another Three?* I glance at the guards, counting the four original monsters I saw earlier. There are two guards from the direction the Obsidian came from, which means it must not have engaged them.

That demon came out of nowhere and ignored other people. Could the Three not see those guards?

Tala and the monster tumble to the ground, both vying to get on top. Its sharpened incisors gnash at her, chomping at the air inches from her neck. The Three ends up above Tala and sinks its claws into her hips, releasing a haunting howl that sounds scarily similar to a victory call. My instructor shrieks, her arms straining against the demon's might.

I desperately flick my eyes back to the guards, still concentrating on the Threes in front of them. Besides Adrian, who seems to have killed his and moved to help another group, there has been no change.

They have their hands full. Tala and I are on our own.

As Tala grapples with the Obsidian, I rush forward, brandishing my sword in a gray arc of scarlet fury. Before the Three can turn around, I swing down with every ounce of strength I have. The blade cuts cleanly through the Obsidian's neck, its black blood spraying all over Tala's front.

The head thumps to the ground and rolls, stopping at my feet. Its lifeless eyes bore into mine, mouth hanging open to expose teeth glistening with venom. The rock surrounding the head crumbles away to ash, leaving nothing but black, lumpy mounds of flesh in its wake. The same goes for the rest of the body, as if the rock is only strong when the monster is alive.

Kicking what's left of the head away in revulsion, I run to Tala and fall to my knees beside her. She's propped up on an elbow, spitting and coughing. I place a hand on her shoulder, but she swats it away.

"You got its blood in my mouth," she chokes, violently scrubbing her tongue with her clean sleeve and gagging. *Is she seriously angry at me after I saved her life?* I almost give a sharp remark back, but suck in a breath when I realize what she means.

There's more than one way to turn, including ingesting their blood that's full of the virus.

In the next minute, Tala will become one of the Obsidian.

My eyes hopelessly scour the rest of our party, but none of them notice our struggle, too consumed with the battle before them. My stomach rolls. As much as I hate Tala, she doesn't deserve this.

Tala lunges to the side, and I stumble back a step, fearing she has already lost her mind. But my instructor grabs one of her short swords in a white-knuckled grip, tilting the blade up to her neck. A thin stream of blood trails from where the steel tip punctures her skin, yet the blade doesn't go in any further.

My gaze locks with Tala's, and I feel the terror resonating

off her in waves. Sacrificing your life so you don't join the enemy ranks is something they emphasize every year of our studies, but following through with it is another matter entirely.

"Help me," Tala begs, the sword at her throat trembling. I open my mouth to ask her what I could do, but she continues. "Kill me."

"Wh-what?" My body recoils in astonishment. I know my question is wasting precious time, but I can't comprehend what she's saying.

"This was how my mother died. I can't do it." Tears fill Tala's eyes, and more shock runs through me.

I scan the skin visible underneath her uniform and find there are no signs of the transformation yet. Usually within the first few seconds, the skin shifts to gray, starting at the extremities, before hardening into rock.

"Tala, wait. You aren't showing signs of turning. Let's just wait a second."

"You want to risk the lives of everyone here?" Tala growls back, though her anger fizzles as she stares at her own hands. Fear and confusion and hope dance across her face until she finally lowers her sword. "How is this possible?"

"I don't know," I say truthfully, just as shaken as she is. Has anyone ever survived ingesting Obsidian blood before? Would this be something Zachary has information about?

We stare at each other in silence, both drowning in our own thoughts, until Adrian runs up beside me.

"Are you hurt?" Adrian asks breathlessly, scanning me for injuries.

He waits for my response before he kneels beside Tala, repeating the question. My gaze moves to the guards, trying to keep Tala's miraculous survival from the forefront of my mind, and I find that the four Threes are dead. Even though

I don't count any casualties, I exhale unsteadily, my blood still pumping with adrenaline.

I killed a Three. It wasn't attacking me, and I snuck up on it, but still.

Adrian helps Tala to her feet as a few guards fall in beside us, and we all slowly maneuver our way to the gate. The rest of the officers start dragging the corroding corpses into a pile.

"Bloody demons. How could this have happened?" One of the guards spits on the ground close to an Obsidian's decomposing body. He rips off his leather half-mask and wipes the sweat from his upper lip.

"Feldin, put your mask back on until we are within the walls," Officer Zypha yells at the guard.

She barely gets the words out before startled shouts spring up from behind us. I pivot with enough speed to briefly blur my vision. Threes materialize from behind trees, black shadows etched in death.

How can there be more? One, two…six of them against the thirteen of us. Tala drops to the ground, still weak and dazed, as Adrian lets her go to unsheathe his weapon. *Well, twelve of us.*

Half of the Threes immediately engage in combat with the guards around the corpses, while the others jump over the fight.

One demon gets a surprise attack on Feldin, the guard who took his mask off. I only have time to let out a strangled breath before the Obsidian's teeth puncture his exposed neck. Feldin falls to the ground, still fighting off the Obsidian that's gone in for a second bite, the sound of tearing flesh an underscore to the screams.

Someone calls for the gate to close, a precaution in case we get overwhelmed. I look around and, for the first time, realize I'm the only student still out here; the rest have made it inside the gate.

"Cassie, no!" Jared's voice echoes behind me as the loud thud seals our fate, reminding us all that we are alone in fighting these creatures.

Feeling nauseous, I raise my still-burning weapon and prepare to fight. But the three Obsidian not in combat dash right past us, not sparing any attention to our group. It takes a moment to understand what they are after.

"They're heading for the gate!" I holler, sprinting after them.

Pandemonium explodes again as guards yell orders to one another, splitting their defenses to defend the academy. The Threes at the gate scratch at the barrier, jumping up and down. *Are they trying to climb it?* My gut twists. *If they can figure out how to climb, then no one will be safe.*

Adrian catches up with me before we reach the entrance.

"There's a small cave northeast of here, about a mile out. It's extremely well-covered, so you'll be safe there. Wait for me to come get you after we finish them off." Adrian's lips curve with tension, his eyes fixed on the Threes. I can hear the pounding of the guard's feet at my heels.

"What? No! I'm not running away. I can fight!" My sputtering falls on deaf ears as Adrian clenches his jaw.

"I'm not asking, I'm ordering you. You've never battled a Three before, and you're not ready. Stop trying to be the hero and get out of here," he barks out, surging forward to slash at the closest Three.

I halt, the guards flying past me with battle cries. Metal carving through rock rings in my ears, and the Threes wail in retaliation. My breathing increases to harsh gasps as indignation washes over me.

Across the field, a severely injured Three that didn't rush the gate continues to bellow in anger and crawl towards the nearest guard, not even noticing its missing leg. Tala is curled against a tree, the heaving of her back the only hint she's still alive.

There's no way I can just leave. This is what I've been training for. I slant my sword parallel to the ground and take a step closer to the conflict.

Trust me, Adrian's voice whispers in my mind. Biting my lip, I sheathe my sword, the fire instantly going out. I turn and run, blinking back the burn of approaching tears.

I have to double back once I realize I've gone too far. It takes two more tries to spot a sliver of the cave behind a giant fern bush and multiple trees. It would have been nearly impossible to spot unless someone was looking for it. *Adrian wasn't kidding.*

A new influx of fury threatens to smother me at the thought of him. I shove it down with a growl, squeezing past a tree to slide into the cave. Heavily filtered by the bush, little light shines into the small cavern.

I have to bend my knees to keep my head from hitting the top of the stone. The floors and walls are smooth and curve inward like a bowl. I crawl to the end of the cave and slump to the ground.

My fingers dig into the sides of my legs as a shudder runs through my body. Shaky breaths soon become too loud in the cramped hole, and I smash my lips against my knee to muffle a frustrated scream.

What do I have to do to prove I'm not a hindrance? I thought Adrian believed in me. My hands twitch uncontrollably as I suck in one strangled gasp after another, sweat stinging my fluttering eyes.

I can't breathe, I think wildly, irrational fear gripping my throat. *I need to get out of here.*

I struggle onto my knees, wobbling on the uneven floor. My fingers jam into rock as I quickly clamber toward the exit. I try to breathe by yanking down my mask, but the oxygen gets stuck in my throat, cutting off my circulation.

With a lunge, I burst through the narrow exit, my shoulder scraping roughly against the jagged stone in my haste. I collapse on the ground, the unrelenting dirt a welcome relief.

The cold air finally breaks free from its entrapment in my throat and I cough, panting, forcing myself to rise. My wobbly legs shuffle me forward until I collapse against a tree, shivering and praying a random Obsidian doesn't find me. My spasming limbs refuse to cooperate anymore. *I won't be able to defend myself even if it's a Zero. I'm useless.*

I watch small birds chirp and dance about the trees, disappearing and reappearing on different branches. The smell of fresh air and oak trees helps to calm my breathing. I close my eyes, listening to the wind rustling through the leaves while waiting for my heartbeat to slow.

A resounding pop resonates through the forest, and my eyes fly open.

Chapter 18

Holding Back

I LEAP TO MY FEET, UNBALANCED AND STUMBLING AS I wrestle the hilt into my hand. The blade pulls out too slowly and it doesn't light, but I'm too focused to redraw the weapon. I struggle not to let my heart vault from my chest as I reassure myself that it was probably just an animal.

Carefully treading toward the source of the noise, my eyes roam over the dense foliage, the leaves tinted brown from the gradually changing weather. My body stays within the sunlight filtering through the trees, an action even the most isolated humans know to do.

If it's an Obsidian, I'll kill it before the monster reaches the academy. Adrian and the rest of the guards already have enough to deal with.

And yet, the image of going up alone against a Three makes my throat convulse. I swallow hard, gripping the sword tightly. *Focus, Cassie. You got this.*

I sidestep a massive tree trunk, and a cottage materializes into view. The stone walls are barely visible under thick patches of moss and vines, with a roof that I'm surprised hasn't collapsed.

Curious, I keep my sword raised and inch closer. The large wooden door has spots of decay, and rust tarnishes the silver knob. My fingertips graze the metal, and it doesn't take much effort for the handle to twist. The door slides open easily.

Inside, the cottage matches the outside with its broken furniture and cobwebs. My feet crunch over dried leaves as I travel across the room to the lone door that's closed. The large space looks like it once held a living room, kitchen, and dining area.

The silence is deafening compared to the natural sounds of the forest. My ears strain to catch any activity besides the creak of the floorboards under me.

The shut door leading to the back of the cabin looms in front of me, which I assume connects to a bedroom or bathroom. I'm fascinated by this little house so close to the academy. Adrian probably knows the story behind this place. I push down the voice that tells me it most likely belonged to a family years ago, before they either had to evacuate or were killed.

Reaching the door, I open it in a wide arc. My head jerks back as black, broken fingers swipe towards my face, but I'm not fast enough. Its fingers dig painfully into my cheek, carving out indentations. The Obsidian tries to latch onto my skin and pull me to its mouth.

I grunt against the burning sensation and use the Obsidian's force as momentum to fall to the side and roll away a few feet from the monster. My eyes scan its face: empty eye sockets, jagged rock around its entire body.

Even as blood pulses from my wound, I give a breathy

laugh, most of my fear sliding away. *A Zero I can take.* One demon, especially one so weak, is a simple task.

The Zero moans, limping toward me and gnashing its teeth with unnatural strength. I dodge as it swings at me again. The Obsidian shuffles closer and I stick my sword into its sheath, yanking it out with enough force to burst into flames.

The Zero stops and takes a few steps back. Even this one knows what fire means.

I leap forward, my sword cutting through the air with a soft whistle. It slides cleanly across the Obsidian's neck, and the body lands on the ground with a thud, where it dissolves into ash.

My sword slips from my grip, and I press a gloved hand against the gash on my cheek. *Ouch, that hurts. I should have brought Serous with me.*

I crouch and use my fireproof sleeve to bat the fire out so the cottage doesn't go up in flames. Maintaining pressure on the wound, I meander outside and sag against the exterior wall. My knees buckle, and with a slow exhale, my body slumps to the ground. Exhaustion hits me, forcing my eyes closed.

I don't return to the cave, positive Adrian will find me eventually. *He might have even heard the fight.*

I'm answered by the beat of racing footsteps gaining on me, but I don't open my eyes. The foot placement is too precise to be an Obsidian. I tilt my chin so it looks like I'm propping my head up on my hand rather than stopping the blood flow. The thought of Adrian knowing I got injured by a lowly Zero makes me want to collapse into a ball and shrivel away.

Adrian appears from behind a tree, slowing once he sees me. He crouches by my side, pulling me from my thoughts.

"Cassie, what happened?" Adrian's voice is dark and rough, his warm hand settling against my unblemished cheek. I fight the urge to lean into it.

I nod toward the door. "I heard a noise and came to check it out. A Zero was hiding inside the bedroom."

Adrian gracefully rises and enters the cottage, his movements accompanied by the sound of doors opening. *He's probably making sure there are none left.* My face pulls into a sour grin. *Maybe I should have done that after the fight. A tip for next time, then.*

Minutes pass before I hear him come out, and I risk a glimpse of his expression. Adrian observes me with unreadable eyes until he finally kneels close, his jaw clenching. "That was your blood in there, wasn't it? You're hurt."

I glance down at the red liquid coating my jacket. *Kind of hard to hide that.* I don't lift my hand away from the wound as I say casually, "I got clipped by the Zero, but it's not a bite. I barely feel it now."

Adrian pauses, his hand hovering near my covered cheek. I keep my eyes lowered, shame flowing through me, shame… and anger. *You're not ready*, he had said. The ultimate humiliation, like shoving everything I want but am unable to achieve in my face.

When I don't remove my sleeve from the abrasion, he stands and walks away. I bite my lip to keep from asking where he's going, but he only drops to the base of a tree with a faint sigh, his long legs stretching out in front of him.

I wait for him to speak, but he doesn't. *He'd better not think I forgot what he said to me.* I scrutinize him in displeasure as he lifts his head to meet my glare.

His azure eyes are an abyss of regret.

"After I graduated, I became a hunter with my best friend, Wick. He died while protecting a family of farmers, and I could have prevented his death. I won't watch another person I care about die." He blows out a long breath. "But I shouldn't have yelled at you. I'm sorry."

By some miracle, I keep my mouth from dropping to the forest floor. *Let's just summarize, shall we? One: Adrian is sharing his past. Two: He cares about me. And three…he cares about me.*

My tongue adheres to the roof of my mouth, refusing to form any comprehensible words. So I remain silent, picking at the ground with the fingernails of my free hand and squishing balls of dirt into tinier pieces. The feeling of mud under my nails gives me something to focus on.

"I'm sorry about Wick. I can't imagine losing your best friend," I finally mutter. The thought of Sara dying is unbearable.

Adrian dismisses it with a shrug, looking everywhere but at me. *I wonder if he will ever tell me the story behind Wick's death. Honestly, how am I supposed to stay mad at someone who bares their soul to me?*

"Why did you become a hunter when you could have worked in the city?" The question has been bugging me since I first found out about his past, and if Adrian is sharing, then I might as well try to get an answer.

Adrian continues to avert his gaze, his fingers tightening around his knees. "I'll never work in the city, and Wick had his reasons for being a hunter. So I chose to help him."

"Ah, makes sense," I respond, even though it makes absolutely zero sense. With the slow, deliberate tone of his words, he's purposely hiding the details. While I'd prefer to know more about why Adrian refuses to go to the city and what Wick hoped to do as a hunter, Adrian's rigid form is screaming at me not to pry. I'm surprised he gave me any information at all. From what I gathered, his usual answer to any personal probing is silence.

I don't want Adrian to be uncomfortable with me present, though. *Think of something else to talk about, Cassie, quick!*

"You need to trust me, too, Adrian. What's the point of training me if you just push me to the sidelines every time danger is around?" The words tumble from my lips before I can stop them. I had repeated them over and over in my head while waiting for him to find me, but after hearing his confession, I meant to tuck them away for later. *What a horrible subject change. Stupid mouth.*

Luckily, the question distracts Adrian from his discomfort. "I know," he runs a hand through his hair, the tips sticking up in different directions, "but there's still so much to teach you."

"Well, it's a good thing we have three weeks now, isn't it?" I tease, throwing a ball of mud at him. It hits the tree above him and explodes into dirt particles that rain down onto his hair and shoulders. He shakes his head, swatting the earth clumps away.

Adrian's lips pull up at one corner into a lopsided smile. "I suppose. But as much as I try, trouble seems to find you anyway." He surveys the open door with a frown before peering at me with piercing eyes. "What am I going to do with you, Cassie?" He says it like a statement.

I mull over a response. My usual snarky comments don't seem to be appropriate here. I suppress a snort. *Like I have the ability to not be snarky. No, not even I am that powerful.*

I sigh and think of Adrian's power as he fought the Obsidian. I've never seen him like that, not even when we spar.

I raise an accusatory finger at him once I realize what my thought means. "I saw you today against those Threes. You're holding back on me during training!"

Shock strikes Adrian's features before he throws his head back and laughs. I've never heard his actual laugh until now, and I shove my blush as far down inside me as possible. I like its velvet quality *way* more than I should.

"We were just bombarded by a group of Threes, then a Zero ambushed you, and that's what you're thinking about?" He chuckles again. "You're very odd, Cassie."

"Being even is boring," I smirk, deciding to take that as a compliment. "You'd better not restrain yourself tonight, or else."

He tilts one shoulder up. "It's your funeral."

Before I can argue, Adrian rises, brushes off dirt from his black pants, and offers me a hand. I grab it and let him pull me to my feet. His hand is rough and calloused against mine, his grip firm.

Once I'm standing, he looks me up and down. "Where's your sword?"

I scour the ground at my feet until I realize I must have left it in the cabin. I nod in its direction, not willing to go back inside to retrieve it. Adrian doesn't hesitate, swiftly vanishing from sight before reappearing moments later with my sword. I briefly hug it to my chest before sliding the weapon into its covering.

Adrian watches me with indecipherable eyes, his vision narrowing on my cheek. It takes a second for me to put together that I had dropped my hand from my face when I snatched the sword.

"Cassie," he starts, but I brush past him before he can touch the wound, starting the long walk back to the school.

The dried blood makes my cheek cold and numb, and it throbs with each step. *Not that I'd ever tell Adrian that.* I hear him exhale before catching up with me. We crunch through the grass, attempting to avoid as many fallen branches as possible.

"What was that cabin used for, Adrian?"

179

"It's an abandoned house, long before the academy was built. We have the occasional hunter that uses it when traveling through the area, though it hasn't been occupied in some time."

I nod. "So how did that Zero get into the bedroom? The door was closed, and there were no signs of it breaking in, were there?" *I should have checked the house for its entry points.*

Adrian slowly shakes his head. "Not that I could see, no. And I've never heard of them being able to open doors."

"Then how could it be in there? It's not like someone would open doors for the Obsidian."

"Huh," he says, as if he finally sees how it doesn't add up. "I'll need to check the cabin out more closely later."

I give a small smile, happy he's considering my input. We walk in silence for a few more minutes before my mind travels to the instructor who survived an ingestion of Obsidian blood.

"How's Tala?" I don't want to ask, but the memory of her terrified eyes haunts me.

He stares straight ahead. "She didn't transform within five minutes, so that's something. I had one of the guards take her to the infirmary to get some tests done."

"Did any more of the guards...?" I can't believe I haven't asked sooner. My heart swells with sorrow at the mental image of Feldin's torn flesh.

"Two others were bitten," he responds solemnly. "It was the most Threes in a group that I'd ever seen. But we killed them all, and their sacrifice kept the students safe."

My sadness doubles when I remember them struggling against the Threes while I ran away. *Could I have saved a life if I'd stayed?*

"Don't get any ideas," he commands, reading my expression. "Protecting the school was their job. There's no guarantee that you wouldn't have died as well if you were there."

I huff, but something in his eyes stops me from disputing him. Adrian's face remains impassive, but his jaw ticks, like he's having a hard time keeping his feelings inside.

I focus on the trees in front of us, giving him as much space as I can. A cool breeze blows through my hair, hoisting leaves into the sky where they flip and twirl. I'm grateful that the beauty of nature survived the harsh transformation of our country, with there being more blood soaking the earth than rain.

I shiver at the recollection of the Threes and how much deadlier they are compared to a Zero, how much speed, strength, and agility they possess. *I mean, they were even trying to jump a gate twenty feet up. Why would they go to the gate instead of attacking humans? It's like their focus didn't allow them to see us...*

An unpleasant idea worms its way into my mind.

"Adrian, I think a Commander was controlling those Threes."

Chapter 19

Phoenix

ADRIAN'S BROWS SHOOT UPWARD AT MY COMMENT. I FLOURISH my hands wildly, snatching a leaf from the air. It crinkles as I crush it in my fist.

Indistinct whisperings float to us from ahead, and I flash my eyes toward the gate. Guards are moving chunks of black flesh into a pile a good distance away from the wall. I don't see the fallen officers anywhere.

Knowing our time is limited, I rush to explain. "Think about it. When the first of the Obsidian arrived, another waited to attack Tala until the others were in combat. And then once they died, a second wave hit us when our backs were turned and our guard was down. They charged the gate even though there were humans right in front of them. Normal Obsidian don't do that. You said it yourself: you've never seen a horde of Threes so big."

My breath quickens with excitement. I unfurl my fingers, letting the leaf particles catch the wind and take off. *I'm right, I know I am.*

Adrian rubs his chin, his eyes narrowing. "If there's a

Commander nearby, and they are trying to get into the school, then the students are in peril." He gives me a sideways glance. "Nice observation. I'll talk to Zypha about this."

Fear overrides my happiness and I knead one hand with the other, suddenly nervous to be out in the open. If a Commander is here, then the academy isn't safe anymore. I suck in a deep breath, the cold air burning my lungs.

As I make for the open gates, Adrian calls my name in a low voice. "You did well today. Against the Obsidian."

I nod, keeping my expression neutral. Jogging into the academy, exhilaration at his praise courses through me until it rapidly fades to uncertainty. *If the demons invade the school, what will happen?*

I look around for my friends as I cross through the metal gate, but the courtyard is empty. The guards must have forced everyone into their rooms as a security measure. The idea of joining Sara in our room while I'm sporting my injury is almost as unpleasant as if I were to acquire Serous from Nurse Dorna. I look down at all the blood coating my jacket, crossing my arms to cover the stain as best as possible.

Burning flesh tints the air, and I whip my head around. A thin trail of smoke rises over the wall and dissipates soon after. Thoughts of using Serous disappear from my mind as the weight of this potential threat to everyone here wraps itself around me. *There has to be something I can do.*

The person I need to see is the only one who's given me inside information on the Obsidian.

Zachary's hands grasp my shoulders seconds after I push the doors to the library open, the scent of leather and worn paper enveloping my senses.

"Cassie, are you okay? Devero just gave word about what happened."

I pull away from Zachary with some effort, surprised by his strength. The man must be doing push-ups in his spare time. I open my mouth to begin my barrage of questions, but Zachary ushers me into his secret office, softly closing the door behind him.

I notice a second wooden chair that barely fits between the table and the overflowing shelf has joined the room. Zachary gestures to the chair while taking the other one, sighing loudly.

"I don't know how there could be an attack," Zachary mumbles, half to himself, dragging a hand roughly across his wrinkly forehead. "We cleared the area just this morning."

I shake my head. "I think the area *was* clear this morning."

Zachary leans forward. "You believe they caught the scent of you all outside?"

I didn't think about that option, but I'm too deep in my theory to second-guess myself. "More like they were led there."

At Zachary's confused appearance, I sigh. *Good grief, they're the ones who taught me about Commanders. Why am I the only one thinking this?*

I quickly relay what I told Adrian, and the scholar's face darkens in a brewing storm with each point I make. His expression is one I've never seen before, a mixed reaction that's hard to place, but it sends a tremor through my hands. While I talk, I grab a blank sheet of paper from the table and fold it over and over again.

Zachary is quiet throughout my speech. When I finish my explanation and pause for his reply, he still doesn't speak, his head lowered in concentration.

Unable to take the silence, I blurt out, "You have experience with Commanders, right? Maybe not you personally, but another scholar?"

"Yes, but not too many. Commanders are a relatively new Obsidian type, and while we know the basics, there is a lot that is unknown. They are so rare, I never thought there would be one here." Zachary's eyes are on the map spread out on the table, scouring it like it holds all the answers. It's a new one, without blights from Obsidian movement yet.

"So, besides having a brainstem and the ability to control other Obsidian, what do we know?"

"The data is sporadic, gathered from about five cities around the country. The information I've gotten from other scholars explains the Commanders differently: they lead the pack or stay behind and wait, they can move slowly or have to be carried by other Obsidian. One trait shared between each group is that the Commanders are ruthless and attack with hordes quickly and efficiently until they meet their goal."

His words echo back to me as though they're coming from underwater, and it takes a moment for my brain to process them. "What does that mean for us?"

Zachary slowly places a hand on the map in the center of Hallow Academy. "It means that if you are correct, and this is a Commander we're dealing with, then it will not wait long before attacking again. Soon enough that we won't be able to call for reinforcements."

"Reinforcements? Did the other places with Commander attacks need that to win? How many locations have succumbed to these attacks?"

"None. There hasn't been a successful invasion so far."

The words should give me a sense of relief, but I can't feel anything remotely similar to that. Not when I'm looking at Zachary's facial expression. "Then what's wrong?"

"Each invaded place had large armies at their disposal to take down the threats and kill the Commanders before they could claim the cities."

So that's what he means by not enough time for reinforcements. We have what, twenty security officers?

I stand, my chair screeching against the floor in a jarring wail of protest until it slams into the wall. My arms fling out, gesturing to the overflowing bookshelves all around me. "You said this study is filled with strategies to take on Obsidian! There has to be something, even just one incident, where a school neutralized a Commander. How many academies have won? How many strategies do we have?"

My harsh breath crowds the room, not giving me any space to think.

For the first time since bringing up the Commander, Zachary raises his head to meet my eyes. The hand laid against the map curls into a fist. While his words are hard, his muted voice softens the edge. "You don't get it, Cassie. There has never been an attack on an academy, only cities. There is no strategy, there is no army."

And then I can finally identify Zachary's expression.

Fear.

Pure terror radiates from his features, an emotion I've only ever seen on people who know they are about to die. His voice catches as he states his remark in a voice like glass, a voice that hollows my stomach and forces me to hold my breath to prevent shattering it.

"We have nothing."

I slowly sink back into my chair at his words, a weight settling against my chest that makes it difficult to breathe. The panic I was feeling seems to drown in the overwhelming numbness, as if my body refuses to comprehend Zachary's damning words.

The sound of Zachary turning in his seat and rifling through endless stacks of rolled parchment easily muffles my shallow breathing. He's muttering to himself, but I can't quite make out what he's saying. I only catch one word, something I've never heard before.

"What's a Phoenix?" I ask, focusing on that to keep myself from cracking.

Zachary stops what he's doing and spins around, eyes wide, like he didn't realize he spoke his words aloud. "I think you are mistaken, child. I did not say Phoenix."

My head tilts at his words, though I don't respond. After all, Zachary has given me a lot of leeway as a student, and I have no intention of being a nuisance to him because of it.

Although that doesn't mean I won't find out about this Phoenix business in a different manner. My teeth dig into my cheek to keep the scheming ideas from my eyes, not wanting the scholar to figure out my slowly forming plans.

"I am sure you will attempt to uncover this yourself, so I'll tell you instead. I don't want you earning the wrath of the headmaster," Zachary says with a sigh, folding his hands together.

I immediately feel guilty for forcing him to do something he clearly doesn't want to do. "I don't want you to tell me if you're going to get in trouble, Zachary. And I won't go looking for it as well."

The older man smiles. "I won't get in trouble if no one finds out that I told you. Which means you must keep this a secret, understood?"

I hesitate. Even though I'm dying to know what a Phoenix is, I still feel unsure that Zachary won't pay a price for it. "Why would you risk it? Why do you trust me so much?"

"I've been following you as much as the headmaster has.

A defenseless child who survived an Obsidian attack, her entire house engulfed in flames while she remained untouched. Curious, don't you think?"

It takes a second to realize what he's talking about. When I do, my jaw tightens against the waves of painful emotions. Why is he bringing up the worst night of my life now?

"I don't understand," I grind out.

Zachary leans back in his seat, eyeing me with intensity. "The Phoenixes arrived three years ago. There were two of them, though I do not know their identities. All I know is that they lived in separate cities, but they simultaneously burst into flames without their skin burning. It was quite a shock for everyone, and news of it traveled fast throughout the scholarly community. They had the power to control fire, the Obsidian's greatest weakness. It was a development that could change the tide of the war.

"Researchers tested them relentlessly to understand how their abilities came to be, but we still don't know what caused their transformation. The city lords decided early on to keep these people secret, for fear that those opposed to this power would interfere in the military's work. At that point, the two were heavily involved with the military's attack against the Obsidian.

"Last year, one Phoenix disappeared, and we have yet to find them. We believe they were killed in action on one of their missions. Ever since, the military has kept the remaining Phoenix such a secret that even the scholars are unaware of the current situation."

"And what does that have to do with me?" It's the only thing I can say while my mind spins at the new information. People capable of wielding fire to kill the Obsidian? It makes no sense that they would want to keep these people hidden.

Wouldn't it be better for us to know of their existence so we have a beacon of hope?

"We found you three years ago as well. At first, the headmaster wanted you to join because of your ability to survive the Obsidian. When word of the Phoenixes reached us, it was rational to assume that you were one as well. That you had burst into flames and caused that fire without harming yourself at all. We watched you, waited for more signs that you could be one of them. So far, there has been no more proof of such a claim."

I fold my arms, fingers digging painfully into my ribs. "Of course not," I answer in a tight voice. "I think I would know if I had magical powers. Powers that, if your thesis is correct, means I blew up my own house."

Zachary pales slightly, the instant response revealing he's never considered that before. I wonder if it's because of the excitement of having a potential warmonger or if being an orphan is so common that family and memories aren't even a factor anymore.

Either way, anger floods through me. Sadness, too. I had thought Zachary trusted me because we were friends and I was getting stronger as a student, but it turns out it's really because he's been waiting for me to show him my innate abilities. *Which I don't have.*

I abruptly stand, tired of my depressing thoughts and the look in Zachary's eyes. "I'd better go see if I can help against the Commander's attack."

With this revelation, I almost forgot that we have much more pressing matters on our hands. Zachary's mouth opens, but I give a half-wave and dart from the room, wishing Zachary had followed the rules and never told me about the Phoenixes.

Chapter 20

Cold and Forsaken

THIS IS OUR FOURTH DAY WITHOUT CLASSES. I'M GOING TO LOSE my touch if we don't resume soon. Staring up at the gray ceiling of my room, I flip another dagger into the air before catching it and repeating the action.

Tala's classes so far have been canceled, with the rest of the teachers too busy to pick up her schedule. "To be determined," was what Headmaster Hallow said. The entire academy was in a frenzy after I so graciously told everyone that a Commander was eyeing our school. Security increased, and all students were quarantined to their rooms for the first day as the school prepared for an ambush.

But nothing happened. Not even a wayward Obsidian wandered too close.

At that point, I felt like the idiot who cried monster. Since Commanders never wait a day before attacking again, the whole assault on the school got chalked up to unfortunate timing. Which makes a ton of sense considering Commanders are so rare in our country.

I should be grateful that our school is not in immediate

danger, but I was just *so sure* it was a Commander that I would have staked my life—no, not my life, more like all the fruit of my lifetime—if given the chance.

Groaning, I roll around to give Sara's vacant bed a dirty look. I've barely seen her around lately, and with all our classes canceled, she and Jared have been ghosts after the first day of lockdown. Of course, I was the one to encourage her to spend time with Jared and not me, since she refused to leave my side after what happened, and the coddling was driving me crazy. It took a lot of persuading to convince her I was okay.

Now I'm wishing I hadn't shooed her away. Without my friends or class, I've never been more bored. *I never thought I would say this, but Tala not teaching class is affecting me negatively.*

Adrian has also been absent. He just narrowly makes it on time for our training and then immediately leaves when it's done. He seems distracted, especially when we spar. *I almost beat him once, and that's bad.* I don't comment on it, though, since I'm sure he's working more to bulk up protection around the school.

Giving another sizable sigh, I fling my dagger into the air with a little more savagery than I intended. It soars upwards until lodging itself solidly in the ceiling, its hilt vibrating rapidly.

"Are you kidding me? Why?" I yell at the dagger in frustration. *How am I going to get that down? How am I going to explain a nice hole in the ceiling to the headmaster?*

Mumbling curses, I angrily storm around the small room, throwing on my hoodie and marching out the door. *I'll deal with that later.*

Moonlight pours into the hallways through the windows, lighting my way more than the torches do. Still steaming, I launch the door to my training gym open as hard as possible.

It swings with a creak, slowing down before knocking into the wall.

That wasn't as satisfying as I wanted it to be. A feral urge to kick the door tingles through my legs.

"Bad day?" Adrian's humored voice resonates from the corner of the room, where I find him bent over the weapons shelf, his trusty white rag in hand.

"Holy crap, you scared me. I didn't see you there." I push the palm of my hand against my racing heart, forcing it to slow down, and walk as casually as I can into the room.

I hadn't expected that Adrian would be here this early, or else I wouldn't have attempted to slam the door. *Why is it that on the one day I come in here throwing a tantrum, Adrian is here to witness it?*

I gesture irritably toward my bedroom. "My stupid dagger got stuck in the ceiling."

Adrian chuckles, which is not the reaction I thought I was going to get, and it somehow makes me fume more. His behavior is bizarre compared to the previous few days. So distant and distracted...but now he has time to taunt me? *Not today, buddy.*

Noticing my fury, he tosses a hand up. "Sorry, I'm not laughing at you, I promise. It's just been a bad day for me, too."

My anger dries out at his comment, and I cross the room quickly. "What happened?"

He sighs, his hair falling into his eyes as he tilts his head down. "Tala's blood samples confirmed the virus is in her system, and we know it's not Serous because the medicine is so diluted it doesn't get picked up when tested. I guess it's such a small amount that it won't cause the transformation, though there's no documentation of that happening before.

The nurse said she might be a little off, more aggressive, as her body rejects the virus, though."

I snort, placing my hands on my hips. "That sounds like her normal attitude to me."

Adrian gives me a look that conveys he doesn't think my joke is funny. "I've been sitting with her while she recovers. A majority of the time, she's not awake, but she keeps mumbling strange things in her sleep." He shakes his head in confusion.

Oh, so that's where he's been lately. With Tala. Here I am thinking he's doing his job and protecting the school. *Silly me.*

I try to smooth out my wrinkled nose, but Adrian catches it. "What?"

"Nothing," I reply, trying to sound indifferent. "I just think it's weird that you're the one who's helping her recover. Doesn't she have a mean best friend who can stare at her while she's sleeping?"

Adrian watches me with narrow eyes until he puts his hands on his waist and leans forward. He's holding back a smile as he asks, "Cassie, are you jealous?"

The floor drops from under me as I blink, my mouth agape. I never thought Adrian would be capable of asking me that question. Even now, his foolish smile sits abnormally on his usually stern face.

I scoff. "Of course not!"

"Then why does this bother you so much?" I can hear the laughter in his voice.

I grind my teeth and throw my hands in the air. "Oh, I don't know. Maybe it's because she's made my life hell from day one, and now she's getting coddled like a baby by the man she's obsessed with. She tried to kill me, you know." *How does he not see how crazy this is?* I want to scream in frustration as Adrian's lips stretch wider.

"You said it yourself that she wouldn't have. While she can be a little ruthless, she's not a murderer."

I work to hold in my shaking rage. *Wasn't he the one to tell me Tala would have killed me in our challenge if he hadn't stopped her?*

Unperturbed by the daggers shooting out of my eyes, he slowly saunters closer to me. His mouth opens, but I cut him off, unable to take any more of whatever's gotten into him.

His teasing isn't really out of the ordinary. We've always bantered easily enough with each other. On a normal day, I would have taken his joking in stride and probably would've given it back to him, but he unfortunately picked the wrong moment. Embarrassment at falsely accusing a Commander is still raw, and, if I'm able to admit it to myself, I've felt very lonely these past three days without Sara, Jared, and even Adrian himself. It's the first time in a while that I've felt so alone.

"Stop," I snarl, smothering the rest of my words. I don't want to end our friendship by spewing out comments I'd regret later.

Adrian's smile falls from his lips as he surveys me intently, his somber expression returning. "I've seriously upset you, haven't I?"

I don't respond, too afraid of what would come out if I did. But Adrian can see it written all over my face.

"I'm sorry," he murmurs, backing away to give me space, "I didn't intend to frustrate you. I was poking fun, but I let it go too far. Of course I know Tala is a danger to you, especially now. Zypha asked me to monitor Tala since she could be a threat to the students, and I accepted. If she was capable of attacking you before this, then who knows what she would do to you now?"

Well.

I feel like punching myself in the face. *Way to let your temper get the best of you, Cassie.* Honestly, I can take a joke. But something about Tala with Adrian makes me want to rip apart the closest practice dummy.

He's watching her to protect me. The thought sends a shiver down my spine.

"I'm way too comfortable around you," Adrian says with a small, sad smile. "I forget to watch what I say when I'm with you."

"No, Adrian, I—" *I want you to be comfortable with me. I don't want you to watch what you say. I won't let the thought of Tala get the best of me next time.* There's so much I want to say to him, but the words get stuck in my throat and I can't get them out.

A young boy appears at the entrance to the door, wringing his hands with his head down, a mop of curly brown hair covering his eyes. "Excuse me, sir, but the nurse asked me to tell you that Professor Tala is conscious."

"Thank you," Adrian responds without taking his eyes off me. "I'll be right there."

The boy dashes out without another word. He seemed frightened to be in the same room with Adrian, though my instructor didn't seem to be offended by it. I wonder how many people are afraid to look him in the eye. With so many people who are either scared of or revere him, does he get lonely, too?

Adrian briefly scans my face with apologetic eyes as he throws on his black security jacket. "We are going to have to skip training tonight, Cassie, and I'm sorry about that. I'll see you in the morning." He's through the door before I can reply.

A frustrated groan escapes me and I fall flat on the mat, my hands rubbing over my face. *How many times am I going to humiliate myself around him?* I couldn't even tell him how I felt, how he did nothing wrong. Well, there could be a little blame, but not enough to make me feel *good* about my response.

Next time I see him, I'll set things straight. For now, I'll have to train without him. I pull myself off the floor and over to the array of weapons. My eyes linger on Adrian's white cleaning rag that's tucked under the steel sword he was polishing. I pick up the weapon, feeling its cold, heavy weight in my hands.

For the millionth time, my mind travels back to everything Zachary said about Phoenixes. Does Adrian know the reason the headmaster wanted me to join the school? Does Tala, and that's why she hates me so much?

Of course, I know how erroneous all of their theories are. There's nothing special about me except for my unique ability to make a fool of myself.

Adrian said it would take some time for the Obsidian blood in Tala to dissipate, but I'm not sure how much more I can take.

Today, Tala decided we should play a new, demented game she created, where five people are blindfolded and try to dodge hard leather balls that the rest of the class is launching at their faces. She explained it as a great opportunity to refine our other senses besides sight, but in reality, I'm sure she just wanted to see me break something.

I land on my back with a thud, my breath whooshing from my lungs. I struggle to climb to my feet as I attempt to quell my haphazard gasps. My eyes strain to see through the black cloth tied across my face, but I'm unable to make out anything. Tensing my muscles, I wait for the next ball to be thrown at me.

Tala was absent all of last week, but classes resumed as normal once the weekend was over. Headmaster Hallow must have deemed her capable of not going crazy. It's now the end of the week, and I regret ever wishing Tala would come back. She's been an absolute menace lately, more so than usual.

Each class has been more insane than the last, and it's not stopping. It's masterful how she can keep topping herself, even when I think there's no way. My ears throb from her constant screaming as she yells at the class to throw harder.

"If I don't see blood in the next ten seconds, everyone is doing laps!"

The other four classmates chosen to be human targets with me moan in unison.

I hear another ball whizzing towards me seconds before it lands solidly on my cheek. The momentum spins me around until I trip over myself and fall to the ground in a heap of flailing limbs. A ringing sensation buzzes in my ears as warm liquid trickles from my nose. I hastily rub it away with my fingers and wipe it on my pants.

"Now that's what I'm talking about! Very nice throw, Joshua," Tala crows with glee, her hands clapping together. I don't need my eyes to picture the satisfaction on her face. I growl and rise to my feet, lowering myself into a defensive position. *Stupid teacher's pet.* I'm not letting another one hit me like that.

Even though my covered eyes see nothing through the black cloth, I close them anyway. Jared drops heavily to the ground beside me with a grunt, the faint thuds of a bouncing ball echoing his fall. The classmates standing in front of me are panting from the extensive effort of splitting skin open.

We've been at this for about twenty minutes, and I can sense it starting to take its toll. Especially since the five of us haven't switched out with anyone yet. Tala isn't even trying to hide her animosity.

The air contorts as a sphere flies through it. *That one's coming right at my stomach.* I stumble to the side just in time for the ball to soar right past me. A smirk edges its way onto my lips. *It's on now.*

The next four balls that are directed at me miss their target, each one angering Tala to no end. By the fifth dodged ball, she shouts at all the throwers to aim at me while the other blindfolded classmates take a break. I jump, swivel, and duck as each ball flies at me, one after another, or multiple at once. Sometimes I'm not fast enough to sidestep, and a hard sphere successfully hits some part of my body, but I keep focused on the next one.

Tala finally calls time and I drop to my back, sucking in each breath like it's my last. I remove the blindfold and raise a trembling hand to my eyes, blinking against the torchlight.

When my vision finally adapts, my gaze sweeps through the large gym. Most of the class is in a similar position to me, some putting their heads between their knees.

Tala is tapping her foot against the stone floor beside the mat I'm currently sprawled on. She's glaring at me with a twisted face that expresses just how livid she is with me for not getting pulverized. I stare back at her with resolution. *She should know by now that I don't give up easily.*

"Class is dismissed for the day," she announces flatly, her eyes never leaving mine. I wearily stand and head towards Sara and Jared, who are waiting for me by the door. Tala steps in front of me before I can pass her.

"I'd like a word with you, Cassidy," she says in even tones.

Any word with Tala won't be pretty. The question is, what

does she want this time? Another challenge? I study her carefully, but her expression betrays nothing of what she wants.

Focusing over her shoulder, I nod to Sara and Jared. They hesitate, faces uncertain, so I wave them away with a calm smile, hoping to get across just how unafraid I am of her. They must see something that comforts them because they nod back and leave.

When the class clears out, silence is the only thing left in the room with us. I cross my arms and wait for her to speak first.

Chapter 21

What You Are

"I KNOW WHAT YOU ARE, CASSIDY," TALA REMARKS, SO LOW I have to lean in to hear her.

Confusion washes over me, and I arch an eyebrow. "If you're about to say a pain in your ass, just know the feeling's mutual."

Tala growls softly, a real dog-like snarl, and the action surprises me. *Do people actually do that?* "I've known it all along. You think you have everyone fooled, but not me. And soon everyone will know, including Adrian." Her lips pull up in a slow, creepy smile. "Enjoy your secret while it lasts."

I give her a hard stare. I have no idea what 'secret' she's referring to, if she isn't just making things up to scare me.

When Tala doesn't elaborate, I lift a shoulder in a shrug and brush past her. My bare arm touches hers as I pass, and she jerks away with a hiss as if my skin hurt her. Frowning at her odd behavior, I keep moving, wondering how much Obsidian blood is still in her system to make her act so crazy.

"Get some sleep, professor," I call over my shoulder.

"You're a parasite!" Tala shouts after me. I turn slightly,

enough to catch the same disgusted glower she's always given me out of the corner of my eye. When she notices I'm listening, she lowers her voice. "You're a monster that I've let roam free for far too long. You'll bring them all down upon us and destroy us. Maybe a part of me had some doubt in the past, but he has made it clear what I need to do to protect this school."

"'He'? Do you mean Adrian, or the headmaster?"

Tala runs her tongue across her top teeth as she peers at me in contemplation, head cranked to the side. She suddenly jerks forward, and for a moment, I think she's going to attack me, but Tala rights herself with a small scoff and strolls away toward the back entrance.

I don't let myself relax until the door slams shut behind her. Tala has consistently been mean to me, but now she's borderline insane. Who does she mean by 'he'? Definitely not Adrian, but maybe Hallow had a talk with her about her fragile, virus-ridden state.

I pause, my breath freezing in my throat. What if Hallow or Zachary said something about me being a Phoenix? Maybe Tala took it seriously and has now moved beyond feeling threatened to something else. It's obvious she's trying to scare me, but why? What's her goal?

For one thing, her threats do nothing to me now. Even if she challenged me, I'm confident I'd put up a good fight. Maybe that's why she hasn't done it again.

I rub my exposed arms after leaving the vacant gym, irritated at the weather for steadily growing colder throughout the day. Tala's statements continue to nag at me, though. *I know what you are. I've known it all along.* Zachary said no one but him and the headmaster ever discussed Phoenixes, so if it's not that, then what else could she be referring to?

Besides, even Zachary told me they don't think I'm a

Phoenix anymore since I've exhibited no signs in three years. The more I think about it, the more convinced I am that she's just trying to mess with my head, make me doubt myself, or become scared of her.

Unfortunately for her, it's doing the opposite. If her empty threats are anything to say about it, I think I'm winning this little war between us.

"What did Tala want?" Sara queries as I walk over to the pair. They had waited for me close to the garden.

"Nothing important," I respond as we head to our small oasis.

With the weekend free of classes, I spend every waking minute training. By the end of the two days, I've turned into a ball of nerves. My heart races every time I think about the trials that are a week from tomorrow. Doubt pricks at the edges of my mind, filling my lungs with each breath. It keeps me awake at night, even when I take sleeping pills.

Images of all my declarations going up in flames as I fail the trials and am forced to repeat a grade continue to pulse behind my eyes with every blink.

A white towel hits me in the face, dragging me out of my inner thoughts.

"Stop psyching yourself out," Adrian snaps.

"I'm not," I bite back, annoyed at my distraction and Adrian for noticing it. I throw down the two short swords and bend to pick up the towel. Taking a deep breath, I wipe my sweaty forehead. Adrian leans against the weapons shelf with his arms crossed.

"Yes, you are. Your aim is off." He points to the old practice dummy, where my strikes left slits inches below the marks he drew for me to cut through. Precision is everything if you're trying to sever their senses and *I know that.*

"I'm just tired since I haven't been sleeping well." I blow out a long breath and pick up the blades, walking past Adrian to put them on the shelf. My heart skips a beat when I pass his long, domineering form.

I still haven't apologized to him after the whole Tala debacle last week. Since the conversation, Adrian hasn't acted differently, so maybe I don't need to say anything. *Or maybe that's a good excuse for you to keep being a coward, Cassie.*

"Have you run out of the sleeping capsules?" Adrian asks in a concerned voice that makes me feel weirdly guilty.

I shake my head. "They just aren't working very well anymore."

Adrian's silent as I bustle around the weapons shelf, not ready to look into his eyes for fear of what I would find. Pity? More concern?

Only when I have perfectly straightened all the weapons on the top shelf, leaving nothing else to distract myself with, do I turn around to face him. I suck in a soft breath when I find him standing right in front of me. The scent of fresh air and pine trees hits me, and I have to fight to keep from hugging, or worse, *sniffing* him. *How does he always smell so good?*

His bright eyes regard me carefully, so intensely that I'm locked in his gaze. His blank mask gives nothing away. Finally, he nods to himself.

"Follow me," he commands over his shoulder as he makes his way to the door. I pause for a second longer, inhaling the stench from years of sweat that is unnaturally perfect at clearing my mind, before jogging to his side.

"Where are we going?" The corridors are empty, multiplying the sound of our soft footsteps through the halls. We turn left into the corridor beside the faculty wing, and I almost trip over my feet. "Why are we going here?" I ask as we enter the security portion of the building.

"I'm showing you something you can't tell any of the other students about. Understood?" His serious tone pulls an agreement from my lips. Intrigue and warmth build inside me at his remark. He trusts me with a place no student has gone before.

The security wing is desolate, which is the opposite of what I thought it would be. I guess everyone is already at their assigned posts for the night.

We wind through the corridors and up a flight of stairs. I follow closely behind Adrian, the torches attached to the wall barely lighting the path ahead of us. Adrian doesn't seem to have any trouble as he glides forward decisively, like he's walked this path a hundred times.

My hand reaches out to tug on Adrian's jacket as we finish yet another set of stairs, a demand to know where we are going perched precariously on my lips. He halts at the top of the stairs without warning, and—like the skilled warrior I am—I plow straight into what feels like a cement wall.

"Seriously?" I groan, rubbing my forehead. He stays quiet and steps to the side as my hand falls limply.

"Oh, wow," I gasp in amazement.

Brilliantly shining stars light up the sky in an array of blues, whites, yellows, and reds. When I observe the sky in the courtyard, the stone walls block most of the view. But here, standing on top of the wall, I can see the stars for miles. *And it's beautiful.* I give a breathless laugh.

"This part of the wall isn't manned very often. I like to come up here when I feel overwhelmed." Adrian ambles to the edge of the wall, leaning against the parapet with his forearms. *It's hard to imagine him ever being overwhelmed.* He stares at the sky with a gentle smile that relaxes his sharp features. "The stars always make me feel less alone somehow."

With the moonlight washing over his face and his serene expression, I can't drag my eyes away from him. *He's just as beautiful as the stars are.* My lips part, and I step closer to him, my insides turning to mush.

"Thank you for bringing me here, Adrian," I murmur.

He turns to me, a shadow of worry passing over his face. "I'm going to be gone next week."

I blink twice as the moment between us shatters. "What?"

"Next week is a field trip for the seniors, and this year, Zypha is putting me in charge of it. I won't be back until the weekend."

Adrian's apologetic voice hardly penetrates my shocked state. I don't even register that I'll be going on the field trip since I'm a senior, my mind focused on one terribly blaring problem.

"B-but the trials are only eight days away. I'm not ready." It's the only thing I can think to say. My voice shakes, and I turn back to the treetops, digging my fingernails into the stone wall. *I thought we had more time.*

"Cassie, you're ready. You can do this, and you'll pass. Trust me." His voice is confident and reassuring. I take a deep breath to calm my nerves, the stars winking at me in encouragement. I think about his previous news to divert my panicked mind.

"So, where are we going for an entire week?" I question, tilting my head to grin at him.

"You won't be there for the whole time, and I'm obligated to keep silent. You'll find out tomorrow, I figure."

"And I thought we were friends," I huff, shaking my head in mock disappointment.

"Oh, we are, but I'm also a loyal academy officer. I can't

go breaking the rules just because I like you, now can I?" Adrian teases with a small smile before moving his eyes back to the sky.

"I suppose not." I follow suit with my heart fluttering in my throat.

Adrian said he likes me. It's strange, but that, more than anything, relaxes my muscles and puts me at ease. I soak in the chilly air and bright sky, my body tingling with rejuvenation.

***

"I heard a rumor," Jared whispers with a sly smirk as we wait in line for our breakfast. I stop my humming and glance at him. My lips still hold the smile that I woke up with, especially since I slept better last night than I had in weeks.

With my stomach growling in hunger, I stretch onto my tiptoes, attempting to gauge how much food remains in the bins. If I don't get my full ration because we got to breakfast late, then there's going to be hell to pay.

"We're leaving the academy this week," he adds at Sara's prompting.

"Oh, wow!" Sara jumps up and down with excitement, firing off one question after another while I freeze.

"T-that's crazy," I stutter weakly, not prepared for Jared's announcement. Too bad I'm a terrible liar on the spot. He surveys my response until his smile fades, eyes squinting in accusation, and I fidget under the weight of his scrutiny.

"You already know." Jared finally states in a matter-of-fact tone. Sara stops jumping and turns to me as Jared continues. "Was it Adrian? Well, it has to be. Who else do you talk to?"

"Excuse me, I talk to a bunch of people." Now it's my turn to shoot Jared a look at his dubious expression. "But it just so happens that Adrian may have mentioned something like that to me yesterday."

"I wish I were dating an instructor so I could know what goes on behind the scenes," Sara sighs. Jared pouts at her, but she's not paying attention to him. We fill our plates with the usual porridge and head to our seats, but I find my appetite has disappeared.

"We are *not* dating," I insist harshly. "And he's not a professor; he's just been teaching me as a favor. Besides, he wouldn't tell me anything else about it anyway."

"And I bet that just *burns* at you, doesn't it, Cassie?" Sara bites into her bread roll with a chuckle.

I sigh. *So much for my good mood.* "He just wanted to tell me he was leaving for the week, so we wouldn't be able to train."

"That sucks," Jared proclaims.

I give him an evil eye. "Yes, it does."

"You can still train without him, though. I bet he's taught you a lot of great practice techniques." Sara covers my hand with hers, giving me a gentle smile.

I mirror hers with a nod. Adrian has definitely taught me a lot, enough so that I can follow our usual routines with little thought of my own.

"Well, let's eat fast so we can find out where we're going," Jared exclaims, shoveling in another bite of food.

It doesn't take us long to scrape our plates clean, eager to hear of our next adventure.

"It's a tradition that we take our seniors on a special field trip the week before the trials begin," Tala shouts, pacing in front of us.

Officer Zypha and Adrian stand stiffly beside her. Zypha

is listening to Tala intently while Adrian stands with his hands behind his back, staring straight ahead. I try to catch his gaze, but he doesn't turn in my direction. I frown.

Tala sucks in a breath and continues. "As head of security, Officer Zypha is normally in charge of this trip, but she has decided that Officer Camson will lead the excursion instead. In groups of four, you all will journey to the closest farm, where you will help cultivate the land for a workday. You will spend the night under the watchful eye of Adrian's security team before traveling back here the next morning. Classes will be held as scheduled for those not currently on the fun experience."

I smirk at her pathetic attempt at sounding enthusiastic. Whatever is happening with Tala still isn't over, because her attitude resembles that of a wet log.

"Why can't we go to the city?" Bryce yells, and more than one person mumbles in agreement.

"There is strict population control within each city. Even in small groups, we wouldn't be allowed in. If you want to live and work inside a city, then you have to earn it," Tala says with disdain. I wonder if anyone here deserves to live in a city in her mind.

"But why do we have to play farmer? That's a job for quitters," Amber whines from the back of the group. More whispers and nods, but no one is brave enough to second the opinion. I think back to the girl who left the academy because of her classmates' bullying. Even the thought of it makes my fingers curl into fists. She didn't seem like a coward to me.

Tala bares her teeth in a wicked smile at the redhead. "We just like to show you kids your fates if you don't pass the trials."

A moment of shock fills the room before it bursts into disorder, everyone talking at once. Confusion and anger crackle through the group. Tala soaks up the puzzlement with greedy eyes while Officer Zypha and Adrian's stony expressions don't change.

You can't repeat a year if you don't pass? My eyes widen, but I don't join the riot. Now that I think about it, I've never seen someone held back a year. We must have just assumed we could stay if we failed the trials. Sara pulls on my arm, and her lips move, but I can't hear her over the discourse. I shake my head at her.

"No one told us that!" Bryce argues over the raging complaints, his lanky arms trembling.

"If you haven't gained the ability to be a successful soldier at this point, you never will," Tala shouts. "Look at the graduation list and tell me that expulsion from the academy isn't a kindness for you. Now shut up and listen!"

The angry comments dissipate, and thick tension falls over us as our eyes rise to the back wall. Tala doesn't need to elaborate to get her intent across. The red academy emblem by those who've died is a beacon of what awaits us, like the blood of our fallen comrades has been spread across the stone wall in a weak effort to commemorate their contribution. But if everyone is dying, who is left to remember them? If the last twenty-five years are any indication, then barely passing the trials is only guaranteeing your death as a hunter.

With my gaze on the wall, I find Adrian's name from four years ago, but I don't stay on it for long. My eyes lower to the second name, one that's been haunting me for the last week, ever since Adrian spoke of his late best friend.

Wick Vyran.

The symbol by his name seems to stand out above the others, even though fourteen of the seventeen graduates that year are also gone. Adrian said he could have prevented Wick's death. I'm not sure what that means, but I wonder how Adrian feels with the constant reminder that only he survived the ruthless job as a hunter. *Does he wish he had never become a hunter? Does he ever want to forget?*

My eyes switch to him, but he exudes what he always does: unshakeable determination.

Once the chatter settles, Adrian steps forward, ready to battle an Obsidian with his full black outfit and stern demeanor. "As Professor Tala said, I'll be taking four of you today, and the rest will rotate out by my team. We will go in order of rank, so the four lowest-ranking students will go first."

He lists the four students, and my breath catches when he doesn't say my name. Based on last month's ranking, I know I've improved significantly, but I've been so used to the bottom that it's almost impossible to accept I'm not there anymore.

My hands clench tighter in anticipation with each group he names. Sara gets called into the fourth group with a rank of fifth, and she squeezes my arm. A dark cloud darts over her face when her rank is called, but it's gone within seconds, not giving me enough time to process whether her distress is real or why it's there.

"And our last group that leaves on the fifth day: in fourth is Jared, third is Naire, second is Emmerick, and first," Adrian finally focuses on me, the pride shining in his eyes making my knees wobble, "is Cassie."

Chapter 22

Fodder

ANOTHER ROUND OF STILLNESS ROLLS THROUGH THE GROUP AS I hold in a gasp. I'm ranked *first*? Even Sara and Jared are gaping at me with astonished eyes. However, no one's expression is as murderous as Emmerick's. He looks as though I've stolen something that rightfully belongs to him. I ignore him. Not even Emmerick can ruin this moment.

Tala growls at Adrian to move on to the next order of business, and I stand stunned as Adrian goes over the rules involved with leaving the academy overnight. *I'll have to ask Sara for an overview of those later.*

"With that settled, the first group: go pack an overnight bag and meet me at the front gates. Everyone else will meet there on their respective days at eight in the morning. Classes can resume as normal now. Thank you for your time, Professor." He turns to leave but pauses after taking a step.

"Cassie, may I have a minute with you?" Adrian asks casually, gesturing to the door.

Tongue still stuck to the roof of my mouth, I nod as my eyes flick to Tala's tense form. By the strain of her jaw, I'm afraid her teeth will splinter. Zypha slides in beside Tala and leans in to whisper in her ear. Whatever Zypha says, Tala's distracted by it, and she turns her full attention to the head of security.

Adrian rests his hand on the small of my back and leads me to the door. My cheeks burn with the heat of his light touch and everyone's gaze. *I'm never going to hear the end of this.*

"I wanted to congratulate you on your ranking," Adrian explains with a warm smile as the doors fall shut behind us. I shove down the disappointment when he draws his hand back, clasping them both behind him. We start our usual loop around the courtyard. With class in session, it's empty except for two playful birds.

"Thank you, but I couldn't have done it without you."

He shakes his head. "I only showed you what to do. You're the one who executed it."

We walk in silence, listening to the birds chirp. It hits me that this will be the last time I see him until the end of the week, and sadness washes over me.

Adrian stares ahead of us, face drawn in thoughtfulness. "Your classmates didn't seem pleased with the new class order. Are you going to be okay here?"

His question makes me laugh. "I'm not worried. You taught me well. One more week and I won't see any of these people again."

"Right," he says, his voice sounding far away. "And you're still planning on being a hunter, even if you can choose any profession you want?"

"Yes, that's the plan."

He hums in response, the distant sound drawing my eyes up to his face. I scan his shuttered expression. *Is he thinking about what happened to Wick?* My mouth opens to ask, but before I can, Astrid shuffles past us with a small bag, heading toward the gate. It pulls Adrian out of his trance, and I lose my chance to ask him.

"I need to gather my team. They should be done with the last outside inspection. Be careful," he says in a low, silky voice. His fingertips faintly graze my shoulder, and then he disappears into the security wing.

I put a palm over my heart to help ease its racing. My shoulder tingles where his fingertips lingered, and I suck in a ragged breath. *How can a single touch affect someone so much?* With sparring and tackling embedded in our training sessions, this is hardly the first time he's touched me. But this one felt different. More meaningful.

The door to the gym swings open, and Sara's head pops out. "Cassie, you'd better get in here or Tala is going to explode." The professor's shouting drowns the last part out, along with the sound of wood hitting flesh.

I wince and follow her back into the building.

I blow out a frustrated breath while rubbing my temples in slow, deep movements. Class today was a bust. I don't think I've ever paid less attention to my studies. All I could think about was Adrian: his crooked smile, his intense eyes, his firm grip. The image of him replaying in my mind is going to drive me insane.

"You good, Cassie?" I jump at the voice and look up to see Jared standing over me in concern.

"Yeah, long day," I sigh. After dinner, I excused myself to sit in the garden. It was the only way I could find some peace from my thoughts.

I pat the white cement while keeping my eyes on the water swirling in the small pond. My favorite spot has been helping me to relax for years, and today is, thankfully, no exception.

Jared sits silently on the bench beside me. I settle my head against his shoulder, soaking up his comfortable presence. The red rays of sunset pour through the few trees in the garden. My eyes drift closed. I haven't seen a true sunset in years, not with that giant wall in the way, but at least I got to see the stars.

I bet I could see the sunset from the top of the wall. If Jared wasn't with me, then I just might have tried my hand at sneaking back up there.

Rapidly approaching footsteps advance on us from the garden's only entrance. Eyes springing open, Jared and I jump to our feet on high alert. Few people are interested in the garden, so there are only a few scenarios where someone would sprint into here like a bat out of hell.

None of them are good.

Sara bursts into view, her brown hair flying around her flushed face. "Emmerick has been cursing your name since dinner. He's throwing out an official challenge."

My stomach drops to give my feet a quick hello.

"It's too early for challenges," Jared gasps, looking at me in surprise.

"He doesn't care about the rules unless you want to explain it to him," Sara snaps, looking visibly distressed by the situation. No one stands up to Emmerick without finding themselves unconscious on the ground.

Suddenly, my mind transports me back to my first year, filled with nothing but challenges and pain, pain, pain. Emmerick was my biggest bully. He would issue ninety percent of the challenges himself, and I never won them. The only thing that I can say with dignity is that I never forfeited either. My stubborn pride was the only thing that kept me in this school.

"Let's go," I state dully, interrupting Sara and Jared's argument.

Wringing my hands together, I follow Sara through the corridors to the unused training room. I pass through the door first to see everyone already waiting for me. Most people, like Amber and Bryce, stare at me with unimpressed expressions, as if I've already lost. They must think my improvement in class won't translate to challenges.

Joshua's lips widen into a malicious grin at my entrance. "Took you long enough," he jeers, and the class parts its semi-circle, revealing Naire and Emmerick in the middle. His cocky stance shows exactly how he thinks this fight will go.

My fingers curl into fists. *I'm not the same girl I was back then.*

I glance around for Raddo, the instructor who always facilitates these illicit challenges, but he's nowhere to be seen. I narrow my eyes. *Sara's right. They're not planning on following the rules, are they?*

"So, how did you get Adrian wrapped around your little finger, huh?" Naire sneers from beside Emmerick.

"Excuse me?"

"If you think sleeping with a guard will help you pass the trials, you've got another thing coming."

The spectators laugh at Naire's comment, and I bite my tongue hard to hold my temper. How *dare* they insult Adrian like this. I was expecting backlash, but not against him.

"Stop being a sore loser," I grind out, trying to keep my cool. Sara steps forward, but I push her back. I refuse to let her fight my battles for me. "I rose to first place on my own."

"Prove it." Emmerick finally opens his big mouth and steps forward, raising a meaty hand into the air. His voice is just like the rest of him: thick and slow. "I challenge you."

Anger drowns everything out and lights a fire within me. I used to dread those three words more than anything else. They haunted my dreams and fueled my nightmares until I had visceral reactions whenever I heard them. Now the only thing I feel is the burning desire to stand up for Adrian, to show them he was right to put his faith in me.

"I accept, only so I can embarrass you in front of the entire class," I bite back, shrugging off my jacket and tossing it to Jared, who catches it in a tight, white-knuckled grip.

"You got this," he says with determination, and Sara nods along.

I shoot them a smile before walking into the center of the room to face my opponent. The class creates a ring similar to the one made for Risa and Ian. I jump and shake out my arms to warm up my muscles. While I work hard to keep my mind focused, I can't completely control my body as my heart races and fingers twitch.

"Are you sure you want to do this?" I taunt Emmerick. He responds with a grunt and charges at me.

Of course he takes the usual head-on approach, and I mean that quite literally. Shoulders hunched downward and head leading the way, he closely resembles a raging Talon wolf. I take a deep breath and bend my knees, waiting. Adrian always says to use a bigger opponent's weight against them.

I hear his voice whisper all the points he's given me about fighting in hand-to-hand combat. I never understood why he focused on that in our training as much as I have at this moment. Who knows how I'd feel right about now if he hadn't drilled combat into my skull?

Well, I do know, and it would be how I usually felt before all the challenges I was about to partake in with my lovely schoolmate.

Only when I can see the sinister glint in Emmerick's eyes do I spring into motion. I drop sideways to a knee and kick my other leg out, swiping it hard in front of him. Emmerick's going too fast to stop, and he rams into my shin before stumbling over it. I hide a wince. *That's going to leave a mark.*

I'm on my feet in front of him instantly. With a roar, I put all the fear, pain, and humiliation he's ever given me into my fist and plow it into his jaw. The force of it spins him in a full circle until he falls face-first onto the mat with a loud thump.

The crowd doesn't cheer like they did for Ian, or for Emmerick in our past challenges. I'm met with silence as I loom over Emmerick's prone body. He doesn't get up, and nobody moves to help him.

"Anyone else have a problem with my rank?" My voice is stiff and flat.

I stare each person in the eye, though most look away. Naire is the only one with a smirk still plastered on her face, her nose ring flashing in the light when she tilts her head up. She jerks her head at our classmates, and Bryce and Joshua step forward, helping haul Emmerick to his feet. The three of them can barely balance Emmerick's weight.

"See you tomorrow, fodder," Naire calls as they make their way out of the room. The rest of the crowd disperses soon after that, unsatisfied with the lack of blood. It's almost a joke how bloodthirsty the new generation of Obsidian hunters is.

"Fodder?" Jared asks from somewhere behind me while tossing me my jacket. It lands on my shoulder and slides halfway down my arm before I have the thought to grab it.

"It's a derogatory term meaning I'll become Obsidian food if I leave the safety of the walls." I exhale slowly. I haven't been called that in a while. Sara's been around me long enough to hear that word whispered to me in the halls when there were no instructors nearby.

Sara shuts Jared up with a look and steps closer to me. "I'm surprised you didn't draw it out."

"That's what he would do. I won't be like him," I respond, walking toward the dormitory.

I don't want to tell her how much I wanted to, though. How much I ached to see him suffer as much as I had over the years, tenfold. *What matters is that I didn't act on it, right?*

I put two fingers briefly to my left temple, pushing them hard into my skin. *All this self-restraint is giving me a headache.*

"Where are you going?" Sara calls after me.

"I'm tired, so I'll be going to bed early. Enjoy the rest of your night together," I smile at her with a jovial wink. Sara's anxious expression slides from her face, and she laughs at my innuendo. The ornery grin slips from my lips once I'm alone in the hallway.

I get ready for bed slowly, running cold water over my bruised knuckles, waiting for them to turn numb. As good as it felt beating Emmerick, especially in less than ten seconds, I have a sinking feeling that the retaliation is going to be much worse. Hopefully, he's not dumb enough to go after Sara or Jared, or else he'll find out how much I was holding back.

I slide under the covers and close my eyes, trying to ignore the unease crawling through my stomach.

―――――――

The rest of the week goes by without incident. Besides the multiple deadly glares Emmerick throws at me every hour, he seems too scared to try anything again. By the fourth day, I've all but relaxed.

By the fourth night, I'm bouncing with energy. *Tomorrow I*

will see Adrian again. Four days without him have shown me how much I enjoyed our training sessions. Well, mainly his company. Being around him makes me feel powerful and protected.

I've never felt this way about anyone else, and it scares me. I try not to dwell on my feelings for too long, afraid of what I'll dig up if I do.

If I admit to Adrian that I like him, then that puts our friendship at risk, and I'm not sure I'm willing to do that. Besides, I'm almost positive Adrian doesn't see me in any way except as a friend. I play out his reaction in my mind.

Hey Adrian, I like you. I mean, I really like you. You're pretty strong and handsome and supportive and handsome...wait, did I say that twice?

Oh, sorry, Cassie, but I don't think of you that way. It's impossible for a warrior, renowned as myself, to be with a student, exasperating as you. Honestly, I'd rather be with Tala than you.

Ouch. Owie times a million.

It's official. My brain is trying to implode itself. If I confess and he doesn't feel the same way, then we can never go back to the way things are now. I'd rather be flattened by a stampeding Obsidian horde than lose whatever is between us.

Besides, what's the point of bringing up my romantic feelings now? I only have the weekend before I graduate, then I'll most likely never see Adrian again.

That thought alone brings its own emotion of unbearable sorrow. Will he forget about me after I'm gone? Adrian will still be here, maybe deciding to take on other students, barely holding on to his fond but distant memories of his very first pupil.

And I'll be a hunter, hopefully saving lives while unable to shake the immeasurable regret of my cowardice.

"How did things get so messy?" I groan, tugging at my hair. My eyes make their way back to the brilliant canvas of lights in the sky to find some solace.

Adrian never explicitly said *I* shouldn't return to the top of the wall. An hour ago, I found myself in dire need of calm as my thoughts continued to tornado through my head. So I took it upon myself to sneak back to Adrian's secret spot.

Even with the night sky, it's hard to focus on its beauty. *Is it going to be different between us when I see Adrian tomorrow?* I rub my palm against the cold stone and stare down at the dark shadows enclosing the oak trees. More than anything, I just want to see my friend again.

"You're not thinking about jumping, are you?"

I whip around and stifle a scream at the black figure next to me.

Chapter 23

More at Peace

THE GUARD LEANS AGAINST THE WALL AND WATCHES MY reaction with a grin. As he walks closer, I squint my eyes to get a better look at him. Brown eyes, mole on his upper lip. Recognition hits me hard.

"I know you. You were there when we got attacked outside." The memory of him standing over me, promising to protect us, flashes behind my eyes.

He stops in front of me, his grin widening. "Why yes, miss, I was. And how did you get up here?"

I scramble for something to say that won't get Adrian in trouble. "I, um…climbed," I finish lamely, inwardly cringing at my lie.

"Really?" He raises an eyebrow and looks over the side of the inner wall toward the smooth stone. Climbing it would be an impossible feat without footholds. I flick a pebble off the wall with feigned disinterest as he looks back at me, forming a small whistle. "That's impressive."

My body tenses as I wait for him to call me out or drag

me away, but he rests his back against the wall, crosses his ankles, and looks up at the stars. I blow out a slow, relieved breath.

"You're Adrian's pupil, right?"

Shock pulls my lower lip into my mouth, and I bite it hard, but the guard doesn't move. There also doesn't seem to be any malicious intent behind his question, at least not from what I can tell.

"That's right," I retort cautiously, just in case my inner lie detector is malfunctioning.

He rolls onto his shoulder and holds out his opposite arm. "Blake," he says with a charming smile. He has a hint of an accent, and I wonder if his family got stuck within our borders when the Obsidian attacked.

I shake his warm hand. "Cassie."

"I know," he says with a chuckle, "but I promise I'm not stalking you. Zypha likes to brag about how Adrian has taken a prodigy under his wing."

Oh great. I shiver against the cool breeze, not exactly jumping for joy to hear that another person believes I'm 'special.' If I saved one person, I'd be happy. I shrug in response, chewing on my lower lip.

"I knew you were something else when you offered to stay and fight that day. Takes real guts to do that." He flips around to scan the treeline absentmindedly.

The trees twist in the darkness, creating ugly shadows full of death and deception. How anyone can stay sane while looking at that abyss of nightmares is beyond me.

"It's my job to fight, but I left the battle, remember?" In the end, my intentions didn't matter...I ran away. The thought still makes me want to punch something, preferably an Obsidian's ugly face.

"No, miss, it's not your job, it's our job. You should have

seen how fast the other students scuttled away at the first sign of danger." He laughs and then ducks his head. "Not that I can blame them. The *idea* of killing Obsidian and seeing them in the flesh are two very different things."

I pull my jacket tighter around myself as another gust of wind rustles the trees, the icy tendrils slipping through my sleeves and leaving behind a trail of goosebumps.

Blake surveys me peculiarly, scratching the side of his scruffy jaw. "You want to be a hunter."

It doesn't sound like a question, and his observation stuns me. I haven't spoken about my goal with anyone except Sara, Jared, and Adrian. I tilt my head. "How can you tell?"

"You have the same air about you that Adrian did when he was your age, but I must admit, at least you know how to smile."

I laugh at his teasing tone. The way he talks sounds like he knew Adrian back then. Blake grins as though he's reading my thoughts.

"I may have graduated with him four years ago," he says with a cheeky smile. "I was barely able to choose this job. Luckily, I performed well in the trials and bumped my rank up a spot. I'm still rather ashamed at how relieved I was to find out I didn't have to be a hunter."

"You shouldn't feel ashamed. You fought the Obsidian bravely that day and stopped them from attacking the academy." My mind goes back to the graduation list, but I don't need the mental image to remember that all the hunters in their grade died, except Adrian. I'm sure Blake understands better than anyone that his increase in rank saved his life... and doomed someone else in the process.

Blake smiles at me. "I'm still trying to find ways to prove that I deserve to be here. That something I did was worthwhile. Forget it, I probably sound foolish."

"You don't, Blake. If anything, I'd say those without resolve are the foolish ones." I match his grin. The guard has a calm presence that makes him easy to talk to. We stand in silence before I have the courage to ask, "So, what are the trials?"

Blake snorts. "Nice try, but my lips are sealed. Adrian would probably be more likely to tell you than I would. Though knowing him, he wouldn't want to give you any advantages that he felt would take the win away from you."

I sigh. *Well, it was worth a shot.*

"Adrian was someone everyone looked up to, and also feared. He trained like a hardened soldier every day. He had all this unbelievable power, but only ever used it when he needed to. I think he was the only top-ranking student to never issue a challenge in our academy's history." Blake stares at the stars, tapping his knuckles on the stone.

I suck in a silent breath at his statement, though the fact doesn't surprise me. A hard exterior doesn't correlate with being a bad person. Adrian always emphasized that the techniques he showed me were specifically for self-defense against humans and aggressive offense against the demons.

"He and Wick were a sight to behold, starting from the day they joined the academy together. They were both so proud to be hunters."

I turn to him, confused by his phrasing. "You mean when they met at the academy, right?"

"No, actually. I don't know the specifics, but they were friends before entering the school. The two of them were inseparable, to the point that most of us believed their bond was the reason Adrian could join the school at twelve." The guard massages one hand with the other, eyes still on the sky.

I should let the topic drop. Adrian is such a private person, I doubt he'd be happy to hear I've been snooping around his past. But this is the most I've learned about Adrian, and I can't stop myself from probing. "Their bond?"

"It's one of many rumors, since neither of them explained their lives before the academy. When Wick turned thirteen, the orphanage tried to send him to Hallow Academy, but he refused to leave Adrian behind. Hunters were called in to assist the staff, but with Adrian's help, the two boys fought off three pairs of hunters. Before things could escalate, Wick said he would go if Adrian could come too. Devero, impressed with Adrian's skills, agreed to his demand."

My fingers fiddle with a loose thread of my hoodie, and I swallow thickly. To think Adrian was strong enough to impede soldiers at only twelve years old. No wonder he's considered the strongest warrior. And Wick must have been just as strong. My heart squeezes once again at how much his death must have devastated Adrian, especially if they were close before the academy. I want to press for details, but I've already pushed more than I should have.

"It's just a rumor, but it doesn't matter now," Blake continues when I don't respond. "After Wick died, Adrian came back to the academy a changed person: broken, I'd say. He threw himself into security detail, but anyone could see that he never got over what happened." Blake's dark eyes slide to mine. "I've never seen him more at peace than when he's walking around the courtyard with you."

"I didn't realize you were such close friends with him." Despite the cold, heat creeps up my neck at his proclamation. If Blake was trying to change the subject, he picked an excellent topic.

My mind immediately switches to all the panic I've been determined to quell. Adrian cracks a few smiles around me, sure, but that doesn't mean he likes me more than a friend. I don't want to talk about my unresolved feelings for Adrian in front of Blake, though. As cool as he seems, I barely know the guy.

"We're not. I'm just observant. You notice a lot when people think no one is looking. For example, you're much more suited for Adrian than Tala," the guard muses softly.

Instantly, my flush vanishes. *Talk about getting doused in a bucket of ice water.* For a random guard to notice Tala's feelings for Adrian, she must be around him a lot outside of our classes.

My face twists at the thought, too distracted to remember I should be cagey around strangers. "So you see how she looks at him, too?"

Blake's smirk borders on a grimace. "Everyone sees how she looks at him. She asked him out about a year ago, but Adrian turned her down. I've known her for a long time; I doubt she's gotten over it."

"Has she always been so..." I bite my lip, searching for the right word.

"Disagreeable?" Blake offers.

I laugh at his expression. "Yes, that."

He nods. "I arrived at the academy when I was thirteen, and by that time, Tala had graduated and was shadowing as a professor. She spent most of her time with the headmaster. Tala was like his daughter, and he spoiled her like she was the most prized possession in Arrynd. I can only assume he treated her that way throughout her schooling. It was as if she expected everything to be handed to her. I guess she thought being with Adrian would be the same way."

Huh. *I can't imagine the headmaster having any sort of familial side.*

Blake glances at one of the torches farther down the wall.

"I should be heading back. It's almost time for a guard change." He stares at me expectantly.

"And I should leave before that happens?" I gauge, dragging out the first word while processing his underlying message.

"Exceptionally wise, miss." He gives me a thumbs-up before jogging back the way he came.

"It's Cassie," I call to him in a joking voice.

"It was nice talking with you, Cassie." Blake spins around and winks with a brief salute before picking up his pace.

I chuckle to myself and start heading down the dark staircase. *I think I just made a new friend.* The thought warms my cold skin.

I'm up early the next morning, excitement coursing through me. The weather is warmer than it has been recently, which in itself increases my mood.

I've always been intrigued by the idea of these farms and their existence outside any walls. I'm almost positive I passed one on the way to the academy when I first arrived three years ago, but I don't remember much about the horse ride except for the blurred trees.

Jared and I meet at the front gate. There's no sign of Naire or Emmerick yet, so I soak in the last few moments of peace before they join us. Being forced to spend the trip with my second-least favorite people—Tala will always be number one in my heart—is very similar to having a pebble in your shoe when going for a run: it doesn't completely ruin your experience, but the constant annoyance makes it significantly less enjoyable.

"Good morning," Jared says, though his eyes never leave the gate.

"Morning," I chirp, looking around. I had expected guards to be here, ready to escort us. "Where is everyone?"

"They haven't arrived yet, but they should be here any—"

The gates swing open before he can finish his sentence. Sara rushes through them and throws herself into Jared's awaiting arms. I smother a knowing grin with my hand. *So that's why he was here early.*

Sara gushes about the trip and everything she saw, arms flying in big gestures. I walk up, barely dodging a wayward hand, and hug her as well.

"You guys are going to have so much fun! Even though it's hard work," she adds, rubbing her arms with a wince.

Sara's group files into the academy, and two guards join them, their eyes scouring the courtyard.

"Where's the rest of your group?" One guard drawls, clearly not impressed with our time management skills. I don't know why he's angry at us; we were the ones who arrived on time.

Emmerick and Naire saunter into view at an infuriatingly slow pace.

"Sorry about the delay." Naire sneers at me. "I just had to pick something up."

"Your dignity?" Jared mutters.

I cover my laugh with a hasty cough as Naire shoots him a filthy glare and pushes past us. Emmerick gives me the same murderous glower he's shown all week and accompanies her.

"Well, this should be fun," I sigh.

"Be careful out there with them," Sara tells me. I pat her shoulder with a smile.

"Let's go, you two. It's past sunrise," the same guard

demands. He flicks his eyes toward the sky above the wall and impatiently gestures for us to move.

I barely contain an eye roll at his restlessness. We must be on a strict timeline. *His new name is officially Time Crunch.*

Jared and I give Sara one more hug before leaving with the guard. He leads us through the open gate to a small wooden cart with two horses attached to it. The guards sit on the front bench while Emmerick and Naire settle themselves on one side of the cart. I climb onto the other side and try to ignore the stares of the people directly across from me.

"It's a thirty-minute ride there," Time Crunch grunts before snapping the whip that ties the horses to the carriage. The horses flick their dull blue manes but don't make a sound as we lurch forward until evening out at a steady pace.

Horses' manes illuminate when they're fed Azura mushrooms, but the guards must not feel the need to activate the light since it's daytime.

The ride is silent, which is fine by me. I lean against the wooden side and watch the trees fly past our increasing speed. With it being daylight, it's hard to feel the fear that hides in the shadows, so I use this time to appreciate the outdoors.

I'm surprised the academy is allowing us to spend the night outside, where protection from Obsidian is much lower. Still, the experience is worth the danger in my mind.

Thirty minutes later, I hold back a gasp when the trees disappear, revealing flat land that goes on for miles down a wide dirt path. The road cuts through the middle of the farm, and we pass a patch of tall wheat, a row of thin trees, and then multiple rows of green plants.

Each row has about three people tending to it. They all wear different assortments of brown sweats, some with makeshift sun visors, and the farmers weave through the plants like extensions of the roots themselves.

The organization astounds me. *How did they create such a substantial expanse of agriculture?*

The answer comes in the form of guards that line the perimeter of the entire field. They all face the surrounding forest with their guns at the ready. *Fire guns?* I've never seen one in person before, but I suddenly get the feeling that this farm is a lot more important than a few fruits and vegetables.

The guards' concern is not what goes on inside the farm, but around it. Their rigid stances form a barrier against the tall trees and all the shadows festering within them. In between each soldier is a large stone pit, though I can't make out what's in them. I wonder how often they have Obsidian attacks here.

The carriage slows down once we reach a white, three-story farmhouse. One of the farmers carries a handful of carrots into the house, and another leaves with two empty baskets.

My heart rate picks up as I spot Adrian and four security guards standing on the wraparound porch, waiting for us.

The six of us jump from the cart, and we follow the guards to file in front of Adrian. My face flushes as I feel his eyes on me, but I blame it on the rising sun. He looks exactly as he did when he left: black suit that every guard wears, piercing blue eyes, and thick, wild hair that blows haphazardly in the wind.

My eyes eat him up like it's been months instead of only a week, and I let out a slow breath. I didn't realize how much I truly missed him until now, finally seeing him safe and unharmed.

"Welcome to Plantation 14. Here they cultivate fruits and vegetables that supply all surrounding homes and facilities, including Netiva City itself. Today, you will each help to pick the food and give thanks to these hardworking people for what they do every day. A guard will escort you to your assigned position." He nods at the men and women beside him, and three guards move forward towards our line.

Adrian jogs down the steps and walks up to me, the shadow of a smile gracing his lips, so small that you could only see it by staring directly at them. Which I am definitely *not* doing.

Chapter 24

Moonlit Deprivation

"Come with me," he murmurs.

The tight band around my heart loosens when he speaks to me, his throaty voice as soothing as ever. He heads toward the fruit trees, and while we walk, I spot Time Crunch leading Jared to a row of tomato plants farther away from the house.

"The first headmaster created this tradition to help harvest as much food as possible before the crops die. It can become challenging to feed people once winter arrives," Adrian shares as we meander closer to the fruit trees.

"I think it's a great idea." It makes me feel useful to know that the food I pick will help someone else get food on their table for dinner. We stop in front of the first tree, and I stare at its fruit. The first four look to be filled with giant purple plumapples.

Adrian picks up a wide wicker basket from the base of the tree and hands it to me. He grins, which in consequence immediately makes me wary. "You have the fun job. Climb the trees and pick the fruit. You can drop them into this basket. When it fills up, bring it to the house and grab another one."

I return his grin and snatch up the container. *That does sound fun.* I rest the handle on one of the tree branches and swing myself up onto the lowest branch. My hands and feet move with ease as I scale to the top.

Being surrounded by plumapples and green leaves, I breathe in the scent of delicious fruit and fresh air. My mouth waters, and I'm tempted to bite into one, but I pick the sphere and lay it in the basket below me. I won't steal food meant for someone else.

The tree takes about an hour to clear, even at my quick pace. When I jump back to the soft earth, Adrian is gone. I move to the next tree and start the process over again. After the third one, my basket is overflowing.

I leap from the tree and reach for the handle, preparing to drop it off at the farmhouse. The woven box barely scrapes off the ground as my arms strain against the weight of my haul. *How the heck can fruit be so heavy?*

"Here, let me help you," a sweet voice says above me.

I wipe my sweaty brow and stand to offer my thanks. My eyes widen at the tiny figure beside me. "Risa?"

The young blonde girl frowns. "Do we know each other?"

I shake my head. "I saw your last challenge. In passing," I add uncomfortably. I don't want her to believe I was cheering for Ian.

She nods and gives me a small smile. Together, we lift the wooden container into the air and make the short trip to the house. We leave it at the steps, where a guard strides up and takes it inside. More empty baskets line the porch, so I choose one at random and head back to the trees. Risa follows me.

I eye the girl while we walk. She hums to herself, and

there's a lightness in her step. "How do you like it here?" I find myself asking.

"I've never been happier," she exclaims merrily.

"That's good." A gentle smile creeps onto my face, and some of the pain I carried in my heart for her dissolves. It's nice to know that even though she left the academy on bad terms, she found herself somewhere she could call home.

The day goes by in a blur of jumping from tree to tree, with a short midday break for a meal of boiled vegetables. As the sun finally sets on the horizon, Adrian calls from under my tree that I'm done for the day.

"Just a second," I answer from my perch in a cherry tree. My upper half pokes out of the leaves, and I stare at the setting sun. It bleeds red, orange, and yellow into the horizon in a brilliant canvas. I hold my breath against its beauty, the one thing the Obsidian can never ruin. I finally get to see a true sunset once again, rather than whatever colors feebly scrape above the wall.

I stay there as long as I dare before climbing down, my feet landing lightly beside Adrian. He's leaning against the trunk with his eyes closed, his stance oozing tranquility. *I've never seen him more at peace than when he's walking around the court-yard with you.* Blake's words whisper in my ear, and I bite my lip to keep the blush from my cheeks.

The overwhelming urge to confess my knowledge of his past bubbles up inside me. My lips tremble with the desire to ask him so many questions, to know which rumors are true and what happened to his family. If Wick's death truly broke him like Blake said, then how did he come back from that?

My mouth opens, but before the words fly out, doubt

234

squeezes my throat and coats my tongue. I'm positive he's more likely to be upset by my probing than flattered. I've always appreciated that Sara and Jared haven't tried prying for memories I'd rather keep buried, so why should I know Adrian's past before he's willing to share it?

"Ready?" I announce, hating to disturb him, but more afraid he'll catch me staring. *I'll wait for him to decide whether he wants to talk about it.* For now, I'll focus on supporting him however I can.

He opens his eyes and inclines his head. We start the trek that I've done at least a dozen times today.

"It's beautiful," he comments. At my questioning glance, he adds, "The sunset."

"I haven't seen one of those since my parents passed." I smile, the memory of the three of us together making me feel warm instead of my usual lamenting bitterness.

Adrian hesitates before responding, his jaw ticking. "Cassie, I—"

"There you are!" Jared exclaims, slinging an arm across my sore shoulders and pulling me away from Adrian. I peek behind me and watch whatever he was going to say get swallowed, his face morphing back to its usual chiseled stone.

Jared opens his mouth to say more, but gasps and sprints away from me when he spots an older farmer handing out small cryberries to the workers. His childlike giddiness makes me laugh while I sense Adrian taking Jared's spot next to me.

As the farmers lumber into the house, I notice the farm guards tossing torches to each other. My feet slow as I stare, curious about what they are doing. How can they all hold torches throughout the night without negating their weapons?

A soldier lights her torch with a twist of flint and then tips the flickering flames to the officer next to her until it catches fire as well. Once everyone has a lit torch, each guard walks over to a stone pit and throws their wooden log into it.

I gasp as the pits burst into a raging fire, lighting up everything around them. I rotate in a circle as more bonfires pop up in the distance, which I assume mark the end of the fields.

"The fires help keep the Obsidian away at night," Adrian says softly.

He gently pushes me into motion, and I blink twice to clear my dazed fascination. Do they use the same Eloyla paste we use on our swords to keep the fires going all night without fear it'll jump from the pits? *That's genius.*

Most of the farmers are heading into the house, their weary feet scraping against the wooden porch. Instead of going into the house with them as I expected, Adrian trails around the side of the residence.

I peer at him. "Where are we sleeping?""

"We have a small camp set up behind the house. There's not much space inside for visitors."

He leads me to the back of the residence, where four sets of tents frame a small fire, close to one of the raging bonfires. Some distance away are more tents where I see the academy's officer uniforms on the men and women standing near their flames.

Loud snoring rumbles from a closed tent that I assume Emmerick is in. I haven't seen Naire anywhere. I turn to Adrian, pushing the spiteful girl from my mind. That I haven't seen her all day is a *good* thing.

"You were right, Adrian. Today was a lot of fun."

"I'm glad," he responds with a smile.

We don't move, and the ever-growing pause swells between us. My heart rate picks up tempo with the beat of all the fantasies overtaking my thoughts. The image of his warm, calloused fingers scraping against my bare shoulder brings a blush to my cheeks.

Mortified, I pray it's too dark for him to notice. I might not even have to tell him my feelings if my body keeps reacting this way when he's beside me.

"Okay, goodnight," I blurt, clambering into what I hope is an empty tent.

I wait until the sound of retreating footsteps reaches my ears before groaning and slapping my forehead. *I cannot believe I just did that!* If I run from him every time my stupid heart falters, I'll never be able to stay friends with him.

Better yet, if I could just stop having a girly freak-out every time he looks me in the eye.

"Way to make a fool of yourself again, Cassie," I whisper, angrily sliding into my sleeping bag. I huff and try to relax. As tired as I am, it takes a long time for my mind to quiet down enough for sleep.

I wake to the uncomfortable feeling of being dragged.

My arms jerk against the tugging sensation, my legs scratching against twigs and rocks. Alarm bells ring in my head, but I can't focus on them, nor can I lift what feels like a massive boulder on top of my neck. It hangs limply off my shoulders and rolls with each ragged movement of whoever's pulling me.

My mouth tastes like cotton balls. I open it, but no sound comes out except for a weak moan. *Something's terribly wrong.* Panic moves like frozen sludge in my veins, helplessly trying to sharpen my senses.

"She's waking up," a gruff voice says above me.

"Well then, dose her again, idiot," a second voice snarls back.

After a few failed attempts, I finally peel open my crusted eyes. The world spins nauseatingly fast, and I force down the contents of my stomach.

"Whaz goin' on?" Getting my lips and tongue to work together feels impossible as I strain to focus my eyes.

Through the blurriness, I can make out the silhouette of lush green trees against the encompassing darkness. I bite my tongue, barely feeling the pain. My mind races to figure out what happened while I was asleep.

A sharp prick at my neck spears through my haze, and I use all my strength to twist my hand free and swat at whatever's piercing my skin. The sound of glass breaking, accompanied by a rough curse, fills the air. A hand grabs the back of my hair and pulls tight. My neck arches painfully, and I blink back unwanted tears, the face of one of my captors finally swimming into view.

"The syringe broke." Emmerick glances up at someone, his face bending in and out of focus.

"I can see that," growls Naire, who steps into my eyesight as well. "But that doesn't matter. You gave her enough that she won't be much of a threat for a while. We need to speed this up before the guards make their next rotation."

I was drugged, my brain processes sluggishly, *and no one knows we're gone*. I grunt at the stab of pain as Emmerick drags me through rocks and shards of glass. The slight throb of my outer thigh is nothing compared to the screaming in my mind and the sick feeling crawling through my flipped stomach.

This is bad. This is bad. Very, very, very bad.

My mind whirls at my options. If I don't do something now, then I'll die in these woods, drowsy and surrounded by my sadistic classmates. *Are they seriously going to kill me?*

I keep thinking I'm going to wake up, or one of them will start laughing and explain that they were just getting back at me for Emmerick's embarrassment during our last challenge. But they continue to drag me farther away from camp, away from any help.

No one will find my body until it's too late. No one will know what happened. I'll just be another casualty in the long line of people who die every day.

The thought of Adrian losing another friend like Wick pushes adrenaline into my veins, and I wrestle against Emmerick's steel hold. I have to fight back. While my struggle may be me just flopping my body like a fish, I'll be damned if I'm going to make it easy for them.

"Stop struggling," Emmerick hisses.

He raises his hand—*get out of the way, Cassie!*—but I don't have enough coordination to dodge. I close my eyes right before his fist connects solidly with my jaw. He lets me go, and I roll three times across the cold ground, landing in a limp pile of useless limbs.

"I've been wanting to do that for a while," Emmerick chuckles.

I slowly drag myself onto my hands and knees, panting with exertion. *Come on, legs, move!*

"This should be far enough," Naire says, walking in a small circle.

I crawl away from them, ignoring the tremors wracking my frame. My body is feebly fighting against however much more of the drug entered my system before I broke the syringe, and the effect is taking a toll.

"Oh, no, you don't," Emmerick guffaws. A beefy hand wraps around my neck, and he lifts me into the air.

Thrashing against his hold, my fingernails dig into the skin of his forearm while my mouth opens in a silent scream.

Cursing, he throws me hard, and my back slams into a tree, which causes what little air I had in my lungs to whoosh out. I gasp frantically, using the bark to prop myself up and to keep from slumping over and eating grass.

The combination of trying to regain my breath while forcing my limbs to work overtime has my head whirling. A part of me wants to give in to the darkness steadily creeping into my mind, but I refuse to let this be the end. After everything I've gone through, everything I've survived, this can't be how I die.

"This looks like a suitable spot." Naire rams my back up against the trunk and begins wrapping something around my body. I'm too busy catching my breath to fight her. The smell of sweat clinging to her clothes makes me gag and hinders my effort to fill my deprived lungs.

Naire stands beside Emmerick to view her handiwork, and the two of them share a victorious smile. My head lolls to the side, and I force my eyes down to my form. Bulky rope ties me to the tree. I attempt to move my arms, but they're stuck under the tight bindings.

My eyes seek to find any sort of compassion on their faces, some small telltale sign that this is just an appalling prank, but my vision zeros in on Emmerick's right hand, his thick fingers lightly grasping an object.

The lethal glint of steel blinks in the moonlight.

A dagger.

Slivers of genuine terror start to build inside me.

"Why?" I choke out, straining against the cords.

Naire laughs. "Not that it's any of your business, but Tala offered us some real nice, cushy jobs in the city if we tied you up out here. Better than anything the school could get."

"And without you, I will be in first place." Emmerick nods

like murder is the most obvious and reasonable way to get what he wants.

My insides sour at Naire's proclamation. So Tala is truly trying to kill me. Our petty fights in the gym are nothing compared to this. I gawk at my classmates with wide eyes, trying to understand how they could do this.

My gaze travels back to Emmerick's hand. *Oh*, I think dazedly, the thought sounding far away in my mind, *they're going to execute me with the knife and feed my body to the Obsidian.*

Naire kneels by my side and wraps her bony fingers around my chin. "Don't give me that look. I'm helping you reach your true potential: as fodder."

Unable to form the words to describe my hatred, I muster up enough saliva to spit in her face.

My assailant garbles a scream, her features contorting beyond rage. She forcefully slaps me while feverishly wiping her cheek with her sleeve, spewing insults fast enough that I can't understand them. My vision dips with the sharp movement, but I can't feel the blow.

A small part of me simmers with disappointment that I didn't get her in the eye.

Naire lets out a controlled breath and smoothes out her shirt, composing herself quickly. "Emmerick and I should head back. By the time anyone realizes you're missing, the Obsidian will have had their fill."

Her hand gestures to Emmerick and he leans in close. I brace myself for the blade, wondering how he's going to do it: the throat, or maybe the heart?

At least I got one good shot at Naire. I try to smile, but my lips only contort abnormally. Emmerick flicks his wrist, and my bound arms strain to block it.

I'm sorry, Adrian. Sara. Jared.

The stinging pain comes after I realize I'm still alive,

relief flooding me only temporarily. The gash on my upper forehead creates a heavy flow of blood. It streams down into my right eye, and I blink furiously to clear it. Emmerick steps back with a grunt of satisfaction.

"Head wounds always bleed more, as they say. Just a little something to excite the demons. I bet their eagerness will even tear the rope to pieces, not that I imagine anyone will investigate either way. You wouldn't be the first student to die at the hands of Obsidian."

Naire gives me one last once-over before pivoting and marching back into the forest. Emmerick follows closely behind until their black clothes melt into the darkness.

Only when the deafening silence roars in my ears do I fully understand how dire my situation is.

Chapter 25

Disheveled Plea

My breath expels in frenzied wheezes, and my hands shake uncontrollably. The darkness envelops me, embracing me like an old friend. I'm far enough from camp that not even a pinprick of fire is visible.

Even fear can't fully take over; it waits patiently outside the numbing bubble my mind wades in.

The trees distort and bend like blades of grass, and my stomach contorts with unbearable nausea. I can't tell what's real and what's not, and the unknown sickens me. *What kind of drug did they give me?*

Broken wails sting my ears, and I pray I'm not the one making them. I'd be able to tell if I could feel my mouth. The rope rubs my arms raw, yet I don't stop my weak wiggles against the secure bindings. I scrub my cheek against my shoulder to gain vision in my right eye, but the blood has driven it closed.

Groans of a hundred Obsidian fill my ears, and my heart stutters. *Too many, there can't be that many.* Trees morph into

Zeros as they crawl towards me. Twos and Threes follow suit in a horde of black rock.

Some tumble to the ground and meld with the earth, while others unravel like dust and scatter with the wind. But there are always more that keep coming.

My heart stalls in my chest before picking up a rapid, unsteady beat, and I hope the overworked organ will give out before the monsters reach me. If I can die before the venom completely overtakes me, even if it's halfway through a transformation, then I won't become one of them.

My head rolls from side to side, wishing the action could separate hallucinations from reality. I want to scream, but that would just attract the Obsidian with hearing capabilities. Being mauled by a horde of demons, helpless and alone, isn't how I expected to die.

Warped bodies creep toward me, and a strangled whimper escapes. The trees bend away from the Obsidian in revulsion. Even my own trunk leans back as death slowly advances.

A hazy ball of light breaks through the darkness, moving faster than the shadows. Each shadow falls as the orange light washes over them, their bodies falling into multiple pieces and dispersing in puffs of smoke.

The light disappears, leaving a single shadow to collect together and form the solid shape of a Three, its black, soulless eyes never blinking. A scream finally rips free from my numb lips, and the monster rushes forward, enclosing a rough hand against my mouth. It hushes me as its other hand tugs at my clothes.

Tears stream from my eyes, and I struggle violently. *I can't go down without a fight.* My foot connects with flesh and it grunts, pinning my legs to the ground with incredible strength.

"Cassie, stop. It's me, it's Adrian," a voice urges in my ear. It sounds so familiar, deep and silky, ebbing the fear before I can place who the voice belongs to.

My vision darkens, and I groan, fighting against the intense need to sleep. When I can see again, the Three has morphed into Adrian. He's pulling the last of the rope away from my limp body, shaking out his hand like the rope hurt. Relief courses through me, so strong it makes my head swim...more than it already is.

Adrian cups my face, his hands warm and gentle. I stare at him hard, trying to keep his features from distorting.

"Are you okay?" His voice echoes a million times in my mind. He shrugs out of his jacket and dabs it gently on the cut across my forehead. I pull away from his touch with a moan, escaping the pain.

Adrian frowns and leans in close with narrowed eyes, inspecting the wound. The brightness of his blue eyes seems sharper than before, lighting up his entire face. His full lips are so close to mine I can feel his breath on my skin, warming my cheek. Shivers run through me at his nearness.

I sigh softly. With my mind in pieces, it seems so obvious that I like Adrian. Why was this a problem again? Nothing matters except having him beside me. I think my lips pull into a smile.

Adrian scans my face, his eyebrows drawing together. He says something that I miss, but it pulls my eyes down to his lips again. Like it's the most natural thing to do, the only thing I can do, I lean forward and press my lips to his.

Oh, hot damn. They are soft and warm and...gone within seconds.

Confused, I stare at the spot Adrian used to be. Was he an illusion this whole time? Sadness washes through me, along with more dread. If Adrian isn't here, then I need to get up and protect myself.

I fight with my limbs to stand, only making it to my knees before I collapse again. Strong arms prevent me from flying face-first into the dirt.

"What's happening, Cassie?" Adrian's alarmed voice rings in my ears.

I hold back a smile. *Adrian is here.* He hauls me up to my feet, and my vision wavers, spinning fast. I shove him away, my knees slamming into the grass and fingers curling into the earth.

With as much grace as one can have hyped up on an unwilling overdose, I retch beside the tree, squeezing my eyes shut as a few tears leak out. A hand rubs my back in slow circles while I empty everything in my stomach until there's nothing left to do but dry heave.

When I finish, I crawl a few feet away from the mess and take deep breaths. My fogged mind clears briefly, and I scan my surroundings. Obsidian remains litter the ground, and everything that has happened comes back to me.

Farther away, I can see glass glinting in the moonlight. I glance up at Adrian, who's staring at me with a mix of worry and something I can't place.

"Drugged," I slur, nodding in what I hope is the direction of the damaged syringe. Adrian follows my gaze and jumps up, striding toward the spot.

I crumble to the ground once more, weak and dizzy. At least purging my stomach has helped to clear most of the murky haze from my mind. With Adrian here, I feel the adrenaline wearing off, and exhaustion tugs at the edges of my vision. My eyelids weigh a thousand pounds, and they pull down to seal my eyes shut.

Adrian wraps his arms around me and lifts my fatigued

body into the air as if I weigh nothing. He hugs me tightly to his chest and my head lands heavily on his shoulder. I couldn't move it even if I wanted to, which is good because I'm too comfortable to do so anyway.

Being pressed up against his defined muscles is the one good thing to come out of this night. I don't open my eyes, trusting he's taking me somewhere safe.

Emmerick and Naire...the thought of them makes my insides flare with rage, and my head fills with all the revenge and suffering I can return to them tenfold. But however sweet my revenge may be, that would guarantee me two enemies for life, ones that may try to kill me again in the future.

No revenge would be worth it, not since we only have a few days left. As a hunter, I'd have no one protecting my back, no Adrian with me if they decide to try again.

Then my eyes pop open, the dark world swirling ominously. The sick feeling comes flushing through my system as I realize Adrian has saved me *again*. I've needed someone to rescue me...*again*! While I'm grateful to be alive, doesn't this prove that I've gotten nowhere with all my work? That I'm still weak?

I try to look Adrian in the eye, but with my head tucked against his shoulder, all I can see is the silhouette of his sharp jaw. "Don't let—I don't—"

The words fall apart before I can say them, getting frustratingly jumbled on my tongue.

"It's okay," Adrian murmurs, his voice a quiet lullaby in my ears. I feel my eyes slip closed against my will, the drug pulling me deeper into darkness. "We can talk about this when you wake up."

"But I—"

"It's going to be alright, Cassie. I'll watch over you while you sleep. You're safe now."

Gently swaying in his arms, barely hearing the last of his words as they slide over me, I can't fight the drug any longer. I sluggishly drag my hand across his firm chest and sigh.

While I may not always like it, he's there for me when I need him, I think, before letting myself succumb to the darkness, safe within Adrian's arms.

———

Whispers invade my sleep until I'm finally aware of a harsh pounding in my head and ringing in my ears. My arm trembles as I raise it to touch my forehead, groaning with the effort. Coarse fabric where skin should be meets my fingers, and my lips twist in confusion. The muttering stops and two bodies huddle beside me.

"Oh, Cassie, thank the universe you woke up!" Sara exclaims, a slight tremor echoing her words. She grabs my hand and I force my eyelids open, meeting her wide eyes. *Why do I feel like I got run over by Time Crunch's cart?*

"What happened?" I croak, my voice cracking twice.

I expected to be in the nurse's office by the way I'm feeling, but the familiar gray walls show I'm in my bedroom. My throat is like sandpaper as I try to swallow. Jared hands me a glass of water, and I drink from it gratefully.

He sits on the edge of my bed while Sara climbs in next to me. The two of us are quiet as Jared begins his rendition of our field trip.

From his version of the night, he woke up to check on me, and I was gone. Emmerick and Naire were asleep in their tents, so he found Adrian on patrol and told him of my disappearance. He searched my tent and rushed into the woods, telling Jared to wait there. Adrian came back a while later with me unconscious in his arms.

"How come I'm not in the hospital?" While I don't mind skipping the exhausting routine of dodging Nurse Dorna's weird experiment questions, this is the first time I've woken up in my bed instead of there.

Jared shrugs, picking at the fuzz on the blanket. "Adrian said something about it not being safe for you, so you were brought here in secret. We made a special trip back at night and everything. I honestly felt like a secret agent. That may be my calling. He said that you weren't injured too much and that all you needed was sleep, so it was okay to keep you here. Thankfully, we've had no classes."

I frown, trying to decipher the important bits of Jared's monologue. He rambles when he's nervous. Jared's been talking like the debacle didn't happen last night. "How long have I been out?"

"Almost two full days. It's about ten at night now," Sara responds, squeezing my fingers. I calculate the difference in my head and let out a curse, fighting with the sheets to scramble out of bed.

"The trials start tomorrow," I shout. *How could I have slept for so long?* Small fragments of my last conscious night begin to form in my head, but I shove them away for now. I have to train, at least one last time.

My two friends voice their opposition, but I break free of their hold and stagger about the room to find a change of clothes. I'm showered, dressed, and out the door before their pleas can convince me otherwise.

I run down the steps and take the familiar route to my favorite training room. Free from my friends, I allow myself time to piece together what I remember about that night.

Images of Emmerick and Naire giving me some sort of drug fill my mind, and I grimace. That they would try to murder me is astounding, even though I never considered them anywhere close to friends. We've been together for three years, yet my life meant nothing to them.

Easily discarded like a dirty old dish rag.

My legs ache when they hit the stone floor, and my muscles strain as though they were just torn to shreds. Either the drug is still in my system, or my body is protesting two days of immobility. *Training's going to be rough tonight.* I can probably throw a few knives at a minimum.

I shuffle into the gym, rolling my stiff shoulders in preparation while walking beside the weapons shelf.

"I was hoping you'd show up eventually," a voice says from beside the door.

I twist around and see Tala standing in the corner like an expert creep. Her clothes are wrinkled, hair in a messy bun. I keep the surprise off my face at her disheveled appearance. It's one of the first times I've ever seen her without her blonde hair slicked back into its neat, high ponytail. I can't say seeing her look so messed up is an unpleasant sight, though.

I eye the door, judging the distance, but she'll be able to get to it before me. *I'm trapped.* My heartbeat jumps as I realize I'm in no condition to fight for my life. *Will this be my second brush with death in the same number of days?*

"I wanted to give you one last chance to drop out of the academy," Tala mutters in a flat voice.

"Oh, so does having your henchmen tie me to a tree in the middle of nowhere count as 'dropping out'?" I demand, angry at her for even showing her face around me.

My fists clench. If I thought I could throw a decent punch in my current condition, I would have ten seconds ago.

"You weren't going to die, as much as you deserve to. This is your final warning," she deadpans in the same monotone voice.

"Are you kidding me? You've lost your mind," I snarl, tensing for the inevitable fight.

"You wouldn't have died. He needs you alive," she states before walking out of the room.

"Who needs me alive?" I shout after her, but Tala doesn't turn as she disappears into the hallway.

Now what was that? *I wouldn't have died.* How in the world does being surrounded and nearly massacred by demons not equal *death*?

Tala herself resembles death warmed over and has obviously gone crazy. What is happening to her? And a better question, who does she think needs me alive? The same person who told her what needs to be done to 'protect the school'? That, more than anything, makes me believe the Obsidian blood has caused her to have some sort of psychotic break.

I shake my head, a slight throb wiggling its way into my temple. *Ugh, I don't have the time to worry about Tala and her ramblings right now.* I face the weapon shelf again, but the nervous excitement I felt when entering the gym has faded.

Without it, I can tell this last workout is going to be brutal.

Footsteps echo from the hall, and I hold in a sigh. *What does Tala want now?* I whip around to lash out at her, to tell her to leave me alone, but the words die on my lips.

Adrian stands in the entrance, cheeks tinted pink from sprinting. A hot flash bolts straight through my heart when I lock eyes with him, and it takes significant effort to keep my face neutral.

"I saw Tala leave from here, so I assumed that meant you were awake. Did she do anything to you?" His dark voice sends chills through my body.

"She just wanted to wish me well on my road to recovery," I smirk as Adrian releases a breath, obviously relieved my sarcasm is intact.

He walks closer, eyeing me carefully. "And are you recovering?"

I shrug with a wave to the bandage still encircling my forehead. "I think this is completely healed up. My arms and legs are killing me, but that probably has more to do with the fact that I haven't moved in two days."

"You should be resting," Adrian mumbles, shaking his head.

"Did you hear me? I've been asleep for two days. I think I've rested enough." Frustration seeps through me, and I turn back to the weapons shelf, picking up a random sword. It feels heavier in my grip than normal. My arm burns with the exertion of lifting it.

Adrian grabs the sword from my hand—with embarrassing ease, I might add—and lays it gently back in its original place.

"You can barely hold the sword. Give yourself the evening off and you'll be fine for the trials tomorrow."

"You don't understand. I was supposed to train this whole weekend. I was—" My breathing comes in quick gasps, cutting off my sentence.

The image of me tied to a tree and defenseless bursts into my mind. I couldn't fight or defend myself at all that night. If Adrian hadn't rescued me, I would be dead right now, despite whatever nonsense Tala tried to spew earlier. My fingers tremble with the effort to control my emotions.

The last thing I want to do is fall apart in front of Adrian.

He bends down and cradles my face. His nose is centimeters from mine, the faint feel of his breath on my lips efficiently squashing the upcoming panic attack. My breath catches, but I force any romantic thoughts from my mind, the 'just friends' mantra still somewhere inside me.

"You're ready for the trials. You've worked hard, and you will do wonderfully. Trust me," he insists in his smooth, alluring voice.

Trust me. I close my eyes and nod in his hold, savoring the heat from his fingers. His hands linger for a moment longer before dropping to his sides. Taking a deep breath to steel my nerves, I glance at him.

Adrian is staring at me with a strange expression, full of analysis and curiosity. If I didn't know any better, I'd think I did something wrong, or at the very least, incredibly abnormal.

Maybe he's wondering why I'm so susceptible to life-threatening situations? Oh, I hope not. I struggle to think of something to say before an idea pops into my head.

"Come with me," I say, gliding past him and out the door. I smile as I hear his footsteps trail behind me.

Chapter 26

Too Deep to See

WE WALK IN SILENCE PAST THE COURTYARD AND INTO THE garden. The soft trickle of water greets us with its small melody of serenity. I take a seat at the end of my bench and pat the spot beside me. Adrian sits down gingerly, his figure comically rigid.

I exhale and stare out at the garden. "This is where I like to go when I feel overwhelmed," I declare, quoting what he said to me a week ago.

Adrian silently surveys the tiny garden. The moon shines on the flowers, giving them an ethereal demeanor. Iridescent fish swim through the pond, and the trees rustle in the wind. I feel the tension slowly leak from his shoulders.

"It makes me feel at home," I continue. "The peace of nature, but none of the danger."

I meant it as a joke, but wince as Adrian stiffens beside me. *Maybe it was a mistake to bring up the dangers of the wilderness.* I risk a peek at Adrian. His face is stone, jaw clenched. It's not a giant leap to assume he's remembering my latest dance with death.

"What do you remember about the attack?" Adrian asks in a forced, calm voice, stretched as thin as the translucent petals of the flowers littering the edge of the small pond.

I weave my fingers together tightly, somewhat nervous about how this conversation is going to go.

My face scrunches as I think. "Most of it is hazy. Emmerick and Naire tied me to a tree and left me for dead. They gave me a sedative, which made me have a lot of delirious dreams. I remember you showing up right before I started vomiting everywhere." I frown. *Yeah, that's a little humiliating.*

Adrian hesitates, slowly extending his arms down his thighs until his palms rest against his knees. His rolled-up sleeves give me perfect access to his forearms, and my eyes trail up the thick cords of muscle. I squeeze my hands to stop myself from touching him.

Not the time, Cassie.

Just like the last time the moon lit up his face, the contrast of white light and defined features is breathtaking. Watching him sends little slivers of heat through my stomach.

A few wayward strands of inky black hair fall across his forehead, barely scraping his high cheekbones as he tilts his head down. I cross my arms in a stronger attempt to halt this incessant desire burning inside me.

Not the time, Cassie!

"I brought you back that night and immediately went to Zypha with what happened. We interrogated both students who went with you on the trip, and they explained that they were following Tala's orders, and she coerced them into it. Zypha had an emergency meeting with Headmaster Hallow regarding Tala's employment."

His voice fluctuates delicately, sharp as glass to soft as satin, a shifting undercurrent beneath his sentences. I tell myself it's a good thing I'm hanging onto his every word, savoring the deep timbre of his voice, because it allows me to detect it.

"And what did he say?" I almost interrupted him when he stated that Naire and Emmerick were 'coerced into it' by Tala. They sure didn't appear coerced to me.

Adrian's gripping his knees with enough force that I see the whites of his knuckles. *That can't be a good sign.* "Tala told the headmaster it was an attempt at team building gone wrong. That there was a miscommunication between her and the students, that this 'exercise' wasn't supposed to be outside the perimeter of the farm, that she meant you no harm."

I almost snort at his words, but hold it in when I look at his facial expression. Adrian does not seem pleased. "So, nothing's going to happen?"

"Hallow seems to believe Tala's reasons were true, but that doesn't mean you still didn't get hurt. She's being put on probation for the trials and all of next year. Tala's allowed to lead the trials, except she can't actively partake in them. The two students involved lost points, but not enough for their ranks to drop. I think both of them are scrubbing pots in the kitchen right now."

I hum in response. I didn't expect anyone to get expelled, but the punishment seems oddly low for a murder attempt, though I guess no one knew that. In the headmaster's eyes, they were pulled into whatever scheme Tala created.

I'm honestly not surprised Tala didn't get kicked out of the school either, if what Blake told me was correct. If Headmaster Hallow thinks of Tala as family, then he'd do what he could to protect her.

It's a sweet sentiment, but one that makes him suck at his job. He should protect the students rather than his crazed adopted daughter. Hallow has absolute authority here, however, so even if we disagreed with his orders, no one could break them.

"He's a coward," Adrian growls, and I glance at him, stunned by his aggressive tone. "He knows that Tala's excuse is fake, yet he's doing nothing about it. Hallow only got his position because it was his father's. He doesn't care about this school. Students are getting hurt, and he doesn't care."

I'm surprised to hear Adrian talk about the headmaster in such a way. He always seemed accepting of anything the headmaster had done. Has his resentment toward Hallow been festering longer than just this weekend?

Adrian drags in a long inhale and peers down at me, his sad blue eyes cutting into mine. "I'm sorry it turned out like this."

"It's fine." I shrug, rolling a tiny pebble between my thumb and index finger until it crumbles under the weight of my anxiety.

I flick the dust away and scrape my right hand against the bench in search of another clump. Having Emmerick and Naire expelled might mean less trouble for me, but I won't dwell on the unfairness of the world. I learned that lesson a long time ago.

"Tomorrow's our last day anyway," I add, feeling my stomach knot slightly at the thought of the unknown trials. Not even my favorite spot and the man beside me can placate the turmoil inside completely. "After tomorrow, I'll never have to see their faces again."

There's no reason to force their expulsion and have them come after me in retribution. Besides, I have Adrian here, and Sara and Jared. I know they have my back, and I have theirs. I've been getting a lot better at accepting their help.

I bite my lip as I stare at the swirling pond. *But have I, truly?* A large majority of me still wants to take Tala on alone.

I'm stronger now, and if she had gone up against me one-on-one without using her goons to drug me, I'm confident that I would have beaten her.

Now that Adrian is aware of the lengths Tala will go to kill me, I doubt I'll be able to get within five feet of her without him at my side. Emmerick and Naire are—I peek up at Adrian's tight jaw and flaming eyes—*most definitely* on his naughty list, so her puppets won't be able to do anything for her either.

Basically, her hands are tied. She threw down her last-ditch effort to get rid of me, and now she's the one alone, with no support, and still seeing my face every day. Ouch. For me, she has become as fierce as a kitten.

And maybe she knows it now, too. Tala left the room earlier without even lifting a pinkie finger toward me, something I doubt she would have done in the past. So why don't I try to win this fight? I have one last day in the academy before I graduate anyway, and some sick part of me wants her there to rub it in her face that she lost. That every insult, every fight, and every attack has been worthless.

It takes a moment to pull myself from my inner thoughts, feeling mildly uncomfortable with their direction. I don't want to become hate-filled and bitter like Tala is. I don't want to watch people suffer…and *enjoy* it.

Adrian is quiet, contemplative. I wonder what he thinks of my answer. Since our conversation is with us facing forward, my side-eyeing isn't giving me a good read on his expression. "You don't seem upset that they tried to kill you, and this isn't the first near-death experience you brushed off."

The gentle concern within the statement is enough that I almost want to cry. *That's not something I want him to be thinking about.* Innocently enough, he touched one of the few subjects that I would rather not talk about with him.

My own feeling of self-preservation.

Before my parents died, I was constantly afraid of dying, of monsters tearing through my flesh while I helplessly watched. After that horrible nightmare became a reality, something inside me broke. Like my survival instincts were hastily wrapped around me in thick, haphazard layers that the Obsidian came in and ripped away with their lamented claws. Leaving me bare, exposed, uncaring.

I should have died with my family.

It's the thought that lies curled in the darkest corner of my mind, whispering its deadly, cursed words like black tar into my guilt-ridden consciousness. *I don't deserve to live when they have perished. My parents were my life, and then they were gone in an instant.*

I couldn't get away from the thoughts after it first happened. Having the goal of being a hunter helped, but even then, I knew hunters didn't live long. Being under the constant threat of danger, actively throwing yourself into hoards, usually isn't compatible with a long and happy life. Being able to help others before I died seemed like a better, more honorable way to go.

Then I met Sara, and later Adrian and Jared. After finding them, I didn't feel so inclined to throw my life away. I wanted to be their support, and to do that, I had to start living for myself.

The change was slow, a crawling pace so imperceptive that I didn't notice the difference until my mortality was shaking my hand with a farewell wave. Being tied to the tree and seconds away from death showed me just how much I wanted to *live*.

Unfortunate timing, but I'll take what I can get.

So yes, I know I want to live, and I know I still want to be a hunter. My drive to save others only increases each year, and now that I'm so close to graduating, I'm both excited and anxious. Excited that I can finally begin my life as a hunter, and anxious because I'll be leaving any family I've made here and becoming a hunter with survival instincts. Will I be able to sacrifice my life for another? I want to say yes, but I keep imagining Sara and Jared's faces when they get the news. Their best friend, sibling, murdered. How could I do that to them?

"That's not the case," I respond, but my voice sounds flimsy even to my ears. Because really, how does one go from planning to throw their life away to fighting to keep it overnight?

Our country is riddled with death; people die all the time. Do I deserve to live any more than the next person? If I had died two days ago, would that have been better for everyone instead of them worrying every day for my safety as a hunter? Not knowing which day would be my last?

I pull my knees to my chest and clasp my arms around them. A soft breeze rolls through the garden, rustling leaves and blowing the scent of dirt and honeydew toward us. I close my eyes and breathe in the fragrance. I visualize the negative thoughts in my head, swirling with hatred and fear, and compress them into a compact ball, smaller and smaller until they are the size of a stone. With a slow exhale, I imagine taking my hands and crushing the rock to dust.

Opening my eyes, I can think clearly again, taking in the small pond, luscious trees, and Adrian. He's been silent this whole time, whether not knowing what to say or giving me space, I'm not sure. He almost looks out of place in his black uniform against the backdrop of flowing white flowers and green vines.

"That's not the case now," I repeat with a stronger voice, holding onto my new conviction like a lifeline. Knowing that

Adrian was present to witness my internal struggle doesn't sit well with me, especially since he isn't saying anything.

Finally, I swallow hard and turn to the officer, who's examining me with a stoic face. I freeze, my heart rate ratcheting up a few notches as I notice the very short distance between us, something I'm acutely aware neither of us is adjusting. Though with how focused Adrian is, eyes sharp and piercing, I doubt he is as conscious of the minimal space as I am.

Satisfied with whatever knowledge he gained from peering into my soul, he leans back and I release a shaky breath. The beauty of the garden and having Adrian so close are making me lightheaded.

"You are much stronger than you give yourself credit for," he murmurs, almost absentmindedly, but with great confidence, like his observation is as simple as stating the sky is blue.

I shrug and let my back thud against the vine-coated wall. *What exactly does he mean by that?* The statement feels random, not quite the word I'd associate with our previous conversation, where I basically admitted my lack of interest in my own life.

Adrian mirrors my action with a soft sigh. "People think strength is the ability to overcome your fears and failures, but I think it has more to do with recognizing those faults and choosing to live with them. To acknowledge they are there, but know they hold no power over you."

My lips slide into a small smile. "So you're saying I'm strong because I have a lot of faults?"

Adrian chuckles. "I'm saying I admire your strength. You have a better understanding of yourself than I did at your age."

"It doesn't feel like that, trust me," I joke, even though his words have warmed my insides and sent a brigade of butter-flies rushing to my stomach.

The whirlwind of emotions I've felt this evening has left me tired, like I've been juggling boulders for hours. The ache settles deep in my bones and graces my temples, but I ignore it, my mind still wild. *Adrian is wrong. I don't understand myself at all.*

A young bird finds its way into the garden, chirping and hopping from one side of the pond to the other.

"A guard told me about your challenge with Emmerick last week. They overheard some students talking about it."

My lips sink into a frown. I don't want Adrian thinking I was going around picking fights while he was gone. Or that I'm using our lessons to bully other students, even those as slimy as Emmerick.

"They said you knocked him out in a single punch," he adds before I can respond, a hint of pride in his voice. "But he deserves more than that."

I pivot my head to scan his hardened demeanor, surprised by the venom in his voice. "I don't want to use my skills on a human unless I have to. It's monsters I'm supposed to battle, not humans."

"Obsidian aren't the only monsters out there, Cassie. Sometimes the corruption is buried too deep to see," he murmurs.

I hesitate, internally flipping through topics to change the subject. Emmerick's broken moral compass isn't something I care to discuss. I settle on my most trusted response when I find myself uncomfortable: sarcasm. "Since when did you become so insightful?"

"I'm always this way. I just can't get a word in edgewise because you normally never stop talking."

His remark pulls a laugh from me, and I lightly swat his

shoulder with the back of my hand. *Which,* I think with a wince, cradling my knuckles, *probably hurt me more than him.*

I tilt my head toward him, another teasing comment dancing on the tip of my tongue, but I catch sight of his playful grin, and instantly, I can't remember what I was going to say. Adrian's full smiles, ever so rare, always send my heart fluttering and scramble my thoughts. Suddenly, it hits me how grateful I am to have Adrian in my life. Without fail, he's been there for me: teaching, supporting, and rescuing me when I need him the most.

The urge to let him know how important he is overwhelms me, and my mouth opens on its own, but I bite my tongue before any words come out. I've never been good at filtering my thoughts, but our relationship is the one thing I don't want to screw up. I don't want to end our friendship because of my big mouth.

Instead, I say, "Thank you for saving me, again." At least with this, I can still let him know how much I appreciate what he's done for me.

"I'm happy I got there in time. Luckily, those two weren't smart enough to cover their tracks. I saw the Obsidian swarming you. One more second and it might have been too late." Adrian doesn't look at me as he speaks.

Ah, so Obsidian really were there. I couldn't tell if they were all made up from the hallucinations or not. I purse my lips, unsure how to respond. His voice sounds fragile, like it could easily break.

He finally dips his head toward me, his blue eyes as dark as the pond at night. "You should work at the academy."

I blink. "What?"

Chapter 27

Crumbling Resolution

"I KNOW YOU WANT TO BE A HUNTER, BUT THE ACADEMY would benefit from your skills." Adrian's voice is low and urgent.

I wait for him to crack a smile or start laughing, but his serious expression never wavers. *He's not kidding*, I think in shock, the wheels in my head ticking at an aggravatingly slow pace.

"There's no way I can work in the same building as Tala for the rest of my life." The thought makes me shudder.

"I've been talking with Zypha, and we've started petitioning for Headmaster Hallow to be replaced. She thinks we have a good chance of Lord Netiva hearing us out. If that's the case, Zypha will be the new headmaster, and Tala will be gone, too much of a risk to stay. That means there'll be a spot available as an instructor here."

My mouth opens and closes with an uncontrollable twitch as I struggle to respond. I have never entertained the possibility of being an instructor. Or anything besides a hunter, for that matter. Adrian's intense stare burns a hole in the side of my head. I turn to face his patient expression.

"The whole reason I joined this school was to be a hunter. I want to help others like me." *You're the one who inspired me to be a hunter,* I almost say, but the words get stuck in my throat.

"You can still do that. Give these students the love and encouragement that Tala never gave. You could change generations of lives with your work. There are plenty of people who can be hunters." He hesitates before continuing. "Don't tell anyone about this, though. No one knows our plans except for a few trusted people."

I nod, my mouth glued shut. Me? A professor? The idea of having any influence on future students is terrifying.

Although, I think as quickly as sap rolling down a tree, *it might be fun to show a new generation all the tips and tricks I learned from Adrian.* Even with this strange turn of events, there's one thing I can't wrap my mind around.

"Why are you bringing this up now? Why do you care if I'm a hunter or an instructor?" It makes zero sense. He should be proud that I'm following the path he once walked himself.

Adrian blows out a long breath, leaning against the stone wall. "When I first saw the Obsidian closing in on you, I was terrified I wouldn't make it in time. I've watched countless soldiers die as a hunter, watched them leave on missions knowing the odds of their survival were slim. It became my way of life, expecting everyone around me to disappear eventually. But the thought that you could leave tomorrow and I would never see you again, only to enter the gym one day and see the academy's emblem by your name...I don't think I could recover from that."

My heart stills in my aching chest. His words aren't exactly a declaration of love, but I definitely mean a lot to him. I sit back and look up at the full moon. It appears so lonely in the sky, always watching by itself. I haven't thought about tomorrow being the last time I ever see Adrian.

I glance up at him, and his eyes regard me cautiously. His handsome, serious face tugs at something deep inside my body. The idea of being without him seems almost unbearable when he looks at me. I swipe my tongue across my dry lips, and his expression changes as his eyes follow the movement.

"Adrian, I—" My breathy voice falters. What can I possibly say to someone I'm too afraid to admit my feelings to? Adrian's eyes take in every moment of my indecision. "I don't think I could recover if you died, either." It's the closest I can get to the truth without explaining my true feelings. Even that admission sends my fingers into a small quiver. I clench them together in my lap.

His lips curve up in a mysterious smile as he leans in close. "Do you remember what you did to me when I cut the ropes tying you to the tree?" His voice is a silky whisper, dark and seductive, that sends a flash of heat through me.

I frantically search my memories for what I could have done to set his eyes on fire, but I come up empty. How is the universe so cruel as to give me amnesia about something like this?

With each passing second, he bends his head closer until my mind fogs and I can think of nothing besides, *oh, man, his lips are so close to mine*. I shake my head as an answer, not trusting my voice to be steady.

"Then let me show you," he murmurs against my cheek. His fingertips lightly graze the bottom of my chin, and he tilts my face up to his.

Adrian's warm lips slide softly across my cheek, and a shiver runs through me at the touch. My eyes close of their own accord, heart racing in anticipation. I wait breathlessly for his lips to reach mine, but they never move from their original position. His soft exhale brushes my skin before he pulls back, sliding his fingers through my hair.

My elation crashes and I deflate, sagging against the stone bench with my heart wreaking havoc in my torso. I keep my eyes squeezed shut, too afraid of the rejection I know is going to be reflected in his eyes.

Stomach in knots, I finally look up into his eyes, and my brow furrows at the sorrow embedded inside them. *Sadness* was not the expression I expected. Conflict, disgust, fear, I was ready for, but not that.

"I loved Wick like a brother," Adrian says, each word a calculated drawl, with a vulnerability not suited to the strength that radiates from him. "When he died, I thought I wouldn't be able to love anyone ever again. But I was wrong." His admission steals the oxygen from my lungs. *Is he implying that he loves me?* "I know it's selfish, but it would mean a lot if you considered living and working here. Of course, if you decide to be a hunter, I will fully support your dream." He gives me a slightly crooked smile, but his eyes are still defenseless in a way I've never seen before.

My mouth drops in shock before snapping closed. Every feeling I've ever felt for Adrian but pushed away breaks free from my chest, and I almost drown in it. My heart longs to be with the man beside me, yet I've never thought of becoming anything besides a hunter. Is that still the most important thing in my life? Am I willing to sacrifice leaving Adrian for good?

Adrian must see the conflict in my eyes because he squeezes my hand and stands, pulling me with him. "It's getting late, and you need to rest. This is an important decision. I don't need an answer right now, so let's talk again after the trials."

We walk back to my dorm in silence, my mind too jumbled for conversation. He bids me goodnight at the door and gingerly presses his lips to my forehead over the bandage, vanishing around the corner before I can respond.

I trace the cheek still burning from his soft lips with trembling fingers. My knees, which had been so strong carrying me this far, finally give out, and I slide down the door, wrapping my hands around my legs.

Adrian wants to be with me. He wants a life with me.

The thoughts swirl around in my mind, and I rotate my head from side to side in silent astonishment. When I started my training with Adrian two months ago, I never thought this would be the outcome.

And what did I do out in the woods? Kiss him, or his cheek? Recite a full love poem? As much as I want to know, maybe the universe is really doing me a favor by helping me forget. *How embarrassing.*

Wallowing in self-mortification and utmost confusion, I don't realize the door has swung open until I find myself flat on my back and looking up into Sara's bemused expression.

"What are you doing?" Sara chuckles, hip resting against the edge of the frame.

"Checking the resistance of the door. It was holding up nicely under my attentive inspection until you foiled my research," I say with a tsk, mustering up my greatest impression of casual.

It would have worked, I'm sure, if my voice hadn't cracked once…or twice. *Yes, because falling through the door wasn't suspicious enough.*

I roll myself up and push Adrian from my mind because if I don't, I know Sara will read it all over my face. Until I figure out what I'm going to do, I'd rather keep my inner turmoil to myself. "I'm surprised to see you awake. Don't you normally go to bed early?"

Her good-natured smile dries up, replaced by an oddly nervous expression. "Actually, I wanted to talk with you."

Uh oh, what did I do? I wrack my brain for any stupid mistakes I've made this week, but I'm constantly making stupid mistakes. The reasons for this talk are endless, but I have a feeling it may be about the field trip.

"Sure," I answer nonchalantly, making my way over to my rumpled sheets.

I scoot across the bed until my shoulders hit the wall above my pillow, and I pull my legs up, giving her plenty of room on my bed. She perches herself lightly on the end, fiddling with a loose strand on the hem of her white shirt. I contemplate throwing out a joke to clear the heaviness in the air, but Sara doesn't seem to be in the mood to fully appreciate it. So I decide to do something totally out of character and stay quiet.

"We're graduating tomorrow, and there's something I need to ask of you before that happens." Sara's voice quivers slightly.

"Anything," I reply instantly. Sara has never asked for a favor before, and after everything she's done for me, I'd give her the world if I could.

"Wait until you hear what I have to say before you promise." Her sad smile draws my lips down, as if her request could be so horrible that I wouldn't grant it to her.

I nod before letting my head thunk against the wall.

"You're at the top of the class now, and that's amazing. I'm so proud of you. We've never really gone into depth about it, but as you know, my original plan was to work in the city."

Was?

I almost voice my question, but with a sickening lurch of my stomach, I realize that the school only lets the top four people join a city. Fifth through tenth place can get into an academy or as guards in outlying facilities, and the last ten people become hunters.

Sara's in fifth place.

My immediate gut reaction is to tell her I'm not choosing the city anyway, so she can just take my spot. But that's not how the system works. I guess they never planned on someone choosing a job *other* than the safest option, because if someone picks another position, then only three students are allowed in a city. Two people got into Netiva City the year Adrian and Wick chose to be hunters.

"I don't want you to think that I'm like Emmerick or Naire, who would do anything to be in the city because they're scared," Sara goes on. My best friend leans in and lowers her voice, and I unconsciously copy her stance. "I haven't told you this, but you deserve to know. I was born inside Netiva City."

The words come out rushed, and Sara immediately sighs afterward as though a weight has lifted off her shoulders. I force a neutral expression, though a current of astonishment whips through me like a crack of thunder. I've never heard of anyone coming here from a city before. We learn little about how cities work since most people don't get the chance to live there. I can't help but wonder who would ever want to leave the city?

"It wasn't by choice," Sara adds hastily, eyeing me. *Wow, I'm a freaking open book.* "My parents are blacksmiths, and they've lived there for years. You need to show your worth to stay in a city. Every year they examine your input to the society, and if they deem you an unnecessary cog in the city's well-oiled machine, then you're kicked out so a more profitable person or family can take your place."

Her voice is bitter, a harsh edge I've never heard from her before. A small knot forms in my insides. "My brother was born seven years before me. The thing with children is that they are yet to provide for society, so the family has to have twenty-five percent more productivity for each child until they graduate and contribute themselves. My parents could *barely* meet that quota with Xavier. They taught him how to shape metal before he could walk.

"And then I was born. They struggled for two years until they were forced to oust one of their children." I can see where this is going, and my heart thumps painfully at what her next words will be.

She shrugs, looking off above my shoulder and blinking rapidly. Her hands continuously weave through the sheets in slow, methodical movements. After a deep breath, she returns my gaze with a weak smile. "It made sense that it would be me. Xavier was already contributing to the family; they would've had to wait a few more years before I could give them any results. I stayed at an orphanage outside the city until I was old enough to be shipped to Hallow Academy. Xavier received an apprenticeship at one of the blacksmithing schools, but I wasn't able to get in myself."

"Sara…" My voice trails off when she shakes her head, putting a warm hand on my knee. With the way her face lights up when saying Xavier's name, they must have been close before she left, even if it was only for two years. That Netiva City tore them apart makes me want to punch a hole through the wall.

"I know all of them are still upset about it. My parents write to me once every few months, and Xavier keeps me posted on everything happening there at least once a week.

I'm still part of the family, something they never forget to put in their letters. I promised them I would work hard enough to return to the city, to be a family again."

"Why didn't you tell me all this?" I rest my hand over hers, keeping my voice gentle. How had she kept this to herself for the past three years?

She shrugs again. "We don't talk about our past. It's kind of our thing. I don't know the details of what brought you to the academy, and that's okay. Our present lives are here."

I nod, immediately deciding to share my past with her once the trials are over. While I could do it now, rehashing my parents' deaths doesn't seem like the best thing to focus my mind. I make a mental promise not to forget. "I understand, but why are you telling me this now?"

Sara's resigned smile completely shatters my heart. "I was hoping you'd say hello for me when you get there. Let them know I gave it my all."

I'm shaking my head before she can finish her sentence. "No way. You're going to tell them yourself."

One eyebrow pops up in amusement. "I appreciate the passion, and I will fight for a spot in the final four, but I don't want to push Jared into fifth place, and the top three spots seem pretty secure. I don't think I could take any of you on in a true fight. Maybe I'll get lucky and Emmerick will mess up so bad he quits," she laughs, swinging her legs over my bed in preparation to stand. As much as she's joking around, I can still hear the raw pain in her voice.

"Sara—" I try again, but she's up and in the bathroom before I can say anything else. I punch my pillow softly with a small groan.

Working in the city has never been an option for me, but if I turn it down, then that's me throwing away the dream she's always wanted, but only I had access to. And I'd also be turning down her sweet request to meet her parents and explain to them what happened. While Sara knows of my aspirations to become a hunter, she must assume that I wouldn't pass up the opportunity of being in the city.

But I don't want to go to the city! That would mean leaving Adrian *and* my desire to be a hunter. I wrap myself up tightly in blankets and try to put my thoughts in order. Sara's my sister; I can't turn down her plea. I'm falling for Adrian, and he wants me to work with him, to be with him. For three years, I've been pushing myself to become the best hunter there ever was, to save people before their fate turned out like mine.

Sleepiness nags at me and I struggle to stay awake. I want to have this all figured out before I go to bed. My body has other plans, though, and I fall into unconsciousness quickly.

Chapter 28

Intricate Maneuvers

MEANDERING SLOWLY AROUND THE COURTYARD, I WATCH TWO young teens swing short swords, pretending to battle each other with full circle spins and high-pitched squeals. It almost brings a smile to my lips. Almost.

Frustratingly enough, Adrian couldn't make it to train one last time. More final preparation talk. And I got up hours before I usually do because I went to bed early last night, so I've been wandering the empty halls until human life started to show itself.

The worst part is that I still haven't figured out what I'm going to do.

I've never been good at making decisions. Each option bounces around in my head like hail against the academy's stone walls during a harsh storm. They all make sense. They all have their pros and cons. *Why is this so hard?*

Groaning, I rub my hands slowly up and down my exposed arms as I watch the sun leisurely creep above the walls. The slight chill in the air makes me regret leaving my jacket discarded by my bed this morning.

A shout of laughter draws my attention back to the sparring kids just in time to watch the shorter girl trip over her own feet, eating an early breakfast of grass and dirt. Sympathy rises within me as I watch her slam a fist into the ground in aggravation. She must be in her first year, her age and lack of knowledge showing.

The taller girl, sporting a mess of curly red hair, laughs as she helps the blonde to her feet.

"I'm never going to get this," the short blonde whines, throwing her sword behind her just inches from my feet.

"Come on, Clara, you need to try harder. Just do it like I did," snickers the redhead again, slapping Clara on the back. Her partner doesn't appear satisfied with the response.

"I'm giving it everything I've got, Ky! You're not showing me anything!"

"You twist your feet too much when you try to attack with your non-dominant side, which puts you in a perfect position to fall."

I blink, finding them both staring at me with wide eyes. It takes a second to realize the comment came from me. Another moment passes, and I scoop up the thrown sword, making my way over to them.

Neither responds as I find myself describing how to properly hold the hilt and the stance that allows for ease of motion. *What am I doing?* It's like my limbs have a mind of their own and they've taken control. But this girl, Clara, reminds me so much of myself. A lot of drive and conviction, but not quite hitting the mark.

If I can bestow even a little wisdom from everything I've learned these past few months, then maybe I can keep the cycle going. Adrian helped me when I was struggling. Now I can help others as well.

My passionate montage slowly withers when I flash my

eyes to my company's faces, both surprised and regarding me with confusion. I feel stupid in my fighting stance while they look at me like I've grown three extra sets of eyes.

"Sorry," I awkwardly mumble, straightening up. Flipping the wooden sword in my hand, I extend the hilt to Clara. She and Ky gawk for long enough that I begin to question if I somehow hit their heads during my demonstration.

Finally, Clara's hand slowly drifts up to wrap around the short sword in a weak enough grip that I don't dare let go of the other end. With my luck, it will fall right on her foot and I'll get in trouble for bullying. *On my last day here, too. Why did I think this was a good idea?*

And then Clara's mannerisms change.

Her fingers tighten, and she crouches to match the stance I was in previously, determination written all over her features. "Like this?"

Ky looks at her friend, back at me, and then copies Clara's posture. She tilts her head up to mine with open curiosity.

I grin.

———

We spend the next hour going over the basics of defense and attack...though mainly defense. It doesn't matter how hard you can hit if you get knocked down by a faster opponent with better defenses. I tell the kids as much.

They soak up every word like eager sponges until a few kids their age call for the girls to join them for breakfast. Ky groans, griping about how rude they are for interrupting our session.

Clara whips her head at me with imploring eyes. "Will you help us again?"

Sadness washes over me. "Today's my last day, unfortunately. But I know you both will do amazing."

Clara and Ky leave the courtyard with heavy feet, and I watch them with wistful eyes. I'm surprised by my feelings; how much I enjoyed teaching them, how happy their success made me feel. It throws a whole new wrench into my already chaotic thoughts.

"You're a much better teacher than Tala ever was," an accented voice laughs from behind me.

I whirl around in disbelief. I scan the field nervously, really hoping no one heard him say that. *A comment like that may send the crazy woman over the edge.*

The brave, *or stupid*, man in question saunters up to me from the security wing with a lighthearted smirk on his face.

"Come on, Blake," I say, grabbing his upper sleeve and dragging him back to where he came from.

"Is this really necessary?" He complains, but doesn't resist my tugging.

I lead us to the back of the courtyard, a few feet away from the security entrance. "Are you trying to get me killed?" I hiss, though a small smile tilts the side of my lips. It's hard to be mad at the guy who's currently sporting a toothy grin.

"I'm just calling it as I see it. Observant, remember? You probably taught them more in that session than they will ever learn from Tala. Well, if she was staying anyway. I guess attempted murder is frowned upon here," Blake shrugs casually, though his teasing smile never falters.

I almost step back, but hold my ground. How does he know about that? Does he know about the plans to get rid of the headmaster? I remember Adrian's words about it being a secret. And yet, with his expectant expression, there's no question he knows exactly whom Tala imposed her murder plans on.

"Are you alright, by the way?" He leans in with a concerned drop of his lips.

I ignore his question, still reeling from his previous statement. "How do you know this?"

He must take my avoidance as "yes, I've never felt better" because his mouth stretches into a secretive smile.

"Well, well, I'm surprised Adrian hasn't told you this juicy little detail. News arrived this morning. Devero Hallow will be gone after the trials tomorrow, replaced by the lovely Zypha Felvor."

"What?" I say, dumbfounded. How did the city decide so fast?

"Yep. It looks like the lord had been looking for a reason to get rid of Devero anyway, so this was the perfect opportunity."

"You still didn't answer my question," I state, resting my hip against the stone wall. Blake knows a lot of information for a random guard, especially since this was an undisclosed decision. "How do you know all this?"

"Because when Adrian becomes the head of security, I'll be his second in command."

"What?" I blurt out again, feeling like an idiot for not coming up with a better response, but he keeps shocking me.

So Zypha will become the next headmaster. I haven't had a lot of contact with her, but from what I've seen, she at least cares about the safety of the students. And Adrian's going to be the new head of security. I wonder how he feels about that.

Still, what confuses me the most is that Blake's even telling me all this. We aren't close, though I do like him. Yet I also liked Zachary, and he was just using me in case I was a Phoenix. Is Blake doing the same thing? "I'm only a student. Why are you telling me about this?"

Blake smiles and tilts his head forward. "I'm sure Adrian would have told you eventually, so it wasn't like you'd never find out. And like I said before, you're a much better fit here than Tala. I think we could become great friends if you were to stick around a while longer." He gives me a wink.

I laugh with relief. Blake wants nothing from me but a friendship. "I don't know what I'm doing just yet. Things have gotten a little…complicated."

"I'll say," Blake chuckles. "Think carefully. I'm sure you'll figure out what's best for you. Be warned that Zypha might approach you with an offer after the trials tonight, so I'd have an answer ready by then. In the meantime, good luck with the trials." He gives his usual salute before disappearing into the security wing.

As soon as he's gone, my smile fades. So, it's official that Tala and Hallow are leaving the school. I wonder what they're going to say when they figure out what's happening, what they're going to do. *Maybe they'll find a quaint cabin in a desolate part of the country and never bother anyone again. Wouldn't that be nice?*

I heave off the stone wall, striding toward the cafeteria. More than anything, I just want this day over with. I've never been good with decisions, and this one is wrecking me mentally. I'm astounded by how much I enjoyed showing those kids some stances and sword techniques, especially when they lit up once they perfected the form.

It was the first moment I could see myself as a professor. Adrian was right; there are many ways to help people. I could change the lives of future generations for the better, so they can go out and do good in the world. To help kids show kindness to others and confidently stride toward their future instead of marching with fear and dread. If I become a professor, maybe I could help kids become independent fighters, rather than mindless, ravenous soldiers.

Yeah, being an instructor might not be so bad.

"You should eat something, Cassie. You're going to need your strength," Sara insists at breakfast, biting into a piece of chicken.

I glare at the food warily. While I can't argue with her statement, my stomach feels like it's shriveled into a tense ball that'll reject anything it's given. While the usual porridge fills most of my plate, there is also some chicken and two entire peaches. Everything but the porridge is reserved solely for the seniors, as it's our last day in the academy.

In the corner of my vision, I see some of the younger kids watching us eat with greedy eyes. I have a strange urge to tell the kids that most of them won't be able to enjoy the feast when it's their time, anyway.

I slice up a small peach and stick a sliver in my mouth. Normally, fruit is my favorite part of any meal, but today it just tastes sour. I sense Sara's eyes on me, and I choke it down for her sake.

"Why are you so stressed? There's a zero percent chance that you'll fail or drop from your rank. And you don't even need that to be a hunter," Jared declares over a mouthful of chicken. He almost cried when we walked into the cafeteria earlier and smelled the meat.

Sara and I exchange a glance before she smiles mildly and looks away. Earlier this morning, she told me that if I want to be a hunter, she wouldn't hold it against me. I didn't respond because I didn't know what I wanted to do then.

Now I know exactly what I need to do. While I've made a

decision, the actual plan is a little trickier to accomplish. I don't want to stay at the top rank, not if that means I deny Sara her future goals.

So that leaves the incredibly delicate task of performing poorly enough that I drop past fourth place, but well enough that I don't fall to the bottom. Which means the stakes have been raised immensely for the trials. If my plan goes up in smoke and I spiral to last place, then I won't have the option to stay with Adrian. I'll have to leave his side, and the thought makes me shudder. *That's not an option.*

"I guess my body likes being nervous," I respond with a shrug.

As much as I want to tell both of them my plan and recent development with Adrian, I have a feeling Sara won't appreciate the risks I'm willing to take for her. She can't change my mind, so there's no point in stressing her out.

After breakfast, the class files into our usual gymnasium, though it looks completely different. We all stand at the doorway as we take in the new changes.

There are two enormous sparring mats placed in the middle of the gym. The center torches cast a reddish-yellow haze over the mats, creating an eerie atmosphere, especially since the professors extinguished the rest of the outer torches. There's a small white tent tucked in the corner, where I can see Nurse Dorna shuffling around it. *So we have a personal infirmary today? That's encouraging.*

Four instructors, including Raddo, Heather Bosts, and Tala, and three high-ranking guards line the front of the mats. Zypha and Adrian each stand beside a different mat. My eyes immediately slide to Adrian, who stands stiffly at the end of the row. Our eyes align, and their intensity helps to alleviate some of my anxiety. He gives me the ghost of a smile and I return it, trying to convey my feelings to him through my eyes.

Tala steps forward, and I fight a wince at her haggard appearance. Dark circles hang under her eyes, and her hair droops in a limp ponytail. Either she's having an extremely off day, or they've already told her she's fired. Both can explain why she appears in pain.

"Good morning, students," she shouts. I absentmindedly rub my ear. Too bad her voice hasn't lost its harshness. "We have finally arrived at the trials. There will be three of them: one in the morning, the next after lunch, and the last in the evening. Tonight, based on your rank and today's results, you will choose your career path moving forward. Whatever you choose will help humanity prosper in these trying times." The woman sounds like she's reciting from a script that she doesn't agree with.

"Our first event," she continues, "is sparring matches. You need to show your endurance and skill. Two matches will take place at a time, and you will spar with all of your colleagues."

I glance around as an undercurrent of unease ripples through the group. That's nineteen duels for everyone; I don't think we've ever done more than ten per person.

"Each round will last one minute. In that time, your goal is to show off as many combat techniques as you can. Your score will be based on that. There are also bonus points if you can knock your opponent unconscious or out of the ring within that minute." She gestures to the staff beside her. "There will be a mix of instructors and guards watching each ring. If you harm another student on purpose, a guard will step in, and you will receive a severe point reduction. Accidents happen, though, so Nurse Dorna is here with us today.

She will heal you enough so that you can proceed to the next round.

"Pretend you are out on the battlefield and fight through the pain. This is your chance to prove that you can survive the harsh world outside the walls. Refusing a match will mean your immediate failure, and you will be escorted out of the academy. Questions?" She blows her whistle after a brief silent period and calls out four names.

Her method is obvious as Emmerick and I step up on separate mats, facing the two lowest-ranking students. She wants these first matches over quickly. And, best of all, I won't be going up against Emmerick or Naire until my last two battles.

Lucky me.

Chapter 29

Relentless Retribution

I STARE INTO THE APPREHENSIVE FACE OF MY FIRST OPPONENT, the girl who fell to last place when I jumped up the ranks. Astrid curves inward on herself, the slouch highlighting her petite form. I hear Emmerick crack his knuckles beside me, and I know he's planning on ending his match quickly. My stomach rolls at the idea of hurting a girl who still looks fifteen. *It's fine. I don't have to attack her. I'm trying to drop my rank, anyway.*

I glance up at Adrian. He's supervising Emmerick's ring, but his eyes are on me. He gives me an almost indiscernible nod before scrutinizing Emmerick with barely shielded contempt. I'm not sure if he's wishing me good luck or encouraging me to do what I must.

Tala blows her whistle to start the match and Astrid springs at me. I easily block her weak attacks. Every motion of her body screams what her next move will be, and I take advantage of it, knocking away punches before she can fully release them. As we fight, I can't help but wonder how she's gotten this far, until I remember I used to be lower than her in rank. The thought slows my aggressive blocking, allowing her to show off combinations and hopefully earn more points.

In my peripheral vision, I notice Emmerick hit his opponent with an uppercut that sends the boy off his feet and crashing to the ground. The poor boy, Carter, doesn't stir. Adrian steps in to carry the unconscious student to the nurse.

I hope the 'bonus points' aren't more than what he would have gotten if he showed more techniques. I grit my teeth, realizing that losing my rank gives the first-place position back to that meathead.

A kick clips my side, drawing me back to my match. Astrid's pale gray eyes are bright with a determination that squeezes my heart. I can empathize with her stubbornness in not giving up. We dance around the ring, showing off a wide range of attacks. We stop when Tala's shrill whistle pierces the air. Astrid bends over, gasping for breath. *Eighteen more matches to go.*

As I step off the mat, Sara grabs my arm. "You're going to drop in rank if you're the only person not ending these matches quickly."

I brush her off with a smile. *That's the plan, Sara.* Even though I know that, the other students' scorn over my supposed weakness makes my jaw clench. I blindly watch the next matches, stewing up a way to fight more fiercely without actually doing damage. A simple jab to the temple won't cause much pain, but it will still knock my opponent out. If I finish every other fight early, then that should be enough to execute my plan without going overboard.

By the time my name is called again, my resolve to finish this next fight has strengthened.

It crumbles when I face my opponent. Carter, Emmerick's previous opponent, has his jaw wrapped in white cloth, which must have broken in the last match. He steps up to me, his sky-blue eyes tinged with weariness. I bite my lip. *How can I humiliate this boy for a second time in two rounds?* The thought rattles loudly in my head and weighs heavily on my heart.

The match is over when the minute is up. Carter shakes my hand, relief etched on all his features. His expression lightens my dread. *I made the right decision.*

The next eight rounds are just as simple and without bloodshed. As I wait for my name to be called again, my eyes frequently linger on Adrian. He observes his ring with his normal steeliness, and I smile at his strength. Did he hold back or give it his all when he was in his trials?

I glance at the tent and count four wounded students being fussed at by Nurse Dorna, ranging from an excessively bleeding nose to a fractured leg, and the idea of sending more classmates to her fills my stomach with queasiness. I refocus on stretching my arm, slowly moving it in a circle.

I haven't gotten an injury yet, but I know that can't last forever. Sara flutters around the mat, launching fast jabs that Chelsea promptly dodges. Their movements are smooth, twisting like willow trees with each offensive strike.

With my gaze settled firmly on the skirmish, Jared walks up, sits beside me, and rubs his palms together. He inhales deeply, and I almost comment on his willingness to breathe in the toxic fumes of sweat and blood. But his seriousness, so unlike him, sobers my humor.

"You can't throw every match, Cassie. We're only going to look worse with each fight," he says solemnly, nodding at Carter and his bound jaw.

"Even if I drop a few ranks, that's fine by me," I reply, hinting at my plans, but even as I say it, I know I can't keep going like this. The first four can choose the city, and the next six can choose either security detail or instruction. With my luck, I'll end up in eleventh place.

More than that, it's not like me to go *this* easy on my opponents, similar to how Adrian went easy on me when we first started training. It's demeaning. I sigh and nod to Jared, who gives my shoulder a brief squeeze. *I can finish these fights without seriously hurting anyone if I can force them out of the ring*, I tell myself.

I'm able to end five of the next seven matches swiftly, though not without earning a few bruises in the process. I hobble off the mat and lower myself to the floor, my right thigh aching with every step from Amber's bony elbows. My palm rubs the sore spot until I give up on easing the pain, deciding to rest my forehead on the coarse fabric of my pants instead. At least I haven't lost a fight, so my score should still be passable.

Feeling the weight of a gaze on my skin, my head lifts and I lock eyes with Adrian, who's frowning in concern. He looks torn, like he's debating coming over to check on me or remaining at his post. I give a thumbs-up and a smile to show I'm alright. A moment elapses before he pulls his eyes off me and focuses on the students in his ring.

My eyes peer sideways at the nurse's station and then around at my classmates. Most are nursing minor wounds, like me. Only those unconscious or sporting broken bones are permitted in the tent. *The instructors want us to feel the brunt of these fights*.

Tala barks my name, and I stand, shaking my leg out. Sara's name is also called, and we stare at each other for a split second before walking into the ring. It isn't like we didn't know we'd end up together at some point, but the thought of us sparring still bugs her. Our eyes connect again and a silent message passes between us.

Our attacks are fast and hard, but each one misses by a fraction of an inch. We skip around each other like our bodies are weightless, striking with expert precision. When the match ends, we laugh and hug in a tight embrace. While we may not have gotten the bonus points, I bet we scored a ton with our combos. I tug Sara off the mat and past Tala's sneering mouth.

My fight with Jared goes similarly. We made a bet to see who could throw the most techniques, and by his unusually focused face, I'm winning. I feign to my left and hurl my leg up in a roundhouse kick. He spins away with a punching combo. Sweat drips into my eyes and I hastily swipe it away, sucking in a ragged breath.

"Tired already?" Jared taunts in between blows. I can see his muscles bunch from the strain of his hits, but he halts the blows inches before they land on me.

"Nothing but a light warmup," I respond, making my point by gently swatting his neck with a backfist. The whistle blows before he can retaliate.

Jared chuckles, giving me a side hug as we weave through the small crowd toward Sara, who has positioned herself in the back. Each student stands alone in varying degrees of exhaustion. She smiles when we reach her and hands us our refilled water bottles.

"Thanks," I say gratefully, chugging more than half of it. The cool liquid pours down my throat, and a soft sigh of relief escapes me.

My muscles cry in objection as I drop my bottle and touch my toes in a long stretch. I keep reminding myself that I only have two more matches left, and then the first trial will be over. *Of course, these next two will be the worst of them.*

Rising from my stance, my gaze falls on Naire. She's already waiting in the ring. Her eyes gleam with malice, one hip protruding with a cockiness that oozes brighter than the torches. The wicked grin on her face tells me exactly who her next opponent will be.

I straighten my shoulders and meet her in the ring, ignoring Adrian as I glide past him. This will be the first match he's judged for me, and my nerves only increase at the thought. It'll be terrible if I get my butt handed to me in front of him after all the training he's given me.

Our arms graze as I advance, and it sends a pulse of heat blooming across my chest. Even though I keep my eyes on the enemy, I feel his gaze on my back. I get a whiff of his normal scent of fresh earth and trees that threatens to make my head spin. Pushing further into the ring, I deeply inhale the sweat and blood around me. I choke back a gag, but it at least helps to clear my mind of Adrian.

My stomach clenches when I look back up at Naire, and I fight the urge to throw myself at her like a feral cat. After everything she's put me through, seeing her smug smile taunting me, I tremble with the desire to show her how much I've learned. She and Emmerick are going to find out just how badly they messed up when they left me for dead.

Naire bends her knees and leans forward, itching to start the fight. I wait for her insults, but she keeps quiet, her eyes cold and sharp. I curl my fingers tightly and wait for the signal. *This is one match I don't mind ending as fast as possible.*

The whistle goes off, and we both spring forward, narrowly missing the other's assault. My upper lip pulls up in a silent snarl as I block strikes meant to debilitate me. I jump away from a heel that would snap my shin if it landed.

So much for accidental injuries.

Naire isn't just going for a knockout, she wants me to suffer. I grind my teeth and dodge her heavy blows. Her vicious attacks leave little room for me to go on the offensive, so I bide my time and wait for an opening.

I feel Adrian's eyes on me, along with the rest of the class. Besides Adrian and my friends, everyone's hunger for blood-lust sends an uncomfortable tingle through my aching body. I'm not sure which side they want to see bleed more. Taking a deep breath, I try not to let their gazes distract me.

My feet are less steady than I'm used to. They drag with fatigue, betraying me with their loud scrapes against the floor in a proclamation of my enervation. The constant sparring matches have caught up with me at the worst possible time. I know it, and soon I'm sure Naire will know it, too. I can't help the thoughts that flood my head as the match continues without excitement. *What if I don't pass the trials? Or if I don't get a high enough score? I'll be separated from Adrian forever.*

My eyes shift to him of their own accord, and I scan the hard planes of his face, his full lips, his pitch-black hair that falls into vivid blue eyes. It takes my breath away every time I look at him, and I'm hit with the realization that I can't bear to lose him.

I suck in a soft breath. *When did Adrian become so important to me?*

As I'm scouring his features, his eyes flash in warning past my shoulder. I silently curse myself for getting distracted and spin around just in time to block a punch with my forearms. What I don't see is the second fist that follows, landing solidly on my ribs.

I stagger away before she can continue raining down attacks. My breathing comes in ragged pants, and my ribs protest with each inhale, though I don't think she cracked any of them.

Naire shoots me a smug smile that burns my insides, and rage crawls over my body like an unpleasant second skin. It pushes adrenaline through my veins and the pain fades away to allow room for blinding, all-consuming *hatred*. Hatred for the girl who tried to kill me. Hatred for the professor who urged her to do it.

Their determination might have been enough to make it happen if not for my sheer obstinacy. I want to laugh at the absurdity of it all. I always believed that my one true enemy was the Obsidian, but it seems everything and everyone wants me dead.

Naire deserves to be *punished* for her sins. There needs to be *justice*.

My spine snaps straight and something inside me splinters.

Heat overtakes the white-hot anger at a frightening pace, like a wildfire engulfing a forest, and ignites a path through my body. Naire must note the change because her twisted sneer falls away, her black eyes shimmering with unease. I blink, my mind adjusting to this new burn, this overwhelming hunger for righteousness. All my thoughts dissipate, and the only thing that matters is disciplining this person full of sin.

The enemy's fist comes flying toward my face and reminds me of my current situation. I blink again. Centimeters before her knuckles touch my cheek, I step to the side and grab her wrist with a speed that is almost faster than I can keep up with. Before I can comprehend what I'm doing, my body takes over and I squeeze her wrist hard, feeling bones fracture under my grip. Broken snippets of vicious satisfaction float through my fog at her strangled scream. Gasps and shouts follow behind me, but I don't let my focus waver.

I inhale the sinner's fear while exhilaration pools in my lower abdomen and radiates through the rest of my being, tingling my extremities with demented euphoria. I tug on her arm until she stumbles close enough for me to wrap my hand around her small, vulnerable throat. The muscles aligning her neck spasm as my fingers flex with the irresistible temptation to silence this foul creature, my relentless grip refusing to let her swallow.

"You're not as tough without your drugs," I spit at her, tightening my hold. A garbled breath is the only response.

I rear back the elbow of my free hand, curling my fingers together, and envision all the bones I want to break. How I want her face to end up after I'm done with her, so wrought with deformities that not even Serous can fix them all.

My teeth grind together as I throw a punch with all the power of an exploding sun. The trapped criminal's eyes close in resignation, and her body becomes limp. Power of limitless control washes over me in complete and utter waves of pure bliss, entrancing my capability to think. The fire continues to rage inside me, burning under my skin and urging me to take action. She deserves this for everything she has done. She brought this upon herself. Retribution is here.

I am the judge, and she is *guilty*.

Chapter 30

Painted Black With Abhorrence

"Stop."

It's as though someone dumped ice water on my over-heated body. The deep, commanding voice shatters my enclosed feelings like glass. A voice I would recognize anywhere. That, even as a hollow frame filled with hate and rage, makes my breath stutter and I come back to myself. I have no idea how, but I'm able to halt my punch before it hits the mark. All the emotions rush into me as fast as they left. They eagerly seize my throat, similar to what I'm currently doing to my opponent, and I choke against the onslaught.

Releasing Naire, I plummet to my knees. My wide eyes stare in horror as she rolls on the ground in agony, clutching her red throat with her one good hand. The marks on her neck, in the exact shape of my fingers, are speckled with painful-looking blisters. *How hard was I gripping?*

The cocoon of silence is gone, and nothing can stop the bombardment of chatter that echoes off the walls in a cacophony of shock and disbelief.

Naire curses my name through her coughs, unable to muster her usual amount of hostility.

My mouth flails desperately as I struggle to respond. My gaze lifts to meet Adrian's, and any sense of an apology falls from my lips. Shame, intense and unwavering in its ability to pull me under, rises like bile in my esophagus. Adrian observes me with a soft compassion that is undeserved and unwanted.

How can he look at me like that after what I just did? I turn inward, unable to move, as Heather Bosts assists Naire to the nurse's station.

Exposed on the floor, I half-expect Tala to argue my expulsion and throw me to the fields for intentionally harming another student during the trials. Not just harming, for this wouldn't be the first time someone got caught in a chokehold. It's the fact that I wasn't stopping, that I was planning on rearranging her face while also continuing to cut off her oxygen supply.

But Tala only blows her whistle and calls for the next match. Maybe she understands I can torture myself better than anything she could come up with, or maybe this has more to do with her not being allowed to get directly involved with the trials.

As two more students shuffle to the edge of the sparring mat, my mind processes dully that I have to get up. My legs, however, are lead blocks cemented to the mat, begging me to collapse to the ground and forget my loss of control.

Move, I growl to myself. Still, I'm a statue. Black flashes in front of me, and I reluctantly raise my eyes to Adrian, who's walking forward. Another bout of pain stabs my heart at his concern. Fragments of my savagery continue to run through my mind and, embarrassingly enough, tears blur my vision.

Tala's tight grip on his shoulder halts his progress, and she snarls at him to focus on the next match. Blue eyes narrowed, face contorted with indecision, he looks seconds away from ignoring her command.

While he's debating, Sara pops up behind me and tugs under my armpits, dragging me back to the corner where Jared anxiously rubs his hands together. The next match starts, though the room is significantly quieter. The weight of my classmates' stares presses firmly against my skin, the force a boulder against my trembling shoulders.

Zypha stops us before we reach Jared. "Cassie," the head of security says in a low voice, one hand resting on the hilt of her sheathed sword. Her green eyes bore into mine, though she's not as angry as I thought she'd be. "I don't want to, but next time I will be obligated to take disciplinary action. Please be careful."

I give a jerky nod and continue past her.

"Are you hurt, Cassie?" Jared's voice drifts down to me as I sink to the ground, my feet too numb to stay upright.

"No," I reply emotionlessly. Once I answer, I'm reminded of the pain in my chest, a faint ache that usually represents a cracked rib. Pushing my palm against it absentmindedly, I bite my lip hard until the tears subside.

Focus on the pain. I will not unravel here.

After a few painstakingly long seconds, the crowd loses interest in my immovable form. Jared and Sara also leave me be, but still hover close by in case they're needed. Their whispers float over to me, soft questions about whether the match will drop my points and where my ranking will be after this.

Their words are a rod of metal stabbing into the back of my head, and I lean against my drawn knees, shoving my forehead into the limbs until it throbs. I'd forgotten about that rule and suddenly, fervently wish I hadn't gone so easily in my previous matches. There's no way I'll be able to stay as a professor now. *Not that I should anyway. I'm no better than Tala.*

I take a deep breath, reveling in how the movement twinges my side. *Calm, calm, calm.* A few more relaxing breaths clear my mind, and the pain fades.

Finally, I can think.

I disregard my emotions to focus on what happened. Detaching myself from the fight, I review it over and over in my head, grasping at anything that could help me uncover what happened. I know I was angry, but I've never been angry with *this* being the result. I remember the fire that washed over me, the way I had no control. My hands *wanted* to hurt Naire.

My overwhelming bloodlust frightens me until I recall that I, during the crazed state, never considered Naire as a person, but as my enemy, a criminal, a sinner.

I was a predator, dead set on justice. But what does that mean? What triggered it? Will it happen again? The unanswered questions leave an acidic taste in my mouth.

Lost in thought, I don't notice Sara until she jerks on my arm. I swirl to her with a blank expression.

"It's time for your last match with Emmerick." Sara's voice is cautious, questioning. Even if I want to skip this fight, I can't, not without forfeiting the trials. But with Zypha's warning, one more misstep and they may still kick me out anyway. I nod to her and smile, demonstrating that I'm fine.

At least I hope I am.

As I tread the measured steps toward the mat Emmerick is already stretching in, it only takes a second to figure out that Adrian will oversee this match as well.

Great.

I refuse to meet Adrian's gaze, unsure of what would happen to the little box I shoved all my negative emotions into. I fold my hands together to hide their shaking and step onto the mat. How funny it is to think, after everything that has happened, I'm afraid for Emmerick's life.

Though Emmerick doesn't seem frightened in the slightest. If anything, his jumpy attitude and grizzly smile show just how *unafraid* he is. Maybe he believes this is his best chance for revenge after our last challenge.

I bend my knees, ready for an attack at any moment.

However, when the whistle blows, his demeanor quickly morphs and he relaxes, his flinty gaze following my every action. I shift my weight as though my ankles will break if I stand too still, but otherwise don't budge from my starting spot. With the fear coursing through me, I'm honestly skeptical I'll be able to attack at all. The only thing I can think about is how I felt getting ready to hit Naire.

I will not slip back into that frame of mind again. Calm, calm, calm.

Emmerick doesn't wait any longer than a breath before he launches himself at me. I sidestep his attacks, dodging and weaving with fluid grace. Through it all, I urge myself to throw some combo moves, any technique, to gain points for the trial, but my arms remain glued to my sides. How can I fight back when there's a huge possibility I could lose control again? My stomach rolls at the spiraling thoughts that carve their way through my eroding mind, painting it black with abhorrence.

One stumble is all Emmerick needs to fly forward and slam his fist into my ribcage, on the exact spot Naire had hit in our match. The shockwave of pain that follows suit is enough to jar me from my descent into madness, and I find myself again, staggering back before his leather boot can find a new home against my intestines. I flinch away from him while simultaneously tossing a kick that he deftly swats away.

"Come on, Cassie," Emmerick grumbles. "I expected this to be fun." He guffaws at my timid strikes, and I want to join in.

What a pitiful mess I've turned into.

Still, I'm grateful he pulled me back from the edge, and some of my usual determination seeps into my bones. I continue to fight back, though my quivering muscles feel like they've lost all strength, and the dance begins anew.

Now, with my thoughts locked away and my full attention on my partner, we battle it out evenly, both unable to get the upper hand. A sharp, stabbing sensation in my left side accompanies every inhale, and I'm positive Emmerick broke a rib.

If I didn't know any better, I would guess he deliberately aimed for the same spot Naire hit earlier. I breathe out harshly at the thought, allowing myself a small amount of reluctant appraisal. It seems I may have underestimated the brute once again.

Before I can place pressure against the wound, his gnashing teeth, clinking together in a warrior's cry, signal another advance. His meaty fist slams into my ear and I crumple to the ground, black dots swirling in my vision. Thick, strong fingers locking around my bicep alert me to Emmerick's presence, and I blindly twist my feet up to wrench out of his hold. I crawl away, counting in my head as my sight slowly returns to me.

One, two, three. Emmerick's feet thud closer.

Four, five, six. His face swims into view.

Seven, eight, nine. He's right on top of me.

No time for ten. Cursing softly, I scramble to my feet. I can feel the anger starting to simmer. Its presence scares me, as if my fury will unleash itself instantly on Emmerick and I won't have the power to stop it. *Relax, Cassie, and focus!*

A shrill whistle echoes through the room, and I immedi-ately slouch. I rub my temple, pushing away the headache brewing between my eyes. But no pain can take away the surmounting relief, a sweet triumph that coats my heart, knowing I had no compulsion to murder Emmerick.

Then another, stronger reassurance enters my mind. *I passed the first trial. I may have dropped back to my comfy position in last place, but there are still two more trials to increase a level…or ten.*

I involuntarily spin around, my eyes seeking Adrian to share in my success. Forgetting in my haste to be through with the fight that Emmerick is incapable of playing nice. I hear him rush toward my back, akin to a wild animal adamant on running me over, one I won't be able to dodge, and I desperately search for Adrian.

But he's gone.

Suddenly he's behind me, thumping Emmerick's chest with the heel of his palm with enough force to knock the oaf backward and onto his butt.

"I'm not sure you heard the whistle." His voice is a deadly quiet that makes everyone standing near the mat involuntarily step away, everyone except me and Tala. His hands hang loose at his side and I can't see his face, but his tense shoulders give away his casual façade. "The match is over."

Adrian radiates enough authority to send Emmerick cowering, but it soothes me like a warm blanket. The safety of his presence nearly turns my legs to liquid, and I fight the urge to slump against him.

More than the desire to coil into him is the impulse to stand as his equal. So I rise to my full height and step up beside Adrian, keeping my face impassive, staring at Emmerick with my arms crossed. Nothing can hide the fire burning in my eyes or the relief lining my features. The bout with Naire feels like a distant nightmare now, but it still wreaks havoc in the corner of my thoughts.

Officer Zypha steps in with a placating smile. "Emmerick, I think it's time for you to take a break. Go cool off before you break any rules. I'm sure you don't want that, right?"

Emmerick clambers to his feet and sulks off as Tala blows her whistle a second time. I still don't meet Adrian's gaze, though I can feel his eyes on me. I slide through the crowd easily enough since most retreat with varying shades of fear or contempt and place myself next to Sara and Jared.

"Congrats on passing the first trial," Tala deadpans with a weak, celebratory gesture. "It seems everyone is moving on to the next trial. While we calculate the scores, go eat lunch and meet us at the front gate in two hours."

"Front gate?" Sara whispers, voicing my confusion. *Are we leaving the academy for the next trial?*

We file out of the gym, rubbing different parts of our bodies that are sure to bruise. I consider running up to my room to grab my Serous bottle for the presumed broken rib, but a tiny, deep part of me wants to feel the pain. Similar to the pain I inflicted on Naire.

I watch the front of our class march through the cafeteria doors, and the idea of eating makes my stomach riot. As does the fact that I'll be sitting with Naire and have to endure the probing eyes of everyone else. And the questions Sara and Jared are bound to ask.

"Hey, guys, I'm not feeling too hungry," I blurt out, biting my lip as my two friends pivot to me with comically similar faces of consternation. "I think I'm going to take a nap before the next trial."

"What? You barely ate any breakfast!" Sara says in a hushed shout. The three of us stopped in the middle of the walkway, causing the other students to shuffle around while muttering rude comments.

"I'll swing by and grab something before we start the next trial. Don't worry, I just didn't sleep very well and need some pick-me-up energy!" I laugh, leaning in to pat them on their backs before heading toward my bedroom. I glance behind me twice.

The first time, I give my hesitating friends a shooing motion and another grin.

The second time, seeing the hallway empty, I take a quick lap around the courtyard and slink into the garden.

Settling onto my bench, I let my head fall against the wall and close my eyes, blowing out a slow breath. Taking a nap is a fantastic idea, but I know there's no way I'll be able to sleep.

Not in my current mental state.

How did I lose myself so much when fighting Naire? Never have I felt...not out of control, more like being controlled by something else. That's the scariest part of all this. I had *no idea* I was capable of that.

If I don't know how or why that happened, how will I ever learn to master it? I don't want to snap and hurt someone, or live in fear of that happening at some random moment. What if I'm hugging Sara and I get angry and break her neck?

Ugh, don't think that. I swallow forcefully against the thick lump forming at the mental image.

After over an hour, agonizingly close to meeting for the next trial, I'm no closer to a solution. I pick a leaf off the vines behind me and slowly tear it into slivers. *Maybe I should drop out and work in the fields where there's less stress. If I'm alone harvesting tomatoes, at least that will keep people safe.*

A small brown package appears under my nose. "Hungry?"

Chapter 31

Not Advice, a Warning

WITH A YELP, I FALL OFF THE BENCH, LANDING HARD ON MY right side. For a second, I lay frozen, blinking at the ants traveling through the cracks in the stone path. *Did I really just do that?*

Scrambling up, my eyes flick to searing sapphire ones and I frown, ignoring my racing heart at his ghost of a smile. He's stretched out on the other side of the bench, still holding up that mysterious rectangular package. *How was he able to sit there without me noticing him?*

My cheeks heat at my obliviousness. While Adrian can move like a shadow, I should have sensed him. "What are you doing here?" I ask, slowly sinking back into my seat.

Adrian shrugs, balancing the wrapped box on his knee. He laces his fingers together on his stomach, looking so relaxed that my fingers itch to push him off the bench. *He shouldn't be so calm around me. I tried to kill someone.* "Your friends asked me to check up on you."

My thoughts evaporate in surprise. So I hadn't fooled Sara and Jared earlier. They still knew something was wrong, and knowing my feelings, they asked Adrian to come here instead of themselves. *Have I told them lately how much their friendship means to me?* "Aren't you busy? Prepping for the next trial, that is."

He tilts his shoulders again, not the least bit concerned. "Zypha can manage without me for a minute."

I shake my head, both touched and annoyed at his concern. "I'm fine."

"Okay, but I'm here if you want to talk." His voice is so tender, it makes me want to bawl.

I swivel to him, burying the feeling under anger. "You mean about when I almost killed Naire? When I lost control of myself?" I look away with a strangled laugh. "Tala's been right all along. I *am* a monster."

A few traitorous tears leak out and I scrub them away quickly. There it is. The thought that's been dancing around my mind for the past two hours, but unable to be voiced aloud.

"You're not a monster," Adrian replies just as hotly. I don't respond, my glare burning holes in the plants ahead of me. "Cassie, look at me."

He waits until I begrudgingly tilt my head toward him. Those bright eyes are blazing, his jaw set in determination. "No one is going to fault you for what you did, especially those who know what they did to you. She deserves a lot more than what you gave her."

My shoulders twist away from him. "I don't care if she deserved it or not. The fact is, I went berserk. I couldn't stop myself, and I didn't want to. I wanted to see her suffer." Biting my lip to keep the tears at bay, I focus on a lazily swirling leaf in the pond. "That's not me."

"I've lost control before, too, and it wasn't pretty," Adrian sighs, shifting his weight without the package on his knee so much as wobbling. "When you lose yourself, there are two things that can happen. The first is that you let the moment define you, take over, until you are nothing but the darkest parts of yourself. Like Tala, like Naire." Delicate fingers graze my chin, and I let the pressure guide my face back to him. "Or you can acknowledge the fear and pain that follows, but choose to rise above it. To conquer it. Like me." A small smile. "Like you."

"But how do I know I won't go crazy again? How will I stop it?"

Adrian's expression shifts to thoughtful as his fingers slowly trace my jaw, then my cheek, creating a pathway of tiny electric shocks. My breath hitches at the sensation, and I fight the urge to lean into his touch. "Because you're strong. The very fact that you don't want to lose control means you won't. You know what it's like now, so you will be ready if it ever happens again."

"I wish it were that easy," I respond, almost breathlessly. Adrian's unwavering faith in me is immense and frightening, only highlighting the exorbitant uncertainty I have in myself. He helped me again today with Emmerick. I wonder what would have happened if he hadn't intervened. Would I have gone all murder psycho on Emmerick as well?

But Adrian, the man who embodies restraint, confessed that he had lost control once.

"What happened to you?" I ask, all too happy to switch the subject back to him. His hand drops from my face, though he doesn't move away.

"After Wick died, I—" he takes a deep breath, "I wasn't in the greatest place. You could say I went on a rampage. No Obsidian within a mile of me survived." Adrian's lips distort into a smirk, though his eyes solemnly scan my face, either waiting for my reaction or for me to stop him.

I keep my features even, an encouraging smile in place, and wait for him to continue.

He gives a light exhale of resignation. "When Zypha heard what I was doing, she and a few guards tracked me down to retrieve me. Something about how I was too valuable to let me throw my life away, but I wasn't paying attention when she was justifying it. I had let myself be swallowed by my grief. I didn't want to stop my killing spree, so I didn't go with them quietly. The five of them could barely restrain me, and no one walked away without some sort of injury. Yet Zypha never held it against me, nor did the other guards. And slowly, I found myself again." The hard edge of his smile eases. "You're already doing much better than I did with it."

I almost argue with him that losing someone like a brother is a lot worse than what I went through, that he's so much stronger than I will ever be. I don't, though. Adrian would just argue the point back, and we'd get nowhere.

So instead, I rest my head on his shoulder. "Your story gives me strength, Adrian. Thank you."

We sit in comfortable silence, listening to the soft chirps of birds and the muffled sounds of people walking past the garden. I can make out a few voices, all from my class. They must be heading to the front gate, which means my moment with Adrian will be over soon.

While I'm searching for something to say, anything that will let me hear his voice again, my eyes fall on his knee.

"What's that?" I ask, pulling my head up.

Adrian follows my gaze and gives a short hum, as if remembering the reason he came here. Long, nimble fingers pinch the package before dropping it into my open palm. Stiff cloth swathes the rectangle, and I tear it open carefully, finding a brown block of compacted grain.

"It's food." Adrian chuckles at my confused expression. "Bars manufactured for those who either don't have time or cannot get a decent meal. It's got enough nutrients to sustain you for up to six hours, though it's not what you'd call gourmet. A staple in every hunter's diet."

I warily sniff the odorless bar before my rumbling stomach forces me to take a bite. "Oh man, this is some seriously awful stuff," I mutter through my full mouth. I've tasted dirt before, *not by choice*, and that was better than this. Still, my teeth tear into the bar for another bite. I hadn't noticed how hungry I was until the food hit my empty stomach.

"You get used to it."

I chew methodically, keeping my mind distracted from the tough crunch of every bite with one eye on Adrian. "Thank the universe I won't have to eat this every day."

"It's not that—" He pauses, his eyes snapping to mine.

I nod at his expression, full of surprise and hesitancy and hope. "I think this academy needs a little more of my optimistic and bubbly personality. The Obsidian wouldn't fully appreciate it like my students would."

"No, I don't think they would," Adrian says, matching my mirth. In an instant, his expression sobers again. "Are you sure? I'd like you to stay, but I also don't want my wishes to influence you."

I cross my legs and wave my hands dramatically, brown crumbs flying everywhere. "Oh no, you weren't a factor at all. In fact, I forgot about you entirely when deciding."

I've never seen Adrian smile so wide, and I forget to breathe, my throat clogging with emotion. *No, I'm definitely not going to have any regrets.*

A whistle cuts through the air, sounding harsh enough that it could only be Tala. The call briefly sends me back to the previous trial, images flashing of my fight with Naire and

Emmerick. *I will not allow myself to lose control again, no matter what we do in the next trial.* My mantra helps mitigate the pain of my memories.

Adrian stands, eyes toward the garden's exit, and I hastily follow suit. I gobble down the rest of the bar, finding it tastes better in big chunks, and roll the cloth inside my fist. There aren't many compost piles outside the cafeteria, so I don't know what to do with my wrapper. I'll just have to find some way to use it.

We round the corner and follow the path toward the front gate. Up ahead, my class, the same instructors, and extra guards all stand with their faces to us, their expressions fluctuating between boredom and irritation. Jared and Sara are whispering to each other with matching grins, and I know I'll be getting some jokes thrown my way soon.

Tala is sporting her usual murderous expression at the sight of Adrian and me together. Her arms wrap around her midsection like vines choking a tree, and barely contained rage emanates from her form. It suddenly makes me wonder why Headmaster Hallow would be crazy enough to allow her involvement in the trials. He either truly doesn't care about the safety of the students, or something else is holding her back from another murder attempt.

Then I notice Adrian walking a fraction of an inch ahead of me, the profile of his face tense as he stares Tala down.

Ah, I think, speeding up to equal our bodies again. *It isn't something holding her back, it's someone.* I'm about to tell him off and explain how I can handle this myself when he speaks in a soft, slightly rushed tone.

"You need to be careful in this trial."

I eye him sideways and smirk. "I thought you said you wouldn't give me advice."

"This isn't advice, it's a warning." He slows our pace minutely, an adjustment only Tala catches.

"A warning about Tala? Trust me, I know."

He shakes his head, which draws my eyebrows up. "This is the most dangerous trial, the one that's the least supervised."

I open my mouth to question him further, but Sara slides up beside me, silently looping her arm through mine and dragging me away from Adrian. Before I can take a step away, his hand briefly wraps around mine.

"This can be reused for another meal," he whispers.

Frozen with heat rushing to greet my cheeks, I feel his calloused fingertips brush against my palm with a gentleness that beguiles his formidable strength. Belatedly, after his hand slides away and Sara helps my feet move again, I realize he was taking the wrapper from me.

I glance back, locking eyes with Adrian. The cloth is gone, presumably stuffed in some pocket. His frown radiates concern, but after a second, he blinks and heads toward the rest of the instructors. He plants himself behind the woman I had been trying very hard to ignore.

It's now impossible to ignore Tala when absolute fury displays itself clearly across her face. She looks remarkably close to blowing up into a raging inferno that will take everyone down with her.

No wonder Sara pulled me away from Adrian, and no wonder Adrian's muscles are taut as he waits for her to make a move.

As much as my skin prickles over Adrian's protectiveness sometimes, I'm grateful for his unmistakable presence and the power that settles over whatever room he walks into. I doubt anyone could stop Tala but him if she attacks.

Our gazes meet, and my shoulders stiffen. I didn't think

someone could possess such undiluted anger. *She's going to strike.* I slowly slide one foot back into a casual sparring stance and cock my head to the side.

If she wants a fight, then I'm ready.

I itch to smile, or blink, but I fear any reaction on my part will set her off. While I wouldn't mind watching Adrian take her down, I'm afraid that somehow this will be my fault and I'll get in trouble for instigating a fight. So I keep my face neutral and wait.

A minute passes. Not enough time for anyone to notice anything strange, but enough to drive me crazy. *I can't keep my eyes open forever.*

Just before the stinging in my eyes becomes too much, Tala moves, but not in the direction I thought she would go. She steps back and swallows, seeming to suppress her hate with that one small motion.

The tension rushes out of me and I sag my shoulders.

"That was intense," Sara whispers to my right, grabbing my hand. *So she noticed.* I tilt my head toward her in response, squeezing her fingers.

"The second trial will be unique because it takes place outside the academy. There's an abandoned town just north of here. Close enough that we can walk without too much of a risk. I will explain further when we get there." Her voice is rigid and clipped, tight enough that anything more may send her over the edge. Tala spins around, marching through the sliver of opening between the main doors. The rest of us wait for the doors to finish being pulled open before following her.

I note her twitchy movements. Since I'm closer to the border of the group, it gives me an almost clear view of her side profile. Between the trees, I think I see her lips moving, but no one is near her. I frown, my brows knitting together. *Who is she talking to?*

"Are you okay?" Jared's voice floats from behind me, and I hastily remove my gaze from Tala to face my friends.

"With what?" I ask, not sure which part of this spectacular morning he's referring to.

"Well, the whole thing with Naire." Sara retorts, and my lips pinch at her hesitant intro.

The female in question leads the rest of the pack, almost as furious as Tala. While I'm doing my best to ignore Naire, I know her wrath is directed at me. She's one of the major reasons I skipped the cafeteria for lunch. I'm positive I'll see retaliation at some point.

"I'm fine. Are you guys okay?" It's not every day you watch your best friend turn evil for a few minutes. I'm sure the whole thing must have bugged them as well.

"Of course we are. But you didn't look like yourself for a second." I nod, biting my lip. "I don't know how to explain it. It was like your eyes were glowing…" Sara trails off, shaking her head. With a half-smile, she wraps her hand around mine and gives it a brief squeeze. "I'm just happy you're safe."

Jared voices his agreement, and I grab his hand as well, though I'm too absorbed in my thoughts to keep the conversation going. Due to my exceptional failure in the first trial, I don't know where I am in my plan to get Sara into the city and become a professor myself. I wish I had asked Adrian if he knew what the new scores were.

I'm going to have to be very careful from now on. My eyes flit through our group, attempting to gauge where each classmate would be in the new ranking. As I'm watching them, I find almost everyone is tense and alert.

Along with the seven original trial overseers, five more guards joined us before we left the academy. Tala said the walk was short, with the path already cleared, but it looks like nobody's taking any chances. The last time we were outside, a large group of Threes ambushed the class, and no one has let it go. Even Emmerick routinely scans the forest, a bead of sweat trailing down his thick neck.

With my aptitude for the wilderness and the constant state of safety with Adrian in the party, I allow myself to turn my thoughts inward again. *Where to even start?*

There's no way I'm in the first-place position anymore, but how far I dropped is the real question. The knowledge that Sara should be within the top four spots is the only fact comforting me right now. So, even if I keep messing up, she should be able to make it back to her family in the city. *At least I haven't ruined that part of the plan.*

What scares me is the strong possibility that I'm lower than tenth place. I need to do better in this trial, whatever it is. Because if I don't, I'll lose Adrian forever.

No pressure.

Tala spares me any more depressing thoughts by stopping and facing us again. My attention is drawn to the wall behind her, similar to the academy's own protection, though the gray stone is shorter and much more weathered. Chunks of rock are missing, with holes trailing up the wall. There doesn't seem to be a door.

"This town was called Karanos once, before the reign of the Obsidian began. The people here were the first to come up with the idea of a wall to protect the people. It took a lot of time and lives to make it happen, but they did it."

Tala puts a hand on the stone, distracted from her animosity by the story. "In the end, their efforts were wasted. Once people realized the wall worked, they flooded to Karanos in waves for a chance to live in safety. Too many people crowded into the town, and with them, the Obsidian came. Hell broke loose before the monsters even reached inside the gates. There were fights everywhere, people murdering others to reduce the population. It was only a matter of time before the Obsidian finally infiltrated the city. There weren't many survivors.

"But their sad story allowed us to create the walls we know today, and it's why there are so many restrictions for anyone wanting to live in a city. Nobody wants what happened here to happen again. Nobody wanted to revive Karanos either, so the desolate town sat for years until the academy was built and we took it over." Tala leans against the stone and crosses her arms. "Inside these walls will be your next trial."

Chapter 32

Masked Essence

STANDING ON TOP OF THE STONE BARRIER, IT'S DIFFICULT NOT to be shaken by the state of the town. Tala's tale explained the destruction that ensued even before the Obsidian got in, but seeing it now is a whole different story.

Karanos is fairly small. I can barely make out the other side of the wall, about two miles away. Inside looks like a disaster that was never cleaned up and left to rot for twenty years: burned buildings, piles of rubble...and Obsidian.

My heart seizes at the first glimpse of their limping forms. From this height, I can count at least ten below me, wandering aimlessly between destroyed houses and broken carts that litter the cracked roads. *What the hell are we supposed to be doing?*

The top of the wall is wide, allowing three people to line up in rows in front of Tala. Similar to the farm's circle of bonfires, torches border the town, except they hang from mounted posts on the wall.

Behind her is a thin steel shed, which she ducks into. Distant sounds of her rummaging through the shed reach me at the back of the many rows of students. I pull myself onto my tiptoes and poke my head around the others to see what Tala has stuffed in her hands. It looks like a giant blob of black leather. She pulls apart a section of the lump and I finally make out a backpack, which she hands to Naire.

A quick routine of gathering backpacks, distributing them, and then filling her hands back up forms. While she passes them out, the other guards and instructors split in half, each group walking in separate directions from the wall. I follow their actions as every so often, one person splits from the group and stops, crossing their arms behind their backs with eyes lowered to the town. They stand rigid, waiting.

They're placing themselves around the perimeter. I try to spot Adrian, but he must be farther down. Feeling disappointed at his sudden disappearance, I face the front again.

It feels like hours until Astrid timidly turns around, her small hands gripping the leather so fiercely that it turns her knuckles white. I give her a soft "thank you" and try for a reassuring smile. Astrid's gray eyes are wide with fear and she turns back around without responding, her thin fingers tucking wayward tendrils of black hair into her bun.

"Whether you work in the city or as a hunter, there will be times when you'll face the dangers of being outside a wall, maybe with nothing but the clothing on your back. You need to gather the tools necessary for survival. This trial will test your ability to make it on your own, to see if you have the skills needed to take care of not just yourself, but others, too. If you're unable to find shelter, food, or weapons in an emergency, then you'll be useless to humanity."

Another winning pep talk, Tala. So inspirational.

"We've placed multiple tools throughout the town that could prove beneficial to your task. Be it food, weapons, blankets, or more. Each item is tagged with a number based on how valuable it is. For example, you might discover a jar of beans with the number five written on the lid. This means the jar of beans is worth five points. The numbers range, but your goal is to gather as many of these objects as possible. You have two hours to get at least fifty points."

I share an uneasy glance with Sara, listening to the uncomfortable murmurs from the students in front of me. Fifty points? We need to locate some big items, or that's a lot of jars to haul around.

"What if we don't reach fifty?" Someone in the middle asks.

A minuscule portion of Tala's sick satisfaction leaks out from her tilted lips. "Then you don't pass. I told you, you're a worthless asset if you can't gather a few measly objects."

Another wave of nervousness ripples through the group. This differs from the first trial by a landslide. Before, we just had to suck it up to move on. Now, there's an actual stipulation to succeed. I unzip my backpack and peek inside. It holds a short unlit torch and a piece of flint, but they take up surprisingly little space. A fair number of items could fit in here.

"The point system directly affects your rank. The more points you have, the better. Obtain the worst items, or not enough, and you may plummet yourself straight to the bottom." Tala's eyes find mine, only confirming my fear that I've ruined my ranking.

Her stare isn't exactly subtle, either. Snickers float through the crowd, the hateful sound making my teeth creak against the tightness of my jaw. *I'll show them who they're laughing at when I beat them by a hundred points.* I huff, backpedaling my thoughts. *No! You can't jump back to the top again. What about Sara?*

Quietly, I zip up the bag and slip it on. This is going to be a little tricky…again. I need to increase my score so that I'm higher than eleventh place, but not much more than that. The best course of action is to hover close to eleventh so I won't need to hold back in the last trial. Because seriously, all this thinking and scheming is giving me a headache.

Of course, this would be easier if I knew how many points the others would get. What if I think I have a good amount, but it's still below everyone, or a lot higher? I rub my temple. *Way too much thinking.*

"The Obsidian are here to keep you focused and on your toes. Remember that your goal is to be silent and efficient, so there are no bonuses for killing them. Choosing to fight places you at a greater risk of alerting the others to your presence. The guards and instructors will jump in if things look deadly, but understand that if you need our help, then you fail. Keep in mind that traveling in groups makes it harder to stay hidden. When you are outside the walls, safety is not always in numbers. You each will start with a torch and flint. If you have to light your torch for any reason, you will fail."

One hundred Obsidian? Failing if you find yourself in a deadly, inescapable situation or if you need fire? Adrian's warning about this being the most dangerous trial echoes in my ears. It's not just dangerous because it's a lot easier to fail; it could also cost you your life.

A sweat breaks out at the small of my back.

"Alright, it's time to get started. The only way into Karanos is climbing down the wall, similar to how we came up."

Everyone at the inner edge of the crowd simultaneously looks over the ledge, including Jared. No one moves.

"Stop standing around, or I'll start the time now!" Tala snaps.

With Tala's encouraging words, the front of the group shuffles to the ledge and files down one at a time. I watch

Sara lower herself and suddenly I'm the last one on the wall. Alone with Tala.

Crap.

I awkwardly shuffle sideways to get to the ledge, not liking the idea of my back to her. Tala stares with a blank face, but her eyes are unyielding. The look pauses me with one leg halfway swung over the edge of the wall.

The only way to describe the feeling in her eyes is dead, uncaring. Not quite lifeless, not as if she's given up and is now hopeless. More like her anger earlier was just for show—because who wouldn't be angry when being displaced from their home?—and that façade has fallen to reveal the terrifying loss of herself and any scrap of humanity clinging to the darkness of her heart.

With that humanity gone, nothing can stop her from killing me at this exact moment.

Tala blinks, anger lighting her eyes and flushing her face. "What the hell are you waiting for?"

I suck in a shaky breath, slide my foot around until it sinks into the first foothold, and descend with weak arms. I progress slowly down the wall, taking care that each foot is secure before letting my hand grab a new cavity.

What I first thought were crumbling sections of the wall when we arrived are actually man-made holes that create an easy pathway. Tala says it is the only way in or out, making it safer than any door since Obsidian can't climb.

My mind flies back to the Three ambush when the senior class was outside the walls. Those monsters appeared to be trying to scale the smooth stone. What would've happened if there were footholds where they did their erratic jumps?

I also don't believe that they stuffed one hundred Obsidian into this town by throwing their bodies over the wall. How did they get an exact number in here with only one section of footholds to facilitate their movement?

My hand, slick with sweat, slips against the stone and I grip tighter, pain lancing through my palm. Once I'm steady again, I lift my hand and see a thin line of blood trailing down my wrist. I give a particularly sharp section of the hole a glare before moving down again. It's not like I can patch the cut now. *Besides, the burning helps me focus...*

Focused until my mind drifts once again. This time, I can't get the image of Tala out of my head. I could have sworn I didn't make up the deadness in her eyes; I definitely didn't fake my abnormal reaction from seeing it. My body knew something was extremely off before my mind did. Whatever happened with Tala was more than just a blank stare.

What confuses me the most is her reaction after our staring match. She wasn't shocked or upset that I caught her expression, the mask of outrage sliding effortlessly back into place, making me doubt that I had seen anything to begin with.

Either she's playing the best game of pretend, or maybe even she doesn't know about the abyss of death swallowing her. Both possibilities mean she's still intending to end my life before she's gone. *If that's true, then I have to stay on my guard.*

Even if she isn't plotting my imminent death, there's still something seriously wrong with her. She's cracking, hitting a breaking point.

Thankfully, I reach the bottom of the wall without incident. Sara and Jared stand close by, and I curl my fingers over the wound as they approach. No need to bother them over some insignificant laceration. Though I'll need to pay attention if I'm holding a weapon. I can imagine myself pressing the cut against a sword and releasing the blade on instinct.

I take a quick inventory of my surroundings. So far, it doesn't appear that any Obsidian heard us enter their playground. The nearest one lurches over the remnants of a wooden cart two houses away. Almost everyone presses against the wall, as though any step forward will draw the demon's attention to us. The Obsidian seem to be Zeroes, so at least they won't have heightened senses.

The muted blow of a whistle jerks our heads up to Tala. I know how loud that thing can get, so she purposely made the sound as quiet as possible. It's a relief to know she doesn't want to kill *everyone*.

"You know the rules. Time starts now."

Half the group immediately launches into the action at her words, but again, I'm consumed by Tala's gaze. Her eyes are harsh, sparked with life. She's looking at me with her usual amount of hate, and I never thought I'd be grateful to see it.

So, either she's currently strategizing my death, maybe waiting until I graduate, or I have an enemy for life that truly loathes me and I'll need to look over my shoulder forever.

Yeah. All of those options stink.

It isn't long until Sara, Jared, and I find ourselves alone, running through sunlit sections of a decrepit dirt road. Everyone else formed their small parties and disappeared somewhere within the town. It became clear early on that Tala was right. Sticking in groups would not only draw the attention of Obsidian but also decrease the chances of earning enough points for everyone.

So far, Jared has a five-point butter knife, Sara has a ten-point blanket, and I'm sitting pretty with a one-point small potato. There's no way this little potato has been here for the last twenty years without rotting. It's easy to tell for most items whether they've been in Karanos since its fall or were placed here for the trial.

Jared found the butter knife in a drawer of a half-burned-down kitchen, the only makeshift weapon with a number carved into the wooden handle. Rust creeps along the edges of the dull blade, making it less effective in a fight than if we had a fluffy pillow.

It took a lot of convincing to give Sara the blanket. She pushed zealously for me to have it, since I didn't do too great in the last trial, but both Jared and I were able to pawn the blanket off on her. As she sighed and put it in her backpack, I caught Jared's eye and smiled at him.

Whether he has faith that I will get enough points to increase my score, or he's focused on protecting Sara, doesn't matter in my mind. It shows he cares for Sara as much as I do, and I'm grateful she has him.

Halfway through the trial is when we run across our first complication. Well, technically, in my mind, we've had a complication for a while now.

The first problem is that I have the most points by far. It's all because of this stupid bow in my hand and the quiver slung across my back. Combined, they're thirty points, giving me forty-six points, where Sara and Jared only have twenty-five each. I'm blaming everything on Sara's persuasiveness and Jared's uncanny ability to cave to anything Sara demands.

When we found the bow and arrows, I fought to give

them to Sara, but I was only at sixteen points and my best friend wasn't taking no for an answer.

I'm horrible with a bow, too! Unless I'm using the arrows as melee weapons, count me out of the fight. But Sara wouldn't budge.

How am I supposed to make sure she's in one of the top four spots if she's doing a better job of getting me up there? And there's no reason for me to reject any points in her eyes because she doesn't know my plan to boost her score. If I tell her about it, there's no way she'll accept the decision. I'd wager she would somehow talk me out of it. *That won't happen.*

Which leaves me now, as the three of us argue over who's taking a seven-point bottle of hydrogen peroxide with two strips of cloth taped to its side, to wiggle my way out of a ridiculous situation.

"Cassie, just take the bottle!" Sara whispers, her lips twisted defiantly.

"No way!" I growl, shoving the glass bottle back into her hands. "If you don't start gaining points for yourself, then you might run out of time. I only need one more item to be done."

"And this can be that one item. Besides, you need more points than us to increase your rank." She thrusts the container into my chest.

There it is. The whole reason for this argument. In her mind, being at the top is a way to show everyone how hard I worked, something she so strongly feels I deserve.

I tilt my head to Jared, silently pleading for him to help me. He's been quiet recently, torn between supporting Sara's decision and giving her more points. From the looks of his scrunched nose, he hasn't decided.

"*You're* taking it, or I'm throwing it onto a roof and then no one will get any points," Sara announces, pleased with her ultimatum.

I, on the other hand, am seconds from throttling her.

I snatch the bottle from her and shove the alcohol into my bag with jerky movements, seething with rage. Something needs to change. I don't believe for a second she'll stop fighting to give me items. She's putting both herself and Jared at risk of failing for the prospect of my reaching the top place again. I love Sara like a sister, but I won't let that happen.

Which is why the second complication is a godsend. I mean, anything that has to do with Obsidian throws us into an unforgiving nightmare, but at least this time, it's useful.

Chapter 33

Hostile Ruse

SOMEHOW, WE FIND OURSELVES PINNED BETWEEN TWO GROUPS of Obsidian, three in each, all dragging their uncooperative bodies toward us. With the sun beating down on them and their energy lowered significantly, we have a higher chance of escape rather than needing to kill them.

We duck behind a shed and survey the situation. Their movements are sedated and jagged, which means they haven't picked up on our presence. Not that Zeros can run, Obsidian get faster the more advanced they are in development, but their speed does noticeably increase when they've locked onto a target.

I briefly debate fighting them, but toss the idea out. Tala didn't elaborate on how much it'll take for the instructors to intervene, and I don't feel like discovering that limit, especially with Tala having the capability to end my trial early. I'm sure convincing everyone else that she was only protecting me wouldn't be too hard, even if I had everything handled.

We huddle in a tiny circle, talking in rapid whispers. We

only have a few minutes before they're on us, and then the escape plan won't matter.

"Okay, what do we do?" Jared asks. He must realize that attacking is a bad idea as well, because he's normally just as likely as I am to suggest combat.

I try not to smile. *Time to enact my brilliant plan.*

"We need to split up. I'll draw their attention away while the two of you sneak off," I announce, bracing myself for Sara's objections. She doesn't disappoint.

"No way!" Sara declares with indignation, mouth thinned and hands balled into fists.

I swing the bow in my grasp. "Look, I'm the only one with a weapon. Your butter knife couldn't cut actual butter, Jared," I add, watching him dig through his backpack. He pauses, glances at me with surprised eyes, and pulls the zipper up sheepishly.

"Well, I don't know about that." Jared gives me an easy smile, not seeming the least bit worried about the six approaching Obsidian.

I continue. "It's also a ranged weapon. I can shoot some arrows and let them chase after me at a safe distance. I won't need to engage in any conflict. You guys keep gathering points, and I'll meet up with you after the Obsidian have dispersed. I'm already at fifty points, so I won't need to worry about getting items until I'm free from danger."

I raise my eyebrows at Sara, daring her to poke holes in my argument. I'm sure she could, but we don't have the time. She peers at the monsters, only ten feet away. She knows as much as I do that the decision needs to be made right now if we don't want to force our way through.

The defeated sag of her shoulders is my signal to heave myself up onto the metal frame of the shed. Most of the roof is gone, but there's enough steel for me to balance my feet.

Adrian and I have never worked with a bow before, mainly because I told him I'd mastered it before coming to the academy. In reality, I just hate bows. Why go for a ranged weapon when you can have the satisfaction of lopping the demon's head off with one clean swipe?

Adrian would kill me if he figured out I lied to him. *Oh, I really hope he can't see me right now.*

I pull an arrow from the quiver and place it on the carved notch, resting the stone arrowhead on my straightened finger. There isn't any Eloyla paste on the arrowhead, but I wouldn't have lit the weapon even if I could have. I'm not trying to win this fight. Battering their bodies with sharp arrowheads should be enough to get their attention.

With a controlled breath to relax my muscles, I close one eye, aiming for the nearest Obsidian's head, and fire.

The arrow, to my surprise, flies fast and straight...right into the tree four feet above the target's head.

Everyone pauses for a second: the Obsidian searching for a living thing, my friends gasping at me in utter horror. If I had the time, I would have laughed at their astonishment.

Instead, I give them a two-finger salute and a brazen smile before launching myself off the roof and sprinting past the Obsidian in the opposite direction of my friends. I can almost hear Sara's exasperated sigh before it's swallowed by the groans of the demons. I slow down after making enough noise to catch their attention, carefully weaving through debris to avoid attracting any more to my location.

I can't believe my plan worked! Even with the thundering of Obsidian behind me, my lips stretch into a winning grin and I fly over a crumpled barrel without breaking my stride. With me gone, they can gather points to share between the two of them. I'm positive that within minutes, they'll be reaching fifty.

I stumble past a small cluster of bricks, the momentary lull in speed giving me a chance to gauge the distance between me and my pursuers. The six of them are still trailing close behind, not allowing the space I require to release another arrow. *As if that would do any good.*

I could go back to a sprint, but that has its own mess of complications. So I pick up a brick and launch it to the left. I'm back to a steady jog before the clay can hit the ground. Another quick peek behind me shows that two of the six hobbled over to investigate, and the others decelerate in the confusion of sound. I let loose a relieved breath. *Not that I was worried.*

My relief at losing the Obsidian is short-lived when I hear two voices that still haunt my nightmares.

"You won't deny us this, right? You're saying you want us to fail the trial?" Naire's voice grates against my ears, and my fingers automatically curl against the wooden bow at the sound.

I ease my pace. The words drift from inside the small home just ahead, her voice flowing out through the multiple broken windows and gaping holes. The house doesn't give much cover from Obsidian, but it could be a shield from the guards on the wall. *Now, what wonderful things could the devil spawn be up to?*

I crouch low, sparing one more look behind me at the pathway void of Obsidian, before stealthily making my way to the closest hole. Beside the crater is a window bare of glass, and I poke the top of my head above the sill, just enough to view what's going on.

Instantly, my next breath stills in my throat as my esophagus spasms in anger.

Emmerick and Naire stand haughtily over Carter, the boy who got a broken jaw in the last trial. The one who went up first against Emmerick. He has glasses on now, which he must have taken off during the sparring matches.

He's sprawled on the ground, cradling his right hand against his chest. Emmerick swings what must be Carter's backpack in his grip mockingly. Naire passes Emmerick her bag, and he starts to transfer all the items from the boy's pack into Naire's.

They're stealing other students' points.

"There we go. That wasn't so hard, was it, Carter?" Naire laughs as she slings her newly filled bag onto her shoulders.

Carter stares at them both with a mix of resentment and resignation, breaking eye contact when they lob his empty backpack onto the ground at his feet.

Unable to let them get away with this, I step through the hole in the wall.

"I'm pretty sure that's against the rules," I state calmly, my temper spiking again when their surprise at my entrance morphs into relaxed smirks. Like I'm not a threat to them.

"I don't think so. Did Tala say that taking items from others is prohibited? If she doesn't state it, then it's acceptable."

As fast as my hands can move, I nock an arrow.

A splinter of hesitation breaks through Naire's confident smile, but within seconds, it's buried again. "Now, now, no need for violence."

"Oh, so you're against cruelty now? What happened to the person who tried to have me murdered?" Sarcasm drips from my voice, and I fight to keep the bow steady. *Don't let them get to you. Don't let them know you have horrible aim.* Threatening them with a weapon seemed like a great idea at the time—really, I just wanted to watch them squirm—but if they call my bluff, I'm screwed.

"You know, I heard your conversation with Tala in the

gym after everything went down. She said she wasn't trying to kill you, so no harm, right?'"

"But you didn't know that, did you?" I roar, my rage seconds away from spilling over. Even Carter, whose strained features relaxed at my entrance, steals a nervous glance around the room, prepared for an Obsidian to suddenly jump through the dilapidated walls. I don't blame him. I'm not exactly using an inside voice at the moment, but my fury is blinding.

Later, I might be uncomfortable knowing Naire was eavesdropping on me, but right now, the fact that she heard my conversation with Tala before the trials began doesn't even register. "You had no idea she wasn't trying to kill me."

I didn't believe Tala when she first said it and I don't believe it now. How Tala thinks tying me up against a tree, drugged and bleeding, doesn't lead to my demise is baffling to me. But I sure as hell know that Naire thought I was going to die that night.

Naire's face is stern, eyes trained on my bow. "Put that down before you hurt yourself. I know you won't use it."

My jaw clenches as I internally curse myself for my failed bluff. I flip through all the strategies in my mind. I could let an arrow fly, knowing it would hit nothing, and call it a warning shot. However, that might trigger them to attack, and while I feel confident in my sparring abilities, I can't simultaneously defend Carter as well.

"Just like you knew I wouldn't attempt to injure you during our last match?" I feel sick just bringing the whole thing up, but I have to keep the upper hand in this conversation. *To protect Carter*, I repeat over and over.

"You got me," Naire sneers, baring her teeth. That's obviously still a touchy subject for her. "I never pegged you as a crazy whore. Killing out in the open and throwing yourself at every guy in sight. Absolutely pathetic."

Don't let her get to you. I want nothing more than to hurl the bow and lunge at her, but that would help no one. "Dump everything in your backpack onto the ground and get out of this house before I change my mind," I grind out. Choking her in the last trial was my revenge. Anything else I do to her will just prove her words right.

Emmerick, who until now stood silently and tried to appear intimidating, speaks up from behind Naire. "The two of us can easily take you."

"Shut up," Naire bites out, running a hand through her short dark hair. I'm sure she's calculating the best way to get out unscathed and with the points.

"You can try." I shift my aim, pointing the arrow at Emmerick's head. That seems to shut him up better than Naire's words.

I ready myself to toss down the bow and jump in with my fists. After a tense moment, Naire grabs her bag from its bottom, unzipping and flipping it over unceremoniously. A variety of minor objects plummet to the floor, including a small dagger and two jars filled with something brown, but definitely not worth fifty points.

"Fine, we'll play nice for now." Naire flings the backpack on and heads to the nearest gaping hole, gesturing for Emmerick to follow. He sends me a scowl that I return before following in her footsteps. Naire stops before stepping outside. "Just pray we don't run into you again. We won't be so generous the second time."

I don't move after they're gone, my muscles tensing as I brace for them to attempt a surprise attack. Once I'm certain they've left, a sigh escapes my lips, and the bow slips from my fingers.

The wood clatters against the ground, startling Carter. His flinch pulls me from my sinking reprieve and I pull myself together.

Wincing at what he must think of me after that conversation, I soundlessly grab his bag and fill it with the scattered items, counting the points in my head. Thirty-two points. What are the odds he'll be able to get enough to succeed and also avoid Emmerick and Naire? I'm sure they'll be on the lookout for revenge now.

"I'm sorry about that," I whisper, holding out his backpack in one hand and the discarded blade in the other. Now that the adrenaline has faded, I feel guilty for blowing up and also implying that I intentionally hurt Naire. "I would keep the dagger on you rather than in the backpack, just in case."

Carter nods, simultaneously snatching up the bag and pushing his glasses higher up the bridge of his nose. His fingers slide over the worn hilt of the knife, and he clutches it to his chest. "Thank you. You saved me from them and from failing the trial. At least now I have a chance."

I prod through my bag, coming out with a small notebook on Obsidian weaknesses worth ten points. "Still, I'd appreciate it if you accepted my apology gift."

"I couldn't possibly, Cassidy. I know I'll be able to find enough on my own." He stands, his face a mask of resolution.

My offering hand lowers, eyes narrowing. I want to argue, but he vanishes behind the brick wall before I can, his footsteps muffled against grass and stone.

My lips pull into a frown, taking in the vacant home around me. From my current position, nothing inside the dingy home is tagged. With half the house gone, it's a miracle most of the roof is still intact. I swiftly scour the living room and kitchen, the bare space squashing my hope until I travel through a narrow hallway that leads to what resembles a home office or personal library.

Books could be tagged.

I wander into the room, taking in the faded book covers laden with dust. Half of the shelves have crumbled with the weight of time and age. I skim through the books on upright shelves, wiping off the grime to read the titles. Nothing's marked. I squash a sigh as I scan the rest of the room, which holds a desk and chair.

The desk looks like a giant piece of wood that got chopped in half, crumbling in on itself in the middle. Still, it was once a magnificent piece of furniture, a darker wood and larger than the one in the headmaster's office. Even the chair, without its back and springs clawing through the leather, has a sense of superiority to it.

I make my way over to the chair, sitting lightly on an edge with no poking wires and take in the desk, unable to shake the feeling that someone important once sat here. I run a hand across the wood until pain shoots through my palm.

Flipping the limb, I groan at my carelessness. Not only did I smear the wood with blood, but the wound on my palm is now covered in dirt. *Great, nothing like an infection to up the stakes.*

I almost go to the kitchen with a prayer that there's still running water, but I grab my backpack instead, the small stroke of luck making me smile. I seize the hydrogen peroxide and throw the bag to the side, placing my good fortune on a section of flat wood. *Now, I just need to clean it up.*

The cloth strips easily peel from the bottle and I lay them gently on my knee. Grimacing from the sting, I pour at least half the disinfectant onto my wound, washing off everything but the most stubborn of dirt. I grab one strip and, biting my lip to repress another grunt, carefully wipe the cut until I'm confident I won't get an infection.

Satisfied with my work, I wrap the second cloth around the wound and tie it off. *I hope I still get the points even if I used half of the item.* If people can steal points, then they should be able to use the items as well.

With slumped shoulders, I rest my elbows on my knees and stare at my newly bandaged hand, pondering my next move. I need to stay away from Emmerick and Naire for obvious reasons. I also don't want to catch up with Sara and Jared before the trial is finished. They might give me all their extra points, and that would have wasted my previous efforts.

I'm already over fifty points, so I could just sit here until the trial is over. That would negate the risk of running into anyone. But do I have enough points to ensure I don't drop in rank? *Ugh, why is this so complicated?*

As I contemplate, my gaze slides past my injury and onto the floor. My brain sluggishly registers that something is off with the wood panels.

Pursing my lips, I slide to a knee on the ground for a better view.

The liquid I poured onto the floor while cleaning the wound isn't pooling like it should, but is slowly draining into the side of one of the wood panels. The rivet is also deeper than the rest of the wood, and upon closer inspection, winds in a rectangle. *Looks like someone was trying to hide something.*

I search the nearby rubble for anything resembling a crowbar. Picking up a long piece of metal and hefting its weight, I kneel beside the drawer, determined to expose its secrets.

It takes a few attempts for the old wood to bend under the weight of my tool, but after a minute, I'm able to pry up the small chunk of flooring. Dropping to my knees, I use my hands to force the wood the rest of the way and peer inside.

A light brown rectangular tube sits in the small hole with a string tied across the center, the edge of the tube soaked from the still-dripping peroxide. I snatch the cylinder up, my fingers curling around what feels like leather, and immediately set to work drying the hide with my shirt. Once the leather isn't soaking, I gingerly untie its binding and hold my breath in anticipation.

Inside rests a long sheet of aged parchment, hastily scribbled words etched into it. The brief thought that this paper has not been touched since the fall of Karanos passes through my mind. Squinting my eyes to read the small ink scripture, I read the first line.

I CAN'T COUNT HOW MANY TIMES I'VE WRITTEN THIS OUT, BUT I CAN TELL YOU THAT THIS WILL BE MY LAST.

I let out a small gasp. *It's a letter, addressed to whoever finds this paper first.*

Chapter 34

Crucial Potential

I CAN'T COUNT HOW MANY TIMES I'VE WRITTEN THIS OUT, BUT I CAN TELL YOU THAT THIS WILL BE MY LAST. I DON'T KNOW WHY I STILL WRITE THESE LETTERS, FORCING MYSELF TO RELIVE THE UNIMAGINABLE TRAGEDY THAT BEFELL ARRYND. THERE WAS ONCE HOPE SOMEONE WOULD LISTEN TO ME, THAT THEY WOULD PUT THEIR FEAR ASIDE FOR A SINGLE SECOND AND ATTEMPT TO UNDERSTAND. I TRIED ONCE, AND IT NEARLY COST ME MY LIFE.

NOW I DON'T HAVE HOPE. ALL I FEEL IS TIRED.

I THOUGHT THIS TOWN, WITH ITS STRONG WALLS AND PEOPLE, COULD PROTECT ME FROM HIM, BUT HE HAS FOUND ME AGAIN. IT IS ONLY A MATTER OF TIME BEFORE HE COMES FOR ME, SO I MUST LEAVE WHILE I STILL HAVE THE CHANCE.

FOR TWELVE LONG YEARS, I'VE BEEN RUNNING FROM HIM. FROM ALL OF THEM, BECAUSE WHAT THEY SEE, HE CAN SEE. I NOW KNOW THE ONLY SAFE PLACE IS SOMEWHERE NO HUMAN INHABITS, SOMEWHERE THE DEMONS CANNOT FOLLOW.

HE TOOK EVERYTHING FROM ME: MY FAMILY, MY LOVER, MY HOME. BUT JUST BY BEING ALIVE, I HAVE THWARTED HIS

PLANS. IT DID NOT TAKE HIM LONG TO DISCOVER MY EXIS-
TENCE, YET THAT MOMENT OF CONFUSION WAS ENOUGH TIME
FOR ME TO TAKE MY CHILD SOMEWHERE SAFE AND RUN ON MY
OWN. I HAVE MISSED HER EVERY SINGLE DAY. NOW I WILL FIND
HER, AND WE WILL HIDE TOGETHER, BECAUSE SOCIETY IS NOT
SAFE. NOWHERE IS.

FORGIVE ME, I AM RAMBLING. MAYBE I DON'T WANT TO
LEAVE AS MUCH AS I THOUGHT. BUT I HAVE TO. I CANNOT LET
HIM CATCH ME, LET HIM WIN. I AM THE ONLY THING STOPPING
HIM FROM KILLING EVERYONE.

IF YOU ARE STILL READING, I APPLAUD YOU. MAYBE YOU
WILL BE DIFFERENT. I DO NOT HOPE ANYMORE, BUT KNOWING
MY EFFORTS WERE NOT WASTED WOULD BE NICE. THE CHOICE
IS YOURS.

IF YOU WANT TO KNOW THE TRUTH, YOU MUST FIND IT YOUR-
SELF. FOLLOW THESE COORDINATES. MY WORDS MAY NOT HAVE
AN IMPACT, BUT THAT PLACE WILL SHOW YOU HOW RIGHT I AM. IT
WILL EXPLAIN WHAT HAPPENED, HOW IT ALL CAME TO BE. WHEN
YOU DISCOVER THE TRUTH, WHAT YOU DO WITH THAT INFORMA-
TION IS UP TO YOU. MAYBE YOU WILL HAVE BETTER SUCCESS
TRYING TO HELP HUMANITY THAN I DID. EITHER WAY, I WILL BE
FAR ENOUGH THAT I WILL NOT KNOW OF YOUR DECISION.

GOOD LUCK.

KENDRA

I read the letter a second time, and then a third, but it still
doesn't clear my confusion. There's a sketched map below
her signature of where the supposed 'truth' is, the circled
location within a large town, a week away from here at most.
But who is Kendra? What does she mean by the truth? I

wrack my brain, though I'm sure that name is nowhere in our history books.

I fold the paper back up inside the leather and gently lay it back into the compartment, closing the wooden lid on top. As a skeptical person, my immediate thought is that this paper is a prank. Maybe a guard put this here to see if people were gullible enough to fall for it. Regardless, I'm not about to go gallivanting through the wilderness on the whim of someone I've never met, even if this supposed truth could 'save humanity.'

I need more information. While I'm still mad at the man, the only person who may have some answers to this is Zachary Cane.

Exhausted from the constant bombardment of unanswered questions, I slowly trek back to our starting point. Every once in a while, I find a tagged item on the ground. I scoop up about half of them, not wanting to catapult my score but also wanting to increase it enough to climb my way back to tenth place.

I lift my gaze, unsure how much time has passed while in my head, and see that most of the guards and instructors have already made it back to the starting point on the wall. Even from this distance, I can see classmates working their way up the footholds, scaling the stone with the speed of someone who'd rather not be sitting in an Obsidian pen.

Did I miss a signal? *Ah, crap. Now I'm going to be late.*

Strapping the backpack across my chest, I take off in a sprint, weaving and bobbing past obstacles and the occasional roaming Obsidian. It doesn't take me long to catch the other stragglers who must have been on the other side of town when the signal was given.

I wipe the back of my hand against my sweaty forehead, thankful there's a crispness to the air. Emmerick and Naire are already on the wall, which isn't a shocker. I'm sure they were squatting close by once they stole enough points from others. No need to take any extra risks.

From the faces of a few students around me, near tears with trembling lips, I can tell they don't have enough points. I debate giving them some of my items, but Jared and Sara choose that exact moment to pounce on me.

"Where have you been?" Sara demands, grabbing my arm.

Their backpacks strain against the fabric, the bulge making me smile. At least they got themselves a hefty amount of points.

"I found a lovely house and took a nap. The bed was pretty comfy, even though the owner hadn't changed the sheets in years."

Jared snorts, but quickly covers it with a cough at Sara's sharp glare. "That's not funny, Cassie."

"Seriously, Sara, nothing happened. I found some items and took in the scenery. That's all, I swear." I make a cross over my heart as a bonus to my veracity.

"As long as you're alright," Jared says before Sara can argue again. He wraps an arm around my shoulder, giving it an affectionate squeeze. My best friend sighs, shaking her head and muttering to herself.

I'm saved from any more questions when it's my turn to climb the wall. I ascend as fast as possible, wanting to be back at the academy already. Reaching the top, a guard immediately grabs my backpack and tosses it to the next person. I watch in fascination at the assembly line of instructors who count all my items before putting them in the shed for next year's placement.

"Ninety-seven points," Raddo declares with a sigh, like he's disappointed I made the cut, and writes the number on a small notebook. I ignore Raddo. The idea of working with him in the future isn't a pleasant thought, but maybe Zypha will get rid of him, too.

Ninety-seven points, not bad. I hope that'll bring me to the sweet spot of tenth place, though it's hard to tell since I have no clue what everyone else got. A guard shoos me away, so I awkwardly shuffle to stand by Astrid and Bryce. Astrid's eyes are red and puffy, and she discreetly tries to wipe her nose every few seconds.

A wave of sympathy hits me, followed by vehement wrath. If Emmerick and Naire stole her items, I'll end them. Not that I have or will ever get any proof that they did, but do I need a solid reason for beating them up?

Nope, you will not go crazy on them, Cassie. At least I could save Carter from their terror, and the knowledge helps to subdue some of my indignation.

Standing on top of the wall, the cold air burning my lungs, I realize I've completed the second trial.

Two down, one to go.

I don't have time to visit Zachary like I thought I would. As soon as we walk through the gate, Zypha explains that the next evaluation will start in a few minutes. Most people don't seem to be bothered either way, yet I feel nothing but relief. *It's almost over, we're almost there.*

No one needed rescuing from the Obsidian while inside Karanos, but four students didn't reach fifty points. Astrid,

Carter, and two others. I feel a pang of regret when I see Carter join the group at the front gates. If I could have convinced him to take one of my items, would he have passed the trial?

I make eye contact with him, and he gives me a sad smile and a nod. I hope that means he holds nothing against me.

Our class watches the four of them march past the front gates toward an awaiting cart, and I wonder where it will take them. To the field close to the academy? Or a farm two cities away? Besides me, no one seems to care what happens to them. In fact, most of the other students' faces return to boredom as the gates close behind the four.

"Alright, everyone. Time for the third trial. Please follow Professor Bosts to your next destination. Good luck," Tala says, sweeping her hand to my old teacher.

Heather Bosts pushes her glasses up her nose with a shy smile, her brown curls just as wild today. She beckons us forward, and we all follow her into the main section of the school.

While I'm happy we get a break from Tala, it makes me anxious that she's gone. At least when she was with the group, I didn't have to worry about a sneak attack. I have to remind myself that Adrian and Zypha are keeping a close eye on her to calm my racing heart.

Tala should not have this power over me. *I am not scared of her.*

The class walks in silence, each person lost in their own world. Maybe they're thinking about their future outside of this, or maybe they're focused on the third trial. Bosts leads us deeper into the building, past the dorms and through a door hidden at the end of the hallway, showing off how truly large the academy is. I didn't even know there was more past our bedrooms.

340

The stairs down feel like they go on forever, the path barely lit by the dim torches lining the right wall.

Finally, the narrow hallway at the bottom of the steps expands into a medium-sized underground bunker with no windows. The walls are jagged, some sections pointing out in sharp stone, and a door at the opposite end of the room seems to be the only other way out of here. All that the room houses is a few benches scattered around the perimeter.

If I had any claustrophobia problems, they would be in overdrive right now.

"This is where you will wait before your trial starts," Bosts explains once we all line up in front of her. "One at a time, you'll enter the next room and begin your individual trial. Your name will be called out depending on your rank after the last trial's calculations. Hopefully, knowing your rank will give you the motivation you require to *rock* this trial." She points to the nearest wall and grins.

Oh, was that a joke? The silence filling the room is uncomfortable. I smile in encouragement as Bosts fixes her glasses and hides an embarrassed blush. She coughs and moves on. "You won't know what the trial is until it's your turn, so those who go last won't have an advantage. First up will be Emmerick."

I roll my eyes as the brute stretches his thick muscles. *I cannot believe he is back in first place.* Bosts gestures to the door and he leaves without his usual intimidation tactics. Luckily, the professor stays behind. I wouldn't have put it past Naire to start something if we were alone.

My two friends and I choose a bench away from our classmates. I try to lean back against the wall, but the stone is unyielding, jabbing my spine like an accusatory finger. Instead, Sara and I each rest our heads on one of Jared's shoulders.

No one talks, but I don't need words to understand how we all feel. This is our final trial. In a few hours, we will choose our placements and go our separate ways.

What will it feel like to sleep alone, the calming snores of my best friend gone? Or to go a whole day without one of Jared's horribly amazing jokes? I bite my lip when I realize Jared will probably go to the city with Sara, where they will be together, safe and happy.

While I'm glad for them, it's difficult to acknowledge that I'll be separated from my two best friends. If I ever get to visit them in the city, will our relationship have changed? Will they be as close as ever, but distant with me? I huff, throwing those thoughts from my mind. It doesn't help to fear the worst. I have to believe that our bond is strong enough to last through the years.

Jared is the first in our tiny group to leave. He's moved to third place in my absence. Sara and I slide together, wrapping our arms around each other. Those who go in for the trial don't come back into this room, so we don't know how Jared did. But in what feels like seconds, Bosts calls Sara's name and I'm left alone.

Naire and Emmerick are gone, so I don't have to worry about them. I close my eyes and try to find a comfy section of the wall. Sara is in fourth place; that in itself gives me more solace than I've felt all day. I'm confident nothing can happen in this trial that'll knock her from her position.

Now to focus on getting myself through this last trial with a high enough rank to stay at the academy. A part of me wishes I still wanted to be a hunter, for the simple fact of not having to worry about such problems. My rank wouldn't matter.

Then I think of Adrian, and I know there's no way I won't fight to be with him. To stand as his equal, someone he can trust with his life. I have to give it my all. *For Adrian.*

I watch each person go by, scan the dwindling room, and my stomach sinks. Currently, eight people have gone, leaving eight in the room. What makes me so nervous is the fact that if my name doesn't get called soon, I'll be past the tenth position. Even with four people gone, the rankings won't move. There will just be six people becoming hunters instead of ten. *And I won't be one of them.*

"Cassie Hale," Bosts announces brightly.

I spring to my feet, my heart stuttering in my chest. Within a few seconds, I'll discover what the last hurdle to my destiny will be. I'm in ninth place, which is an immense relief, so all I have to do is pass. If I can do that one crucial thing, I'll succeed.

Pressure builds inside me as I walk over to the professor, her kind eyes locking with mine in silent encouragement. I almost think I'll pass out before I get to her, but before I know it, she's opening the door for me and pushing me through.

The first thing that hits me is the sound, like a million people talking at once.

My eyes blink rapidly as my vision adjusts to the near darkness, the torches hardly more than glowing embers. When I can finally see again, I struggle to keep my mouth closed.

I'm standing in a large arena. The area is circular with high walls and a wide gate on the other side of the room.

Above the gate is a space cut from the stone, a box to watch all the fights. Inside holds Headmaster Hallow, Adrian, Officer Zypha, and what feels like every other instructor and guard in the whole academy besides Tala. They all quiet down when they notice me gawking in the center.

While the number of people makes me nervous, I shove

the feeling down as my eyes shift to Adrian. His steady gaze is already on me, which immediately settles the antsy energy vibrating through my fingers.

Headmaster Hallow steps forward, placing his hands on the ledge. He stares down at me with a vaguely disinterested expression. "Cassidy Hale, this is your final trial. To pass, you must kill three Obsidian, however you see fit. That's the only rule for this trial. After your third kill, you will be done. Do you have questions?"

Seems simple enough. I shake my head.

"Choose your weapon, and we will begin."

I follow his gesturing hand, spinning around. Behind me is a thin shelf with various sizes of swords. I run my finger gently over the metal bar as I take in my options.

I pick up a long sword and its scabbard, attaching it and the weapon to my waist.

After a moment of hesitation, I swipe an already sheathed dagger and tuck it at the small of my back, secured by the waistband. *Can never be too careful.* I turn back around and nod at Hallow.

"Release the first Obsidian." The headmaster's voice echoes through the chamber. This will be the first time he's seen me in action, and I want to show him I don't need special powers to take down a demon.

I lower my head as I wait for the gate to open, pulling up the mask around my neck to cover my nose. When my eyes meet the ground, I find dried black blood and ash drench the entire floor, along with glossy red stains. *Not just the Obsidian have gotten hurt in these trials. I hope none of this blood came from Sara or Jared.*

The sound of metal clanging in front of me drags my eyes from the splatters. The gate works on a pulley system, and the metal wheels haul the thick steel gate upward.

As soon as it's up, an Obsidian lunges at me.

It's faster than a Zero, but I'm ready for it. After fighting a Three, this is nothing. Its crooked fingers stretch for me as I adjust my feet into a fighting stance. Ducking the clawed swipe, I scan the monster's face.

Eye sockets sunken in, smooth, black rock where the nose used to be. I don't need to see the frayed skin that cups its ears to know this One relies on hearing. *They must all be Ones, most likely with different senses.*

Instantly, I stop and wait, barely allowing myself to breathe. The One also halts, its head unnaturally bent to the side. Someone in the viewing box coughs, and I use the distraction to my advantage. While the Obsidian jerks its body toward the noise, I grasp the hilt of the sword and yank it out with enough strength that the flint built into the scabbard lights the sword on fire. In a wide arc, using as much power as I can muster, I aim the flaming blade at its neck.

Its head flies off in one clean swipe, the fire shattering through its tough exterior. I turn away before the head can reach the floor.

You can't do that with a stupid bow, I think, my eyes on the people in the box. Most watch with blank expressions, but there are a few appraising nods in there, including Adrian.

My chest swells with pride. Even better than demonstrating my potential as an instructor is knowing I'm also showing off how well Adrian taught me.

Hallow calls for the second one, his eyebrows raised like he's surprisingly impressed. *Or that's how I hope he feels.*

I bend my knees and raise my sword. If possible, I want to end these next two Obsidian just as quickly.

The gate, which lowered immediately after the first monster came out, starts its slow crawl up again. I prepare myself for another instant attack, but nothing comes out. I don't even hear any groans that always follow triggered Obsidian.

I stand, head tilted in confusion, and glance at Hallow. His face mirrors mine, as do everyone else's in the group. *So this hasn't happened to the others yet. Strange.*

Luckily, everyone stays quiet. After a minute, I can hear it. The dragging of feet, the chattering of teeth. I focus back on the gate, watching the shadows for signs of movement.

Chapter 35

Breakdown

Two Obsidian sprint out at a speed I'm not prepared for. Within seconds, the first one's on me, digging its razor claws into my upper forearm. The fabric of my jacket tears, and the sharp pain of perforated skin radiates from the limb up into my collarbone.

Luckily, the demon grabbed my free arm, so before it can sink its teeth into my covered neck, I swing my fiery sword up with brutal strength. The Obsidian's claws spring from my arm, and the demon jumps out of the way before the blaze can reach its mark. I stifle a gasp at its quick reaction.

This is no One I'm dealing with. It wouldn't have been fast enough to dodge that attack.

I glance at my injured arm. Four puncture wounds shine through the torn jacket, but I can still flex my fingers, which means it didn't cause any serious damage. I take hold of my weapon with two hands in an unyielding grip.

In front of me, the two Obsidian hover near the gate, seeming to size me up like I am them. I take in their features, the flaming sword a modest shield against them, and my heart sinks past my stomach to my feet.

Threes. They're both Threes.

The blood rushing past my ears almost blocks out the chaos of the viewing box, but with this moment free of fighting, I risk peeking at the viewers.

Some people rush from the room, whether to help me or to make sure the school hasn't been invaded, I can't tell. Those who stay are watching with grave expressions, including Hallow. Zypha's turned away from me and she's barely holding someone back, her tight bun unraveling with her effort. She leans in, shouting in a man's ear as she wraps her upper extremities around his arms and chest.

A head of midnight black hair comes into view, and I realize she's detaining Adrian.

I don't think I've ever seen him so angry before. His face is flushed red, and he's yelling at Zypha, grappling against the older woman's constraint. Zypha's head cranes to the side and her lips are moving again, her features firm yet exuding sympathy. Two more people step forward to restrain Adrian with her, but even then, they struggle against his strength.

I understand two very important things at that moment.

The rules never stated that the Obsidian had to be a One. Hallow specifically said the only rule is to kill your three Obsidian. While I'm sure Adrian could overlook this tiny detail since these Threes are dangerous, the others, including the headmaster himself, don't have a soft spot for me. I bet two Obsidian were accidentally released before, which is why they made the rule so vague. They probably weren't Threes, but nothing in this life is fair or easy. Hallow would uphold the law of the trial. You either kill your monsters or you don't pass.

The second important fact is that I'm alone in this. Zypha

is stopping Adrian from coming to save me, from ending the trial. As much as he wants to, Adrian can't come to my rescue this time. I need to kill these Threes. Not just to pass the trials, but to stay alive.

Out of the corner of my eye, I see the Threes move in unison toward me. The only good thing is that I have *some* experience with Threes. I've encountered their speed and strength before, so if I can kill one, going up against a single Three may not be that bad.

At least that's what I'm telling myself.

They come at me from both sides, clearly trying to trap me. I dive out of the way and they collide with each other, throwing their gangly bodies off balance. I'm back on my feet and dashing toward them while they're still gathering their bearings.

Brandishing my sword, I slice deep into one of their arms. It leaps back from the weapon and emits an enraged moan, snapping its teeth at me.

In the same swing, I rotate my hold on the sword and viciously drive the hilt backward toward the other demon. The hilt slams into the Three's cupped nose and, while it doesn't break its hardened skin, the blow disorients the enemy for a split second. I duck into another roll, coming up behind the flailing, discombobulated Obsidian. With another thrust of my sword, I run the blade through the back of its knee.

It goes down, arms still attempting to grab me. Raising my sword to execute the monster, I almost miss the blur of black in my peripheral vision.

I forget about the one on the ground and spin around, coming face-to-face with the hurt arm Three. The stench of decay as it screams at me is overpowering, and my eyes fill with water.

It reaches for my throat with its uninjured limb. Unable to

fully see, I jerk back out of the way. My foot lands on the floor Obsidian, until it wiggles away, leaving nothing underneath to steady me.

I fall, the fingertips of the hurt arm Three grazing the leather on my neck. While the jacket can resist a bite, it isn't strong enough to protect from their knife-like claws, and they easily slice through my skin.

Hitting the ground hard, I gag as the breath gets knocked out of me and blood fills my mouth. The second I need to catch my breath is all it takes for one Three to jump on me, its claws slashing without mercy. Lifting my free hand to block the blows, my outer forearm immediately gets shredded against the savage attacks. Pain blooms up my arm and into my shoulder, yet I'm too focused for it to distract me. Not with the block buying me time to think of a plan.

As smart as a Three is, there are still things it could learn. Like stopping the arm that is actively holding a weapon, or going straight in for the bite rather than for debilitation.

Has an Obsidian ever not gone for the instant kill? The demon must be toying with me.

I stab at the Three and it leans to the side to dodge the flame, which gives me enough leverage to twist my hips and throw the monster off me. I'm on my feet again, gasping, tucking my torn arm against my stomach while surveying the battlefield.

Unfortunately, I'm on the opposite side of the room where the weapons wait, the two Obsidian blocking my path. One is hobbling on its busted knee while the other's arm hangs limply at its waist.

At least I'm not the only one with an injury. The problem is, I'm the only one who needs blood inside their body to survive. The fact that black dots are swimming in my vision, and the increasing trail of blood I'm leaving wherever I go, tells me I'm losing *a lot* of blood.

I can feel it dripping down my neck, onto my shirt, and off my arm, but I know the demons didn't hit any vital arteries. I'd be dead already if that were the case. The most important thing is that I stay bite-free. Serous can heal any injury except for that.

This time, I have to take the offensive. If I don't end this soon, I'll die before anyone can reach me.

With a scream, I launch myself at them. My attacks are wild and desperate, and the Obsidian easily evade each one. Before they can turn the attacks back on me, I quickly change tactics, trying to throw them off.

It works...mostly.

Instead of another wide arc, I propel my sword forward at one of their torsos. Rather than fully jumping out of the way, the Obsidian takes a step back and leans away from the flames. Halfway through the lunge, I switch my assault again, moving faster this time, and slash into its exposed left leg.

When I feel the blade cut cleanly through the body, I give a silent 'thank you' to whoever sharpened this weapon.

Without its leg, the monster falls to the ground, scrambling and attempting to stand again. Knowing the second Obsidian will be on me at any moment, I slash down one more time as I drop into a roll. The floor demon's right arm separates in two.

As I leap out of the rotation, a flood of dizziness hits me, and I stumble.

Blood loss. It's all I can think before the mostly uninjured Obsidian strikes me while my vision is fuzzy. Deadly nails rip through my right thigh, pulling a ragged scream from my throat. Its grip on my leg is far scarier than any scratch, though. A grip means it's holding my leg for a bite.

I throw my whole body to the side, falling hard on my injured left arm but also freeing myself from its grasp. The bloodied limb snaps at the elbow from the impact, and another cry leaves my lips. *Damn, I think I broke it.*

The pain is easy to disregard against the rush of adrenaline and I spring to my feet, fighting a wave of nausea. The Obsidian that's missing two limbs slowly drags itself toward me with its good arm.

Wow, that's persistence, I think, dazed as the world spins around me. The other is sprinting toward me, much faster than its counterpart.

I stagger out of the way at the last moment, letting the monster run right past me. My right leg almost gives out with the jarring motion, but I force it to keep me standing. With its back to me, I raise my sword and let gravity do most of the work, coming down onto the demon's upper forearm. The steel slides through the rock, and the Obsidian smacks into the wall with its momentum.

This is my chance. I switch the hilt of my sword to my injured arm with a strained grunt. The hand spasms with the sword's weight, the pain almost overwhelming, but I'm able to withstand it by letting the tip of the blade rest against the stone floor.

While the Three spins around, I twist my newly freed hand and grab the dagger that somehow didn't dislodge from my waistband. Gripping the smaller blade, I slash the metal against the long sword until the dagger catches fire as well. The pressure is too much for my broken limb and the sword clatters to the ground, the flames struggling to cling to the Eloyla paste.

Relying on muscle memory—*is someone extinguishing the torches?*—I throw the dagger.

It thunks into the demon's arm and keeps going, landing

solidly in the stone wall, pinning the Three in place. The Obsidian attempts to jerk free, but the dagger holds. With its other arm missing, the Three is unable to pry the blade free. Stuck, it screams in rage, the harsh movements etching a hole around the knife. From the look of it, the monster will be free from its entrapment in minutes.

I take a step back, a terrible choice on my part, and my right leg finally gives out. I drop hard onto a knee and watch multiple parts of my body pour blood, making a small puddle on the floor.

I need to kill them. I blink slowly. The floor demon is too close for comfort, still dragging its body toward me, teeth clicking together.

I need to kill them, I think again. *If I don't, I fail.* My thoughts holler at me to move, to pick up the sword and finish the job, but my limbs won't cooperate.

Kill them, Cassie. Kill them, kill them, KILL THEM!

I fall backward, staring at the ceiling, the edges of my consciousness filling with darkness. Hearing a groan beside me, I use all my strength to turn my head. Only a few feet away is the Obsidian, half of its extremities gone, yet it eagerly picks up the pace at my nearness.

I close my eyes, not particularly in the mood to watch death creep closer and closer. Pain washes over me, the wounds littering my body seeming to seize control.

Unable to stand it anymore, I let myself drift into nothingness.

This time, it doesn't take me long to realize I'm in a dream. But not just any dream: *the* dream. The nightmare. I almost forgot what my old home looked like; the sleeping pills kept this nightmare away for so long. The flower-patterned couch, the bright yellow curtains, and the small fireplace that was always lit.

When I open my eyes, I know I'm in a dream for the simple fact that I'm observing myself stare with wide eyes at the sliding glass door that leads outside. I'm floating by the front door, unable to do anything but stare.

The Obsidian are here, but my old self doesn't know that yet, eyes looking past me at the front door. Being a bystander in this horrific event has never happened to me before. I've always seen this unfold with my own eyes. *So what's going on?*

The glass shatters with a deafening boom.

My younger self gags at the rotten stench, rubbing her eyes and tripping. The Obsidian stagger in, moans gurgling past black tongues. They overcome my parents almost immediately, capturing their struggling bodies and sinking their teeth into flesh.

The monsters drown out Young Cassie's screams, and I struggle from whatever binding is forcing me to watch this over again from a new, unwelcome viewpoint. My father tries to light himself on fire, but a demon bites into the fleshy part of his wrist before he can.

The younger me drops the sword and scrambles backward until her shoulders hit the wall. I refuse to look at my parents, already knowing what awaits if I do. Hearing everything is bad enough.

It's hard to witness my complete breakdown, how my younger self doesn't even make an effort to get away. I can see it in her eyes, dull and drained of hope. She doesn't even care that an arm coated in shiny black rock is inches from her face.

Finally, she moves. A sob tears from her throat once the Obsidian touches her. Since I've been here many times, I almost feel the snap inside me, the feeling of something splintering. *This is where I pass out,* I think with relief. *Now I wake up from this nightmare.*

But I don't.

My younger self convulses violently before letting out an ear-piercing scream.

Wait. What?

With the screech, an explosion of fire erupts from my father's discarded torch, dousing the nearest Obsidian in flames. They lurch away, but the flames rapidly engulf them before they can flee. Over the demons, the furniture, and even my parents.

Everywhere except for my younger self's limp body. The fire parts around her as if she's behind a shield.

Young Cassie's face is expressionless as she lies in what looks like sleep, the fire never drawing close enough to touch her.

A few minutes later, Adrian and Tala burst in.

My stomach coils in tight knots, pushing up against my esophagus in a desire to expel its contents. *What is this?*

My mind whispers a word in Zachary's voice, but I force the thought away. *No way. There's no way!* I refuse to believe that what I just witnessed is reality. My mind is creating a horrific version of the night because I was asleep when it happened. My horrible imagination is messing with me because Zachary told me how he and the headmaster thought I was a Phoenix.

As I sink past the floorboards into dark space, eyes heavy with sleep, my new theories help relieve my fears. It's impossible that the scene was real. Even if it was, how could I see it now if I had no recollection of it happening? I'm positive my mind is playing a cruel trick on me.

So why do I still feel uneasy?

Chapter 36

Shattering Sanctuary

SUCKING IN A RAGGED BREATH, I SWIFTLY SIT UP AND immediately get flooded with dizziness.

"Hey, it's okay. You're safe." A warm hand caresses my back, and my muscles relax at the velvet voice.

Vision clearing, I find myself in an unfamiliar bed with Adrian kneeling beside it. He's so close I can see the flecks of silver in his crystal eyes. Still trying to get my breathing under control, I scan the room, which is mostly bare except for multiple different weapons mounted on the wall. It's pretty spacious, bigger than the room I share with Sara, and definitely not the hospital wing.

"This is my room," Adrian says, answering the question in my eyes.

"Oh." It's the only thing I can think to say as my mind scrambles for how I possibly landed myself here. Then I finally process his words. "*Oh.*"

I'm in Adrian's bed, wrapped up in his sheets. Each inhale smells like him, and I'm surprised I didn't figure it out sooner. *I really hope my face isn't as red as I feel like it is.*

Adrian steps away, lowering himself into a chair. He scratches the back of his neck without meeting my eyes, and I'm happy to know I'm not the only one affected by my presence here.

Needing a distraction, I cast my gaze over the room once more, but this time, my eyes linger on the dresser. I don't know how I missed it the first time, but more pieces of paper than I can count cover the top of the wood's surface. My eyes squint, and I realize I've seen similar thick paper before, stuffed inside Sara's bedside table. They're letters, except these are clean and smooth, without markings to indicate they've been opened. Does Adrian have family alive? But then why would Blake say Adrian came from the orphanage, and why wouldn't he read them?

I open my mouth to ask him, but he breaks the silence before I can.

"Tala's missing, and I didn't want to take any chances while you recovered."

My inquiries dissipate at his words. *Tala is missing?* How is Tala tied to this? And speaking of *this*, how did I get here?

The third trial.

The two Threes.

I'm scrambling off the bed faster than I can form any words. When my feet hit the cold floor, my knees buckle and I pitch toward the ground. Adrian wraps his arms around me before I land and helps me sit on the edge of the bed. He goes back to his chair, surveying me with an unreadable expression.

I take a deep breath. "So it was Tala? How could she have possibly snuck in such strong Obsidian?" It's not like she could have asked them politely to follow her into a building with more than a hundred people and not kill anyone.

"We don't know for sure, since there's no evidence of her

involvement. But her being missing during the third trial and her continued absence aren't helping her case."

"What happens now? Did I pass?" As much as I love talking about Tala, there are more important things to discuss.

Adrian's sad look is all the confirmation I need. "It was a tough debate. Some said that because you incapacitated them, you should pass. Others argued you should fail because you didn't kill them. In the end, we had to settle on a compromise. You passed because you held your own against a higher level of Obsidian, but because you would've been bitten if a guard hadn't stepped in, your rank immediately drops to last place."

Last place. I should be grateful that I passed at all, but the only thing I can think about is that I'll never see Adrian again after today. My eyes roam over his features, memorizing his beautiful face. *I'll have to live my life without him.* Pain clenches my stomach, and I almost double over from the wave of emotion, so potent I taste the sorrow on my tongue like an expired piece of fruit.

"Cassie, what matters most is that you're alive." His voice is gentle, so gentle I have to turn my face away.

"Right," I choke out, blinking back the tears.

Adrian sighs while I observe his expression from the corner of my eye. Concern creases his face and he opens his mouth, but he closes it with an exhale. After a silent moment, he stands and offers me a hand. "You've been sleeping for a few hours. Everyone is in the gym for the ceremony, but we should be able to make it before it starts."

My trembling fingers settle into his palm, shaking as fast as my stuttering heart. I unsteadily rise to my feet, gripping his hand like it's the last time I'll ever be able to touch him. *Maybe it is.*

After a few steps, my balance comes back to me, so I hastily let his hand drop from mine. Looking down, I find I'm dressed in a fresh pair of gray sweats and can only pray that Nurse Dorna changed me before I came up here.

The wordless walk through the hallways is strained, at least on my part. I can't believe this is my last day at the academy. I couldn't complete the trials. Even if they were rigged against my favor, I still should have beaten the Obsidian.

Just go back to your original plan. Be excited to know how many families you'll save from future horde attacks. I try to pump myself up, because really, it was only a few days ago that I was still dead set on being a hunter. It shouldn't hurt this much to go back to it.

But I didn't know the life I could have with Adrian existed a few days ago. Now that I do, knowing I have to let it go is excruciating.

Adrian and I travel through the last door and cut across the courtyard to save time. I can see the entrance to the main gym, a few feet from the cafeteria. All grades are required to view the ceremony, and then there's one last meal to celebrate the graduates. For me, the rest of the night will be bittersweet. *Adrian, Sara, Jared. I'm leaving everyone I love behind.*

In the gym and cafeteria, the torches go out, dousing everyone in a dull blue haze from the small quantity of Azura mushrooms scattered about the walls. I pause halfway across the courtyard. The full moon is high in the sky, so even though it's nighttime, we can see around us.

"What was that?" I ask as Adrian stops with me. He glances at the guards lining the front gate, both of whom have spun around to search for the source of the instant darkness.

"Probably just wind—"

Bright light flashes from the main entrance, followed by an ear-splitting detonation.

I'm knocked off my feet by the force of the blast, even though I was a good distance from the front gate. My back slams into the ground, ears ringing, and I'm too stunned to move. Someone grabs my arm and hauls me to my feet while I stagger at my loss of bearings. There's screaming, but it's muffled. I look up at Adrian's face, streaked with dirt from the explosion.

"Get to the gym and tell the others!"

I strain to hear his warped words. *Tell them what?* Adrian's fierce expression doesn't leave much room for a conversation, though. After I nod, Adrian lets me go and dashes past me.

I swivel to see where he's going and get my first glimpse of the damage. There's a giant hole in the middle of the double doors, with the metal falling to pieces on the ground. *An explosion capable of shattering steel doors? How is that possible?* The gate is bent inwards toward the academy, which means the bomb must have come from the outside. There's not even a fire from the blast, just smoke.

But what's worse than seeing our academy exposed to the outside are the Obsidian making their way through it. A quick scan shows they're just Zeros, but their sheer number is overwhelming.

Oh no, please, no, I think, wondering if I'm still trapped in the nightmare of my past. But this time, it's not three people under attack. It's over a hundred.

Icy tendrils of fear instantly weave their way through my body, freezing my limbs. The demons swarm the guards at the entrance within seconds, while the two on the wall scramble for arrows. Then there's Adrian, surging into the fray with no gear but his sword, the orange haze of his flame almost entirely consumed by black bodies.

I'm rigid only for a moment before I force my legs into action, launching into a sprint toward the gym. Some instructors must have lit extra torches because dim light settles in a fog over the crowd of people.

"Obsidian have breached the front gates!" I scream over the confused murmurs. My directions to help the younger students head for the back exit get swallowed by the mayhem that explodes before me.

I can hear the wails of the demons right behind me, already broken free from Adrian's line of defense, so I dart inside the gym and fling the doors shut. Most of the guards understand my plan, and they begin pushing tables in front of the door to keep it closed. The gym doesn't have locks since it's available anytime, which now seems like a design flaw.

Luckily, there's another door at the opposite end of the gym that leads farther into the academy, hopefully to secret rooms similar to the one we had our third trial in. A large force hits the doors and the tables screech against the impact, lurching a few inches forward. We shove them back into place with our shoulders, absorbing the blow as another hit from outside shudders the door. *This won't hold for long.*

"Are there weapons in here?" I have to yell to be heard, even though the guard is right next to me.

Though I can't discern much description of her features in the dim light, I can tell she nods. "Right back corner. They were moved for the ceremony."

I leave the guards to keep our barricade up and make my way to the far end of the gym. Bodies cram together, pressing against one another, making it difficult to squeeze through. If we don't find some semblance of order before those doors get busted open, then we are all dead people walking.

"Get to the back entrance! Grab a weapon and be ready

to fight! Find an empty room and lock the door!" I call out orders to as many people as possible, ushering the kids to the instructors who are keeping themselves together, or asking older students to follow me to the weapons.

I remain vigilant for Jared or Sara, but I can barely see the profile of the person next to me, let alone through the massive throng of panicked students. There's a steady flow of kids filing out the small doorway, so I can only hope they made it out of this mess safely.

When I finally reach the corner, most of the weapons are gone. I parcel out the rest as best I can and grab a short sword for myself, tying its sheath around my waist. It isn't my favorite weapon since it has less reach, but it's better than nothing.

I shout my next order to the little following of older students I collected on my way here. They're only a year or two younger, but they all stare at me with expectant and terrified faces.

"We need to—" A hand grips my shoulder and spins me around. I lift my gaze to Officer Zypha, whose expression is the most ferocious I've ever seen.

"You have to get out of here," she bellows over the echoes of screams filling the cavernous room.

I shake my head. "If there's any chance of surviving, we need to take these Obsidian down while the only entrance they have is the front door." I point to the barricade. "Running away now will just spread them throughout the whole academy."

"They're already all over," she responds, and my head rears back in surprise. "They got through one of the back entrances that only a few people know about. Someone must have let them in."

My immediate thought is Tala, but I force it away. While

the woman hates my guts, the smile on her face when teaching the younger kids proves how much she cares about this school. There's no way she did this.

The head of security continues, pulling me from my thoughts. "You need to warn Zachary. I know you've spent a fair amount of time with him. He won't know what's going on until it's too late."

"What are you going to do?" I don't ask her how she knows that. Now's not the time for personal questions.

Zypha gives me a small smile, her white teeth flashing in the faint light. "You're right that a great deal of demons are trying to get into this room. I'm going to get all the students out of here, and then I'm going to let them in. The instructors will protect the students. The guards and I will kill as many as we can here."

"You can't!" I yell. Ten of them against a hundred? She has to know that's suicide.

"I'll do what I must. Please, leave now before it's too late!" Zypha thrusts me toward the entrance, where fleeing students have slowed to a trickle. A look behind me shows that my group of students disappeared while we were talking.

Officer Zypha's back is already to me, shouting commands to the remaining guards. None of them show fear, just determination. More torches are being lit, and a few guards are breaking wooden chairs and tables to stack in the center of the room. Fire is the only way to survive this encounter, and they know it. *If it's all Zeros, maybe they'll have a chance.*

I grip my sword tightly and dart out the door, hoping above anything else that I'm not leaving the guards to die.

As I progress toward the library, the hallway is eerily quiet and does nothing to soothe my nerves. If anything, the silence puts me more on edge.

Every once in a while, my ears pick up a faint scream or the sound of something heavy hitting a wall. Hearing that makes me itch in a completely different way. Whenever a wail echoes through the corridor, it takes all my energy not to head straight for the noise. I can help them, protect whoever it is, but I can't save them and Zachary at once. The endeavor to keep my fears in line, to not think about how the screams may be from Sara or Jared, is strenuous.

But I have a job to do. Zachary's whole reason for being at the academy is to defend and expand our history. He's probably the most valuable person at this school. If the Obsidian destroy what's inside the library, then everything this academy is protecting will vanish.

As Zachary's friend, I can't let that happen. While I may not have appreciated the real reason he befriended me, I know he's a good person with good intentions.

I grab the hilt of my sword as I round the last corner, trying to keep my breathing even.

The thick double doors to the library are wide open.

Have I ever seen these doors open like this before?

No, I haven't. I slow down, softening my footsteps, and glide forward silently. Preparing myself for the worst, I creep my way through the open entrance.

Chapter 37

Unreachable Forgiveness

Books scatter the ground from broken shelves, the wood splintered at odd angles like something rammed into them multiple times. Fire licks up the corner of the room where a lit oil lamp shattered. Only when I pass the first row of shelves do I see the multitude of Obsidian ash covering the floor.

I'm too late.

Picking up my pace, I lap the room, half to search for Obsidian and the other for Zachary. The librarian is nowhere to be seen, but none of the monsters here are alive. When I reach the front once more, I close the doors to ensure no more unwanted intruders can enter.

I suck in a ragged breath to steady my nerves. He has to be here. He killed them all. But then why wouldn't he put out the fire? I march over and stomp on the flames until only charred dust remains.

His office! He must have hidden himself inside with the most precious pieces of history. I run back to the far end of the room, my hand swiping around the edges of the shelf. Relief hits me when my fingers find purchase, allowing the shelf to unfurl.

For a gut-wrenching moment, my breathing stops as my eyes take in the man sprawled on the ground. Then his labored breathing echoes through the tiny office, and my heart sputters into its regular rhythm once again. A thin shelf props his back up, his limbs limp, eyes closed.

"Zachary." I rush to his side and collapse onto my knees beside him. His eyes open, though they are frighteningly unfocused. I lean away, checking him for injuries.

Stifling a sob, I spot it.

A clear impression of sharpened teeth printed into his right forearm, the center of each indentation weeping blood in a futile attempt to rid itself of the fatal disease.

His entire hand and forearm are gray, and if I look closely enough, I can see the slow crawl of death making its ascent to his elbow. His fingertips have already hardened into shiny black rock.

"Oh, Zachary," I moan, my hands hovering over his body, desperate to do something, to *fix this*. But there's nothing to be done.

He gasps, leaning forward rapidly. "Cassie," he grunts, eyes finally connecting with mine. I jerk back on my heels at his action, instantly ashamed of my response. In the end, he'll know how scared I was of him.

But Zachary doesn't seem to mind; his attention rests solely on the bite mark. He pauses, tilting his head toward the mark like he's trying to identify what it is. His gaze returns to me, lips thinned in concentration.

Then he's up, surging forward with enough strength that it knocks me to the ground. My heart skips a beat, a brief image of him attacking me sparking behind my eyes. Yet

Zachary moves as though I'm not in the room, stumbling around and throwing papers to the ground. I stand, slinking into a corner as he whirls around the room, unsure of what I should do. Is this him or the virus?

The librarian pulls out a piece of rope that is tying a group of scrolls together. They fall to the ground unnoticed as Zachary rips off the remaining fabric of his sleeve up to his shoulder. The discoloration has spread above his elbow into the upper arm. He wraps the rope tightly above the dark section, so tightly that blood trickles down from pinched flesh.

I shuffle closer, eyes wide as I take in the alteration. Miraculously, the venom's invasion has slowed.

"This is only a temporary fix," Zachary wheezes, leaning heavily on the shelf. "Nothing can stop the transformation now, but it will help me stay around long enough to leave with no regrets."

He turns, fingering through a massive stack of papers before shoving them to the side. Opening a drawer, Zachary gives a sharp inhale of excitement and pulls out a small piece of parchment paper, smoothing it out on his desk the best he can with one good arm.

Red marks cover most of it, with arrows and Xs over parts of what appears to be topography. Recognition hits me. I've seen this type of paper before, in this room weeks ago. It's a map, though not of the academy like the others were. A wide black circle occupies the bottom left corner.

"What is this?" I ask softly, impressed with his ability to stay calm even though he must know he only extended his life by a few minutes.

The fact threatens to pull me under, the urge to curl into a ball almost irresistible. But there is a reason Zachary still needs to be alive, and I will help him accomplish anything he wants. This moment shouldn't be used to wallow in grief.

"It's—" Zachary gasps, swaying slightly before focusing again, tapping a trembling finger in the circle, "it's research. Based on my cal-calculations, it's where the Obsidian were created."

"What? How do you know?"

He shakes his head. "No time...to explain. I couldn't leave. I-I wasn't positive enough to...send others. Deadly area." His deep brown eyes lock onto mine. "Too late to consider anywhere else. Pl-please. May help us stop them."

I stare silently, processing his words. Zachary doesn't know about the letter I found during the second trial. The writer, Kendra, said she knew the truth, but didn't explain what that truth was. Though it doesn't take a genius to understand she was implying it had to do with Obsidian.

I told myself I wanted to find more answers, and this is it. Zachary's right. I have to go to this location to at least validate his research. As a hunter, I should have the time to investigate. I roll the paper up tightly, fold it in half, and stick it in the back pocket of my sweatpants.

"I promise you," I state, hit again with the realization that this is the last time I'll see my unexpected friend. Even now, dying and in pain, he knew exactly what I needed. "I promise I'll get to the location. If there's anything to be found, I'll find it."

Zachary sinks to the ground, as if waiting for my promise was the only thing keeping him up. "I know...you will."

I kneel beside him, unable to take my eyes off his arm. The virus has escaped past his makeshift tourniquet, giving it full access to his heart and the rest of his body. I bite my lip, knowing a decision needs to be made.

If I were bitten, I would rather die than become an

Obsidian. If Zachary doesn't want to die, and I let him turn, then he may end up killing students. The question here isn't whether I should kill my friend, but if I do it while he still has humanity left.

At least, that's what I know I *should* do. I'm not sure I have the strength to end his life if he doesn't want me to. The weight of this decision slowly crushes me, the pressure of it compressing my throat. *I can't do this. I'm not strong enough.*

A warm hand gently presses against mine. My head flips up, the surprise allowing a few tears to leak out without my consent.

I don't know if Zachary sees the conflict in my eyes, but he squeezes my hand. Or maybe his body is seizing because suddenly tremors rack his frame. *Time is running out.* "I will not...put this on you. My one last c-contribution to society."

From what feels like thin air, there's a dagger in Zachary's hands, and I finally comprehend what he means. I almost laugh through the hysteria. *Always thinking about what's best for society.*

"Thank you," I cry, but I don't think he can hear me. Even though there's black foam beginning to drool from the corner of his mouth, he puts the blade to his throat. "Thank you for everything you've done for me."

I turn my head away, shutting out the sounds of his death, allowing the tears to fall freely now. Through it all, I keep a grip on his fingers, refusing to leave him in his final moments.

Even after he goes still, I don't—*can't* let go. If I let his hand drop, then I have to face reality.

The reality that Zachary is dead.

The way to the library was empty, but retracing my steps, I'm unable to walk ten feet without running into a demon. Maybe I'm more reckless and they're drawn to me. A part of me is glad for it. The more they attack me, the less they attack others.

I want to rip apart every Obsidian to avenge Zachary, to make them suffer. I follow whatever corridor has an Obsidian in it, ready to exterminate every single one myself.

A trail of lumpy flesh and ash follows behind me as I slice into the monsters without so much as a misstep. I've run across a few students as well, and each one brings me off the ledge of hatred a bit more. I direct the kids to the nearest safe room and continue my death march.

The only thing keeping me going is the drive to find my friends. I need to find and protect Sara, Jared, and Adrian.

Adrian. Even just thinking his name plunges me into an icy lake of fear and worry. The last time I saw him, he was heading straight into the worst of it, surrounding himself with what looked like a hundred Obsidian. No one could have survived the onslaught.

Don't think like that! Adrian's stronger than ten regular guards. He's still alive. I just need to locate him.

I barge through another set of doors that lead to one of the larger gyms, mainly used for storing equipment around its perimeter. Yet today, rot accompanies the usual stench of sweat. A sea of moans and blackness and death overruns the gym, and I step back from the oppressive weight of their presence.

There are pockets of Obsidian remnants dispersed on the ground, so someone must have tried to do some damage here. Other discarded bodies are shaking, pulling themselves up and joining the monsters. One glance at their smooth black heads with sunken eye sockets confirms that those Obsidian were recently humans.

Strangely, my loud entrance hasn't disturbed the nearest ones yet, though I know it's a matter of time before they notice me. The only reason I can think of for why they haven't detected my presence is that there are people still fighting on the other side of this Obsidian barricade.

I could go in blazing, try to cut a path down the middle to get the survivors. I survey my surroundings, noting the tall pieces of wood stacked up against the wall. *Best to survey the battleground first.*

Being as stealthy as possible, I sprint to the most stable-looking pile. Sliding my short sword into its sheath, I climb the stack, focusing on my foot placement and cushioning every step. As I go, my mind mulls over my next move. There are far too many of them to just jump into the fray with my one weapon. *Could I distract some? Get them out of the room somehow?*

The sheer amount of them surprises me. With this gym set further back in the academy, all the monsters in here bypassed students to fill up this space. Were all the students hiding here, and that drew their attention?

Even if there were a lot of students, it still makes no sense that the Obsidian wouldn't run off and chase down stragglers in different sections of the academy. I ran into a few on my way to the gym, but for as many as had swarmed the gate, it was a minuscule fraction. Is this where they all went? *But why here?*

All my thoughts fly out of my head as I reach the top of the planks and can finally see below. Instantly, I turn to mush, not even noticing when my legs are incapable of supporting me anymore and I crash to my knees.

Sara and Jared fight, surrounded and separated from

each other, with a circle of Obsidian crowding in on each of them.

They are small orange bubbles trapped by shadows. How they endured for so long is a miracle in itself, a luck that is near-depleted. Sara is closest to me, and I can see the resolve on her face as she continues to cut down demon after demon. Tears stream down her cheeks; she must know the fate that's a few claws away from claiming her.

I wonder who she's thinking about. Her life at the academy or her family in the city?

Jared is a little farther away to my right and also a sight to behold. I can't see his expression from here, but he doesn't stumble as he keeps death at bay.

However, once every few seconds, when his sword is motionless as he waits for the next one to rush forward, I can see how frequently his sword shakes. I doubt he's that scared, which means he's exhausted. He steps toward Sara's position, but the Obsidian push him back, refusing to let them reunite.

My stomach twists so hard I'm positive I would have vomited if my body had anything in it to throw up. I stand and pull my sword out, but it's too slow, the friction unable to produce any flames. I barely notice.

This can't happen. I can't let them die. Even as I agonize over the best way to save them both, the space around them shrinks.

Sara flicks her eyes up, her gaze sliding past me before honing in on my form. "Cassie!" she screams, still working in a hasty circle to keep it from dwindling even further. "Cassie, save Jared! Please, I'm begging you!"

And I realize she understands as much as I do that the odds of both of them making it out of here alive are near zero. *I can't make this choice. Not my family. Not again. I can't lose them again.*

Jared, head rising when he hears Sara's voice, spots me as well and I scour his face. The acceptance in his eyes, the slight curve of his lips that always carries a joke, emanates from him. His voice fades with the distance, but I'm able to discern what he mouths.

Jared raises his sword high, blade pointed inward.

"NO!" The scream tears from my throat, ringing my ears with its anguish.

My sword bursts into flames, larger than if I were to have used the sheath. The fire is hot as it whips close to my face, but I don't feel the heat, my insides scorching like the fire beside me. *I will not let my family die again!*

Filled with rage, I leap off the wood. The massive blast of fire sends the Obsidian into a frenzy. In the few seconds it takes to fall, time seems to crawl to a halt, allowing me to watch the next events unfold with perfect clarity.

Jared's sword is inches away from carving into his own heart.

Sara, who had been watching me until the sword exploded, jerks her head around to stare at Jared through the break in the massive throng of bodies.

The Obsidian, desperate to get away from my blaze, charge Jared, knocking into him before he can end his life. I hear the clatter of his sword hitting the stone floor and watch helplessly as my brother gets swarmed with Obsidian until I lose sight of him.

"Jared!" Sara bellows and immediately starts toward him.

I land directly onto an Obsidian and thrust my sword into its skull. Working as fast as I dare, I cut down any monster standing in my way. *Please, Jared. Please, please, please. You can't be dead. Please don't be dead.* The words chant in my mind, burning along with the rest of my limbs.

When I reach the spot Jared was, the only person I see is

Sara. My heart, which had been suffocating under the weight of all the pain, finally shatters.

Sara's eyes widen in horror when she sees me, and she stops searching, like my presence confirms there will be no getting Jared back. Her sword slides from her fingers. "No, no, no, no. Jared! Jared, please!"

She's in no condition to fight. I need to get her out of here. I focus on one task at a time, ignoring the tears running down my cheeks.

I grab her arm, and she's in too much shock to fight me. I progress quickly toward the entrance, cutting in a wide arc that will hopefully prevent the Obsidian from reaching Sara while she's incapacitated. She bawls, calling Jared's name and cursing me at the same time.

I keep a straight face, but inside, I'm falling apart with her. *Jared, I'm sorry. I'm so sorry, please forgive me.*

We make it to the exit and I fling the door open, throwing her outside before jumping through the threshold and slamming it closed. I expect the Obsidian to bombard the door immediately, but nothing comes. *Aren't they going to follow us? What bizarre acting Obsidian.*

"We have to go back," Sara screeches, frantically reaching for the door handle.

I step in her way, blocking her access to the room. "It's too late, Sara. He's gone."

My vision blurs as my heart constricts. While I want to as well, we can't go back into that room. The Obsidian would swarm us instantly. *I lost Jared. I will not lose Sara.*

Stinging pain slams into my cheek with enough force to snap my head to the side. I press my hand to the spot Sara slaps, not even able to open my mouth before she's on me again, pummeling my chest with her fists.

"You can't stop me," she howls, her face contorted with fury and grief. "I told you to save him, and you didn't!"

I grab her wrists. She tries to pull away, but I hold tight. "Stop it, Sara. I won't let you die, too."

"Jared's dead. He's dead, and it's your fault. You killed him!"

I drop her wrists, her words hurting me more than the punches. My lips move, but I can't form any words. I lick them and try again, my voice breaking halfway. "I promise you, I did everything I could to save him. If I could take his place, then I would."

My words do nothing to console her. She drops her head, sobbing into her hands. The sound grinds the fragmented pieces of my heart into dust and I go to wrap her in a hug, anything to help ease our shared suffering.

When my fingers touch her shoulder, she spasms and lurches back, pushing me away from her. "Don't touch me! You killed Jared!"

Anger breaks through my sadness, and I almost lose myself in the grief and shock. "You think I wanted to let Jared die?" I yell hoarsely.

"*I would rather he be dead!*" Sara screams, and I shrink away from the hate radiating off her. "He was going to do it. He was going to end his own life, but your sword stopped him. However you lit your sword, it gave the Obsidian the chance to attack him. Now he's one of them." Her voice loses its hysterics, the emotions draining from her features. "I guess you're right. You didn't kill him. You just fed him to the enemy."

I wrap an arm around my stomach, trying not to crumble at her accusation. I don't remember putting my sword in its sheath, but I knew I needed my sword lit, and somehow it happened. That flame was the reason the Obsidian tackled Jared.

Now that Sara points it out, in my desperate attempt to save his life, I may have doomed him to an eternity as the monster he's sworn to destroy. "I didn't—" I choke on my tears, my voice barely above a whisper. "I didn't mean—"

"I hate you," she cuts me off, straightening up with a blank expression. "I will never forgive you for this. If I ever see you again, I'll give you the death Jared deserved to have."

She turns and walks away without looking back, leaving me in my misery. I call her name, begging her to stop, but she disappears around the corner without responding. My feet carry me a step further and then seize, shoulders twitching in place. My hands go to my hair, gripping the strands tightly against the pounding reverberating through my head.

Zachary is dead. Jared is an Obsidian. Sara is gone, wanting nothing to do with me. Some tiny part of me still clings to the hope that she's just angry and, after some time to grieve, we can repair our relationship. But a bigger part feels sick, knowing the likelihood that I just lost my sister is extremely high.

I groan, pulling my hair harder. Jared tried to take his own life to make sure he didn't become an Obsidian, but I stopped him. The fear of losing my family only ended up costing them anyway.

It's happening again. I lost my family *again*.

At the peak of the undiluted pain, so immense in its strength that my vision dips, I remember Jared's last words he mouthed to me seconds before the end.

'*It's okay. I love you.*'

My limbs begin to burn, each nerve igniting in an explosion of fire. The heat crawls over my body, suppressing my thoughts into one focused intention.

Justice for Jared. The innocent have to be avenged, and I will incinerate the guilty.

Adrian was right that I would recognize the loss of control when it happened, but I don't stop it this time, don't stop to think about the consequences that may arise from letting the inferno take over. I let the sensation wash over me, freely giving my power away.

Anything to make the pain cease.

Chapter 38

Flame Horizon

I SLIDE BACK INTO THE GYM WITH PURPOSE AND CONSIDER THE room full of evil. A quick estimate puts their numbers at about fifty. *Fifty sinners who need to be purged from this world.*

At least thirty piles of ash litter the ground, the remaining Obsidian shuffling around without intention. I walk up to the closest one, and its head flies off before the demon can sense my presence.

Now that I've made myself known, they all stagger toward me. I smile, ready to crush these unworthy souls under my heel.

I cut a path to the middle of the room, wanting to be at the center of it all. Having them on all sides will be more of a challenge. The Zeros are simple creatures, effortless to kill. I dispatch them before they even realize I'm there. This is too simple. So simple that the satisfaction I should receive at righting the world is minimal.

When I reach my destination, I survey the room once more while my sword blurs in a fiery haze around me.

My eyes drift past the swarm to a lone figure standing at the back wall.

A sinner who has chosen evil. My lips curl into a sneer. *Worse than the ones I currently kill.*

Tala leans on the door at the back end of the gym, arms folded, eyes on me. Seeing her in the flesh after so long, everything falls into place. All of this is *her* fault. She tried to kill me, and when that didn't work, she ruined my life instead. An eternity of suffering is not enough of a punishment for Tala's actions.

She opens the door and saunters into the next room, closing it behind her. The criminal is trying to run away again. *I won't let you escape that easily.*

I advance at a full sprint, leaving the Obsidian alone except for those directly blocking my path. *I can always come back for them later.*

Mouth watering, I near the door, knowing justice is on the other side.

My name reaches me from across the hoard of Obsidian, and I instinctively turn, annoyed that someone is halting my vengeance.

At the opposite end, still halfway through the door, is Adrian. *A good man, worthy of life.*

"Cassie, what happened?"

By the concern in his voice and the speed at which he got here, I'm assuming he ran into Sara. *Someone who has been harmed by the evil in this room.* Reoriented to my goal, I pivot and reach for the door handle.

"Hold on, Cassie. Wait for me." Even from here, I can hear the sounds of fire shattering rock. He's making his way toward me, but it will still take some time for him to get through the wall of death separating us.

Hopefully by then, Tala will have paid for her crimes.

I stride through the door. Before my eyes can adjust to the dim room, something heavy hits me in the back of the head and throws me out of my lethal mindset, jarring me back to myself before I crumple into unconsciousness.

The harsh inflection of a voice is the only thing that halts me from gripping the back of my throbbing head and groaning. I lie completely immobile as my senses slowly return to me.

I'm dizzy, which isn't fading like the fogginess is. After a few seconds, I can make out the words of the person talking.

"How much do you want me to take? You wanted her alive before, but is the blood sufficient? Can I kill her now?"

The voice is easily recognizable as Tala, and numbed anger washes through me at the hopefulness in her voice. She's begging to kill me, but who's she talking to? From her tone, I wouldn't be surprised if she tagged the word 'master' after her sentences.

There's a pause before she speaks again. "Will four vials be enough? It hurts to touch her." Another pause. "I'm positive she's one of them. Isn't what she did in the other room proof of that?" Pause. "Of course, sir. The cabin's sample will be nothing compared to what you'll get today."

Confusion fills me. Tala's speaking as though there's someone in the room, but no one else is talking. And what does the 'cabin sample' mean? I wait, hoping she explains herself or the person she's getting orders from appears and I can identify them.

I wait until a pinch in my forearms forces my eyes open, and I instinctively roll away from the pain, a fresh wave of nausea hitting me at the motion. *I'm so stupid.* How it took me this long to understand that she's taking my blood is beyond me.

I end the roll on my knees, gasping slightly as a cold sweat breaks out over my skin and my fingers quiver with the exertion. Protruding from the bend of my left inner elbow is a thin cylinder tube, the access allowing blood to pour from the needle onto the floor in a steady stream. I yank the needle out with a wince, covering the hole with my thumb.

Tilting my head to the side, I finally get a good view of Tala, who's still kneeling beside where I was, gripping an empty vial the length of her hand. Three filled vials line the ground near her left foot.

She really is trying to bleed me out. Getting woozy from the amount of blood lost, I move past her to the other figures tucked in the corner.

The four Obsidian are still, their bulging black eyes staring in our direction. From their facial features, they appear to be Threes. I tense, ready for them to attack me and Tala...but they don't move. If I didn't know any better, I'd say they were statues.

"She's awake." Tala stands, scooping up the bottles and putting them in a small bag that's wrapped around her waist. "What would you like me to do now, sir?"

I need to distract her from whatever she's planning, to give myself time to recover. My eyes settle on the Obsidian. "Who are you talking to?" I ask, a bead of sweat trailing down my temple. I've never heard of a demon speaking, but I'm running out of explanations for Tala's craziness.

Tala cocks her head to the side like she's listening to something. *Or someone.* I strain my ears, but the only thing I hear is our breathing. She nods. "He has chosen not to reveal himself yet. The less you know, the better it is for him."

"I don't understand." My legs tremble as I rise. I lean

heavily against the wall for support, but at least I'm on my feet. "Who is 'he'?"

The familiarity of the words hit me. I've said them before, in the main gym when Tala called me a monster. "Is it the same person who told you what you need to do to protect this school?"

"Yes," Tala says quickly and then cringes. "I mean, that's none of your concern."

Almost all her words must be coming from the man giving the orders. But how am I supposed to gather information about him if she's forbidden from saying anything? I think back to that day in the gym. She said something else then, too. "You had Emmerick and Naire tie me to the tree to give me to this person, right? That's why you said I wouldn't die. He needs me alive. But what does he want from me?"

Tala narrows her eyes but doesn't respond, presumably heeding her new orders. "Enough talk," she eventually states. "He says we need to go."

"I'm not letting you go anywhere," I growl, though the threat is pretty empty. Even if I'm at a disadvantage, I can't just let her take my blood and give it to a stranger. Who knows what that person will do with it?

I creep a hand to my belt to grab my short sword, preparing for battle. While I may be shaky, I still have a chance. My fingers slide across my belt, unable to find the hilt.

Dread lances my stomach, blooming across my chest. *Of course they'd take my weapon away.*

Tala offers a twisted smile and marches to the door, her next words drifting from over her shoulder. "Don't worry, you're coming with us. There's someone who would like to meet you."

Without a signal, the frozen Obsidian sprint in my direction. Before I can even flinch, their cold, hard claws wrap around my arms. My heart rate spikes as the demons tug me toward the door Tala just went through.

I thrash, kicking out my legs and landing blows on their shins, but the monsters barely note my efforts. They aren't even trying to bite me, which is the basic instinct of any Obsidian. They must be following orders, being controlled by something.

'Adrian, I think a Commander was controlling those Threes.'

My words after the attack on the academy during our excursion outside come back to me. I was right. There *was* a Commander there, trying to get into the school. But why didn't it attack the next day? Why would he wait a month to attack again?

Through my wrestling, my eyes land on Tala, who's waiting impatiently at the threshold for us to follow. An unpleasant thought worms its way into my mind.

Is she being controlled, too?

Tala had always been mean to me, but she didn't start trying to kill me until this past month. Did she just snap, or did something push her to do it?

If that's the case, how did the Commander get hold of her? When did she truly start becoming deranged? I think through the panic, unable to shake that I'm missing a few crucial details to figuring this all out. I gasp as memories flood me.

How Tala gagged and spat into the grass after I chopped the invading Three's head off in front of her.

'You got its blood in my mouth.'

'I know what you are. I've known it all along.'

'He has made it perfectly clear what I need to do to protect this school.'

"Tala, you're being controlled by a Commander! You

have to fight it!" I scream, doubling my efforts to escape the Obsidian. Adrenaline pushes through my veins, wiping away my dizziness at the blood loss. If she's able to take me away, then I probably won't survive the outcome.

I need to explain my findings and pray that she listens to me. If I can just get the idea into her brain, maybe she can defeat the Commander's power over her. Once the blood is out of her system, then the Commander will have no grasp on her anymore. "You have the virus in your system, and that allowed—"

The Obsidian let me go as Tala grips my throat and slams me against the wall. Her face is beyond rage, so much so that it paralyzes me.

"The virus isn't in my system; it's a part of me," she spits, gnashing her teeth together. "Do you know how painful it's been to be forced to look at you, to touch you all these years? I was fine until you showed up, slowly driving me insane."

My mouth opens, but Tala squeezes tighter and I choke on the pressure. Her whole body aligns with mine, pinning me in place. I can barely wiggle my legs. She has me trapped with a strength I've never seen from her, and I stare at her with wide eyes as she continues.

"I didn't realize who I was, why I hated you so much, but Henderson told me. He showed me how to embrace myself, how I'm not a monster. What you are, that's the true horror."

What I am? What does that mean? And who is Henderson? Tala doesn't seem to know what she's saying, or maybe she's too angry to care. She said being around me physically hurt, that I was the one to push her over the edge. Her ramblings aren't making sense.

If I don't get out of the chokehold soon, I'll die at the hands of a madwoman.

Tala leans in close, her cheek almost touching mine. Black

spots dance across my vision. "I thought I would die like my mother did, but then I found out the truth. Obsidian blood ran through my veins at birth, and ingesting the fresh blood helped me unlock my potential. I am not one of you, and I am not human. Do you understand, Cassidy? I couldn't turn because I'm already an Obsidian."

I can't tell what's causing me to suffocate more: the aggressive grip on my throat or Tala's words. *She's one of the Obsidian? That's impossible. She's human.* If I could speak, I'd tell her how crazy she sounds.

Across the room, the door flies open with a loud bang, revealing Adrian covered in black ash and blood with only a handful of Obsidian left behind him. He closes the door to keep them out.

Adrian looks like an avenging angel, one I forgot followed me. He blanches at the sight of us, yet doesn't hesitate, stepping forward with resolution.

"Stop or she dies," Tala shouts, easing up on my throat, and I gasp. I can only suck in a sliver of air, but it's enough to keep me from passing out.

I barely notice my hand raising until it's pressed to the mouth of an Obsidian. My body stiffens automatically, ignoring the importance of oxygen, knowing a single twitch could force the demon's teeth into my unprotected palm.

Adrian tenses as well, his face contorting in anger. "Tala, what are you doing?"

"We won't be able to leave with her now. Not with him here." She disregards Adrian as she waits for a response.

Adrian's mouth dips in a confused frown, but he doesn't know that she's connected to the Commander. With Tala focused inwardly, Adrian raises his sword behind his head, as if he's going to launch it rather than run forward himself.

But he wavers, not releasing the sword. It doesn't take me

long to figure out he can't hit Tala or the Obsidian without likely hitting me as well.

"Do it," I shriek, watching Tala nod to whatever the Commander says. "Do it!"

I lock eyes with Adrian, discern the torment and fear radiating through them, and I understand instantly he won't risk it. He won't do anything that has a chance of killing me.

He lowers his sword and sprints toward us.

Tala peers at him with a blank face. "She will die because you're here."

My old professor grips the satchel full of my blood and disappears through the door along with the three standing Obsidian. I sink to the ground without her holding me up, jolting the arm still painfully gripped by the demon.

The Obsidian's mouth widens over my hand. *Please, no, anything but this.*

Sharp black teeth pierce the fleshy underside of my wrist, and my entire body explodes in agony.

The Obsidian falls as its head gets severed by Adrian's fiery blade. I slide to the floor, writhing in pain, unable to stop the screams ripping through me. A thousand hot needles impale my skin, stabbing over and over. It feels ten times worse than any time I've lost control.

Then I think about how Jared went through this exact experience moments ago, and I find the pain isn't that bad after all. It was only a matter of time before I got what I deserved.

Through the unbearable torture, I can feel my body spasming, my numb limbs hitting the floor repeatedly. Then Adrian's face appears above me, absolute anguish written all over his features.

"Oh, Cassie, no," he begs hoarsely, his hands wrapping

tightly around my bitten arm. "Please don't leave me. I don't want to lose you, too."

"Y-you need to kill…" I can't finish the sentence through the chattering of my teeth, the sting of fire closing my throat.

But Adrian understands what I'm trying to say. He buries his head in my neck, and I can't tell if I'm the only one trembling. "I can't," he moans.

Then he jerks back with a gasp, his forehead red from where it nestled against my skin. "You're burning up."

I don't know how it feels to become an Obsidian, but I don't remember Zachary's skin sizzling with heat. *What's happening to me?*

"Get back!" I howl at Adrian, my suffering distorting my voice to a screech I've never heard before. He stumbles away in bewilderment.

The searing agony reaches a crescendo, and my mouth stretches in a wordless scream. Fire explodes from my body, caressing my skin, though to me it feels like warm water. It engulfs me, curling around me like a blanket. I open my eyes as the pain lessens and take in the flames dancing around me, swirling in a bubble of crackles and light. I feel complete with this blaze that belongs to me.

I rise to my feet, stronger than I've ever felt before. The world around me is hazy with reds and yellows as the heat increases in intensity.

My eyes lift to Adrian, who's staring at me with uncertainty and astonishment. He observes the fire as it clings to my clothes without burning them. He tries to move closer, but has to retreat with his hands shielded out in front of him. Beads of sweat dot his skin.

The fire only persists for a minute before it dissipates, yet it doesn't leave me for good. I can still feel it within my body, still raging on, a comforting presence inside my veins. I silently hold out my arms and find no graying or hardened skin, like I had never been bitten.

I didn't turn.

"Cassie?" Adrian asks tentatively.

"I'm a—" I begin in disbelief, but swallow the rest, unable to say the actual word through my incredulity.

I start forward in hesitation, but collapse on the ground, the overwhelming energy draining out of me. Adrian pulls me into his arms and calls my name. I try to answer him as I struggle against the intense urge to fall asleep, but I'm not strong enough.

I'm a Ph—

My eyes roll back into my head before I can finish the thought, taking all my unanswered questions with me into unconsciousness.

Chapter 39

Harrowing Revelations

MY MIND IS BLESSEDLY BLANK AS I WAKE UNTIL THE EVENTS of what happened before I fainted surge through me. The academy, Zachary, Jared, Tala, and then becoming a human torch.

With great effort, I peel my eyelids apart. I stare at the ceiling, pinpointing the lodged dagger that, weeks later, is still clinging to its perch above my bed.

I'm in my dorm room. The room is dark, which at least means I'm not on fire. *But an Obsidian bit me. I should be one of them right now.*

Testing my body, I cautiously turn onto my side. The movement is effortless with no pain, so I sit all the way up without triggering vertigo. Whatever occurred, I'm definitely not an Obsidian, though I feel different. An energy I didn't have before flows through me.

Facing Sara's clean bed, a wave of sadness hits me. Then I get a closer look. Her clothes, the small trinkets she liked to keep at her bedside, are gone. I stand up, wincing as my bare feet hit the cold stone floor, and pad over to her bedside. I shuffle through her drawers, her closet, her side of the bathroom. Nothing.

She's gone. Sara's gone, and I'm never going to see her again.

A different type of pain washes over me, but I blink the tears away. There will be time to mourn Sara's disappearance later. As long as she's okay, that's what matters.

I'm so busy staring at the empty bathroom sink, I don't realize something is off with my reflection until my eyes meet my own in the mirror.

My irises, once a simple hazel color, are a deep shining gold as though the sun itself swims in my eyes.

"What the—"

The door to my room opens and Adrian walks in, his face grim. It shifts to surprise when he sees me standing there, then relief.

"You're awake," he breathes, striding toward me like I don't have two torches for eyes. I step back when he gets close, still trying to wrap my head around my new appearance. He stops, his face concerned. "Are you alright?"

I give a short, slightly frenzied laugh. "Do I look alright? What happened to me?" I gesture to my face, blinking rapidly like the action will force my eyes to change back.

Adrian pauses, narrowing his eyes while he debates his next move. Finally, he motions for me to sit on my bed with him, but I take Sara's so we are facing each other. "Tala got away. Once she left, the rest of the Obsidian fled as well. By the time I came back to find her, there was no trace of where she had gone. We deduced she was the one who set the explosion off at the gates, though we are still trying to figure out how she found the resources to do it."

Indignation fills my lungs as I take a deep breath, frustrated that Tala escaped and that she would allow the

Obsidian to kill so many people just because she realized she wasn't fully human. *If that's even true.*

"You were bitten," he continues, "but instead of turning, you caught on fire. After the flames subsided, I took you to Nurse Dorna. While you had no injuries, you were burning up, and I was afraid you'd die from it."

I bite my tongue to hold back my questions. His haunted face shows just how scared he was. "That was two days ago; you've been asleep since then. Your skin is still hot, but it doesn't hurt to touch you anymore. We monitored you the whole time for signs of the transformation, just in case it were to happen."

"But I'm not an Obsidian," I whisper weakly, still reeling from his words. *My skin is hot?* Rubbing my hands together, they don't feel any different to me.

He shakes his head. "No, but Dorna detected high amounts of the virus in your blood, as well as something she's never seen in a human before. Nobody could explain why you didn't turn, at least not until we found Hallow's old documents."

So the virus is in me, but it has no effect. *What if something inside me changes and the venom takes over?* The thought makes me feel queasy. "What documents?"

Adrian observes the emotions flitting across my face. He stands and ignores my question. "You must be hungry. I'll get you some food. Also, the new headmaster wanted to talk with you when you woke up."

A bolt of anger shoots across his face when he says the word 'headmaster,' yet it's gone in an instant. Adrian hesitates, like he wants to say more, but sighs and wordlessly leaves.

I remain seated and try to sort through my chaotic thoughts. The *new* headmaster wants to see me. Adrian must mean Zypha, who was planning on succeeding Hallow after the trials were over.

But why would he be angry with Zypha? Unless she voted for me to fail the trials. That night seems so long ago now, a distant memory. I wonder if they kicked Hallow out or if he died in the onslaught.

Just the thought of the attack pulls my mind to my old instructor. Tala's escape doesn't sit well with me, especially after the little speech about who she is. Maybe what happened to me also happened to her. Did she get bitten at some point and not transform into an Obsidian?

If that's the case, then wouldn't that make me an Obsidian right now? *No way.* Even now, we're not similar. I don't feel like murdering anyone. Except maybe her...and the Commander.

The bigger problem is that the Commander is still out there somewhere. He wanted me alive, took my blood, and then tried to turn me into one of his minions. His motives are all over the place, and his end goal is still unknown. *What is he going to use my blood for?*

Then a more urgent thought: *why me?* What is so special about my blood that he invaded the school to get it?

Tala had said something when I was feigning sleep, something about how the cabin's sample was nothing compared to the blood she was getting from me then. What cabin? My old home? I haven't lived there for years. If that was the case, why would he wait three years to attack the school?

Unless he didn't know I was here and just attacked Hallow Academy for the hell of it. But then, Commanders are supposed to keep striking until they either die or achieve their goal. So did his goal change?

Think, Cassie. What didn't seem right? What questions did you have that never got answered?

The cabin with the Zero, the one who was mysteriously hiding in the bedroom. I had asked how an Obsidian could have found its way into a closed room if they didn't know how to open doors. Just like how I thought Obsidian couldn't climb walls. *They can't, not unless being directed.*

I freeze, my fingers twisting tightly in the sheets. When the Zero cut my cheek, I bled all over the floor of that cabin. The Commander must have found it, and something about my blood made him change his plans to seek out more. Is that 'something' the same thing Nurse Dorna found along with the venom?

He needs my blood for something, but what?

I shove those questions aside, the smallest inkling of panic beginning to weave its way through me at the revelation.

Needing a distraction, I head back into the bathroom to stare at my form in the mirror. Why did my eyes change color? Because I'm some mutant Obsidian? Tala wasn't able to turn into a fiery ball, though.

And then I remember my last dream, when I witnessed Dad's discarded torch explode into fire on its own, the same thing that happened to my sword when Jared was about to die.

'A defenseless child who survived an Obsidian attack, her entire house engulfed in flames while she remained untouched. Curious, don't you think?'

'I think I would know if I had magical powers. Powers that, if your thesis is correct, means I blew up my own house.'

The mirror shatters as my fist flies through it, slicing my knuckles open. I stare at the blood dripping onto the stone counter, the red liquid now studded with shimmering gold flecks.

All this time, I thought Tala was crazy, but she was right. *'Will four vials be enough? It hurts to touch her.'* My skin burned hers whenever we touched. That's why she always avoided me, why she wanted to ship me off to the fields instead of coming to the academy. Tala knew what I was before we both knew what Phoenixes were.

I am a monster. Just not the same type of monster she is.

I peek down at my bloody pants and am shocked to find they're the same training outfit I wore the night of the invasion. *They must have been too afraid to touch me to change it.*

Pain spears my head, threatening to overtake my mind, but I force it down. I don't have time to fall apart, not yet.

I numbly strip off my clothes and throw them in a corner. The little routine of feeding the Azura mushroom before stepping into the shower helps to calm my mind. I pretend the stream of cold water is wiping away more than just old blood.

Maybe if I stand here long enough, I'll forget about everything that happened. Of Jared and Zachary's deaths, of Sara revoking our friendship, and even of my parents. But I can't stop my thoughts as they churn through my head.

Adrian said that the Obsidian scattered before they were all killed, which means Jared may still be out there murdering people.

Were the Obsidian drawn to me because of what I am? Is that why they attacked my family? Am I the reason my parents died?

Bending over, I heave, though my empty stomach has nothing to purge.

I bring misfortune to those around me, that much I've figured out. And if I stay here, stay with Adrian, more tragedy will befall him again. I won't allow myself to bring any more heartache to Adrian than I already have. The only person I care about who's still with me.

Stepping out of the shower, I get dressed swiftly before wrapping my fingers around a miniature first aid kit, not in the mood for Serous to fix the wound itself. I falter, tilting the package to look at my hand, the one that broke the mirror. The pain faded a while ago, but I assumed that the throbbing ended because my mind was focused elsewhere.

Smooth, unbroken skin covers my knuckles. Not a single mark to attest to the cuts that happened only ten minutes ago.

All the times I questioned if I took Serous when my minor injuries mysteriously mended come flashing back, along with the comments from others about how fast Serous seemed to work on me.

I try to remember if I healed myself when I lived with my parents before the Obsidian attack, but my mind comes up empty. Did causing a fire for the first time unlock some latent ability? So why couldn't I use the power at any time, and why was the healing slow enough that I never noticed?

I know little about the subject, except for the brief explanation Zachary had given to me in his study.

Zachary! With everything that took place, I forgot about the map he gave me, his last dying wish, to figure out if his hypothesis was correct.

My hands dive into my old pants, and I breathe a sigh of relief when I hear the paper crumple. I pull out the map and scrutinize it, memorizing as much as I can in case I lose the paper. As I read it, I can't help the nagging feeling that I've seen a map similar to this one. *What other maps have I read recently?*

I choke on a gasp. The location Zachary drew is almost identical to the coordinates Kendra wrote in her letter. I didn't get as good a look at hers, but I can almost guarantee they would lead to the same spot: Pellema, where the Obsidian made their first appearance.

Does that mean Kendra was right? That she truly knew how the Obsidian came to our world? I curse myself for not bringing the letter with me. It's still sitting in its hiding spot in Karanos.

I need to find her letter again, and then I need to figure out what this location is hiding.

Zachary said it was dangerous, not that I require any extra incentive to go alone. I'm not putting anyone else at risk.

I'll sneak out before anyone can notice I'm gone.

I know exactly what's within Hallow's old documents. How people randomly caught fire and were swept into the military. How they thought I was a Phoenix as well.

If the military is eager to replace the Phoenix that died, I'm sure it's only a matter of time before they figure out where I am and come to collect me. I don't want to end up as a mindless soldier, one who's unable to go where they want. *I have to leave now.*

I don't know how, but I will end this war. I am the reason the demons attacked the academy and my family. If I don't stop the war, then their deaths will have been for nothing.

I quickly fill a bag with necessities and head toward the door, but waver with my fingers on the handle, my heart refusing to let me leave just yet. It seems exceptionally cruel to abandon Adrian without saying a word, a goodbye he doesn't deserve.

Briskly heading to my bedside table, I shuffle through the disorganized drawer until I find an unused piece of paper and a quill. I scribble a brief note, hoping he won't hate me too much for this decision, that he understands why I have to do this, that he knows how much he means to me.

I set the note on my pillow and sling my pack onto my shoulders, preparing myself for the tricky task of leaving the academy without being caught. I don't think the guards would stop me, but Adrian sure would.

I take a step forward and stop, watching as the knob turns on its own. *Oh crap, he's back way faster than I thought.*

Whipping my head wildly around the room, I grab the incriminating note and stuff it in my back pocket. Wrestling out of the backpack's straps, I fling it toward Sara's bed. It slides across the stone floor and disappears underneath the frame as the door swings open.

Chapter 40

A Purpose Reborn

"BLAKE," I SAY, SURPRISED. MY EYES IMMEDIATELY LIFT PAST him, but the man is alone. A small streak of disappointment flares through me. I lock it away, annoyed with myself for letting my emotions take over. It's only been twenty minutes and I already miss Adrian. *You need to let him go, Cassie.* "Er, I mean, what are you doing here? Adrian said…"

I drift off, gazing into Blake's sad eyes. *The new headmaster wanted to talk with you*, Adrian had said. I shake my head. "I don't understand."

Blake sighs. "Zypha didn't survive, nor did Hallow. Lord Netiva offered the position to Adrian, but he declined, so I got it instead."

He closes the door and leans against it, his eyes taking in my new appearance.

I'm not paying much attention to his inspection. A jolt courses through me at his words, as well as sorrow. I knew Zypha didn't have great odds when she took on the Obsidian in that gym, but I still had hope. While there's no sympathy for Hallow's death, Zypha didn't deserve to die that way.

Also, why did Adrian refuse the position? I almost ask Blake, but he takes a large breath and moves further into the room.

He passes by without a word, though I tense as he gives me a wide berth. Of course he would fear me. It only makes sense, given that I don't know how to manage my powers. *I could set him on fire, or lose control and attack him.* The thought hits me hard, and my feet shuffle away from him on their own, my fingers trembling.

I stare at my clenched hands as he lowers himself onto Sara's bed, too afraid to meet his eyes. *I don't want to see the fear there.*

"I read Hallow's notes. You're a Phoenix." The word sounds foreign on his tongue, probably because he's never heard of Phoenixes before. I remember Zachary saying they were a thoroughly kept secret.

My head snaps up at his words. There's no fear in his voice.

Blake gawks at my eyes with reverence. I tear my gaze away, uncomfortable under his wondrous scrutiny, as though I'm some god who has descended to save Arrynd.

"I had no idea people like you existed," he whispers, still in awe.

"Stop looking at me like that," I bite back. He shouldn't be looking at me like that. Doesn't he know the academy was attacked because of me?

Blake shakes his head, pulling himself out of his trance. When his eyes reach mine again, he's more focused, yet they still hold a touch of worship. "The military sent word this morning that they have left the city today to come get you. You should be ready to join them in the next few days."

"W-what?" I stutter, my head rearing in shock.

Blake leans forward in urgency. "They need you to win

this war. We've already lost so much, you won't be of help anywhere else."

I swallow hard, surveying Blake's imploring expression. While I don't know the specifics, the military let a Phoenix die under their watch, and I doubt they'll let me go to the origin on my own because I made a promise to a friend.

My mouth opens but immediately closes again. What do I say to convince Blake to let me go?

I don't get a chance to say anything as Blake continues to speak. "Please, Cassie. You could save us all."

At his words, something inside me cracks. "Save us all?" My voice rises, the feeling of hysteria beginning to bubble up inside me, and I jump off the bed. "I nearly strangled Naire to death in the first trial, and Jared turned because of my abilities. I can't control this part of me. Anyone who gets close to me suffers. *I can't save anyone.*"

Blake stands as well, his hands out in a placating gesture. "The military will help you control your powers. They're the only ones with experience on—"

The door flings open and Adrian stalks into the room. He must have heard me yelling. "What's going on?" He scours my features before a dark look spreads across his face. Adrian whirls on Blake menacingly. "I told you, she's not being shipped off to the military."

Blake flushes, anger replacing his admiration. "And I told you, as Headmaster, I have an obligation to the students, to the future of our country. Are you going to let these powers go to waste?"

"She's a human being!" Adrian shouts, taking a step closer to the headmaster. "If you think—"

"Stop it!" My voice breaks on a sob, and I struggle to hold in all the overwhelming feelings threatening to consume me.

It's almost mind-blowing how messed up my life has

become. I lost my family, my two best friends, and soon the one who's defending me from being abused as a puppet. If that isn't proof of all the destruction that follows me, I don't know what is.

I turn to Blake. "You told them about me?"

My voice is small and pitiful. Blake and I weren't close, but we were friends. To think my abilities changed his perception of me this much. Maybe I'm a completely different person in his mind.

He falters, lips pinched, the only semblance of regret I've seen from him so far. "They reached out to me, actually."

If Blake didn't tell them, then who did? I nod silently, feeling empty inside as Blake gawks at my changed eyes. "I'll do it," I say with a defeated sigh.

Adrian's appalled expression tears at my heart. "Cassie, you can't—"

Blake steps forward and cuts him off, a genuine smile on his face.

"You are going to save us all," he says again, and blood fills my mouth as I clamp my teeth down on my tongue to smother a response. The headmaster turns to Adrian. "She's prohibited from leaving this room until they get here. Wouldn't want anything to happen to her before the military arrives, right?"

Blake peers at me for confirmation of my obedience. I nod, watching the man cross the room and disappear without a second glance. The room is quiet only for a moment before Adrian exhales sharply.

"I won't let them take you," he says harshly.

I shift my attention to him. He doesn't regard me any differently and, instead of happiness, the thought troubles me. He doesn't understand what being a Phoenix means. "That's not your choice."

Even though I have no intention of joining the military, I can't have Adrian discover my plan to escape from here.

"Cassie—"

"Is Sara alright?" I interject, needing to know she made it through that night.

Adrian sighs at my harsh tone, understanding the warning within my words for him not to push the subject. "Yes, we had the graduation ceremony the morning after the attack. She passed at the rank of first and chose the city." He hesitates again before adding, "I offered for her to stay at the academy until you woke up, but…"

I nod. *Sara didn't want to stay.* Her last words echo in my ears. If she left, then that means her vow never to see me again, to kill me if she ever did, is real. As gut-wrenching as that fact is, at least she's alive and able to live with her family again.

"Who else didn't make it?" It's the question I'd been dreading, but I have to know. If Sara ended up in first place, then both Naire and Emmerick died in the attack. While the fact doesn't stir up much sympathy within me, I brace myself for Adrian's next words.

"It's hard to tell who fled the academy and who transformed, but…more than half of our staff and students combined. Most of the younger kids survived, being shielded by the staff and older students. Ten students from your class are unaccounted for."

I fight a gasp at his words. The death toll is a lot larger than I thought. Ten people, companions I've been training, eating, and living beside for three years, are gone. With four people leaving the trials early, that means only six of us survived.

Adrian walks over to me and brushes away the tears I didn't know were falling. "It's not your fault, Cassie."

I push him back, and he lets me. "It's not my fault?" I laugh. "*All* of this is my fault! The Commander was here for me! They all died because of me! Everyone should hate me. I did this. You should hate me. Tell me you hate me!"

Let me go, I plead in my mind.

"I don't hate you," he whispers, slowly moving toward me. "Even if you are a Phoenix, you're still the same person I fell in love with. Nothing will change that."

I stagger away from him, at his words that are daggers to the heart. I don't want to hear them. How can I leave when he just told me he loves me?

Another person who loves me. Another one that will die if I don't do something about it.

As if movement hurts, I pivot to the door. Fingers curling around the doorknob, I steel myself and harden my heart. Adrian deserves so much better than me. Maybe he doesn't see that now, but he will eventually.

"Everything has changed," I reply, and walk out the door.

The academy is in ruins. It's hard to keep the surprise off my face as I walk through the hallways I've trekked a thousand times. Even now, after everyone in the school spent the last few days cleaning and repairing the front gate, rooms, and corridors, there's still debris littering the floor. Broken benches, chunks of stone, torn clothing. Destruction is everywhere.

I halt in the middle of a hallway when I spot two young teenagers huddled against the wall, their hands clasped together. The curly redhead and blonde hair tug at a memory, like I should recognize them. "Are you okay?" I probe gently, kneeling beside them.

When their heads flick up to gape at me, I realize why they look so familiar. It's the kids I offered a brief lesson to on the morning of our trials, Clara and Ky.

Relief at their safety settles over me, even as I take in their puffy, red-stained eyes.

"Are you hurt?" I ask, tilting my head when they flinch at my words. My hand raises, but before I can rest it on Ky's hunched shoulder, she scrambles to her feet.

"Stay away," Ky demands in a shaky voice, creeping backward. Clara follows, if only because Ky is tugging on their interlocked fingers.

I stay on the ground, frowning at their actions. *Are they scared of me?*

With a sick lurch of my stomach, I comprehend what their gazes are focused on. My eyes, the golden glow a signal that I'm not human. "I won't hurt you," I whisper. Clara's face crumples, and she turns her head until blonde strands of hair cover her face.

They don't respond. The two kids, who were so excited by my help and begged me to teach them again, swivel and sprint down the corridor.

I bite my lip to keep the tears from falling. *Their reaction is understandable*, I tell myself. *I'm different now, how else should they behave?* It takes a minute for me to stand once more and continue to wander through the hallways, my hands wringing together.

Ky and Clara aren't the only ones to react to my appearance. Everyone I cross in the hallways either stares at me in fear or runs away like I'm an Obsidian. No one knows what a Phoenix is, and it's clear on their faces that they have no idea what happened to me. Just that I'm not normal.

Each student I meet, each stained stone I spot, cements in my mind that I have to leave as soon as I can. I won't wait for the military, won't be some pawn to be sacrificed when I can figure out what truly happened thirty years ago.

I'm sure the Commander has made significant progress in whatever nefarious plans he has for my blood. Who knows how long I have until he tries to come back for me? He may already be on the way for another attack.

I have to go.

I spin around and quickly make my way back to my room. I don't know where Adrian or Blake are, but I pray neither one catches me during my grand escape. Both of them would be problematic in their own ways.

I breathe a sigh of relief when my door closes securely behind me, and then I dive to the floor by Sara's bed. Crawling under the wooden frame, I drag out my abandoned backpack. I go through one more sweep of my room, adding any supplies I missed in my rush to flee an hour ago.

My eyes dip to my pillow and I still. *Should I write Adrian another note? Give a goodbye?* I sigh, turning away from the bed. A note may just give Adrian hope that I secretly want him to follow me. Better to just disappear with no trace.

Opening the door, I poke my head out and scan the hallway. Thankfully, it's deserted, and the space gives me a moment to breathe easily.

I need a plan first. If I attempt to waltz out the front door, someone will alert the headmaster and he won't let me out of his sight until the military gets here. And if Adrian finds out about my plan, there's no way he won't try to come with me.

I need to get out of here with some stealth, so it forces Adrian's hand. He's needed here more than with me. My mind flips through all my options, analyzing the half-formed plan I started before Blake walked in.

Zypha mentioned that extra Obsidian were able to invade through a backdoor, and somehow Tala got two Threes through the bottom of the academy and into the arena for the third trial with no one knowing. There has to be a secret entrance close by. That's where I'll start.

Okay, luck, help me out. You owe me one.

I take a deep breath and slip into the hallway, easing the door shut behind me. The corridor thankfully remains empty, and I allow a sigh of relief to escape my lips. I need to gain distance between me and my room before anyone notices I'm gone.

I take one step and stumble as a voice echoes through my head. I glance over my shoulder, expecting someone to be standing right behind me, but the hallway is vacant. A chill slides down my spine when I realize it's coming from inside my mind.

The whisper is smooth and dark, mesmerizing in a way that makes my skin crawl. I should have guessed that by being bitten, the venom in my veins has left me vulnerable to him, to whoever Henderson is.

Tingles spread across my inner left wrist at the words. My gaze drops to the sensation, to the shimmering outline of Obsidian teeth printed into my skin. The only scar I have that didn't heal with my powers or with Serous.

Hatred fills me. It douses the fear, reminding me of why I'm leaving the school, why I'm leaving Adrian. I will find the Commander, and I will stop whatever he intends to do with my blood. His voice reverberates around my skull as I stalk through the hallway with a rejuvenated purpose.

"My experiments with you are only just beginning, little bird. Together, we are going to change the world."

End of Book One

Author's Note

Obsidian Reign was inspired by all the YA books I loved to read when I was younger. There's something magical about getting sucked into a world, living and breathing and fighting alongside the characters you cherish. I feel like I've lived a thousand lives, and I'm honored to add one more world for us all to enjoy!

Thank you so much for reading *Obsidian Reign: Book One in the Crimson Shadows Trilogy*. I hope this story reminded you how powerful, brave, and special you already are.

If you've fallen in love with Cassie's story, please consider writing a review. Your words help new readers discover her story and mean more to me than you know.

Acknowledgments

If I were to name all of the people who helped create this book, it might be as long as the book itself. Even if your name isn't written here, please know that I see you, I feel your support, and I'm endlessly grateful that you are a part of my life.

First, thank you to my husband. More than anyone, you've seen the lows, the moments of doubt, and you have never wavered in your compassion and support. Thank you for not going crazy when all I talked about was this book, especially when I was convinced I had. I love you with my whole heart.

Thank you, Mom, not only for believing in this book, but for believing in me every single day of my life. You've been there since the very beginning, back when I would wake up before school to scribble silly stories into my notebooks. You've always known when to cheer me on, when to push me forward, and when to remind me that I could do this. Because of you, I found the courage to turn my childhood dream into something real. Everything I create carries a piece of your love, your strength, and your faith in me.

To my dad, for making me laugh with the dumbest jokes and for never failing to cheer me up. I know you'll be there for me, giving advice I probably won't take and hugs I'll always say yes to. Thank you for getting into the mindset of a young, angsty, love-struck female teenager so you could relate to this book better. Every step of this journey has been brighter because you were there.

Thank you to my English teacher friend, Katie, for being the first editor of my book when it was...not very polished. Thank you for not being afraid to tell me how much it sucked! No, I know you didn't actually say those specific words, but it's much funnier to say that you did. Once I finished crying, I dug in and changed the book so it could become the beautiful thing it is now.

Thank you to my sister and my sister-in-law. Whether it was sharing your excitement, checking in on how things were going, or just being there when I needed a break from it all, your support means more than you know. Your kindness and belief in me helped make this journey feel a little less daunting and a lot more special.

Cassie has so many people rooting for her, but none more so than Sydney, my best friend. Your unending enthusiasm and motivation have been my main source of dopamine since we met. Thank you so much for always being there with a radiant smile to lift me up, and for being my personal hype woman. I can't wait to keep reading my books to you in your living room and laugh when you fake vomit over the banister during an intense scene.

Finally, I want to thank you, the reader. I may not be able to tell you in person how much your support means to me, but just know that I see you, and you are the reason I stuck with this book when I wanted to give up. If this book had any sort of positive impact on your life, then the years of writing, editing, and sobbing into my pillow have been completely and utterly worth it. Thank you for choosing my book.

About the Author

Madalyn Leigh is a YA fantasy author who lives in West Virginia with her amazing husband and two wonderful cats who try to dodge her cuddles. When she's not immersed in her or another author's world, you can find her playing Dungeons and Dragons with her friends, board games with her family, and gardening with her husband.

Ready for Book 2? Follow me for more information on the release of *Flame Horizon: Book Two in the Crimson Shadows Trilogy*!